THE STAG & THE OWL

Destined – Book Four

Michele James

PRAISE FOR THE DESTINED SERIES

The Lion & The Swan

"What an amazing book! Well developed characters, complex and entertaining plot, beautifully described details and settings. Very difficult to put down. It cries for a sequel! Book two, hurry! ~ conniecutie

"The purity of love between Assad and Oona is undeniable and beautiful. I adore Oona's strength and dedication to her sister. Assad was the perfect alpha, sensitive, strong, and passionate. Great, and moving tale." ~ Andrea

The Stallion & The Tigress

"Love these books! Fun, witty, sensual and adventurous!!! Should be made into movies!!" ~Laura L. Sockey

"The strong woman (and the way her chief rival woos her) is wonderful. Especially because the leading lady is every bit as strong as her suitors! She chooses! I love the horses and the races and the way historical places and people are shown. This book stands alone, but it's also so cool that when you read Book 1 The Lion and the Swan, you get some of the backstory of this romance. Can't wait for Book 3 in this Destined Series. ~Kathleen Canney Lopez

"In this myth, the heroine, as her nickname suggests, is as powerful if not more so than any man. The men melt at the sight of her, but only one man will do, no matter the obstacles and there are many. The races by themselves are beautifully rendered. Kudos to the author for this romantic masterpiece. The book although number 2 of 3 is complete and stands alone." ~Plume Sobriquet

The Eagle & The Lynx

www.**BOROUGHSPUBLISHINGGROUP**.com

THE STAG & THE OWL
Copyright © 2021 Michele James

ISBN: 978-1-953810-63-2

For Jim. My man.

ACKNOWLEDGMENTS

Thank you to Elizabeth Archer and Michelle for the honest reads and critiques. And to KCL for all the tech help.

THE STAG & THE OWL

CHAPTER 1

The Spyglass

Roark placed the thick, concave glass lens into the end of the leather tube, wiped it clean with the hem of his tunic, and set the spyglass to his eye. He focused on the shoreline and took in the bustling docks where two small boats were tied to *The Rover*, the trade ship he'd sailed in on from the Green Isles to the port of Sea Ridge. The ship was being loaded with the goods his laird's son, Leif, had traded for with their prized Highland wool. He moved his gaze west to where six warships were docked at their own pier with two guards at the gate. Warships he'd learned Sea Ridge's King Jerrik kept ready to sail at a moment's notice.

He moved the glass to the left and found the road leading from town to the king's compound of long houses built on the last flat expanse of ground before the mountain jutted up behind it. He trained the glass to follow the winding path. Halfway up the road, he spied a horse and rider accompanied by a huge, shaggy brown hound coming down from the palace.

The horse was a dark, leggy roan with a black mane and stockings. As they got closer, he saw the rider was a young woman and was intrigued as she turned the horse off the road and cut across an open field, abutting a beach west of the warships.

To his amazement, she pulled off her boots and tied them to her saddle. Then she tucked her skirts up under her seat, exposing a pair of long, lean legs. She urged the horse, a mare, into an easy gallop up the deserted beach away from the ships and docks, and then she gave the horse its head and leaned forward in the saddle, racing in a full gallop along the shoreline, her mass of waist-length earthen brown hair streaming behind her.

He admired the line of her legs from her slim calves to her shapely thighs, and the way her hair flew about her like a living creature. He was in awe at the ease with which she and the mare moved as one. After a few laps along the beach, she tucked her skirts higher and rode the mare belly deep into the water. Raising her arms high above her head, she arched her back, her face to the sky, and smiled as the last sun of winter started to set over the western horizon.

"Damnation." Roark lowered the spyglass, only to lift it back up, finding her bare legs first and slowly raising his sights from her wet skirts tucked under her seat to her slim waist and up to where her damp tunic clung to the swell of her breasts. "Double damn." He lifted the glass to her face. She was far enough away to make her features blurry, yet close enough to see she was looking straight at him. "Bollocks."

He raised his hand and waved, and after a moment she lifted a hand and held it up to him. She cupped both hands and made like she was looking through a spyglass. Roark held the glass up and grinned as she tilted her head first one way and then the other, like a curious little owl. She waved and then turned her mount around, untucking her hems from her waist belt and letting her skirts drop down around her legs while returning to shore.

Roark groaned.

The knock of a small boat coming alongside the ship brought him back to where he was and why, and he stood at the ship's rail as Leif climbed up the ladder and stepped on deck.

Roark nodded down at the small boats full of furs, spices, and bolts of worm weave, a rare, pricey cloth that the merchants of Sea Ridge were known for, along with several barrels of oils and wines. "Looks like a successful day at the trade market," he said.

"It was." Leif clapped Roark on the shoulder, grinning from ear to ear. "I met the king's eldest son, Anders, who invited us to sup with his family tomorrow noon whilst telling me all about the feasting and revelry to follow in celebration of Spring's Eve."

"And?"

"And the entire royal family will be at the festival, including Princess Alina."

"Will there be masks?" Roark asked.

"There will," Leif said.

"Good." Roark nodded. "Our plan is falling into place."

"You mean yours and my father's plan," Leif huffed, apparently forgetting how Roark had been coerced into helping form and execute these plans.

Roark and Leif had both sat in on the meetings with Laird Roger and his spies, but where Leif had been more interested in flirting with the serving maid, Roark had paid attention, which was why he'd insisted on bringing masks and headdresses for the spring festival.

"It was you who got us our invitation to sup with the king's family," Roark said, smoothing Leif's ruffled fur. "An invitation that will get us close to the princess."

"True." Leif puffed out his chest, and then turned his attention to the crew as they brought up the bounty to stow in the ship's hold. "Put the dry goods in the aft of the hold," he ordered them, though they were all experienced seamen who'd been sailing and trading on *The Rover* for years while this was his first voyage. "The furs and cloths go in the fore."

"Aye, yer lairdship," Roy, one of the older seamen said, and then looked to Murtaugh, the captain of the ship as soon as Leif turned his back.

Making sure that Leif wasn't looking, Murtaugh dipped his head in answer to his man's unspoken question, and then met Roark's gaze with a shrug, knowing he wouldn't tell their laird's son.

Having lived in the laird's house since he was ten and two, Roark loved Leif like a brother, but that didn't mean he was blind to his faults: arrogance born of breeding and privilege, and a handsome face and athletic body of which he was too proud.

He went down into the hold and gathered a clean tunic and breeches. "I'm going to the bathhouse," he told Leif. "You want to come?"

Leif lifted his arm and gave his pit a sniff. "Nah, I went yesterday. A bowl of water and a washrag'll do me fine for a few more days."

"If all goes as planned, we'll be sailing home day after tomorrow," Roark reminded him.

Leif waved him off. "Another six days without bathing and I'll finally fit in with this stinking crew."

Roark chuffed. "And you wonder why the crew hasn't taken to you."

It being the day before the spring festival, there was a line for the bathing tubs at the Portside Inn. Roark spent his time waiting drinking ale, which was called beer here, and casually questioning Digby, the proprietor, a genial, talkative man who ran a clean, honest establishment.

"I saw a girl, a young woman, with long brown hair riding a roan with black stockings along the shoreline today," he said. "There was a big, brown hound with them."

"That'd be Princess Alina on her mare, Brynja," Digby said. "The hound's name be Beast, which is what he is, and why the princess can ride without escort around the docks and town."

"She rides with an escort otherwise?"

Digby nodded. "She and her mother, the queen, they don't ride anywhere without a guard or three with them."

"If the mother looks anything like the daughter," Roark said, "I can see why."

"Aye, they're both beauties they are," Digby said. "The king, he's a mite protective of them."

Roark nodded. This was good to know. "What kind of ruler is King Jerrik?" he asked.

"King Jerrik be fairer than most from what I hear sailors from other parts say," Digby continued. "Sea Ridge has more than prospered under his and the queen's rule. Our trading's ten times what it was before them, which brings all kinds of other business as well, and there's no slavery. Here, a person works for fair pay and pays fair taxes."

"Which go into the king's coffers?"

Digby shook his head. "They get put right back into the community. Which is how we have such good roads, docks, and warehouses, and why if a family's having hard times through no fault of their own, they won't go cold or hungry."

"How does the king pay for his household then?"

Digby grinned and touched the side of nose. "Three of those ships in the harbor are King Jerrik's," he said. "He has another two at sea. He was a rich trader afore he became king,

and he's an even richer trader now."

12

"I see." Roark emptied his cup and pushed it forward for a refill. "What about the jarls he forced out? The one's whose lands and property he took without recompense when he became king?"

Digby shook his balding head. "Don't know nothing 'bout that, unless you be asking 'bout his murderous uncle and his yellow beards." He glanced over at the entrance to the bathhouse where two sailors from southern climes by their looks and dress, were coming out. "You're next," he said.

***

"You'd better get going, missy," Hamar told Alina. "Else you'll be late for supper again."

She unclasped her apron and tossed it onto the pile of dirty aprons worn by the stable hands. After her ride along the shoreline, she'd been helping the stablemaster dose the yearlings for worms with a paste of hyssop, fennel, and garlic. Her hands and arms were covered with the paste and horse slobber. Splashing water over her face and arms, she dried off with a towel and then wiped her tunic and skirts with it. It would have to do. She had no time to change.

"Here she is," her father said, eyeing the telltale stains of dried seawater on her skirts as Alina slid onto her seat at the high table to her mother's left. "You rode along the bay shore today, I take it?"

"I did. Then I helped Hamar worm the foals, which is why I was almost late," she said as the servants laid trenchers of food on the table.

"We have stable hands for that," her father said with an indulgent grin.

"I know." She grinned back. "But Hamar says the foals don't vomit it back up when I dose them."

Her mother, who never met an animal she didn't like other than a snake, smiled and shook her head. "You and Hamar and your concoctions."

"One would almost think she was Hamar's daughter," her father teased.

"Still not amusing," her mother chided, though her eyes crinkled up at the corners.

Alina grinned at the old jest between her parents and tucked into her supper of salted cod, boiled beets and carrots, hard cheese, and rye bread. Glad to have a full, sated belly, she'd be gladder still when the first tender greens of spring sprouted and the stone fruits in the orchard budded and ripened.

Tomorrow, the carpenters would move the glass panes on the roof of the greenhouse to welcome the spring sun, and Alina would plant seeds for broccoli, cabbage, and spinach in the raised beds she'd been tending all winter. Once the seedlings were hardy enough and the last frost had come and gone, they would be transplanted into the outdoor gardens.

Her father had designed the three removable panels to take seasonal advantage of the sun, along with a permanent glass window in the three walls without a door, an expense that had paid off by affording them an early and extra harvest of vegetables, and a constant store of fresh and dried herbs for which cooks and healers traveled from a hundred leagues away to buy and trade. Alina loved trading herbs and knowledge with them, and had learned of many exotic herbs and their uses, several of which now grew in her greenhouse.

The glass panes reminded Alina of the man on *The Rover*. "I saw a man on a ship with a looking glass today when I was riding," she said.

"A looking glass?" Her father, who loved inventions of all kinds, set down his fork. "I've only ever heard of one. Did he seem able to see from a distance?"

"He did." She recalled his reaction to her stopping and staring at him.

"How far?"

"His ship, *The Rover*, was the closest to shore, so maybe fifty fathoms."

Her father's blue eyes lit with excitement. "I'll have to seek out this man and his looking glass."

"No need," Anders said from his seat to their father's right. "I met the owner of *The Rover* today at the trade market and invited him to sup with us tomorrow noon."

Alina's twin, Anders was tall, blond, and blue-eyed like their father, with a smile and a body that made girls swoon, and a personality as outgoing as his smile. In contrast, Alina was of medium height and build with brown hair and green eyes like her mother, though without her mother's sweet and open disposition.

She was, as her mother often said, born an old soul, a bit of a loner who preferred the natural world of sky, sea, earth, and animals to most people. She would never have invited someone she'd only met today to sup with her family tomorrow. Even someone as interesting as the man on *The Rover* promised to be.

"What's his name?" she asked Anders.

"Leif."

"That's a Northman's name," her father said. "Doesn't *The Rover* sail out of the Green Isles?"

Anders nodded. "It does."

"What does he look like?" Alina asked.

The head of every person at the high table swung in her direction. She seldom asked about any of the hundreds of sailors who came to Sea Ridge to trade, and then she'd only ask about the goods they were trading rather than the men themselves. At ten and nine years of age, she was old enough to have wed and then some.

It wasn't that she was indifferent to a good, intelligent, handsome man: it was that she'd never met one who'd caught or held her attention in a way that made her want to marry. Her mother had met her father when she was only eight years old and had proposed marriage to him then and there. Until Alina met such a man, she was content remaining single and unwed.

"Why do you ask?" Anders said.

"Oooh, Alina liikes Leeif," her younger brother, Aaron, sang.

"Leave Ali alone," her youngest brother, Aleksi, said, shoving Aaron.

"Boys," their mother scolded.

"I'm interested in the man's looking glass," Alina answered Anders and ignored Aaron. "I was wondering if this Leif is who I saw on the ship with it, is all." She gave Aleksi a quick wink.

"Tall, blond, blue eyes, short beard," Anders told her.

"Then he's not the man I saw on the ship," she said, disappointed, though she couldn't have said why. Other than the strange pulse of recognition she'd felt when she'd discovered him watching her.

"Is he bringing the looking glass with him tomorrow?" her father asked.

"I'll send word in the morning to make sure he does," Anders assured him.

CHAPTER 2

Spring's Eve

Alina smoothed the soil over the cabbage seeds and glanced out the window facing west into the courtyard for about the hundredth time. The higher the sun rose in the sky, the more edgy she became, which was ridiculous. This man Leif was coming to sup with her brother and her father, not her, and wasn't even the man who'd been watching her from the ship, according to Anders's description.

Still, she couldn't shake the nervous energy that had kept her awake half the night and up at the first light of dawn. She kept telling herself it was the change from winter to spring, and the excitement of the upcoming festivities. But even she didn't believe it.

She ran her fingertips across the feathery leaves newly sprouting from her fennel plant, a gift from a healer who'd traveled to Sea Ridge from the southern shores of the Mid Earth Sea last spring festival, and concentrated on working compost into the soil around the bulb without injuring it. She heard men's voices outside and turned to the door as it opened and her father walked in, the looking glass in his hand, followed by Anders and a tall, blond man who looked more Northman than Green Isler.

"Leif MacKinnon," her father said, "meet my daughter, Princess Alina."

"It is an honor, Princess," Leif said in the Northern tongue with only the slightest hint of an outsider's accent. He stepped forward, holding his hand out and smiling as if he expected her to swoon at his feet.

"The honor is mine, Leif MacKinnon," she said, staying where she stood and holding her hands up, palms out, to show they were covered in soil.

"This is Roark MacInnes," her father said as a man with wavy auburn hair brushing his shoulders and a short beard of the same auburn curls stepped from behind the others. The man from the ship yesterday.

"Princess Alina." His voice was deep and rich, and he spoke with a heavy accent. Dressed in a clean white linen tunic and leather vest, he was tall, though not as tall as his companion, built for power with a broad chest, slim waist, and strong, muscular legs by the way his leather trousers fit him. His face and neck were covered with freckles matching his dark auburn hair, but the most arresting thing about him was his eyes. They were the color of rain, and Alina was standing on solid ground, drowning in them.

"Alina?"

"Huh?" She pulled her gaze from Roark's and looked to her father. "What?"

"I was about to explain to Leif and Roark how we move the glass roof panes seasonally, but since they were your idea, I thought you might want to."

"The, ah, glass panes," she said, clearing her throat and gathering her wits. She pointed up to the ceiling. "As you can see, we have three separate panels of glass, all of which can be mixed and moved with the other solid panels of the roof." She glanced at her audience. Her father and Roark were looking up at the panels. Anders and Leif were looking out the open door.

"We move the panels from season to season to get the best use of the sun," she continued. "Today, we positioned one each west, south, and east. In the summer we put two panels facing north and one east, in the autumn, two south and one east, and in the winter, two south and one west."

Roark held his hands up thumb to thumb, turning a slow circle around the greenhouse as if framing and following the sun's seasonal arcs. He lowered his hands. "Brilliant," he said, grinning at Alina with the heat of a summer sun.

Alina took a deep, cooling breath. "It, ah, gives me, gives us, the ability to start seedlings a moon earlier than if we had to sow seed outdoors," she said, warming to her subject and Roark's interest. Or maybe it was his melting grin. She turned to the herb bed. "I can grow many herbs year-round that would normally die out in the winter."

Roark stepped over and stood by her, inspecting the herbs while her father gazed up through the glass panes with the looking glass and Anders and Leif stood outside the door, talking between themselves.

"I saw you on the beach yesterday," Roark said, his voice low. "Riding your horse."

"I know."

He smiled and she flushed from head to toe. She reached down and ran her fingers over the fennel leaves. Either that or run them through his auburn waves. He reached down and touched the feathery leaves too, his long, blunt-tipped fingers brushing hers and sending a surge of awareness up her arm. He leaned in closer to her. "You smell of cherry blossoms," he said, his voice a husky whisper.

"I, ah, I was in the orchard earlier," she stammered. He smelled of soap, sun, and salt air. "The first cherries of the season have ripened."

"Come on," Anders called from outside the doorway, causing Alina and Roark to startle. "The tables are set up outdoors and they're carrying out the food. I for one don't intend to start the night's festivities on an empty stomach."

Alina met her father's grin and shook her head. Anders loved a good celebration.

"Did you bring masks for tonight?" Anders asked Leif as the rest of them filed out of the greenhouse.

"We did," Leif said. "They're in our packs back at the gate." He slowed down to walk beside Alina, forcing Roark to walk behind them. "What will you be tonight, Princess?" he asked her. "I'll be a bear. A big, strong, hungry bear."

"I prefer to keep it a secret," she said, and heard a male chuckle behind her. "I find it more interesting that way."

Roark and Leif took seats across from Alina at her family's table, giving her an unfettered view of the two men who couldn't have been more different. Where Leif was loud, outgoing, and overly sure of himself, Roark was quieter and took the time to think before he spoke. He watched and listened to what people did and said, and though he didn't seem to be shy or bothered by the attention he and Leif were attracting, he didn't seek it either.

Except for Alina's.

He watched her with those rain eyes and smiled his bone-melting smile at her and spoke with her more than he did with anyone else at the table. Alina reveled in it while trying to politely ignore Leif, who insisted on interrupting their conversation with some inane question or comment while ogling her like she was some prized broodmare. Aware of her mother's increasingly curious gaze as she observed the three of them, Alina tried to focus on her meal, though she couldn't help stealing glances at Roark, and he at her.

"How are you enjoying your food?" her father asked the men as a maidservant filled their cups with more beer.

Roark glanced at Leif, who was busy ogling one of the maidservants. "The food is delicious, sir," he answered her father, "and I'm not just saying that because I've been eating ship food for a fortnight."

Her father laughed. "Ah, yes, the food is one of the few things I don't miss about sailing, though I did enjoy tasting many an exotic food in many far-off lands."

"I would enjoy hearing of some of these lands," Roark said.

Her father eyed Roark with his piercing eagle's gaze, and to his credit, Roark didn't shrink or shirk, but sat up straight and met and held her father's gaze. "I think you would much rather see some of those lands for yourself."

"Not enough to become a sailor," Roark said without apology. "I'm more a man of the earth than the sea."

Her father nodded. "May I see the looking glass again?" he asked. "What do you call it?"

"A spyglass," Roark said, handing it across the table to her father, who held the lens end up, inspecting it.

"How does this lens work?"

"It's convex," Roark explained. "A refracting lens, which converges the rays of light coming in into a wider field of view. It bends the light so you can focus on one point. You can take the lens out and look at it," he told her father, who did exactly that, turning it this way and that and holding it up to the sky.

"Would you be interested in trading for this?" he asked Roark, putting the lens back in the tube.

"If I were to trade it, King Jerrik, it would be with someone like you who appreciates it for what it is. However, I cannot." He cast a quick glance at Alina. "Some things are priceless."

"Yes," her father said with raised a brow as he handed the spyglass back to Roark. "Some things in this life are."

Roark put the spyglass into a special sheath attached to his waist belt, and her father turned his attention to Leif, who was speaking loudly with Anders about beer and women.

"You two speak our Northern tongue well for Green Islers," he said to Leif.

"My mother is from the west coast of the Northlands," Leif told him. "She's spoken her native tongue to me since the day I was born, and to Roark every day for the past ten years."

"That explains it then," her father said. "As well as your Northern looks. Have you been to the Northlands before?"

"No," Leif said. "This is my first time here, and Roark's."

"How has your trading gone?"

"So well that we plan on leaving tomorrow," Leif said.

Alina looked at Roark, unable to hide her dismay. "So soon?"

"I'm afraid so," he said, and seemed disappointed.

"We've finished almost all of our business here," Leif said, "and will set sail sometime tomorrow, depending on how much beer we drink tonight." He laughed at his own humor and slapped Roark on the back. "Roark has been anxious to be done here and on our way home."

"What are you anxious to get home to?" Alina asked.

Roark pressed his lips tight and shook his head.

"My sister," Leif said, grinning broadly at Alina as if he hadn't just shot an arrow through her heart. "His betrothed."

"Oh." Alina dropped her gaze from Roark's. "I see." She saw that she was no more than a bit of fun and flirtation for a man whom she had thought different from most. Apparently, she'd thought wrong. She tried to smile like this revelation meant nothing to her, like she too had only considered him a bit of fun for a day. Unfortunately, she was terrible at hiding her feelings.

"Gwyneth and I have been betrothed since I was ten and she four years of age," Roark said, his smile fleeting as Alina lifted her gaze back to his. "Our families arranged the betrothal, which is why I was sent to study under Laird Roger, her father."

Alina forced a smile. "Then she is a lucky girl, indeed," she said. And she meant it. Any girl betrothed to a man as handsome as Roark, with his keen mind and rain eyes, would be. "I'm sure she's as anxious for your return as you are to return to her."

Roark let out a wry chuckle. "On that," he said, "you are more right than you know."

Alina blinked and tilted her head, as if that would help her understand his meaning any better. As if understanding would change the fact that he was betrothed to another and leaving tomorrow and she would never see him again after tonight.

"I, on the other hand, am not betrothed," Leif proclaimed, and it took Alina a moment to realize he was addressing her. "I would be pleased to offer myself as your partner for the evening's festivities, Princess Alina."

"Thank you," she said with polite indifference. "But I have no need of a partner tonight."

"Suit yourself," he said less politely.

"I usually do," she assured him. She caught Roark's quick half grin, stood, and dipped her head. "If you will excuse me, I should go prepare for the night's festivities."

***

Roark was only half listening to the middle-aged stable hand named Pavel, who had taken a seat next to him after the royal family left the table, his mind going over and over Alina's reaction to the news he was betrothed and leaving tomorrow.

"They caught me trying to steal the queen's hair comb in the village I grew up in, poor, half-starved, and beat regular by my pa," Pavel said, catching Roark's full attention. "They were sailing back here to Sea Ridge, bringing the queen to her new home. They could've cut me hand off for thievin', but gave me a chance to sail with them, to learn a sailor's trade." He chuckled. "I got so terrible seasick on the journey they let me train to be a stable hand instead. Here I've been since." His jovial manner turned serious. "They gave me a new life, a good life, King Jerrik and Queen Alyssa did. Even kept me on after some trouble I got into with the king's uncle. Most would've turned me out." He met Roark's gaze head on. "I learnt my lesson about lying twenty years ago. Nothing good ever comes of it."

"No," Roark agreed. The lies of omission kept sticking in his throat. The knowledge of what he was about to do to the king's family, to Alina, weighing heavily on him. "It doesn't."

He considered going to her, to the king, and confessing all, or going back to *The Rover* and refusing to take part in Roger's scheme, or even walking up into the mountains never to be seen again.

Yet no matter what he chose to do, other than take part in the plan, the repercussions would affect not only his family, causing them to lose Roger's and likely many other lairds' trade and alliances, but the hundreds of families who depended on the lairds for their livelihood. Not to mention the shame his family would suffer because of him. He drained his third cup of beer and looked around the courtyard, spying Leif by the beer casks flirting with a buxom blonde as if he didn't have a care in the world. As if what they were about to do wasn't weighing on him in the least.

Roark stared into his empty cup and covered it with his hand when Pavel held a full pitcher of beer over it. "No, thank you," he told Pavel. "I've had enough." Enough to dull the sharp pangs of guilt pricking his conscience, yet not so much he would muck things up. He stood. "It was good to meet you."

"And you, young Green Isler."

He walked aimlessly through the growing crowd of revelers, trying to distract himself from what the night would bring. He patted the vial of White Milk, known here as the Oil of the Dream Flower, in his tunic pocket. He'd traded a bolt of finely woven highland wool for the drug and hoped he wouldn't have to use it on Alina, though he would if it came down to it. For her sake as well as theirs.

Dusk turned to night and the hum of the gathering rose in volume as the torches were lit and the crowd parted, opening a pathway as Alina walked with her parents and Anders from their longhouse to a newly cleared area in the courtyard. Roark made his way to the clearing's edge as the family took their places, the king standing in the middle as the queen, wearing a lynx throw over her shoulders and carrying a harp, sat on a stool near the back of the clearing. Anders went to one side, and Alina the opposite.

She wore a long-sleeved gown of fern green worm weave, the lowcut bodice skimming the swell of her breasts and nipping in at her slim waist, the skirt flowing down in panels flashing iridescent green and gold around her legs, which looked even longer and leaner close up.

Her mane of burnished cedar was pinned up with combs of gold and copper, showing off the graceful line of her neck, and was crowned with a wreath of winter lilies and snowdrops. Around her throat she wore a delicate chain of filigreed copper, from which a lustrous gold pearl the size and shape of a dove's egg dangled in the hollow between her breasts. Alina was a beautiful young woman, even dressed in workaday linens with soil-covered hands, but seeing her dressed like this was a revelation.

Roark stood spellbound.

"Welcome everyone to the festival of Spring's Eve," the king announced. "I hope you are enjoying the hospitality of our city." Shouts and whistles broke out and the king smiled and waited for them to die down. "To start the night's festivities, we will sing and play the song of The Spring Maid, the Sun God, and The Lord of Winter."

The crowd fell silent as the king moved to Alina's side of the clearing and she walked to the center of it, knelt down, and tucked into a tight ball. The queen strummed her harp, and Alina began to sing of the cold and the endless snow, her voice thin and reedy, then growing fuller and stronger as she slowly unfolded and rose, unfurling her arms and reaching for the warming sky she sang to.

King Jerrik stepped into the clearing, jutting his head this way and that, singing in a low, guttural growl, calling to the winds and icy snow. Spying Alina, the spring maiden, standing and swaying as if blown by a gentle breeze, singing with a voice as pure and clear as water rippling over stone, he spread out his arms with his fingers clawed and enveloped the Spring Maid in the Lord of Winter's icy hold, blowing and moaning his victory over her as she shrank back into a frozen ball.

Anders's voice rang out, rich and sure and strong, singing the warmth back into the sky and life back into the earth as he strode into the clearing, head high and shoulders back, the Sun God reclaiming his world. He stood over the Spring Maid, singing to the heavens of light and heat and rebirth as the Spring Maid slowly thawed and rose again. Standing in the Sun God's warm embrace, her brilliant smile reflecting the sun's light, the Spring Maid sang of the new life stirring within her as she and the Sun God held their arms out to the rapt gathering and sang together. They beamed as their voices reached a glorious crescendo.

Roark met Alina's shining eyes and swore under his breath. "Damnation."

"What do you think you're doing?" Leif grumbled in Roark's ear as Alina and her brother and parents clasped hands and bowed to the audience's wild applause.

"What do you mean?"

"The plan was for me to get close to the princess," Leif said. "Not you."

Roark resisted the urge to plow his fist into Leif's face. "Plans change," he said instead. He hadn't chosen to be part of Roger's plan. In fact, he'd argued against it many times, but it hadn't made any difference. The only choice they'd given Roark was to join them or refuse and risk severing all ties, leaving his family shamed and shunned. "It doesn't matter who gets close to the princess," he told Leif. "As long as one of us does. You and I will simply swap roles in this. The end results will be the same."

Leif chewed on it a moment and then slapped Roark on the back. "It's just as well," he said. "She's too plain and high speaking for my tastes."

***

Dressed in her green gown and a short cloak of gold and brown owl and hawk feathers sewn onto a leather liner, Alina stood on the outside edge of the crowd gathered around the musicians and peered through the eye holes of the feathered mask that covered her nose and tufted out from her cheeks into the shape of an owl's wings, the eyeholes and edges of the mask studded with stones of topaz and amber.

"Looking for somebody?" a deep voice said from behind her.

She turned around and looked into eyes the color of rain from beneath a headdress of buckskin adorned with a stag's eight-point antlers. "It seems he's found me," she answered, accepting the cup of drink that Roark held out to her. She took a sip. "How did you know I prefer honey mead to beer or wine?"

"It was what you drank at supper." He leaned in as close to her neck as his antlers allowed and inhaled. "You still smell like cherry blossoms," he said, his warm breath tickling the small hairs on her nape.

"You smell of moth-eaten deer hide," she said, stepping back and putting some distance between them.

Roark laughed, low and mellow. "You should have smelled it before I aired it out for three days."

Alina wrinkled her nose. "I'll take your word for it."

The musicians started to play a reel and Roark lifted his chin toward the people dancing. "Would you like to dance?"

"No. Not really."

"What would you like to do?"

Alina hesitated. He was leaving tomorrow and she'd never see him again. Even if by some unlikely happenstance they did meet again, he was betrothed, soon to be married to another. She'd already be dreaming about his quick wit, slow smile, and rain eyes for days and nights to come. Did she really want to make it harder on herself?

"We can do whatever you want, Alina," he offered.

The sound of her name spoken with his thick Green Isles burr decided for her. "There's a lake behind the compound," she said. "We could go there and talk without having to yell over all these people."

The corners of his full lips lifted and his cheeks rose. "Lead the way, my lady owl."

The light of a waxing quarter moon shone down on the reflective surface of the lake, and contrary to Alina's nerves, the waters were calm and still. She led Roark to a little cove on the eastern shore with a bench made from a fallen log.

"So," she said as they sat next to each other, close, yet not touching. "Tell me about you and Leif."

Roark put down his headdress on the ground and ran both hands through his hair. "Yeah," he chuffed. "Me and Leif."

"Would you be friends with him if you weren't obligated to his family?"

Roark stared at the lake for a long moment and then shook his head. "I honestly don't know," he said. "Leif's not all bad. I mean, he has his faults." He gave Alina a quick, sideways glance. "We all do."

"But?"

"But he really can be an arrogant, overbearing ass." Roark laughed as if he'd surprised himself by saying this out loud, and then he turned and faced Alina, his knee touching hers. "Don't get me wrong, he can be funny and sometimes generous. Life with him is never boring. He's a good man to have your back in a fight, and in truth he's more a brother to me than my blood kin. I love him, but I don't always like him."

"I understand what you're saying," Alina said. "I love my twin, Anders, yet we are nothing alike."

"What about your younger brothers?"

"Aaron is ten and four, and wants to be a sailor like our father and my mother's brother, his namesake, were. My father would let him sail tomorrow, he's already two years older than my father was when he joined the crew of the *Sea Eagle*, but my mother, who cannot bear the thought of losing her son as she did her favorite brother, has made him promise to wait another two years."

"And your youngest brother?"

"Aleksandr," she said with a fond grin. "Aleksi is ten and the spitting image of our grandfather, King Aleksandr, in looks and temperament and horse craziness according to our mother." She lowered her voice to a conspiratorial whisper. "You must swear never to tell anyone else this," she said. "He's my favorite."

Roark lifted a hand in solemn oath. "I swear it."

Alina laughed, her heart light and happy. She took off her mask and met and held Roark's smiling gaze. He reached out and gently lifted the gold pearl from her chest, her skin tingling where his fingers had touched.

"*Tha a braegha*," he said, twirling the pearl in his fingers. He gazed into Alina's eyes, his own warm and soft as a summer rain. "*Tha thu braegha*."

Alina's heart stopped, stuttered, and beat triple time. "You think I'm beautiful?"

Roark sat back and his jaw dropped. "I do," he said after a moment. "I think you're beautiful and intelligent and kind. You can ride a horse like the wind, and sing like a nightingale. I'm impressed, yet somehow not surprised you understand the Green Isles tongue, and, damnation, woman, you really wear that gown."

Alina's heart beat even faster, and almost jumped out of her chest when Roark let the pearl drop from his fingers to the hollow between her breasts.

"How many languages do you speak?" he asked, his voice low and intimate.

Flustered by his voice, his nearness, his presence, Alina had to concentrate to answer him. "I, ah, well, my Northland, your Green Isles, my mother's native Rus, my great-grandfather's Desert tongue, and my Uncle Han's Far Eastern, so, five?"

"Is that all?" he said with a teasing grin.

"My father learned even more from his travels and always thought it a good thing to know the language of the people he trades with. It turns out I have a knack for it as well."

"Apparently," Roark said with a low chuckle. "Will you say something in the Far East tongue?"

Alina stared at the strong line of Roark's jaw, his full lips, high cheekbones, and broad brow. *"Ni ye hen piaoling*," she said in the singsong cadence that could mean the difference between a compliment or an insult.

"What did you say?"

"You're beautiful too."

"No." He shook his head. "I'm not."

Alina tilted hers. "I think you're a handsome man," she said truthfully.

"You don't have to say that." He flicked his fingers at his cheek. "I know these freckles don't appeal."

"They do to me." Alina lifted her hand and hovered it over his cheek. "May I?"

He nodded and visibly braced himself. Alina touched her fingertips to his cheek and down to the edge of his cropped beard. His skin was warm and his beard soft. She grinned and met his watching gaze. "Why would you think you're not a handsome man?"

"Because women have been shuddering at my marked face and crawling over me to get to Leif since we were boys."

Alina scoffed. "Men like Leif are as common as grains of sand on the beach," she said. "You, with your earth-kissed skin, hair of fire, eyes of rain, and soaring mind, you're as rare as the pearl I wear, Roark."

"You called me Roark."

"It is your name."

"Yet never have I heard it spoken so." He smiled slow and easy, and melting. "Thank you," he said. "For your words. How you see me." He laughed, short and harsh. "If only I could trade Gwyneth for you. It would be like trading the poorest weave of burr-ridden linen for the finest of worm weave."

Alina's heart skipped a beat, or three. "She doesn't think you special?"

"She thinks me ugly and above myself."

Alina laid her hand over his on the bench. "I'm sorry for you then. Is there no way out of the marriage?"

Roark shook his head. "Not without destroying the alliance between my family and hers, an alliance responsible for the peace, wealth, and well-being of both our families and hundreds of others. Our alliance requires me to do many things against my will and better judgment." He turned his hand and twined his fingers through hers, then he lifted their hands and placed his lips on the back of her fingers. "I've never wished it otherwise as much as I do now."

Alina's fingers warmed where his lips had touched and her heart had yet to resume anything near to a normal rhythm. "What if you could say or do whatever you wanted right now," she asked him earnestly, "without consequence or repercussion?"

Roark held her gaze for an eternity, his rain eyes pouring into hers, and then he held their entwined hands to his chest and lowered his mouth to hers.

His kiss was hungry and demanding while giving, stoking Alina's hunger and causing an insatiable need to surge through her veins. She moaned into his kiss and he let go of her hand and scooped her up onto his lap, one large hand cupping her backside and the other roaming the length of her back, pressing her close.

He kissed her as if he couldn't get enough of her, and she held nothing of herself back, clasping his arms and kissing him with everything she had until they were both panting. He took her head in his hands and broke their kiss.

"Marry me, Alina," he said, his voice as ragged as his breath.

CHAPTER 3

Taken

Alina swayed in Roark's arms and focused her desire-hazed eyes on his. "What?"

"If I could say or do whatever I wanted without consequence or repercussion," he said, his voice low, his eyes shining silver in the moonlight, "I would ask you to marry me."

Warmth flooded Alina. She smiled and laughed, feeling light and happy. "If I could do or say whatever I wanted without consequence or repercussion," she whispered, "I would answer you ye-mmpphh."

She clawed at a hand holding a cloth over mouth, staring wide-eyed at Roark, silently pleading with him to help her. He stood there looking ashamed and not at all surprised, and Alina realized with a sinking feeling that he was in on whatever this was. She threw her head back, hitting whoever was gagging her from behind square on the chin. Their hold slackened, and she reached for her waist blade, but another pair of hands grabbed her by the wrist and wrested the blade from her grasp.

"Restrain the bitch," Leif ordered in the Green Isles tongue.

A third pair of hands grabbed her from behind and pulled her off the bench. She landed on her back with a thud and tried to roll over on her side and get her hands and knees under her, but was pushed down and held there by three men whose faces loomed over her, cursing her and each other as she kicked and thrashed. The gag fell out of her mouth and she took a big breath in to scream out, only to have the gag stuffed harder and deeper into her mouth. Breathing furiously through her nose, she was losing air and strength, and the fear that had surged through her veins and given her a burst of energy was turning to cold, blood-freezing dread.

"If you'd be quiet and take it like a good girl," Leif said in her Northern tongue while standing over her with a gloating grin, "it would go much easier on you."

"Fuck you," Alina screamed, though it came out a strangled shriek. One of the men holding her raised his fist and Alina glared at him.

"Don't think I won't hit you, you Northern bitch," the man threatened in his Green Isles tongue.

"Enough," Roark commanded, and the man withdrew his fist. Roark knelt down beside her, his beautiful, treacherous rain eyes holding hers. "You won't be hurt," he said in her Northern tongue. "I swear it, as long as you cooperate and stop fighting."

"How could you?" she cried, and though her words were muffled, he understood their meaning.

"I am sorry, Alina. Truly."

She closed her eyes and rolled her head from side to side. How could she have been so foolish? It was all a trap, and he'd been the bait. All he'd had to do was look at her and smile at her and speak a few intelligent words and she'd walked with him, no, she'd led him to the lake, alone. She'd let him kiss her and she'd kissed him back. Worst of all, she'd believed he wanted to marry her after knowing her for a day. She'd almost told him yes.

"Help her up," Roark said in the Green Isles tongue, and the three men lifted her to her feet. "I'm going to pull your gag out and tie it around your mouth," he said in her Northern tongue. "You must swear not to call out." Alina nodded, wondering why he kept switching from the Green Isles tongue to the Northern tongue when he knew she spoke both.

He pulled the gag and she opened and closed her mouth while he unfurled it, wound it tight, pulled it over her mouth, and wrapped it snugly around her head. "Is that too tight?" he asked. Alina shook her head and he leaned in close as he tied the gag. "Forgive me, my lady owl."

Alina grunted in response, throwing daggers with her eyes as he took a piece of rope from the man who'd raised his fist to her.

"I'll tie her hands," he said, taking her wrists in hands that had been pressing her body close to his only moments ago. He bound her wrists together and ran a finger between her skin and the rope. "I'm going to relieve you of your cloak," he told her, unclasping it and tossing it to one of the men, who also held her mask and his headdress. He pulled his waist blade and Alina reared back. "I'm only going to cut off some of your gown," he said. "To throw those who'll come looking for you off our tracks."

Alina stood shaking and panting as Roark cut jagged strips of her gown away, leaving her legs bare to her knees. He held his hands up to her, and then slowly reached for the left sleeve of the gown and nipped the seams open with the tip of his blade. He tore the sleeve off at the shoulder and handed it to the same man who held her cloak and mask and strips of her gown.

"What about the pearl necklace?" the man, a big, burly greybeard, said.

"No," Roark told him. "We have what we need for the ruse."

The man grunted and headed off for the woods with a redheaded man carrying a small bucket and the third man followed, erasing their tracks with a branch of leaves.

"The plan worked," Leif said in the Northern tongue, meaning for Alina to understand. "I have to say I had my doubts, but you played her like a fiddle." He slapped Roark on the back. "Who knew you were such a good actor?"

"Yeah," Roark said, meeting Alina's glare. "Who knew?" He double-checked Alina's binds, his hands lingering over hers and giving them a gentle squeeze. "We should go," he said, taking her by the arm and leading her into the woods.

***

"You're right-handed?" Roark asked as he untied the ropes around Alina's wrists, though he knew she was. It was one of the many details he'd discovered about her. He'd never wanted to be part of her kidnapping, even if all the horrible things Roger said about her parents were true. After meeting King Jerrik and Queen Alyssa and talking with Digby and Pavel and others in the city of Sea Ridge, he had serious doubts they were. Still, he'd gone along with it for the same reasons he'd explained to Alina for going along with marrying Gwyneth. Too many people depended on it. On him.

Alina nodded and her eyes grew wide as he clapped an iron cuff around her left wrist and locked the short chain on the cuff to a larger chain attached to an iron pole in the middle of the hold, which would allow her to stand, sit, or lie on her bed of furs until they reached the Green Isles.

"If I take your gag out," he asked her, "do you promise not to scream?"

She shook her head, her green eyes blazing.

"Screaming will do you no good," he told her. "The ship's hull is too thick for sound to carry, and you'd only end up with a raw throat."

She looked around the hull, snorted, and nodded.

Roark untied the gag. "I'll make sure it stays off as long as you keep to our bargain."

"You're a fucking liar," she hissed. "Why should I believe a word you say?"

"I never lied to you, other than the lie of omission."

"Like omitting the real reason that you came here?" she huffed. "Which means everything you said to me, my brother, my father, was based on a lie."

"Not everything," he said. He folded the linen gag and wrapped it around her left wrist to cushion her skin and bone from the iron cuff and lowered his voice to a whisper. "I meant everything I said and did at the lake."

She opened her mouth and snapped it shut, his betrayal reflected in the green depths of her eyes. "That makes all this so much worse."

"I know." He'd flirted with her and gotten her to trust him. He'd lured her into a trap while becoming trapped himself by her wit and beauty. Then he'd kissed her. The memory of it still warmed his blood and other body parts. "I am sorry, truly."

"If you were truly sorry you would—"

"What are you talking about?" Leif demanded as he came down the ladder. He glanced from Alina to Roark and laughed. "The princess doesn't look too happy with you," he said in their Green Isles tongue. "Too bad. The way you two were going at it, she would've spread her legs for you in no time had we not shown up." He laughed at his own crude humor. "I think your chances of swiving her now are slim to none."

"Shut up, Leif."

"Why? The bitch can't understand a word of what I'm saying."

"She may not," Roark said. "But I do. Don't talk about her that way."

Leif sauntered over to Alina and her eyes narrowed to slits of green ice.

"How about if I take what she was about to give you?" Leif asked.

Roark fisted his hands to keep from wrapping them around Leif's neck. "Your father wants her whole and in one piece," he reminded Leif. "If her father pays the ransom and discovers her sullied, who knows how he would exact his revenge?"

Leif shrugged. "It would almost be worth it," he said, grinning salaciously at Alina, who had the good sense not to react. "Still, you're right, my father wouldn't be pleased if I took her before he had a chance to." He chucked Alina under the chin, jerking his hand back as she snapped at his fingers. "Oh, she'll be a fun one to break." He met Roark's scowl and laughed. "Don't worry, she's yours to protect until we get home, then she's my father's to do with as he will."

Leif climbed up the ladder and Roark met Alina's icy glare.

"Congratulations on a plan well executed," she told him. "I know it was your plan, your trap. Leif doesn't have the brains or the cunning. Well done, you. I'm sure your laird will reward you generously."

"Alina."

"Don't Alina me. We are not lovers, not even close, despite what Leif thinks, despite whatever you thought." She chuffed. "Nice touch, asking me to marry you. It certainly kept me off guard. Too bad we were interrupted before I could give you my answer, which would be a big, fat no."

She was lying. Roark knew it. She knew he knew it. Her eyes, her smile, her kiss had already answered him before she'd started to say yes, before Leif had grabbed her and her eyes had filled with Roark's betrayal.

"I can only say I'm sorry for my part in this so many times," he told her, leaving the rest of what she'd said alone. "I can't make you believe me. Still, Leif's right. You're mine to protect while we sail, and I will. I swear it."

"Was Leif right about his father doing what he will with me once you're home?"

"Roger knows you're worth more to him alive and intact," Roark said. "Leif was trying to scare you." *And me.* He lowered his voice to a whisper and spoke to her in his Green Isles tongue. "Nobody except me knows you speak our language. It would be wise to keep it our secret."

Alina eyed him warily. "Unless this is part of your trap too. You'll forgive me if I don't believe you, or anything you and your cohorts say in front of me, supposedly thinking I don't understand."

"I could forgive you anything, my lady owl," he said.

Embarrassed by his admission and the startled expression on her face, he turned and climbed up to the deck.

***

The muted voices of the crew floated down into the hold and Alina heard the sounds of an anchor being hauled up and sails being hoisted followed by the snap of sails filling with wind. The ship groaned and lurched forward. They were setting sail under the light of the moon and, if the wind held up, would be out of the bay and out of sight by dawn.

From what she knew, it took three days to sail from the east coast of the Green Isles to Sea Ridge, as the wind typically blew eastward, which meant it would take twice as long to sail back. She pulled her lips back in a feral grin. Once her father figured out who'd taken her, he would be on his swiftest warship and fast on their stern. Longboats didn't depend on wind. They sailed when it was convenient. Otherwise, they were powered by oars pulled by ten and two big strong, heavily armed Northmen. Six days would be plenty of time for a longboat to catch up to the heavier, slower trade ship.

Giving in to the exhaustion of the day and the rolling, lolling motion of the ship, she removed her boots and lay down on the pelts, making plans for any number of scenarios, determined to be ready for whatever came and refusing to even consider that she might never see her home again.

When she woke, she was still alone in the hold, which was dimly lit by the gray of dawn filtering down through the open hatch to the deck. She used the chamber pot next to her pile of pelts, grateful her moon-flow had ended three days ago, one less thing she'd have to deal with during this ordeal.

Roark came down the ladder and gave her a quick half-smile, which she returned with a hostile glare.

"Have you used the chamber pot yet?" he asked.

"I have. Perhaps you'd like to carry it up and empty it," she said, and then added in her mother's Rus tongue, "Perhaps the gods will be vengeful and spill it all over you."

Roark quirked his brows but didn't ask her to translate. He didn't have to.

"Perhaps you'd like to carry it up to the deck and empty it," he said. "Get some time top side in the fresh air."

Alina grudgingly held out her arm and Roark unlocked the iron wrist cuff. She considered pretending to trip and spilling the chamber pot's contents on his head as he followed her up the ladder, but with her recent luck she'd be made to clean it up. Plus, she didn't want to lose her chance to be deck side.

The crew stopped what they were doing and watched as she poured her piss over the side, rinsed the pot out with a ladle full of seawater, and set it down on the deck next to the bucket. She lengthened her spine and filled her chest with brisk, salt-tinged air, and took in her surroundings with Roark standing no more than two paces from her, watching her every move.

"I'm not going to jump over the side if that's what you're worried about," she told him. "I've decided to be an accommodating prisoner while I wait for my father's longboats, what you call warships, to catch up to you." She faced west and smiled as the eastward wind blew her hair back, and then she faced east, where her homeland was a shrinking line on the horizon. "I hope you and every man on this ship have made peace with your gods," she said loudly enough for others to hear. "My father's retribution will be swift and merciless."

"If he figures out to look for us at all," Leif said from behind her. He stepped up to her other side with a smug grin. "We covered our tracks and left pieces of your gown and cloak to make it look like you were dragged off into the woods by some wild beast. We even left a trail of pig's blood to complete the ruse." He chortled and lifted his chin toward Roark. "That was his idea."

"My father will figure it out," Alina said. He wouldn't stop his search for her until he had absolute proof she'd been dragged off and killed.

"Maybe," Leif said. "Maybe not. Even if he does, it'll take him several days of searching for your body first."

"His longboats sail three times as fast as your barge of a ship with the wind at your back," Alina countered. "And you are sailing against the…" Wind. Which had stopped blowing eastward and now blew west.

Roark put his nose to the wind, while Leif showed no signs of noticing it had shifted in his favor. If he had, he'd have surely been gloating by now. Either way, there was nothing Alina could do about the wind, but she could get some answers.

"Why am I here?" she asked Leif.

"You're here at the pleasure of my father, Laird Roger MacKinnon," he answered her. "You're his prisoner until your father pays a king's ransom for you, the terms of which will be presented to him in a fortnight's time when *The Rover* sails back to Sea Ridge and presents your father the ransom demands."

"Why me? Why my father?"

"Because you're your parents' only daughter and they ruined my family."

Alina tilted her head at Leif. "How so?"

"They banished my father and uncle and their families from Sea Ridge for being loyal to their liege, taking their wealth and lands as their own."

Alina chuffed. "My parents did this? When?"

"Twenty years ago, when your father became king and your mother his queen."

Alina furrowed her brows. "The only people my father banished from Sea Ridge then were his uncle Fenrir's family and the yellow beards who'd followed him, after they'd attempted to murder my mother and father, and my father killed Fenrir in a trial by combat."

"Lies," Leif spat.

"No," Alina said. "They're not." The entire kingdom of Sea Ridge knew this story. "Was your father one of Fenrir's men?"

Roark, who'd been listening intently, cocked his head at Leif.

"You'll find out in due time," Leif said. "I've told you all I'm going to until then."

Alina still had one question. One point to make. "If your family was brought to ruin by my parents, how is it they're wealthy, landed lairds in the Green Isles?"

"My father still had some friends and family left in the world not swayed by your parents' lies."

"Lies?" Alina snorted. "Fenrir's own wife and son testified against him at his trial. His wife confessed they killed my father's mother and made it look like she took her own life. That Fenrir smothered my father's father, his own brother, while he slept. His son confessed his father ordered the murders of my father's two brothers who'd preceded him to the throne, as well as an earlier attempt on my father's life, which took my mother's brother instead."

"What were they supposed to do?" Leif bellowed. "When the choice your father gave them was to lie or die?"

"That's not—"

"Time for you to go back in the hold," Roark said, stepping between Alina and Leif. He picked up the chamber pot and held it out to her. "Now."

Alina snatched the pot and jerked her arm away as Roark reached for her elbow.

"You first," he said, pointing toward the hatch to the hold.

"Why?" she snapped. "Afraid I'll hit you over the head with it?"

"Yes."

Alina flung a few of her Uncle Han's favorite curses at Roark as she climbed down the ladder, and glared daggers at him when he picked the iron cuff up, waiting with irritating patience until she finally held out her left arm and he clapped it around her wrist.

"Is it true?" he asked, his voice low. "What you said about this Fenrir and his yellow beards?"

"Every word."

"Why should I believe your version and not Leif's?"

Alina met Roark's gaze and held it. "Because my version was witnessed by two hundred people."

***

Roark stood at the ship's bow, the sun on his face, the wind at his back, Leif's and Alina's words swimming round and round inside his head. For ten years, he'd been listening to Roger's and his brother's, Donald's, stories of the young, upstart Jerrik showing up after years at sea to take the throne of Sea Ridge from his dying brother and keeping the younger brother from assuming the throne he'd been trained to rule while Jerrik had been sailing across the known world. Not only had he forced his way onto the throne, but he'd brought his young and inexperienced Rus wife, an outsider, to rule as his queen.

According to Roger and Donald, the new king and queen had run rampant over the kingdom, displacing long loyal jarls and karls with their own people and concocting a tale of lies and treason against Fenrir and his sons and loyal guard, whom they'd denigrated as yellow beards, in order to strip them of their lands and titles and send them into exile.

Roger and Donald had been two of the banished guard and had fled with their wives and children and widowed mother, who'd contracted a virulent sickness that had taken her life along with those of Roger's and Donald's infant sons on a long and winding journey, which eventually landed them in the Green Isles, where their uncle, Ronald, welcomed them into his home.

Aging and without a living wife or children, Ronald had named Roger his heir. He'd died six moons later of a wasting sickness, and Roger had become the new laird of North Shore Keep and Donald his chief counsel. Leif, Roger's eldest and only living son, had been three years old at the time, and Gwyneth had been born at the keep four years later.

Now Roark was helping carry out the MacKinnons' revenge on King Jerrik and Queen Alyssa by kidnapping their only daughter and delivering her to Roger to be held for ransom. He laid his hand over the vial of White Milk in his tunic pocket and shook his head at his luck, which was either really good or really bad, depending on how he looked at it.

Not only had the kidnapping gone off without a hitch, but the wind had shifted in their favor as if on cue. As if the fates had ordained everything that had happened was meant to be. Yet by a cruel twist of those same fates or the gods or dumb fucking luck, Roark had fallen head over heels in love with Alina the moment he'd spied her racing her horse on the beach, legs bare and hair flying.

He told himself over and over Alina would be kept safe, that she was worth a king's ransom whole and intact. Yet he couldn't ignore Leif's salacious interest in her, or his threat of leaving her for his father, which could have simply been Leif spouting off. Or not.

Roark shook his head and toed the deck with his boot. Roger was many things, but foolish wasn't one of them. He had to know

Jerrik's retribution would be swift and merciless should anything happen to Alina.

"Damnation."

"Sir?" Roy stood holding a bowl of the morning's porridge. "Captain said you'd likely want to take the princess her breakfast yerself."

Roark took the bowl down into the hold and held it out to Alina, who sat on her pile of furs glaring at him.

"Unfortunately, it doesn't taste any better than it looks," he said as he handed the bowl of half-congealed groats with a boiled egg sitting on top to her. "But it'll fill your belly and keep your bowels moving, which can be a problem on a ship."

"So I've been told," she said, taking the bowl from him and peering at its contents.

He sat down beside her as she took one distasteful spoonful, swallowed with a grimace, and then another. He recalled the delicious food he'd eaten at the festival. Princess Alina had likely never been forced to eat such a piss-poor excuse for a meal in her life. Still, she finished the bowl without complaint. Something Gwyneth never would've done. With Gwyneth, the porridge would've ended up on the floor or the wall and the entire ship would've heard about it.

"Do you want more?" he asked when she handed him the empty bowl.

"No. That was quite sufficient."

He glanced up at the open hatch but saw no one lingering about. "I've heard Roger's and Donald's telling of how they came to be in the Green Isles many times over the years," he said, speaking low. "Will you tell me your version again, in more detail?"

She told him of her parents' long, strange courtship, of how her father happened to be in port when his brother, Bard, died of a wasting sickness, how his family had begged him to assume the cursed throne. She told him of how her Uncle Aaron died saving her father from a rock slide, of her father sailing east and marrying her mother in her home before bringing her to Sea Ridge as his bride and queen.

She told him of Fenrir's and his wife, Ermelinde's, campaign of lies and betrayal against her parents, of how her father had believed their lies, as had his father, causing them both to deny their wives.

She told him how her father began to doubt Fenrir's lies, how he and his men set a trap for Fenrir and his yellow beards, of the public trial that followed, where the water scryer and the stable hand who'd spoken against her mother confessed their lies, forced on them by Fenrir.

She retold the rest, how her father had killed Fenrir in a trial by combat that Fenrir had demanded, how Jerrik had then banished Fenrir's widow and two adult sons and their families from Sea Ridge, along with the yellow beards loyal to him, when by rights, he could've had them all killed. The events had been witnessed by hundreds of people. People who'd chosen to stay at Sea Ridge under Jerrik's and Alyssa's rule and had prospered there along with the thousands of others who emigrated there. Facts, she reminded Roark, he'd seen with his own eyes.

"Thank you," he told her, taking her empty bowl and climbing the ladder back up to the deck.

If he'd had been back at North Shore Keep, Roark would've taken a long ride through the countryside to go over all he'd heard, seen, and done since the *The Rover* had dropped anchor in the port of Sea Ridge. But all he could do on the ship was pace back and forth across the deck under the curious watch of Leif and the ship's crew.

He'd heard Roger's and Donald's story so many times he could repeat it by heart, along with their grievances against King Jerrik and Queen Alyssa, at whose feet they placed all of their ills and troubles. Which weren't that bad, considering Roger was now a wealthy, landed laird of a keep in a prosperous port town, and Donald his right hand and chief counsel, several steps up in rank and wealth from men at arms for this Fenrir.

As far as Roark could tell, their only real losses had been those of their elderly mother and infant sons on the journey to find a new home. Hard losses, true, but losses both men griped less about than their banishment.

Listening to Alina's version of her father's ascension to his family's throne, Roark had been struck by two particular coincidences. One was the stable hand who had confessed his lies at the trial, and the stable hand Pavel, who'd told Roark, unasked, about some trouble he'd gotten into twenty years ago due to Jerrik's uncle, and how he'd learned his lesson about lying because of it.

The other was Jerrik's brother, King Bard, dying from a wasting sickness, which had actually been a slow poisoning by Fenrir's orders if not his hand, which sounded uncannily similar to how Ronald, the old laird of North Shore Keep, had died six moons after naming Roger his heir.

A hand clapped him on his shoulder from behind and he stopped his pacing.

"What are you thinking so hard on?" Leif asked.

"I was thinking on how well our plan to kidnap the princess worked out," Roark told him. "Wondering how it'll turn out."

"It'll turn out with our father ransoming the princess for enough coin to set all of us up for life," Leif said. "For you and Gwyneth to start your married life in a grand fashion. That was the plan, wasn't it? As you yourself said, it's gone amazingly well."

"So far."

"So far?" Leif spun Roark around by the shoulder to face him.

"Any number of things could happen between now and when the ransom is collected. If the ransom is collected."

"What do you mean if?"

"King Jerrik could kill Murtaugh when he presents the terms of Alina's ransom and send his warships to attack the North Shore and take the princess back rather than pay."

Leif shook his head. "My father will make it clear in his demands that Jerrik's precious daughter will die at the first sighting of any warship. Jerrik wouldn't dare chance it."

"He could pay the ransom, retrieve his daughter, return to his home, and then send his warships to attack."

Leif snorted. "You worry too much," he said. "I'm sure my father has thought of any and all possibilities and made plans to deal with them."

"If he has, he hasn't mentioned them to me."

"He doesn't tell you everything. As smart and important as you think you are, there are some things he keeps to himself or tells only Donald or me, his true son."

Roark let the insult slide, but not the point he was trying to make. "If Jerrik is the vindictive bastard your father says he is—"

"If he's what my father says he is?" Leif spouted. "What sweet poison was the bitch pouring into your ears down there?"

"She only complained about the porridge."

"She took her sweet time complaining then."

Roark shrugged. He'd have to be more circumspect in his dealings with Alina for the rest of the voyage. Leif may have been a hothead who sometimes did stupid things, but he wasn't a stupid man. "Your mother and aunt will be pleased with the bolts of worm weave you're bringing home," he said, changing the subject. "Gwyneth will look pretty in the blue. Did you promise Edna a gown?" he asked about the neighboring laird's daughter, whom Leif was generally known to be courting.

"I did."

"What about Jenny?"

Leif grinned. Jenny was the maidservant he was not so secretly spending time with.

"No gown," he said. "I did buy her a night shift of sheer worm weave from an innkeeper's harlot."

"For her, or for you?"

"Now why would I wear... Oh, I get it." Leif laughed and slapped Roark on the shoulder. He continued to laugh to himself as he walked away from Roark and toward the ship's prow.

CHAPTER 4

At Sea

The day's light from the open hatch had dimmed to dusk when Roark carried a bowl down with Alina's supper.

"Mutton stew," he said, handing her the bowl and sitting down beside her. "And the last of the bread. Tomorrow it'll be back to salted meat and hard tack along with a few carrots and turnips."

Alina said nothing. She had no real appetite and only ate to keep her strength up, sneaking side glances at Roark, who apparently meant to sit with her until she finished eating.

"May I go deck side?" she asked, handing him her empty bowl. "I could use some fresh air and movement. You can tie my wrists together if it makes you feel better," she added when he hesitated. "If you don't believe me when I say I won't try to get away." She smoothed what was left of her torn and tattered gown. "Besides, where am I going to go? I'm in the middle of the sea, hundreds of leagues away from land, with nothing but the shredded gown on my back."

Roark eyed her tattered gown and went to a chest and pulled out a linen tunic and pair of trousers and tossed them at her feet. He motioned for her to stand and unlocked the iron cuff.

"Put those on," he said. "When we go topside, stay by me."

He turned his back to her, and Alina quickly doffed what was left of her once favorite gown and shivered, as much from the chill of the oncoming night as from the fact she was standing naked no more than two paces from Roark. She pulled on the trousers and tied the stays, then donned the tunic, which was soft and well-worn and a decent fit, as were the trousers.

"Whom did these clothes belong to?" she asked, pulling on her boots.

"A stable lad."

Alina chuffed. "You really did plan this all out."

"Not all of it," he grumbled before turning around and facing her, his mouth quirking at the sight of her dressed like a boy. He swept a hand toward the ladder. "Ladies first."

Alina stepped up into the cool night air and breathed in the tang of salt and sea. She'd sailed with her father on several short voyages to neighboring ports through the years, and always thrilled to the feel of a ship beneath her and the open sea and sky beyond her. Though sailing as a prisoner with six seamen and Leif watching her every move took away much of the thrill.

She stood at the stern with her face into the chill spring wind, shivered, and crossed her arms.

"Roy," Roark called out from beside her. "Fetch a pelt from the hold for the princess, will you?"

"Aye, sir," the seaman with flaming red hair said before disappearing into the hold and coming back up with a pelt Roark laid over Alina's shoulders.

Alina pulled the pelt's edges close and rubbed her cheek on the thick, rich fur, fighting a sudden urge to cry.

"Alina?"

She met Roark's concerned gaze, which somehow made it harder to hold back her tears. "My father's pet name for my mother is Little Lynx," she sniffed. "He gave her a lynx throw as a wedding present, and it's her favorite to this day."

"She wore it last night," Roark said. "While you sang and she played the harp."

"Meadowlark," Alina whispered, swiping at her welling tears and wishing she was sitting with her family around the hearth fire and singing along as her mother played. "That's what she named her harp."

"She played beautifully."

Alina drew a shaky breath in and blew it out. "You can always tell what she's feeling by what she plays."

"What's your tell?"

"My tell?"

"How can a person tell what you're feeling?"

Alina held Roark's intent gaze for a long, interminable moment, and then dropped her eyes to her feet.

"I don't have a tell," she said.

Roark cupped her chin and lifted it until she was staring into his rain eyes. The corners of his mouth lifted and his eyes crinkled. "Yes, my beautiful green-eyed owl, you do."

Alina's cheeks flushed hot and she pulled the lynx throw closer around her shoulders, wondering what he thought her tell was and refusing to ask him. If he answered with something kind, she'd burst into tears in front of him and the entire crew. And she refused to do that. She looked up into the darkening sky and found the Big Bear and the North Star to the starboard and the Hunter to the portside with the Lady in the Chair to the starboard bow. They were sailing west, southwest.

"Is the looking glass handy?" she asked.

He grinned. "Stay here," he said, as if she had anywhere to go. "I'll get it."

Roark disappeared into the hold and Alina gave Leif her back as he sauntered over to her.

"You won't be so high and mighty once we reach my father's house," he said. Alina could actually feel his hatred boring into the back of her skull. "Roark's protection will mean nothing to you there."

She slid a sideways glance at Leif as he moved away and Roark's head popped up out of the hatch. Roark watched Leif for a moment and then came up on the deck and over to Alina.

"Do I want to know what that was about?" he asked her.

Alina shrugged. "He told me once I'm handed over to his father, your protection will mean nothing," she said, trying her best to act as if Leif's threats were idle.

Roark held the spyglass out to her, and when she took hold of the leather tube, he laid his hand over hers and pulled the spyglass and her to him. "I swear to you, Alina, no harm will come to you as long as I have breath."

Alina stared into silver eyes as deep and reflective as the sea on a glassy day. "You don't know how much I wish I could believe you," she said.

"Oh, I have an idea," Roark said with that slow, easy grin of his that made her melt from the inside out. "About as much as I wish you would," he whispered in his Green Isles tongue.

She glanced over at Leif, who was standing at the bow, speaking with the captain. "How?" she said in her Northern tongue. "How can I ever trust you again after you trapped me and abducted me? You flirted with me, lied to me, and kissed me. You proposed marriage to me."

"That kiss and proposal were the most honest things I've ever done in my life."

***

That kiss and proposal were the most honest things I've ever done in my life.

The fever dream of Roark's words plagued Alina as she paced around the ship's deck in the brisk morning air, running round and round her mind as they had from the moment that she'd walked away from him last evening, and through a night of fitful sleep.

A restless sleep she'd woken from too many times to count to find herself lying next to him, staring into the deep, silver pools of his eyes reflecting her own confusion back at her.

"I swear," Leif said loudly enough for both Alina and Roark, who stood at the stern looking through the spyglass, no doubt searching for any signs of her father's longboats, to hear, "you're pacing as much today as Roark was yesterday. What is it with you two?"

"I'm not used to inactivity," Alina said pointedly as she passed Leif, who sat on an overturned bucket, drinking his third cup of beer for breakfast. "Nor, I would guess, is Roark."

Leif lifted his sloshing cup up to Alina. "We all deal with it differently, Princess."

"What did they say?" one of the crewmen, a dark-haired, dark-eyed man who looked like the crewman checking the anchor rope enough to be his brother, asked in heavily accented Green Isles.

The other crewman, who was slightly stockier, shrugged. "Not sure," he said and glared at Leif. "Something about sitting on your lazy arse all day while others are working their arses off."

The slimmer man snorted and Alina turned to hide her grin.

"Ha, ha," Leif groused. He jutted his chin toward Roark. "How's standing around staring through a spyglass working?"

"How's keeping an eye out for those who might be coming after us not working?" the stockier man said, and spit.

"You better watch yourselves, you Pict bastards," Leif snarled. "Or my father will have your bog hides."

"Me and my brother be the captain's men," the stocky man said. "Not yer father's. We're paid to get a job done and we be gettin it done. You don't like what we say to you whilst we're working, get off yer arse and be useful. Otherwise, shut the fuck up."

"What did you say to me?" Leif bellowed as he stood on unsteady feet.

"I said I'm tired of listening to ye jawin and thinking yer better'n us."

"I *am* better than you, you black-eyed boggers," Leif huffed as the red-headed sailor named Roy and the cook walked over and stood to either side of the brothers, arms crossed and jaws jutting. "My father—"

"Laird Roger," Roark said, stepping between the sailors and Leif, "would expect all of us to stick to the job at hand and not be fighting among ourselves." He pointed the spyglass east. "So far, I've seen no sign of us being followed, but that could change at any time." He looked from the men to Leif. "I suggest we get back to it, or would you rather chance waking Captain Murtaugh and Gall from their sleep to deal with the lot of you?"

The men grumbled and went back to their duties while Leif stood glaring at Roark.

"You had no right," he snarled.

"I had every right," Roark growled back. "Your father entrusted me to see this plan through and to keep your hotheaded temper in check."

"No, he didn't."

"Yes. He did."

"Don't think I won't ask him when we get back," Leif grumbled.

"Do. But be ready to explain why."

Leif drained his cup with one long swallow, the beer dripping down his chin into his beard, and then he threw the empty cup onto the deck. "What are you looking at, bitch?"

Alina stepped back at the vitriol in his voice and the rage in his bloodshot eyes.

"Leave her alone, Leif," Roark said, his voice deadly calm. "She has nothing to do with this. She doesn't even understand what was said."

"She understands you took her side and theirs against me well enough," Leif said, whipping his arm out toward the crew, who listened and watched and made no pretense of hiding it.

Roark took a deep breath in and blew it out, shaking his head and grinning good-naturedly. "You're drunk," he said. He slapped Leif on the shoulder and kept his hand there. "You should go below deck and sleep it off."

"Yeah, yeah." Leif let Roark guide him to the hatch. "Sleep sounds good. Not much else to do on this stinking barge."

Roark helped Leif down the ladder and Alina made her way over to the crew. She knew Roy spoke the Northern tongue, and she addressed herself to him. "I'm Alina," she said. "May I know your names?"

The two who could be brothers and the cook looked to Roy, who spoke for them. "I'm Roy," he said. "This is Dwyer, and Kerry and Kerwin."

"Roy, Dwyer, Kerry, Kerwin," Alina nodded to each man in turn, and then looked from Kerry to Kerwin. "Brothers?" she asked. Roy nodded. "Twins?"

"Close enough," Roy said. "They were born only ten moons apart. Kerry here," he pointed to the stockier brother, "be the oldest, and Kerwin be his baby brother."

The brothers, knowing they were being talked about, grinned and jostled each other.

"I have brothers," Alina told Roy. "My twin, and two younger brothers." She thought of what they must be going through, how worried they must be for her, especially Aleksi, who tried to hide his soft heart behind a tough exterior. "I miss them," she sniffed and did nothing to stop the sudden welling of tears in her eyes. Better to let these men see her as a person, a sister and a daughter who'd been ripped from her family.

Roy translated what she'd said and the brothers nodded in sympathy. Alina glanced around. There was nobody else topside.

"Whatever Laird Roger is paying you to take me to him," she said, "my father will pay you double." She held up two fingers. "If you turn around and take me back."

"First 'a all," Roy said, "Roger isn't our laird." Alina widened her eyes as if this was news to her. "Secondly, your father's more likely to kill us for taking you than he would be to reward us for bringing you back."

"Not if I told him I promised your safety," Alina swore.

Roy translated what she said for the others, and Alina heard the name Roger spoken as the men whispered among themselves with plenty of curses and hand gestures.

"Despite our personal wishes," Roy told her, "the decision is Captain Murtaugh's."

"And the captain will not go back on his deal with Roger," Roark said from behind her in the Northern tongue. "No matter how much your father might pay him." He stepped up and stood beside her. "To help you do what you're asking them, they would not only have to mutiny against their captain, which could get them killed, but what if they did manage to get you back to your father? Even if he didn't kill them, what do you think Roger would do to them and their families?"

***

Roark steered Alina away from the men as Roy explained what he'd said to her.

"I hadn't thought of the consequences to their families," she said, sounding contrite. They stopped at the rail to the bow. "You understand I had to try?"

"I do," Roark told her. "In truth, I would've been disappointed if you hadn't."

Alina tilted her head. "Why?"

Roark grinned. "I thought an owl's favorite word was who," he said. Alina tilted her head the other way and Roark's grin grew wider. "One of the first things I noticed about you, other than your legs," he said, and was gratified to see her cheeks pinken, "was that you're not a woman of faint heart or timid manners. You have a certain boldness and infinite curiosity."

"Most men I've met don't consider those to be good things," she said.

"Most men are idiots. Have you ever considered that?"

"I have," she said with a wry grin. "Many times."

Roark laughed, quick and short, and wished for about the thousandth time since he'd spied her on the beach that they could have met under different circumstances. However, things were what they were. He was her kidnapper, taking her to Roger, a man who may have lied about his reasons for having her abducted, if not his family's entire history for the past twenty years. All so Roark could keep the peace between their families and marry Roger's daughter, a spoilt brat of a girl who cared even less for him than he did for her. He ran a hand through his hair and toed the deck with his boot. He was an idiot.

"Tell me of this place you're taking me to, this North Shore Keep," Alina said. "Tell me about this Laird Roger."

Roark leaned his back against the rail and gazed westward. "North Shore Keep is the manor and the lands Roger inherited from his uncle, Ronald, not long after he arrived in the Green Isles. The town of North Shore is a small port on the northwestern shore of the Long Firth, which you would call an inlet or a bay. The ships sail in and out of the firth and trade up and down the coasts of the Green Isles and across the North Sea to the shores of your Northlands and on occasion south to the lands along the Mid-Earth Sea."

"The land?"

"Is rich and arable enough, though not so rich and arable as the land of Thorn Bush Keep, my family's home, which is farther northwest and inland up the Long River." He smiled, thinking of his days as a young lad, fishing and hunting with Logan, the gamekeeper, of swimming in the river and running through the woods, of riding over green fields.

"You miss your home."

"I do." Nobody at North Shore Keep had ever realized this about him, or if they had, they'd never mentioned it to him or shown him any empathy. Somehow, it didn't surprise him Alina had. "It's a land of running rivers, rolling hills, green fields, and dense forests," he told her. "Beautiful, bountiful country, rich with woods and game." Her bright eyes were as green as those fields and her smile as gentle as the hills. "Unfortunately, we have no trading port and North Shore has little farmland or woods for lumber, so our clans, our families, sealed an alliance to benefit both places."

"Your betrothal to Gwyneth."

"My betrothal to Gwyneth." He gripped the bow's rail. "As a second son, it was deemed the best use of me."

Alina laid her hand over his and gave it a gentle squeeze. "I'm sorry for you then," she said. She removed her hand, and Roark felt the absence of her touch. "Almost as sorry as I am for myself. The difference being, you're being used by your family while I'm being used against mine."

"Your parents," he said, "they haven't, they didn't… I mean as a princess your marriage would be valuable politically."

Alina shrugged and gazed out across the vast distance of the sea. "They knew arranging a marriage for me would never work." She looked at Roark and gave him a rueful grin. "The women in my family have a long history of marrying the man they fall in love with at first sight."

"Like your mother did your father."

She nodded. "Kingdoms have fallen and risen because of their marriages," she said. "My great-grandparents' love story is legend in much of the world. My great-grandmother, Oona—"

"Your great-grandmother was Oona the Swan?"

Alina tilted her head. "You've heard of her?"

"The story of Oona the Swan and Asad the Lion is known throughout the High Lands," he said, still trying to register Alina was their great-granddaughter, yet somehow not surprised. It certainly explained her otherworldly green eyes, and how drawn he was to her, like a moth to flame. "It's quite a love story."

"So it is. So is my mother's and my grandmother's."

"I'd like to hear them someday," he told her. "To learn about the women in your family and how they fall in love at first sight."

"I'd like to tell you them, someday," she said with the faintest of smiles. "But for now, tell me of Roger. Is he like his son, Leif?"

"Only in looks and arrogance," Roark said with a wag of his brows, and Alina's smile widened. "Where Leif's arrogance is a result of being the only son of a laird, born with fair looks and charm that run skin deep, Roger's is born of a natural shrewdness and cunning and a propensity to use both for what he wants without any consideration for how it affects others."

Alina's smile flattened and grew grim, and Roark stared hard into her attentive eyes, wanting her to understand this about Roger. To fear him. For her own sake.

"And what he wants more than anything else in this world," he told her, "is revenge against your father and mother."

***

Dressed in the stable boy's trousers and tunic, her hair braided and stuffed up under a woolen cap to keep her identity a secret from any onlookers, Alina stood on the bow of *The Rover* as it sailed into North Shore port. The firth they'd sailed west through, the Long Firth, was an inlet close in size to the bay at Sea Ridge, with rolling hills, sparse woodlands, and small towns along the shoreline, unlike the jutting mountains and dense forests of her homeland. Unlike the large, thriving port of Sea Ridge, the port town they pulled into was small and shabby with only one dock and no obvious warehouse, its most distinct feature a large, wooden-framed, cross-beamed gallows with three ropes hanging from it in the middle of the town square that opened onto the dock.

The wind had blown westward the entire voyage and *The Rover* had made its home port in four days, two days earlier than expected. Even so, they were greeted by a full contingent of the laird's household waiting on the dock, including a tall, lanky grey beard dressed in a richly embroidered linen tunic, leather vest and trousers, which were called breeches here, and a short cloak of red fox. The man shaded his eyes with his hand, searching the deck and stopping at Alina.

Leif bounded down the gangplank almost as soon as it was lowered and embraced the man.

"Welcome home, son," the man said, breaking Leif's embrace. "I see your journey was successful."

"That it was," Leif said with a huge grin. He signaled imperiously at Roark, who took Alina by the elbow, giving it a gentle squeeze as she clutched the sack that held her tattered gown and the lynx pelt Roark had gifted her. She reached for the pearl that normally hung at her throat, her only other personal belonging, but found only air. Roark had taken it from her yesterday, claiming that he would keep it safe for her.

He'd told her of the MacKinnons, and so she knew the tall, white-haired woman with the ermine short cloak now hugging Leif was Lynette, his mother, and the pretty blonde dancing beside her was Gwyneth, who hadn't yet even looked her betrothed's way. Roger, however, stared at Roark and Alina as they descended the gangplank with a smug smile on his long-chinned, sharp-angled, Northman's face.

Roark stopped in front of Roger and let go his hold of Alina's elbow. He stepped forward and clasped Roger's arm.

"Did you have any trouble?" Roger asked with only the slightest Northern accent to his Green Isles tongue.

"No," Roark said. "It went surprisingly well."

He stepped back, and Roger and Alina took each other's measure. Looking at Roger was like looking at an older version of her Uncle Tryggr. Same height, build, high-boned cheeks, and grey eyes. All fairly typical of a Northman.

Roger gave a signal and Roark took Alina by the elbow and led her toward a wagon pulled by two draft horses with two saddle horses tied to the back. Roger gave his wife a hand up onto the wagon as Leif helped Gwyneth and then jumped into the back. Roark untied the saddle horses from the wagon, booted Alina up onto the back of the shaggy little dun mare, and then mounted the sturdy, dapple grey stallion.

They rode behind the wagon, traveling northwest along a road cut deep with wheel ruts through rolling hills dotted with small herds of white, tan, and brown sheep before the road turned north through a village of thatch houses, many of them little more than huts, the men and women and children there stopping to watch them pass.

Most of the children were barefoot, and their parents dressed in threadbare tunics and work aprons. Alina looked at Roark, who met her gaze, and she nodded purposely from the ragged serfs to the richly dressed laird's family, who sat on cushions and blankets and laughed and talked among themselves while enjoying a meal of fruit, bread, and cheese, never once asking her or Roark if they were hungry, or even glancing at the dirt-poor villagers.

"I know," he told her. "This is what I'm trying to prevent more of. What I'm hoping to change."

By marrying Gwyneth and keeping the alliances between lairds and clans intact.

Another quarter league up the road they came to the gated entrance of a two-story manor house with several small buildings and what looked to be a stable with a paddock situated over several acres of cleared land.

They rode up to the front doors of the house, where a middle-aged couple dressed in the plain work aprons of house servants stood waiting. Roger and Leif helped Lynette and Gwyneth down from the wagon and the servants followed the ladies into the house.

"Bring our guest to my private chambers," Roger ordered Roark, and then he and Leif strode into the house.

Roark dismounted as two stable hands came trotting over to take their horses' reins. Alina swung her leg over the dun's rump and startled as Roark's hands grasped her around the waist and lowered her to the ground.

"Welcome to North Shore Keep," he said, giving her waist a quick squeeze before letting go.

He pushed the thick, wooden, double doors to the manor house open and Alina followed him into the entrance hall. To the right of the staircase leading up to the second story was a dining hall with one high and several low tables and chairs, and an open door to the kitchens, from which the enticing scents of bread baking and meat roasting wafted. Roark turned to the left, leading Alina through a common room with a large hearth and sitting area full of chairs and tables to an ornately carved door he knocked on.

"Enter," a man's voice said from the other side.

They walked into a room with wood-paneled walls hung with richly detailed tapestries, a thick, woolen rug, and heavy wood furniture.

"Take a seat," Roger said. He sat behind an oak desk with curved legs and clawed feet, and indicated a cushioned bench along one wall. Leif sat on a chair with an upholstered seat next to his father's table across from them. "First of all," Roger said in the Green Isles tongue, "well done, both of you. Well done indeed."

"Thank you, Father." Leif sat taller in his chair. "That bastard Jerrik will be in for a surprise when he finds out his precious daughter isn't dead but being held for ransom."

"Surprise isn't what he'll be feeling," Roger said. He looked at Alina, who lifted her chin a notch at his perusal, and smiled without showing any teeth, putting her in mind of a cat playing with a half-dead mouse.

"What do you mean?" Roark asked.

Roger smirked. "I mean the plan has changed."

"How so?"

"However I say it has," Roger snapped.

Alina sat back at the angry tone of his voice and Roark stiffened and said nothing more. From what he'd told her about Roger, he wasn't a man to be challenged, especially in front of others, even if it was assumed they couldn't understand a word of what was being said.

Smoothing his tunic, Roger addressed Alina. "I am Roger MacKinnon, laird of North Shore Keep," he said in her Northern tongue. "You are my prisoner here for the next fortnight at least, when *The Rover* sails for your home again. Behave yourself and you will not be mistreated. Try to escape, and you will regret it."

"I won't try to escape," she answered him, glad that her voice didn't quake or crack. "As I told Roark, I plan on being an accommodating prisoner while waiting for my father to come for me." She pressed her lips into a thin smile. "And he will."

"I am sure he will," he said. He tapped his chin with his forefinger and then looked to Roark, whose expression was one of unconcern, though his posture was as rigid as a stag in a hunter's sights. "How did you trap the bitch?" Roger asked in their language.

"Roark was great," Leif jumped in when Roark hesitated. "He flirted with her and wooed her until she led him," he said, laughing, "to a secluded lake." Leif glanced at Roark, who shrugged nonchalantly while Alina sat staring straight ahead as if she didn't understand every word of Leif's humiliating recitation. "You should've seen them, Father, cooing and kissing while me and the others snuck up on them."

"Well, well, Roark." Roger chuckled. "I wouldn't have guessed you had it in you."

"He would've had it in her," Leif said, smirking at his own crude jest, "if we hadn't showed up when we did."

"Ha, ha," Roark said affably.

Alina sat as stiff and silent as the stone lodged in her throat. At least Leif hadn't mentioned Roark's proposal of marriage or Alina's almost answer.

"You're sure Jerrik will think her dead?" Roger asked.

"Gall dragged Kerry so it would look like a wild animal dragged her off into the woods," Leif told him. "We left bits and pieces of her gown and mask and cloak and gobs of pig's blood along the trail."

"Good, good." Roger tapped his chin and smiled as pleased as a cat that had finished toying with the poor mouse and killed it. "I want Jerrik and Alyssa to grieve for their daughter, to know how it feels to lose a child and have your family torn apart."

He stood and walked around the table to stand in front of Alina and stare down at her for a long moment. "You are your mother's daughter," he murmured, and then he went to the door and opened it. "Peg, Jenny," he called out. "Come take our guest to her chambers."

Two women dressed in plain brown long tunics and scrubbed white work aprons scurried into the room. The older one, who looked to be the same servant who had greeted the family on their return from the docks, was middle-aged, buxom, and round-faced with curly brown hair poking out from under her white linen cap. The other woman was a younger version of the first. Alina started to stand and felt Roark tugging down on the back hem of her tunic, a tacit reminder that she shouldn't have understood what Roger told them.

"This is Peg," Roger said to Alina in her Northern tongue as the older servant stepped up and curtsied. "And this is her daughter, Jenny, they will take you to your rooms." He eyed Alina from capped head to boots as she stood. "They will provide you with clean and proper clothes and will fetch you for supper when it's served." He sniffed as Alina stood and pinched his narrow nose. "Tomorrow you may bathe."

Alina ignored his dig and followed the women out of the room and up the stairs to a hallway with doors to what she assumed were bedchambers lining the back and sides of the house, connecting to a walkway along the front side with tall, narrow windows along the wall opened enough for air flow and arrows, much like her family's long house.

"Here we are, Lady," Peg said, pushing open a door to a room on the far side from the staircase.

"You speak the Northern tongue well, Peg," Alina said.

"Thank you, Lady. Lady Lynette taught me and Jenny."

"Alina, please." She was hoping to make friends with these women. She could use as many as she could get while here. "Even in my home, nobody calls me lady."

"Alina," Peg said, her round cheeks rising. She turned to the gawking Jenny. "Hussht, girl," she said. "Show Alina here around the room whilst I get her some clothes."

"Yes ma'am." Jenny bobbed her head as her mother bustled out of the room. She gave Alina a shy smile. "This here's the bed," she said in a heavily accented Northern tongue as she pulled back the red drapes to a canopied, four-poster bed. "These here are the chests to put your belongings in."

Alina nodded, not bothering to explain the only belongings she had were the clothes she was wearing, her tattered gown, and lynx throw.

Jenny opened the wooden shutters to the one window in the room and Alina went to look out of it. They were twenty feet high at least, with a thorny bramble bush growing directly below the window and not a tree within fifty paces. She turned away from the window with a heavy sigh.

"I'll bring you some soap and water and a washing cloth," Jenny said, pointing to the wash basin. "My mother should be back with some clothes soon."

"Thank you." Alina sat on the bed as Jenny shut the door behind her and slid the outside bolt with a thud. She laid back, her legs dangling off the edge and giving her back a good stretch. At least this prison had a soft bed, unlike the pile of pelts on the ship. But unlike the ship, this room wouldn't have Roark's steadying presence lying next to her through the night.

She stared up at the red canopy, recalling what had been said in the laird's private chambers. If Roger and Leif knew she spoke their Green Isles tongue, they'd hidden it well. Roark had tugged on her tunic to keep her from giving her understanding of their language away. Why would he have done that if not to help her keep her secret? She grinned, remembering how he'd teased her about "why" being her favorite word.

He'd also warned her they wouldn't be able to speak together often or freely here, not without raising Roger's suspicions. Something neither of them wanted to do. Roark, to keep peace in the household, and Alina to keep from being locked up for the next fortnight, or longer. The way she figured it, if *The Rover* wasn't setting sail for a fortnight and it took three to six days to reach Sea Ridge, depending on the winds, and another several days for her father to amass her ransom and then another four to six days to sail back here, that was closer to a moon of imprisonment for her. She sighed and folded her legs onto the bed, curling into a ball and stretching her back in the opposite direction. Either way, a fortnight or a moon, she was determined to not give Roger a reason to keep her locked up in this room day and night.

The bolt to the door scraped open and Peg came in carrying a bundle she handed Alina. "Here's a clean long tunic, an apron, and a pair of woolen stockings," she said. "It can be plenty cold here though it be spring."

"Thank you," Alina said, not mentioning compared to Sea Ridge, where there was still snow on the mountains, or the icy winds whipping across the deck of *The Rover*, it felt almost balmy here.

"Supper will be in a bit," Peg said as Jenny carried in a pitcher of water, a washing cloth, and a bar of soap. "Clean up and one of us'll come for you then."

***

Roark sat at his usual seat to the right of Donald and Leif, who sat at Roger's right at the high table, with Lynette and Gwyneth and Myrna, Donald's wife, sitting to Roger's left. Alina was seated at one of the low tables with Peg, Jenny, and Craig, Peg's husband, and the other house servants. A second low table held the laird's six men at arms and their wives and children, while the stable hands ate at tables in the kitchen along with the cook staff.

As a princess, even one being held prisoner, Alina should have been sitting at the high table. Certain Roger had seated her with the servants as an insult as much as to hide her identity, Roark was even more certain she was more comfortable there than she would be sitting anywhere near Lynette, Gwyneth, or Myrna, a sour-faced woman whose grudge against Alina's family was second only to Roger's.

She'd been a young wife with an infant son when Jerrik banished them from Sea Ridge, and had lost her son to the same sickness that'd taken her mother-in-law and Roger and Lynette's younger son. She'd miscarried several babies after that, leaving her, if not her husband, childless. Donald had at least six blond-haired, grey-eyed by-blows he acknowledged living in the villages surrounding North Shore Keep, though he only helped support the mothers of his four sons and did nothing for the mothers of his daughters. Or his wife. Theirs was as unhappy a marriage as Roark had ever seen, for which Myrna blamed Alina's parents.

The kitchen servants brought out trays of fresh baked ryes and aged cheeses and roast mutton with the last of the winter roots and the first of the spring greens, welcome food after four days of ship fare. Tucking into his meal, Roark was glad to see Alina eating heartily and speaking with Peg and Nessa, Gwyneth's maidservant, a sweet-natured girl who generally bore Gwyneth's temperamental ways with a resigned complaisance.

"Brother," Gwyneth said loudly to Leif in the Northern tongue. "Tell us how you were able to capture the princess."

Roger clicked his teeth at his daughter, who either forgot or didn't care Alina's true identity was supposed to remain secret, while the servants who understood the Northern language perked up.

"It was easy as it turned out," Leif answered in kind, making sure Alina would understand what he said. "I made friends with her twin brother and got us invited to the spring festival where Roark flirted with her and smooth-talked her into taking him to a secluded area. We followed and waited until they were so wrapped up in their lovemaking that we walked right up and nabbed her."

"Lovemaking?" Gwyneth asked, her blue eyes wide. "The princess and Roark?"

"Aye, sister. If we hadn't taken her when we did, your betrothed would've been swiving her, no doubt."

Gwyneth stared down her nose at Alina. "Did you not know he was betrothed? To me?"

Roark furrowed his brows. Gwyneth couldn't have cared less about him as a man, or her betrothed. In fact, he'd bet coin she was sweet on Munroe, the youngest of Roger's men-at-arms, and he on her.

"Well?" Gwyneth demanded.

"I, ah, I did know," Alina said, her cheeks flushing pink.

"Yet you thought it fine to make love to him?"

Alina glanced helplessly at Roark, who could do nothing but sit there with his jaw clamped tight.

"I was, we were both, quite drunk, my lady," Alina lied. She shrugged unconvincingly and Roark bit down on a grin. She really was a terrible liar.

Gwyneth's high-pitched laugh clawed its way up Roark's spine. "I would hope so," she said, apparently buying the lie. "A woman would have to be drunk to make love to such a freckle-faced ginger willingly." She looked at Roark and made a disgusted shiver. "Ugh."

As used to Gwyneth's vitriol as Roark was, he wasn't used to seeing its effect on Alina, who sat back as if she'd been slapped. She looked to Roark, her expression full of the same sympathy she'd shown him during their talks about his betrothal to the harpy while aboard the ship. He looked away quickly and plastered a well-practiced mask of indifference on his face. "To each his own," he said.

"You want to swive the bitch?" Gwyneth screeched in their language, and every person in the room jerked their heads up. "Be my guest. Maybe the Northern whore can teach you a few tricks to liven up our marriage bed."

"Enough." Roger slammed his fist down on the table. "There will be no swiving of or with my hostage," he said in the Green Isles tongue. He glared from one end of the room to the other. "By anyone. As a virgin she's worth her weight in gold where she's going. Do I make myself clear?"

Where she was going? "You mean back to her home?" Roark said.

"Of course," Roger answered. He was, Roark was beginning to understand, an accomplished liar.

CHAPTER 5

Horses

Alina sank down into the hot bath water with a weary sigh. A small chamber of wood and stone with a hearth fire to heat the kettles of water, the bathhouse held two wooden tubs, a small table of soaps and oils, and washing and drying linens. Though it wasn't as private or as well appointed as the bath chambers in her family's long house, after four days on a ship and yesterday, it felt good to soak and wash the stink off herself.

Unsure of how long Peg, who sat guard outside, would allow her to stay in here, Alina dunked her head underwater and then scooped a handful of soap and sniffed, smelling rose and lavender and bracing rosemary. She stood and lathered her hair and her body from head to toe, and then sat back down and dunked and rinsed, breathing in the clean scent of the soap and lounging in the warm, wet heat of the water, determined to enjoy it for as long as she could.

She hadn't slept well last night despite being in a big, soft bed. Her mind had been racing with everything that'd been said at supper, especially Roger's comment about where she was going. She could tell Roark didn't believe Roger was sending her home. Something was going on, and she had to find out what.

Leif's bawdy story and Gwyneth's cruelty were horrid, but not as worrying as what Roger had said.

Poor Roark. Stuck between his obligations and a lifetime with a horrid woman who couldn't see his worth. Alina padded the tub's edge with a rolled-up linen, leaned her head back, closed her eyes, and thought of Roark. He was everything she wanted in a man: handsome, kind, and intelligent, who kissed like no other man she'd ever met.

She would be twenty years old in a little over a moon's time, and she was a princess. A princess who'd been kissed and to whom marriage had been proposed by six men. Six men whom she'd never come close to responding to the way she had to Roark. Yet, he was her abductor and played an integral part in her capture. Nothing she could say or do would change their circumstance.

Her fingertips were starting to prune. She stood and stepped out of the tub, toweled herself dry, and wrapped the towel around her hair. She eyed the woolen stockings Peg had given her and ignored them. It was nowhere near cold enough to wear those itchy things. She shook out the brown linen long tunic and was holding it out in both hands when the door burst open and Lynette and Myrna sauntered in, their gazes of honed steel leaving a trail of cuts as they razed her unclad body.

"She's Alyssa's whelp all right," Lynette said in the Northern tongue as Alina quickly slipped the tunic on over her head and yanked the skirt down her hips and legs. "If her green demon eyes weren't proof enough, her harlot's body is."

Myrna smirked. "I remember how the little strumpet would strut around, smiling and flirting and tempting every man who looked her way."

Alina's jaw dropped at their naked hatred. She closed it with a snap. Her parents had always been open about how her mother had been accused of infidelity by Fenrir and his yellow beards, of how her father, an admittedly jealous man where her mother was concerned, had briefly believed them, until they'd been proven to be lies. Lies that these women, wives of two of those yellow beards, continued to spread.

Lengthening her spine and squaring her shoulders, she met the women's vindictive glares. "Is there a purpose to this?" she asked. "Whatever this is?"

"We wanted to see for ourselves how alike you are to your mother," Lynette said, her voice, her smile, dripping venom. "Our spies tell us that though you look like her, you act more like your true father than the cuckhold king who's raised you as his."

Alina chuffed. "You mean Hamar, the stablemaster, I assume." The looks on their faces were almost worth the inquisition. Alina laughed, short and harsh. "Did you really think my parents would try to keep what happened a secret from their children when the entire royal household witnessed Fenrir's accusations, as well as the trial where they were proven false? Where his own family admitted he was a lying, scheming murderer?"

"Admissions they were forced to give upon pain of death," Myrna spat. "Lies that were sold as truth and caused our family's banishment. That took everything from us."

Roark had told Alina about Myrna's losing her infant son on the journey here, about her inability to carry a babe to term since, and she was sorry for her. But not sorry enough to stand here and listen to this.

"You were both there, you know the truth," she told the women. "Yet you've held on to your grievances, based on known lies for over twenty years. You've not only held on to them, you've fed them and nurtured them with your hate until you can't see how twisted and pathetic your obsessive need for revenge against my family is."

Myrna stepped up to Alina and slapped her across the cheek. Hard. "My only regret," she hissed in the Green Isles tongue as Alina held a hand to her stinging cheek, "is that I won't get to see their faces when they find out what really happened to you." She smiled, as thin and cold as ice over treacherous water. "Though it is a poor trade, an only daughter for two sons."

Cackling like two hens, they left the bathhouse as abruptly as they'd entered. Alina tore the towel from her head, threw it on the floor, and stormed out after them right into Peg.

"Oh my," Peg said, eyeing Alina's cheek, which she knew without seeing was red and welting. "Oh dear."

"It's nothing," Alina said, catching sight of Lynette and Myrna as they headed for the manor house. She glanced around the yard, wishing for somewhere she could go to walk off her still-seething anger, and saw Roark leading the dapple grey he'd ridden yesterday from the stables toward her and Peg.

"What was that all about?" he said in Alina's language, lifting his chin toward Lynette's and Myrna's stiff backs as they entered the house.

"Nothing," Alina said, looking everywhere but at Roark.

He looked to Peg, who pressed her lips tight and shook her head.

"Alina?" He cupped her chin and lifted her head, cursing as he spied her cheek, which had stopped stinging but still emanated heat.

"Damnation." A low rumble rose from his chest. "Who slapped you?"

"It doesn't matter."

"Damned if it doesn't. Roger swore to me that you wouldn't be harmed while here."

"Apparently his wife and sister-in-law took no such oaths."

"Excuse us for a moment, Peg," Roark said, taking Alina by the arm and walking her and his horse over to the paddock. He tied the horse off to the fence and took Alina by the shoulders, holding her so that she was facing him. "Tell me," he said.

Alina shook her head and dropped her gaze, embarrassed. She glanced at the manor house, from where she was certain Lynette and Myrna watched them.

"Alina." Roark cupped her chin and held her gaze. "Tell me, my lady owl."

"Lynette and Myrna came into the bath while I was naked. They spoke of how I looked and acted like my mother, like a harlot."

He ran the pad of his thumb along her jawline. "They were—"

"Being bitches, I know," she said with a short, harsh laugh.

"What else did they say?"

"Oh, the same old lies about my family that their family has been spewing for twenty years."

"Which one slapped you?"

"Myrna."

Roark gently ran the backs of his knuckles down her tender cheek. "I'm sorry," he said. "Though not that surprised. Myrna's disappointments in her life and marriage have soured her. Her soul is as withered and dry as a raisin."

"I can handle Myrna and Lynette and whatever venom they spew at me," Alina said. She glanced around, making sure there was no one close by listening. "What bothers me is something Myrna said and echoed Roger's words last night. In Green Isles tongue she said her only regret was that she wouldn't be able to see my parents' faces when they found out what really happened to me. That it would be a poor trade, a daughter for two sons." She held Roark's intent gaze. "Why would she want to see my parents' faces? Why did she say it in Green Isles tongue, thinking I wouldn't understand her?"

"I don't know," Roark said. "Yet."

Alina shook her head. "Something's wrong. Roger said plans change. What's he up to?"

"Everything's wrong," Roark rumbled. He clamped his jaw, rubbed his beard, and toed the ground with his boot. "I know this is a big ask, especially after my part in bringing you here, but I want you to continue acting the good, submissive prisoner waiting to be ransomed, and I swear to you, I'll find out what's really going on."

"And then what?"

"Then we'll know what we're dealing with and what to do about it."

"Why?"

Roark grinned. "Why what, my lady owl?"

"Why are you helping me?"

Roark cocked his head at her, stepped in to her so their backs were facing Peg and the manor house, lifted her hand in his, and kissed the backs of her fingers. "Because."

***

Roark tied off Artur in a copse of oak at the edge of the port town and focused his spyglass on the docks where the contents of *The Rover*'s hold were being loaded by the crew onto a wagon bound for North Shore Keep under Captain Murtaugh's supervision.

Kerwin and Kerry had no great love or loyalty to Roger. If anyone would tell Roark what he wanted to know, he figured it'd be them. He'd simply have to keep his eyes and ears open for a chance at finding them alone, away from Murtaugh or Gall, or anyone else who could be Roger's spy. The man was one of the most untrusting, suspicious people Roark had ever known, and he was beginning to see why. It was looking more and more like his and his family's lives here were built on lies large and small.

Too many things had been said and done to erode what little trust Roark had put in Roger's word to begin with, and he was finding it harder and harder to believe anything Roger said about the whole sordid mess.

Roark had seen, heard, and borne witness to how the city of Sea Ridge thrived and prospered under King Jerrik and Queen Alyssa. After meeting Alina and her family, he was more inclined to believe her version of how Roger and Donald had been banished. In truth, he was more inclined to believe her about anything, and not only because she filled his thoughts and dreams day and night.

"Come on, Artur." He untied the stallion, jumped onto his saddle, and urged the horse into an easy gallop. "You and I could both use a good run."

He was settling Artur back in his stall when he heard the stable hands discussing what to do with a foal that had been born to a first-time mother four days ago and wasn't getting the milk it needed from its skittish dam.

"I wish old Lloyd were here," the newer, younger hand named Fergus said about the stablemaster who'd left against Roger's wishes to tend to his ailing mother right before *The Rover* had sailed for Sea Ridge. "He'd know what to do."

"Aye, 'cept the laird'd have yer head if you went to Lloyd about it," Gare, the older hand, said. "I know some of what to do, but old Lloyd, he kept his potions to hisself and swore he'd take them to his grave afore he let the laird have use of them."

Roark stepped out of Artur's stall and over to the brooding pen where a long-legged, flaxen-maned, chestnut mare Roger had bought specifically as a broodmare, intending to sell her foals to other rich lairds and their ladies as saddle horses, stood pressed against one wall. Her ash-grey foal, its ribs visible beneath its dull coat, lay prone in the stall.

"I may be able to help you," he told the frowning men.

Walking from the stable to the manor house, considering how to phrase his request so that Roger would agree with it, a flash of blue at the edge of the orchard caught Roark's eye. It was Gwyneth in a blue skirt holding hands with Munroe as he pulled her deeper into the cover of the trees. Roark snorted and shook his head.

Not that he cared one whit that his betrothed was stepping off into the bushes and doing who knew what with another man, but they were so obvious about it. It was as badly kept a secret as the fact that Leif was sleeping with Jenny.

He went to Roger's private chambers and knocked on the closed door.

"Who is it?" Roger called out.

"Roark. I need to talk to you about Etain's foal."

"Enter."

Roark stepped into the room and stopped cold. He'd interrupted a meeting with Roger, Donald, and Leif. A meeting he hadn't been asked to attend.

"What about the foal?" Roger asked.

"The mare will have nothing to do with him and Gare and Fergus need help to save him. I told them I'd ask you about letting the princess take a look at him. Seeing as how she and her family are so well known for their stables and their knowledge of horses."

"Not a bad suggestion," Roger said agreeably. "Especially if she knows even half as much as her father, the stablemaster, does."

Alina had told Roark about Fenrir and the old water scryer and the untrue rumor that Hamar, the stablemaster, was Alina's and Anders's true father, which was easy enough to refute. One look at Anders, her twin brother, was all a person needed to tell that he was Jerrik's son. Still, Roark knew better than to contradict Roger. He said nothing.

"You will keep guard over her," Roger said. "Make sure she doesn't try to escape."

"I will."

Roger flicked his hand. "Go then. A dead foal is worth nothing to me."

***

"Gare, Fergus, this is Alina." Roark introduced her to the stable hands in their Green Isles tongue. Both men doffed their caps. "Alina, this is Gare," he said in her Northern tongue, introducing the older hand, a moon-faced man with a balding pate and kindly brown eyes. "And this," he said, introducing the flame-haired younger hand, "is Fergus."

Alina nodded to the men and then opened the gate to the brooding pen, holding her hand up to all three men. "The mare is scared enough," she told Roark, who translated. "The fewer people coming at her, the better."

"You be careful, miss," Gare warned. "She's right skittish and tried to bite Fergus when he brought the wee foal to her earlier today."

Alina waited for Roark to translate again and then nodded her head in thanks. This would all go so much more quickly and easily if she didn't have to pretend ignorance of what they were saying, but Roark was right, it was important to keep this one advantage over her captors.

The foal was lying in the straw on its belly, legs tucked and barely able to hold its head up. She knelt at his head and lifted his lips. "His gums are pale and tacky to the touch," she said, more to herself than the men watching, who couldn't understand her except for Roark. "His eyes are dulled and starting to sink into his skull." She ran her hand over its matted coat, stretched thin over its ribs and pelvis, and lifted its tail.

"You're nothing but skin and bones, poor baby, and your tail is covered in shit and flies." She swatted the flies away and stood, ready to chew Gare and Fergus out for letting the foal get this bad, but they both looked so worried, and Roark had told her about the stablemaster leaving abruptly and how they were both new at the job. "If we don't get some milk into him soon," she told Roark, "he won't live another day." She met the hands' worried frowns. "He might not anyway." They may not have understood her words, but they understood her meaning by their downturned mouths. "Does the keep have milk goats?"

"Aye," Roark said. "The farm keeps a herd for cheese making."

"The foal will need three to four bucketsful a day," she said. "We can start with two for now. Make sure the buckets are clean before you use them. And get me a blanket for the foal."

Roark told Gare and Fergus what she said word for word, and Fergus took off running, while Gare disappeared into what Alina assumed was the tack room. He came out and handed her a blanket, with which she covered the foal.

"We'll get some good milk into your belly soon, baby," she told the foal in a singsong voice, tucking him in tight for now. She stood and dipped her hands into the bucket of water it looked like the mare hadn't touched and scrubbed at them, and then she grabbed a handful of the cleanest straw she could find the farthest from the foal and rubbed her hands dry with it. "What's going on with you, Etain?" she sang softly to the wall-eyed mare, angling her body sideways so she wasn't standing or staring head on to the mare. "Did that strange, scary little creature come out of you?" She squatted down and looked at the mare's udder, which was swollen and lopsided and both teats crusted over. "Does he keep shoving that rude little nose of his into your sore udder?" She stood slowly and stepped closer to the mare's head, still not looking her in the eyes. "I'd like to help you feel better," she crooned. "If you'll let me."

Alina walked around the brooding pen, describing what she saw with a soft patter. "The water bucket is full and clean, though untouched, as is the hay in the feeder. The straw on the floor is fresh and clean, the stall itself is roomy and away from the other horses and there's no tack hanging from the rafters to frighten you." She turned to Roark and Gare. "Where's her usual stall?"

Roark translated for her and then Gare. "In the middle of the stables, between the two plow horses."

"How about we take you back there?" Alina sang to the mare, letting her sniff her hands before slowly reaching for the lead rope dangling from her neck. "How would like to go back to your old stall, where things are familiar and your big, calm, steady friends are around you?" She led the mare around the foal, keeping herself between them, and followed Gare to Etain's old stall.

Once inside, Etain nickered to the horse to her right, who nickered back. "There you go," Alina crooned. "This is much better, isn't it? Safe and sound back where you belong. The strange little creature can't get to you here, pretty girl. I promise."

Alina turned to Roark. "Will she normally let Gare handle her? Is she still eating and drinking?"

Roark told Gare what Alina said, and reported back what Gare said. "He says she's always been a little tightly strung, though not naturally mean, and she is still eating and drinking, though very little."

"Tell him to apply a warm, wet compress to her udder, and then gently wipe the crusted milk and dirt off. If her teats are raw, he'll need to rub some healing balm on them. Double her grain and add alfalfa to her feed if they have it."

"Should he try to milk her?"

"No, she needs to dry up, not produce. If he can tend to her, I'll tend to the foal."

Roark told Gare what Alina said and turned to tell Alina what Gare answered, grinning as he caught her with one foot hanging mid-air, remembering to make herself wait for him to translate.

"Gare can take care of the mare," he said. He followed Alina back to the brooding stall. "What can I do to help?"

"I need a soft brush, a washrag and drying linen, a bucket of warm water, and the mildest soap you have."

Roark went into the tack room and came out with everything but the bucket of warm water at the same time Fergus returned with a full bucket of goat's milk. He sent Fergus off to the kitchens for a kettle of hot water to make the bucket of warm water, and hunkered down beside Alina, who was arranging the brush and soap and linens on the blankets edge.

"What else?" he asked.

Alina glanced at the bucket of milk, which the foal was too young and too weak to drink from on his own. "I'll need a drinking horn," she told Roark. "And some small linen rags to make teats out of."

Fergus returned with the kettle of hot water and Alina poured it into the bucket she'd washed her hands in. Roark sent Fergus back to the kitchens for a drinking horn as Alina dipped the washrag in the water and wiped the crud from the foal's eyes and mouth, and then she rubbed some soap onto the rag and washed his hind end.

Fergus returned with a drinking horn and Roark cut a hole in the end of it and rasped the edges smooth. After drying the foal with a towel and rubbing some warmth and blood back into him, Alina dipped her finger in the goat milk and slipped it into the foal's mouth.

"He's suckling," she said, pulling her finger out and dipping it back into the milk and then his mouth. "He's weak, but he's suckling."

Fergus breathed a big sigh of relief and went to tell Gare the good news. Roark held up the drinking horn to show Alina the hole he'd made, stuffing the tip of his little finger in and out of it.

"Perfect." Alina grinned, starting to feel hopeful.

Roark pulled a strip of linen through the hole and then filled it halfway with milk. "Here," he crouched down beside Alina and held the horn out to her as milk started dripping from the linen teat.

"If you could hold it to his mouth," she said, wrapping her arm around the foal's neck and bracing one hand under his jaw while gently prying his mouth open with the other and stuffing the linen between his lips. "Come on, baby," she cooed, inserting a finger into his mouth next to the linen teat. "There you go, baby," she said as the foal began to suck. She pulled her finger out and beamed as the foal continued to suckle. "There you go, Ash."

"Ash?" Roark said.

Alina gave him a sheepish grin. "Every living thing deserves a name of their own."

"Ash," Roark repeated. He took in the foal's coat, a light roan now that the dirt and mats had been brushed out. "It suits him. His coloring."

"Hopefully his spirit as well," Alina said. "He'll need a strong one to survive this and rise from the ashes." The foal stopped suckling and she pulled the horn from his mouth.

"If your spirit rubs off on him any," Roark said, plugging the teat hole with his finger, "he'll be kicking his heels up and tearing around the paddock in no time."

Alina grinned at the compliment. "Fingers crossed," she said. "How much did he drink?"

Roark eyeballed the horn's contents. "A quarter of the half horn. Is that good?"

"It's not bad. We don't want him drinking so much at once that he makes himself sick, especially after days of going without much of anything in his belly." She ran her hand down the foal's neck and her voice caught when he laid his head on her knee. "Poor Ash wore himself out getting cleaned up and eating." She kissed the foal's forehead. "We'll let him rest before we offer him a little more milk. The trick is to be patient, to build his appetite and his ability to digest little by little." She lifted the foal onto her lap and tucked the blanket around him. "He'll need to be fed constantly for the next two to three days at least, it'd be best if I could stay here with him."

"I'll speak with Roger," Roark said. "The fact that he let you tend to the foal at all bodes well for him letting you continue. I'll be sure to point out how much coin he'll make if the foal lives. I've already sworn to watch over you and make sure you don't try to escape."

Alina lifted her chin a notch. "I'd never willingly leave a poor creature alone to die when I might save it. But I might not be good to my word if Roger isn't seeking to ransom me to my father."

"I understand," Roark said. He sat down next to Alina and gently stroked the foal's head and neck. "I can sit with Ash if you want to check on Etain."

"I should," she said, hesitating.

"I promise to be gentle with him," he said. He lifted the foal and settled him on his lap. "Go. See to Etain. We'll be right here."

***

Alina woke in the dark of night to a small hoof in her belly. Ash was sleeping beneath the blankets between her and Roark, his back snuggled up against Roark's belly and his head tucked under Roark's chin, having instinctively drawn closer to Roark's larger, warmer body. Alina reached under the blanket and smiled at the living heat of the foal's body, which had been as cold as death when she'd first laid hands on him.

She stretched and yawned and lay there enjoying the sight of Ash and Roark sleeping, and the lack of wheezing or crackling from the foal that would've meant he'd gotten some of the milk in his lungs.

Ash had taken to the horn with the linen teat so well Alina had to pull it away from him the last four feedings to keep him from overfeeding. Roark had stayed by their sides the entire time, helping Alina feed and care for Ash and watching him when she would check on Etain, who had calmed down considerably once she was in her old stall. She even let Alina hot soak her swollen udder without complaint.

Roark twitched and snuffled, and Alina reached a tentative hand out and pushed an auburn curl falling onto his cheek behind his ear, admiring his high, broad forehead, angled cheekbones, full mouth, and strong jaw. She ran her fingers down his cheek and through the soft curls of his short beard, and then dropped her hand and laid it under the blanket over Ash before doing something really foolish like kiss him.

She closed her eyes with a sigh, reliving their kiss for the thousandth time. A kiss full of heat, desire, and passion that still stirred her insides. A kiss seared into her soul. Which made everything that happened after so much worse.

Roark had betrayed her. Roark, who'd seemed truly interested in her greenhouse, in her, a woman who rode with her skirts hiked up and mucked around with plants in the dirt. Roark, whom she'd had deep, interesting conversations with as they sailed across the North Sea. Roark, who'd slept beside her on the pile of pelts in the ship's hold, who slept beside her now in the straw on a stable floor. Whose presence she'd missed last night and couldn't seem to sleep without, even in a big, soft, comfortable bed.

Roark, whose rain eyes were staring into hers as if they could see her every thought and mirror her every feeling.

He reached his hand under the blanket and laid it over hers. "It'll be all right," he said, his voice low, deep, and resonate.

"What will?"

He smiled, slow and easy. "Everything."

Alina chuffed. It was either that or cry.

She was being held prisoner in a strange land by a man nursing a twenty-year-old grudge against her family and was likely using her as a trap for her father, surrounded by women who'd as soon spit at her as look at her. She was lying in a bed of straw in the middle of the night trying to save the life of a half-starved foal with a man she no longer seemed able to sleep without, who she'd kissed once and wanted to kiss again.

"How?" she asked him. "How will everything be all right?"

Roark gave her hand a gentle squeeze. "I'll make it right." He twined his fingers through hers, and though her breath caught, the tightness in her chest eased. "I swear I will."

"You don't know how badly I want to believe you."

"About as badly as I want to prove to you that you can," he said with a sheepish grin. "Though I admit I'm off to a poor start."

"Only poor?" Alina chided.

"Terrible?" Roark's grin turned wry. "Horrible? Abhorrent?"

Alina laughed softly. "Keep going."

"Unforgiveable?" His grin was gone and his expression serious.

Alina swallowed her heart and opened her mouth to say, what? That his betrayal had cut so deeply because she had believed him, his smile, his kiss, his proposal, and she was almost as angry at herself for falling for him as she was at him? That she could forgive him anything when he looked at her the way he was looking at her now?

Ash stirred and let out a weak whinny. Untwining her fingers from Roark's, Alina pushed the blanket off her and stood.

"Ash needs feeding."

CHAPTER 6

Goats and Cats

Roark spent the morning fencing off half the brooding stall for the three nanny goats chosen to be Ash's milk donors, while Fergus and Gare built two hay mangers, one for the foal and one for the goats. According to Alina, the foal was days, if not a fortnight, away from feeding on his own, but Roark figured it never hurt to be prepared or optimistic.

He'd spoken with Roger earlier that morning before breakfast, and Roger had agreed to let Alina continue tending to the foal. When she came back to the stables after breaking her fast, she'd changed into the tunic and breeches she'd worn on *The Rover*, which Roark had to admit were much more practical for mucking about in a stable.

They also showed off her legs and backside, which didn't go unnoticed by either of the guards Roger had posted outside the stable's door despite Roark's promise to keep watch over her. He'd seen their dropped jaws and open leers when she'd walked past them, and Gare and Fergus both were having a hard time keeping their eyes off her bottom, though they at least had the good grace to look abashed when Roark caught them ogling.

Roark was nailing the gate separating the goat pen from the foal's pen into place when Alina, who'd been tending to Etain, entered the pen and Ash whinnied and stood on shaky, spindly legs. The first time he'd stood without help.

Alina beamed. "Look at you, my big, strong lad." She petted the foal, who stumbled over to her and pushed his nose into her leg. "It's coming, you little tyrant," she said good-naturedly as she poured milk into the horn, for which Roark had built a holder so she could fill it by herself. She grinned as Ash let out a loud whinny and then plopped down in the straw. "Did you wear yourself out?" she cooed, sitting down next to him and holding the horn so he could latch on, without her having to hold his head up.

"He's already much stronger than he was yesterday," Roark said, swinging the finished gate back and forth.

"He is," Alina agreed with a happy sigh. "Thank you for thinking of penning the goats here. That'll make feedings go much easier."

Roark chuckled. "You should've seen Fergus's face when he realized he wouldn't have to be hauling buckets of milk half a league twice a day."

Alina laughed, the happiest he'd seen her since they'd kidnapped her.

"When Ash is stronger, he and the goats can be kept together," she said. "It'll give him the sense of being part of a herd."

"Speaking of his herd." Roark lifted his chin toward the door where Fergus walked in with three goats on lead ropes. Roark waved him over to the new pen, where the goats went straight to the manger filled with fresh hay and alfalfa. Ash glanced sideways at them, never slowing his suckling.

"Beer," Alina said.

"What?" Roark wasn't sure he'd heard her right.

"Beer," she repeated. "It'll help the goats produce more milk. They should get a cup each every day."

Roark translated for Fergus.

"Me da used to give ale to sows who werena making enow milk to feed their piglets," Fergus said, grinning and nodding at Alina, who was doing her best to act like she didn't understand a word he was saying. "I'm on it," he told Roark. "Though cook'll likely be asking you 'bout it later, making sure I'm not swindling the laird's ale stores." He tipped his cap to them and headed out of the stables.

"You've earned yourself another admirer," Roark told Alina.

"Another?"

"Aye, lass," Roark said in his Green Isles tongue. "Along with Ash and meself."

Her cheeks flushed a becoming pink before she turned her attention back to the foal who was still suckling away. The door creaked open and Roark looked up.

"Roger and Leif are here," he warned Alina, and then stepped out of the pen to greet them. "Laird Roger, Leif."

"We met Fergus on our way over," Roger said in the Northern tongue. "He said you ordered beer for the goats."

"I did," Alina answered him. "It'll help them produce more milk for the foal, who, as you can see, has improved greatly."

"I see." Roger flicked a quick glance at the foal and beaded his eyes on Alina. "I suppose it helps to have someone born and bred with the blood of a stable hand tending to the foal."

Alina ignored the slur to her parentage, at least outwardly. "The dam, Etain, is doing better as well," she reported.

"Humph." Roger flicked his hand toward the mare's stall. "She'd better take to her next foal, else she's of no use to me."

"She's young, she'll do better if you wait out her next breeding season," Alina told him. "Let her recover from this foal while watching and learning from experienced broodmares with their foals."

"Is that what your stablemaster father taught you?" Roger said with a sneer.

"It is what Hamar taught me," she said, and then she turned her back to Roger and tended to Ash, who'd drained his horn. Roger turned and strode out of the stables with Leif on his heels.

***

"Wait your turn, mama," Roark told the yowling stable cat whose newborn kittens were sleeping in the box he'd made them in the vacant stall across from Ash and the goats. He dipped a bowl into the milk bucket and set it down for the cat, smiling as she lapped it up. He'd learned from Alina a nursing mother always needed extra food, and over the past three days, mama cat had learned Roark and Alina were easy touches. As had Smokey, a gray and white newly weaned kid who'd been bullied by the other goats and brought over to be a stable companion for Ash, and was now stuffing his nose into the pocket of Roark's breeches, where he kept special treats like pieces of carrots or apple. "You are incorrigible," he said, laughing as he pulled a carrot top out and gave it to the bleating kid.

He reached for Ash's nursing horn to refill it and stopped. The foal had his head in the bucket of milk and was drinking on his own. "I don't suppose you could keep this new accomplishment a secret?"

"Keep what a secret?" Alina said, startling Roark. She stood outside the gate and he stepped aside and motioned toward the foal, who still had his head in the bucket, drinking his fill. Alina beamed. "This is good news, it means he...oh. It means he doesn't need me here day and night feeding him. I have no reason to stay out here away from the manor house and the people in it." She met Roark's bittersweet gaze. "You and I can go back to sleeping in our own bedchambers. Alone."

Staying out here with the horses, the goats, and the cats, practically living in the stables together for the past four days, had been a reprieve neither of them wanted to end. "How long do you think we can hide this?" Roark asked.

She shrugged. "If Ash continues to nurse from the horn as well, Gare and Fergus may not notice for another three or four days. Do you think they'd help keep it a secret if they knew?"

"I think they'd want to, for your sake," Roark told her. "For their own, they dare not. Roger wouldn't take it kindly if he found out they'd kept it from him."

"They've been so kind to me," she said. "I wouldn't want them in trouble."

Roark sat down in the straw, leaned his back against the wall, and patted the space next to him. Alina slouched down beside him, petting mama cat as she bumped and purred, rubbing against her breeches. Breeches he knew she liked wearing, and wouldn't be allowed to once back in the manor house.

He took her hand in his, twined his fingers through hers, and lifted her hand to his lips. He hadn't kissed her on the mouth since the lake, though they'd spent the last four nights holding hands and staring into each other's eyes, using them to say what they dared not speak or act on.

"We'll keep it our secret as long as possible," he vowed. He tucked their hands in his lap, looked around, and grinned. "Horses, goats, and cats." He chuckled. "I'll miss our little world here when it's gone."

CHAPTER 7

Plans

Roark tied the cover over the lens and slipped the spyglass into its sheath at his waist belt. As far as he could see, neither Murtaugh or Gall were on *The Rover* as it was being loaded for the voyage back to Sea Ridge. But Kerry and Kerwin were. He walked Artur to the docks and tied him off to a post.

The secret of Ash drinking on his own had lasted only a day. Alina hadn't wanted to deprive Ash of the chance to feed when he wanted, and so they'd left the bucket of milk out as they always had. Yesterday Gare had come upon the foal drinking from the bucket. He'd been apologetic about telling Roger. Roark and Alina had assured him they understood.

Gare had also told Roger that it would be good for both the foal and the mare if Alina could continue tending them throughout the day, freeing him and Fergus to tend to all their other duties, and Roger had agreed.

Roark figured it was as much to keep his wife and sister-in-law happy as to help out Gare and Fergus, but no matter the reason, it allowed Alina to be with the animals she loved rather than trapped in the manor house with people who hated her.

When he'd ridden out on Artur this morning for the docks, she'd been overseeing Ash's and Smokey's first time out in the paddock under the watchful eyes of Roger's guards, laughing at their antics as the foal and the kid gamboled and tumbled in the grass.

"Ahoy, the ship," he called out as he stepped onto the gangplank.

Kerry poked his head over the railing. "Roark. What brings you here?"

"I was out for a ride," he nodded toward where Artur was tied off, "and saw the ship being loaded up. Thought I'd come by and say hello."

"Glad you did," Kerry said as Roark stepped on deck. "Always good to see you."

Roark clasped his arm and then Kerwin's.

"How's the princess?" Kerwin asked.

Roark told them how she'd only been at the keep a day before she ended up tending Ash. He told them about Smokey and Mama Cat, and how Alina still wore her breeches and tunic.

"Sounds like her," Kerwin said. He'd never been shy about his admiration for Alina. He looked to Kerry and pressed his lips into a thin line.

"What's wrong?" Roark asked, and went fishing when neither brother answered. "You don't agree with what Roger has planned for her either?"

Kerry bit. "Do you?"

"No," Roark said. "I never wanted any part of it from the beginning, but like you two, I had little to no choice. Now that I know her…"

"It don't feel right," Kerry said.

"It ain't right," Kerwin added. "She don't deserve it, none of it, even if what laird high and mighty says about her parents is true."

"No," Roark agreed, "she doesn't." No matter what the new plan was. If Roger concocted it, she didn't deserve it. Roark glanced around the deck, making sure they were alone. "To be honest, lads, after what I saw and heard at Sea Ridge, I have my doubts about the laird's version of his family's banishment."

"Even if it were true," Kerwin said. "The princess is an innocent in all of it. She don't deserve to be taken and sold in no slave market."

Roark did his best to hide the shock jolting through him. "Of course, she doesn't," he managed to say. He cleared his throat and scuffed his boot on the deck, trying to think. "At least she'll have you two looking after her on the voyage," he said. "How long a sail do you expect it to be?"

"A moon's sail at least through the Mid Earth Sea to the desert port," Kerry said. "Then we have to stay until we've traded all the goods and the princess is sold to some king, special like for his pleasure house. Roger's orders."

Roark didn't even try to hide the rage building up inside him. Roger was exacting his revenge on King Jerrik and Queen Alyssa with some twisted play on their family's history. By selling Alina as a pleasure woman as her great-grandmother, Oona the Swan, had been. He spat his distaste out onto the deck.

Roger was many things, but stupid wasn't one of them. If he sold Alina as a slave in some desert port, and Jerrik found out, he had to know that the Northman king would sail into North Shore with his warships and raze the town, the keep, everything to ashes. Which meant he had no intention of telling her parents, ever. His revenge would be letting them think her dead for the rest of their days while secretly gloating over the fear and degradation she'd be living through for the rest of hers.

"You said you sail in ten days' time?" he asked the brothers.

"Aye," Kerwin said.

"Do us all a favor," he said. "Don't tell anybody we had this conversation."

The brothers looked from each other to Roark. "What conversation?" they said in unison.

***

"There you go, my faerie girl," Alina said as she removed the lead rope from Etain's neck. It was the mare's first outing in the paddock since foaling Ash. Alina watched the high-stepping, flaxen-maned, chestnut beauty dance and prance around with a happy smile. "I bet you're as fast as my Brynja on those long legs of yours."

Brynja. How Alina would love to be riding her along the sea's shore right now, free as the wind. She glanced over at the stables where Gare sat on a bench outside working on braiding leather straps into a bridle and keeping an eye on her along with one of the laird's men-at-arms, who sat on the bench beside him, whittling a piece of wood.

Everywhere she went outside of the manor house, one of Roger's men followed, which was still better than being inside the house. Peg and Jenny were friendly enough, but Lynette, Gwyneth, and Myrna never hesitated to show their hatred. She couldn't be in their sights without their eyes boring holes into her like maggots in a days'-old carcass.

She shook her shoulders and squared them. She was a princess of the Northlands, born and raised. She could deal with these women for another fortnight and a half. She had to. What she didn't have to do was subject herself to them any more than was necessary.

She wandered over to an old oak in a grassy corner of the paddock and sat down under its shady branches, leaning her back against the trunk. She hadn't slept well last night, alone in the bed without Roark nearby. She'd felt his absence keenly since he rode off on Artur, his big, powerfully built, dapple grey stallion, this morning.

"He'll be back," she told Etain, closing her eyes and leaning her head back. "He won't leave me here alone."

She woke with Etain next to her, the mare's long legs folded up beneath her, her head bobbing in the dappled sunlight under the oaks sprawling branches. By the sun, they'd slept their way well into the afternoon.

"What does it say about me that I sleep better on the ground amongst horses than in a clean, soft bed in a house?" she asked the mare, standing and stretching her back.

She slipped the lead around the mare's neck and led her past the sleeping guard and Gare into her stall. Smokey and Ash were curled up together in their pen, Ash's belly rounded and the milk bucket half empty.

"Gare." She nudged the stable hand's shoulder. "Gare." He woke with a snort and blinked up at her. "I'm returning to the house now," she said in her Northern tongue, using hand gestures pointing to herself and then the house.

He stood and left the guard snoring away, walking Alina to the front entrance himself. "Best of luck, lassie," he said as she pushed the door open and walked in.

The ladies of the house were sitting and sewing in the common room, and Alina turned for the kitchens. She'd barely eaten any breakfast in her haste to get out of the house and out to the horses, and her belly was grumbling.

"Alina," Lynette's commanding voice stopped her in her tracks. "Where are you skulking off to, girl?"

Alina turned and faced the women. "To the kitchens."

"We serve breakfast and supper here," Lynette told her. "The staff have enough to do without worrying about feeding you special meals. If you're hungry this early in the day, I suggest you take the time to eat a sufficient breakfast, unlike this morning."

"Yes, Mistress," Alina said, biting her tongue to keep from pointing out the half-eaten tray of sweet cakes on the table between Lynette and Myrna. "I'll keep it in mind."

"See that you do," Lynette admonished. "You're not here to be coddled."

Alina chuffed.

"What was that supposed to mean?" Myrna huffed. She tossed her sewing aside and strode over to Alina. "I asked you a question, little miss high and mighty bastard daughter of a stable hand and a cuckolding mother."

Alina laughed, short and quick. What was it with these women that they kept spewing this same tired lie over and over? Did they really think if they said it enough it would somehow be true?

"Well?" Myrna demanded when Alina still didn't answer.

"Well, what?"

"Don't take that attitude with me," Myrna squawked.

She drew her hand up and back and swung at Alina, who'd been taken by surprise in the bath chambers, but not this time. She grabbed Myrna's wrist mid-air and held it as the older woman struggled and squirmed. "I may be the laird's prisoner," she said through grit teeth, throwing Myrna's hand down, "but I will not willingly take such abuse. Not from you. Not from anybody."

Myrna rubbed her wrist and smiled. "Oh my dear," she said smugly in her Green Isles tongue. "You have no idea what humiliations and abuses await you."

***

By the grim set of his jaw and the silver glint in his eyes, Alina could see there was something bothering Roark the moment he sat down at the high table for supper. Myrna, on the other hand, looked overly pleased with herself.

It'd taken every bit of Alina's willpower not to recoil at the woman's vile threat of humiliation and abuse in a language she thought Alina ignorant of this afternoon. To remain calm and simply walk away when she'd wanted to scratch the smug smile off not only Myrna's face, but Lynette's and Gwyneth's too. To scream at them, demanding to know what she'd done to deserve such blind hatred.

Instead, she'd climbed the stairs to her chambers and paced and brooded at the unfairness of it all, missing her parents and the rest of her family so much it felt as if her heart had actually dropped out of her chest.

And then she remembered who she was.

She was the daughter of Alyssa, who'd killed men who'd tried to kill her. The grand-daughter of Sahar, who'd been the first woman to ever ride in and win the great races. Who'd also been abducted by an enemy of her parents and escaped with the help of Aleksandr, the bastard son of King Maksimillian, and they'd survived the wilds together.

Because of her grandparents' time in the mountains, they'd made sure their children knew how to not only survive but thrive in many different wildernesses. Lessons Alina's parents had passed down to their children.

She knew how to make a fire and build a lean-to. How to hunt and fish with snares and sharpened sticks, and how to skin and cook what she caught from squirrel and rabbit to deer and elk. The women in her line had survived so much horror, and Alina knew she could too. She knew how to take care of herself in the wilds and the language here.

Her pearl necklace would pay for her passage home on a ship. She would have to ask Roark for it back the first chance she got and then make her escape. She may have promised to stay and wait for her father, but she believed Roger had lied about ransoming her back home. Myrna's little threat today had only strengthened that belief.

The only thing she hadn't decided was whether to tell Roark. She wanted to trust him, and she could certainly use his help, yet every time she thought of confiding in him, she remembered how he'd betrayed her, and the look on his face when she'd realized what he'd done. The same look he had on his face now as he met and held her gaze from the high table.

Making sure to eat her fill, Alina surreptitiously packed a few scraps of mutton for mama cat into her skirt pocket, along with a piece of hard cheese for the first of what would be her secret larder. She drained her cup of beer, called ale here, more to build herself up for what would likely be some time alone in the wilds than from any real liking of the brew. She was trying to figure out how to grab some cherries for her hoard when Gare came into the dining hall, cap in hand.

"My laird," he said, when Roger deigned to acknowledge him. "The foal's turned colicky and it's Fergus's day ta home. I could use the princess's and Roark's help with the wee, poor thing."

Alina looked to Roger, and tried to seem more curious than worried, as she wasn't supposed to understand what Gare had said.

Roger met her gaze with irritation and then looked to Roark, who was halfway out of his seat. "Go," Roger said with an impatient wave of his hand. "This damned foal is starting to cost me more than he's worth."

Alina sat on her hands as Roark walked over to her. "Gare needs our help with the foal," he said in her Northern tongue. "He thinks it has colic."

Alina stood and pretended to think about what she'd already decided on. "Tell the cook to boil water enough for a pot of tea," she told Roark. "I need a handful each of dried peppermint, dandelion, chamomile, and meadowsweet if she has them. Tell her I'll measure and steep them. I'll go change into my tunic and breeches."

She grabbed a handful of cherries and made herself walk, not run, up the stairs, where she quickly wrapped the cheese and cherries in a linen square. It wasn't much, and she'd hoped to stash away more before she left, but it was better than nothing. If she got the foal over his colic in good time, there was a chance she could slip away from the stables in the dark of night.

***

"Slow down, Alina." Roark pulled on the sack of herbs she was carrying as they headed for the stables.

"But, Ash—"

"Is fine. Gare and I made the colic story up so I could get you away from the house." She slowed her pace to match his, her head tilted, waiting for him to explain. "I went to the docks today and spoke to Kerry and Kerwin." He hesitated, hating to tell her what he'd found out, but she needed to know. "They're preparing *The Rover* to sail in ten days, only not for Sea Ridge." Her head tilted the other way. "They have orders to sail through the Mid-Earth Sea to a desert port, where you're to be sold as a slave, and not as any slave, but as a pleasure woman."

Alina stopped walking, and Roark gently tugged her by the elbow in case they were being watched from the house. No guard had come out yet, but he figured one of them would as soon as they finished their supper.

"He wants me to be sold as my great-grandmother was."

"That was my take on it too," Roark said. They'd reached the stables, and he pulled her to the far side of the building where they couldn't be seen from the house. "I don't believe Roger intends to ever tell your parents you're alive. He has to know your father would wreak havoc on this place if he found out. Knowing Roger, he'll send spies to report back to him how deeply your family grieves to savor his sick, twisted revenge without fear of retaliation."

"I have to leave this place," she said, her face pale in the moonlight. "Now."

"Yes," Roark agreed. "You have to leave this place, but not now. Not tonight. I have a plan, if you'll trust me." She said nothing. "I know I betrayed your trust, betrayed you, but I swear on my life, I will never betray you again."

The door to the stables opened, and Gare came out, peering around the corner. "Sorry, I couldn't tell what I was hearing."

Alina strode past Roark and Gare and straight for the brooding pen, where Ash had his head in the milk bucket, drinking away.

"He's fine," Gare said with a sheepish smile to Alina. "Really."

Roark translated and Alina gave Gare a shaky nod.

"Gare," Roark said. "Can you wait outside the door and warn us when anyone's coming?"

"Will do." Gare tipped his cap to Alina and shut the door behind him, giving them some privacy.

Smokey shoved his nose into the pocket of Alina's breeches and she shooed him away. "That's not for you." She pulled out a linen square and unfolded it, revealing a chunk of cheese, a handful of cherries, and some meat scraps. She removed the meat scraps and rewrapped the cherries and cheese and put them back in her pocket. "Here, mama kitty," she called, and the cat came running and meowing. "Here you go, mama," she said, tossing the meat to her.

"What, or who, are the cheese and cherries for?" Roark asked.

"For me. For later."

"How long have you been stashing food for your escape?"

Alina blinked her big green eyes, trying to look innocent and failing.

"This is the first of it," she admitted. "I intended to keep my promise and wait for my father, but after what Myrna said today…" She shook her head.

"What did she say?"

"She, in Green Isles tongue, she told me that I had no idea what humiliations and abuses awaited me."

"Damn them," Roark ground out. "Damn them all for lying cheats."

The door creaked open and Gare let out a soft whistle. Roark snatched the bucket of milk away and Alina knelt beside Ash and propped him up by his belly, as if feeling it. Gare entered the stables carrying a steaming kettle of water, followed by Lara, one of the kitchen maids.

"How's the wee thing doing?" Lara asked as Gare handed the kettle to Roark.

"Too soon to tell yet," Gare told her. "We've got him standing, which is good. Now we need to steep the tea and get some into him. We'll be walking him half the night through to help get things moving again."

"Good," Lara said, her cheeks dimpling. "I'm sure with you taking care of him, he'll be fit as a fiddle by morn." With a quick dip of her capped head, she turned and headed for the door, leaving Gare staring gape-jawed after her.

"Go," Roark told the moon-eyed man. "Go and talk with her while you can before she has to return to the house."

"Are they courting?" Alina asked as Gare practically ran after Lara.

"If they weren't before," Roark said, "I'd wager coin they will be from tonight on." He sat down and leaned his back against the wall, patting the straw beside him. "We need to talk."

She sat next to him as Ash and Smokey nestled up against her. "Talk," she said.

"You're right about getting away from here," he said, speaking softly so he could hear if the stable door opened. "I'll do everything I can to help you. I owe you that much, at the verra least." She said nothing, nor did she look at him as she leaned her head back against the wall, staring straight ahead. "I'm simply asking you to wait—"

"For what?" Now she was looking at him. "Why?"

"There's a ship sailing in seven days from the southern shore of the firth," he said. He pulled her pearl necklace from his tunic pocket and held it in his open palm. "I've spoken with the captain and he's willing to take you to Sea Ridge for the price of your pearl."

She took her necklace. "Is this captain trustworthy?"

"As trustworthy as I can find in so little time. He owns his ship and isn't beholden to any laird. As far as I can tell, nobody outside of the keep and *The Rover*'s crew know you're here or who you are. Roger's managed to keep your presence a secret."

"So that my father won't hear any stray gossip." Alina took a deep breath in and let it out. She met Roark's gaze, her own guarded. "If I agree to wait and sail on this ship…"

"The Sea Maid."

"If I were to sail on *The Sea Maid,* how do you propose I get to it?"

"That'll be the tricky part," Roark admitted. "They set sail with the morning tide, so you'd have to show up at dawn the day they leave. Any earlier, and Roger could find us and take you again. It's the closest port to North Shore, so it's the first place Roger will look. Any later, and you'll miss the ship, and then we'd have to make a run for another port and hope we find another ship setting sail before Roger finds us."

"You keep saying we. Do you plan on sailing with me?"

"No. Once you're safely away, I'll come back and try to misdirect Roger. Besides," he added with a rueful grin, "your father would kill me for my part in this, and rightly so."

"Not if I explain things to him," Alina insisted. "Not if I tell him how you helped me escape. He understands making mistakes, big mistakes, and atoning for them."

Roark's gut twisted. "My atonement to you will be making sure you get safely away," he told her. "Say you'll let me do this for you. It eats at my insides I was a part of bringing you here. I knew it was wrong even when I believed Roger only wanted to ransom you back to your family. I can't bear to think of you being sold by some slave trader to be kept as a pleasure woman for some desert king." He reached over and pushed a stray lock of her hair behind her ear.

"Please," he said, cupping her jaw and gently rubbing the apple of her cheek with the pad of his thumb. "Let me do this for you. Let me save us both."

She leaned her cheek into his hand and held his gaze, her own sad yet determined. "I'll wait."

Roark blew the breath he'd been holding out. "Good," he said. "Good. Thank you for trusting me, especially after what I—"

"Stop." She covered his mouth with her hand. "Stop beating yourself up over what's been done. It's in the past now. A past neither of us can change."

He laid his hand over hers, pressed his lips to her palm, and lowered their hands. "You're an extraordinary woman, my lady owl. I knew it the first time I saw you, watching you race your horse along the shoreline through my spyglass." He grinned. "The two of you were flying."

"Can I ask you something?" she said, breaking the silence that'd fallen between them.

"Does your question begin with why?" he teased.

The apples of her cheeks pinked. "Part of it does."

"Ask away."

"You told me on the ship you meant what you said to me at the lake when you kissed me and…"

"Asked you to marry me?"

She nodded, her cheeks flushing darker.

"I meant it." Roark cupped her chin and held her gaze. "I still do."

"Then why haven't you kissed me again?"

When Roark remembered to breathe, he took a slow, deep breath in and let it out with a ragged sigh. "Because," he told her, "when you leave here, leave me, it will be like severing a limb. If I kissed you again, it would be like cutting my heart out."

"Oh."

Roark stared into eyes as green and faceted as cut emeralds, eyes reflecting the same recognition and desire coursing through his veins since the moment he'd spied her racing her mare on the beach.

"Ah, damn." He pulled her to him. "Either way, I bleed out." At least this way he'd die with the memory of her lips on his. Lips that met his for a hot, hungry kiss. Her hands clung to him as desperately as he held onto her. He sucked his breath in as she slid a leg over his lap and groaned as she straddled him.

Clasping her to him, he slanted his mouth across hers, his hunger growing with the warm, wet, taste of her lips on his, the feel of her full breasts pressed against his chest, of her taut backside moving in his hands, the slight friction of her breeches rubbing against his, causing his cock to swell and grow.

He broke their kiss, running both hands back through her hair and gazing into her eyes, heavy-lidded with desire. Roark may not have been the womanizer Leif and Donald were, but he'd known a few intimately, including the older, experienced widow of a neighboring laird. Yet not a single one of those women had made his heart swell even bigger than his cock.

Until Alina.

Swaying back in his arms, she smiled at him through lowered lashes, shy and sweet and so damned sensual that Roark closed his eyes with a growl. What he wanted to do was lay her down in the straw and make her his. To claim her, body and soul. Yet he was honor-bound to get her back to her father, safe and sound. And virginal. He touched his forehead to hers, his breath as ragged as his voice. "I cannot. We cannot."

"I know." Her voice was a raw whisper, her breath a soughing sigh. "I know."

He hugged her to him. "You have no idea how much I wish it were otherwise," he whispered hotly in her ear.

"Oh," she said, leaning back with a shaky smile. "I have more than an idea."

A quick, short whistle brought them both to attention. "Someone's coming," Gare said, shutting the door Roark hadn't heard open behind him. "Pretty sure it's Leif."

Roark grit his teeth as Alina scrambled off him, her gaze lingering a moment on the visible bulge in his breeches. She pushed her hair back and smoothed her tunic as Roark stood, and then she slipped a lead rope around Ash's neck and got him to his feet. Roark opened the gate and loosened the stays of his breeches.

When Leif entered the stables, Alina was slowly walking the foal back and forth along the open area between the rows of stalls while Smokey jumped and ran circles around them. Roark was raking a pile of straw in the brooding pen and Gare was milking one of the nanny goats.

"My father sent me to check on the foal," Leif said in the Northern tongue as he leaned against the gate to the pen, ogling Alina's trim backside with a wolfish grin.

"As well as on us, no doubt," Roark added.

"No doubt," Leif said as Alina turned the foal around. "Especially her."

Alina lifted her chin as she approached Leif. "I've told you and your father many times I won't try to leave here. I'll wait for my father to come for me. I'm always under guard, and besides, where would I go? What would I do? I don't know the land or the language and I have nothing to pay or bargain with for passage on a ship."

Leif reached out and twirled a lock of Alina's hair around his finger, making it impossible for her to move away from him. "A sweet thing like you," he said. "You have plenty to bargain with."

"Leave her be, Leif," Roark growled. "Now."

Leif unwound her hair and Alina backed away from both of them. Behind him, Roark heard the scrape of Gare's stool.

Leif stood at his full height and puffed his chest out. "How dare you tell me what to do," he huffed. "I'm the son of a laird."

"As am I," Roark said, refusing to back down, not this time. Leif may have stood a head taller, but Roark outmuscled him by two stone at least. Still, he would try reason before brute force. If they got into a fight over Alina, it could spoil their plans in any number of ways. "Your father has commanded she remain a virgin until her father has paid the ransom. I'm only making sure his orders are followed."

Leif snorted. "You're only sore you can't take her maidenhead yourself."

"True enough," Roark admitted, surprising Leif. "But not sore enough to go against *our*," he stressed the word, "laird's wishes. Besides," he said, still speaking in the Northern tongue so Gare wouldn't understand what he said, "what would Jenny do if she found out? She'd stop warming your bed, no doubt."

"It would almost be worth it," Leif grumbled, "to knock the Northern bitch down a notch or three." He slapped Roark on the shoulder, their standoff forgotten. "No matter," he said in the Green

Isles tongue. "She'll get her comeuppance soon enough. So, what shall I tell my father about the foal?"

"Tell him the foal is improving, but is not out of danger yet. We'll likely be here, the three of us," he said, indicating Gare, "the night through tending and walking him."

***

Alina rode Etain at an easy trot around the paddock under a horned moon. It felt good to be on a horse's back again, even if it was in a fenced area in the middle of the night. She patted the mare's arched neck. "Good girl," she told the high-stepping, smooth-seated mare. "Thank you for letting me saddle and ride you. I promise you we'll be racing over the countryside soon."

It had been Roark's idea for Alina to ride Etain in the paddock after they'd settled Ash and Smokey in their pen for the night. Roark intended for Alina and the mare to be used to each other when they rode for the ship at the southern port. He'd spiked the guard's ale with a few drops of White Milk he'd admitted to buying to drug Alina, and hadn't needed to use. He'd used a much more potent drug: himself. All he'd had to do was talk to her and smile at her, and mesmerize her with those rain eyes of his, and she'd fallen right into his trap.

"She's really settled under your care," Roark said as he rode Artur alongside them. "Too bad the *Sea Maiden* isn't set up to transport horses or you could take her with you."

"My mother would fall in love with her. She's such an elegant, high-spirited horse. Aren't you, my faerie girl?"

Etain nickered and Roark chuckled. "Keep this up, and she'll swim after you all the way to Sea Ridge."

"I'll be sorry to bid her farewell," Alina said. She gave Roark a bittersweet smile. "And others." She tried to read his expression, but there was no moon to aid her. "At least she'll have you and Gare to look after her."

Roark said nothing.

"What will happen to you and Gare when it's discovered you helped me escape?"

"If it works out as planned, nobody except us will know Gare was involved. After you're safely away, I'll go to my family and seek their protection. Unfortunately for Etain, she'll have to be returned to Roger as a peace offering."

"You'll seek your family's protection," Alina said. "Are they likely to give it?"

Roark shrugged. "As likely as not."

"And your betrothal to Gwyneth?"

"If I'm lucky, our betrothal will be broken."

"Along with your family's alliance with Roger?"

"Most likely."

"Fucking Roger," Alina spat. "I would've kept my word and stayed for my family to ransom me. But now? I cannot and will not stay. I will not let myself be sold into slavery."

"I know," Roark said. "Nor would I ever let that happen to you."

"I only wish you and your family hadn't been dragged into this."

"My family put themselves into it when they made an alliance with Roger," he said, sounding more bitter than she'd ever heard him. "They put me into it when they sent me to a man of his ilk and betrothed me to his daughter for their benefit."

Alina moved Etain alongside Artur and laid her hand on Roark's arm. "I am sorry for you. You're a good man, in spite of who raised you. You deserve better."

He laid his hand over hers and gave it a gentle squeeze. "I used to tell myself my feelings and happiness didn't matter. It was worth sacrificing for the good of my family and Roger's, and all the people whose livelihoods depended on our alliance."

"And now you'll sacrifice it all for me." Alina couldn't let him do it. She couldn't be the reason so many people's lives were destroyed. She'd stick to her original plan and escape on her own, keeping him and Gare out of it.

"No, my lady owl," Roark said.

"No what?"

"Don't try to escape on your own. Don't feel responsible for what happens after you're gone."

"How could I not?"

Roark grasped her by the arm and both horses stopped. "Do you truly think I could continue on here as I have been, knowing what I do about Roger?"

"No," she said. "What will you do?"

"I'll find out everything I can about him and his family before I get you free of him, and once you're safely gone, I'll tell my father all I've learned and hope he listens."

CHAPTER 8

Flight

Alina woke to the unfamiliar feel of a soft, warm bed. Stretching and yawning, she rose and went to the window and opened the shutters. By the sun's position, she'd slept until noon, but then she hadn't come to her room until before dawn after spending the night pretending to take care of a colicky Ash, and talking and riding with Roark.

She splashed cold water on her face and shivered as it trickled down between her breasts, where the familiar weight of her pearl hung. She dressed in her long tunic and apron, brushed and plaited her hair into one long braid, and crept down the stairs, keeping an eye out for the ladies of the house. No doubt they'd scold her for missing breakfast, even though she'd been tending to Ash all night, at least as far as they knew.

The house was quiet as was the common room, which was unusual, as the ladies normally sat sewing and gossiping this time of day. She walked over to the closed door to Roger's private chambers and pressed her ear against it but heard no voices from inside the room. There was nobody in the dining hall either, which boded well for Alina's chances of scrounging something to eat in the kitchen. She started to push the door open and stopped at the low, angry sound of a man's voice.

"I told you not to lay with the laird's son, did I not?"

"Yes, Father," Jenny's tearful voice answered.

"And this is what has come of it," Craig scolded. "Have you told Leif about the babe yet?"

"Yes."

"What did he say?"

"That he'd claim a boy bairn, but no girl."

"Ach," Craig spat. "Just like his Uncle Donald, he is. He'll claim a son in case his wife-to-be does'na bear him one."

"What if the babe's a girl?" Jenny cried. "The laird'll send me and the bairn packing for sure."

"Dunna worry, daughter," Peg soothed. "We must hope and pray the babe's a bonny boy with blond hair and blue eyes like his father's. He'll claim it sure, then. If it's a girl, we have kin in the south who'll help find you and the bairn a place in some other laird's keep."

It was wrong of Alina to have listened, she knew, but she'd be long gone before the drama of the baby's birth played out. She'd tell Roark before she left, knowing he'd do all he could to help Jenny. Otherwise, it was none of her business. She pushed the door open. "Good morning," she said cheerfully, pretending not to notice how Jenny quickly turned her tear- streaked face away or how Peg's cheeks were extra pink and Craig's frown etched deep in his forehead. "I know I woke too late for breakfast, but was hoping I could grab some bread and cheese?"

"Of course, of course." Peg swiped at her cheeks and bustled about the kitchen, pulling a loaf of rye and a wheel of cheese from the larder. "Help yourself."

"Thank you, Peg." Alina cut a slice of bread and cheese each and headed for the door to the courtyard. "Where is everybody?"

"Gare drove the laird and Donald and most of the men to the docks this morning," Peg told her. "The ladies rode along with them, intending to do some shopping."

"And Roark?"

"He rode off on that stallion of his early this morn," Craig said. "Didn't say where he was going or why."

Which meant he hadn't slept at all.

"I'm off to the stables," she said. When Craig looked about to follow her, she waved him off. "Stay, rest, relax. I swear I won't try to leave."

She reveled in walking across the yard to the stables without being watched, and breathed a sigh of relief when she found the stables empty of people, though the sight of Artur's empty stall made her heart do a little flip. She only had seven, no, six more days of

Roark's company. Selfishly, she wanted as much time with him as she could get.

Etain came up to her stall's gate and whinnied and Alina stroked the elegant mare's forehead. "You're such a beauty, my faerie girl. I wish I could take you when I go home."

"You're not going home, you Northern bitch," Leif said from the open doorway. "You're not going anywhere, other than on your back, knees up."

He closed the door behind him, blocking her way out, his intent as clear on his face as his words had been. Alina glanced around, frantically searching for something, anything, to use as a weapon. She grabbed a bucket of oats and swung it at him as he closed in on her.

"This is going to be fun," he said, jumping back as she swung the bucket again.

Still swinging, Alina backed up to the brooding stall, where she spied the mucking rake leaning against the inside wall. Grabbing the bucket with both hands, she swung it with all her might and heaved it at Leif's head, throwing the pen's gate open as he ducked. Slamming the gate shut behind her, she grabbed for the rake. Leif vaulted over the gate and landed on top of her, crushing her to the ground with his weight as Ash and Smokey bolted to the far corner of the pen, bleating and whinnying.

"You can't get away from me, Princess," Leif rasped as Alina clawed at the ground, trying desperately to gain some traction. He sat on her back and grabbed her wrists, pinning them to the ground. "You may as well give up and give in. Who knows, you might even like it." He flipped her over onto her back and sat pelvis to pelvis on her, holding her wrists above her head and grinning salaciously at her breasts as she squirmed beneath him. "That a girl," he said with a lecherous grin, his breath reeking of beer. "Keep moving like that for me."

Alina froze. She was hopelessly, helplessly outweighed and outmuscled. She had to think, and think fast. She wiggled a little beneath him and smiled as suggestively as possible without spewing bile.

"That a girl," he said roughly. "That's how I like it." Holding her wrists with one hand, he groped her breast with his other, mauling and pinching her flesh. He leaned down and bit her on the shoulder and Alina bucked up against him. "Oh yeah," he groaned into her neck. "Do that again."

Twisting her head toward his, Alina took hold of his earlobe with her teeth and clamped down, hard.

"You bitch." Leif jerked his head back, leaving the tip of his lobe in Alina's bloody mouth. "You fucking whore." He slapped her across the cheek, knocking the piece of his ear from her mouth. Repositioning his hold of her wrists, he sat up and thrust a knee into her belly, settling all his weight on it.

Her vision hazy, Alina grunted and groaned and fought for enough air to breathe, much less scream, as he untied the stays to his breeches and freed his engorged cock. Alina gasped for air and sanity as he lifted his knee from her belly and straddled her, his cock waving in the air as he pulled her skirt up her legs.

She screamed what little air she'd managed to suck into her lungs out.

***

Roark jumped off Artur and hit the ground running, throwing the stable door open and following the echo of Alina's scream to the brooding pen, the sight of Leif pinning her down, shoving a knee between her exposed legs, sending him into a murderous rage.

"Get off her, you son of a bitch," Roark roared as he jumped over the gate, grabbed Leif by the hair, and yanked his head back. He slammed his fist into Leif's nose, growling with satisfaction at the crunch of cartilage beneath his knuckles.

"Wha da fug," Leif yelled as he pinched his nostrils to stop the gush of blood.

"What the fuck?" Roark thundered back, followed by his right fist into Leif's jaw. "You're trying to rape her," he raged, throwing his left fist into the other side of Leif's jaw. "Her," he growled, throwing an uppercut to Leif's chin, his rage barely abating as Leif slumped back on his knees, his face slack, his flaccid cock sagging against his thigh. "And you ask me what the fuck?"

Grabbing the unconscious sack of shit by his tunic, he dragged him off Alina, who lay shaking on the ground, her eyes wild and unfocused. Slamming the back of Leif's head on the ground for good measure, Roark knelt beside her and scooped her into his arms, holding her tight and whispering into her ear. "It's all right, Ali. You're safe now. I have you. I have you, Ali girl."

She leaned back in his arms, her gaze slowly focusing on his. "Roark?" she whispered hoarsely.

"Aye, my lady owl. I have you. Leif can't hurt you anymore."

She turned her head and eyed the pulpy mass of Leif's face with a shudder, licked the blood on her lips, and threw her arms around Roark's neck. "Thank you," she rasped as another shudder racked her. "Thank you for being here, for stopping…"

"Shhh." Roark stroked her hair and held her close. "It's all right now. Everything's all right."

"No." She rolled her forehead against his shoulder. "No, it's not." She lifted her head and met his worried gaze. "I have to leave here. Now."

She dropped her arms from around him and tried to stand, but only made it to her knees. Roark stood and pulled her up with him. "You're right," he said, supporting her by the elbows as she grasped his upper arms. "You do need to leave here, now. We both do."

"But—"

"I'm not letting you go alone."

They gagged the still-unconscious Leif and tied him to a gate post, leaving his breeches open and his cock flagging. Bruised and bloody, his nose broken and the tip of his ear missing, he'd have a lot of explaining to do. Roark would bet coin on him lying about who attacked who, and why.

"I should slit his throat and be done with the cur," he said, giving Leif's leg a kick.

"No," Alina told him. "Helping me escape is one thing. Killing Leif would be another altogether. They'd hang you for his murder."

She was right. Yet it didn't mean Roark liked letting the rapist bastard live. "What if I cut his stones off?"

"He'd bleed out," she said, "and they'd still hang you for his murder."

"How can you be so calm?" All he wanted to do was take his rage out on Leif. To make him pay with his pound of flesh.

Alina met and held his gaze, and Roark could see the wildness still in her eyes. "I'll fall into a weeping puddle later," she said. "Right now, time's wasting."

Alina saddled Etain as Roark rolled two saddle blankets together and tied them up with a lead rope and then he filled a small sack with several handfuls of oats and stuffed it into Etain's saddlebag. He had his waist blade and spyglass on him, and his short blade was sheathed and tied to Artur's saddle, as was his waterskin.

Roark stripped Leif of his waist belt and blade and the small dagger he kept in his boot and handed them to Alina, who strapped the belt and blade around her waist and tucked the dagger into her boot. If all went well, they only had to make his family home of Thorn Bush Keep half a day's ride from here. If not, well, they'd deal with things as they came.

"Ready?" he asked.

"Almost." She went into the brooding pen and gave Ash and Smokey each a hug and a kiss on the nose. "Be well, boys," she told them. Swiping a tear from her cheek, she closed the gate behind her and led Etain out of the stables.

Roark shut the door behind them, whistled for Artur, who was grazing on a patch of grass, and led him to the back side of the stables, where Alina was waiting on Etain. He tied the bedroll to Artur's saddle, swung up into it, and turned the stallion's head north.

They rode hard and fast, staying off the road and avoiding the villages and farmsteads as they made their way northwest along the Long River, the woods growing thicker and the paths narrower the closer they got to Thorn Bush Keep. They spoke little during their flight, and only out of necessity when they did, concentrating on where they were going and getting there as quickly as possible without being seen or injured.

Although Roark had told Alina his family would protect him if he helped her escape, it was more to get her to accept his help than believing it to be true. That was before he'd beaten Leif to a bloody pulp.

It'd been ten years since he'd lived with his family, and he and his father had never been close. While he didn't think his father would turn him and Alina over to Roger or his men, he wasn't willing to bet their lives on it.

Dusk was falling when they made the keep's southern border and Roark led them deeper into the western woods. Half a league in, they rode up to a small cottage nestled in a glen and Roark pulled their horses up at the clearing's edge, their appearance heralded by the baying of hounds.

"What is this place?" Alina asked, sidling Etain closer to Artur.

"The gamekeeper's house," he said as a man stepped out of the front door, a huge, rough-coated coursing hound at each hip and an arrow set to fly at the bow in his hands. "Logan," Roark called out. "It's me, Roark."

Logan lowered his bow and arrow, commanded the dogs to stay, and stepped forward with a big grin on his face. "I'll be damned," he said. "If it isna himself." He glanced around out of habit, and seeing nothing or nobody else, waved them over. "Come on down, lad," he said and eyed Alina. "You too, lassie."

Roark dismounted and went to Alina, not that she needed his help, but he liked the feel of her slim waist in his hands as he guided her to the ground. She leaned into him as he took the reins of both horses into one hand and tucked her under his shoulder with the other.

"Alina, this is Logan. Logan, this is Princess Alina."

"Princess?" Logan's brows rose and he took in her long tunic with Leif's belt double looped around her waist with the blade in its sheath. He took in her and Roark's more than disheveled appearances, the saddle blankets rolled up and tied off on Artur's saddle. "Not that I'm not glad to see you, laddie," he said to Roark. "But why are you here and not at the manor house?"

"It's a verra long story, my friend," Roark said. "One I look forward to telling you over a cup of ale or five. First though, do you have any fodder for our horses and a place they can't be easily seen?"

***

"Well now," Logan said as he stood from the table after listening to Roark tell him the gist of how he and Alina had come to be on his doorstep. "It's a good thing I've a stag dressed and ready for the manor house. I was gunna take it over on the morrow, but think I'll be taking it over tonight instead." A handsome, middle-aged man with curly brown hair, sharp eyes, and the lean, well-muscled body of an outdoorsman, he touched the side of his nose and grinned. "In case a certain, arrogant laird or his men show up looking for you and your lady friend."

"Thank you," Roark said as Alina soaked the juices of her second bowl of venison stew up with her third piece of bread. "I'm sorry to put you in the middle of all this. You were the only person I knew I could trust."

"Other than your lady mother, of course. Who I'll be telling you're here."

"Of course." Roark stood as Logan put on his cloak and cap and went to the door.

"Flossie and Courser'll let you know if anyone's coming besides me," Logan said, giving the two hounds Alina had been sharing pieces of bread with a hand motion that had them both sitting at alert. He tipped his cap to Alina. "Throw the bolt behind me," he told Roark.

Alina washed their dirty bowls in the bucket, the hounds at her side, and then she sat down on the blanket Roark had laid out next to the hearth's fire. She yawned and patted the blanket beside her. "Tell me about Logan, and why you trust him more than your own father."

"Caught that, did you?" Roark asked as he sat down beside her.

Alina nestled into Roark, and he wrapped an arm around her shoulder and tucked her in close.

"Thorn Bush Keep is held through my mother's line," he said. "She grew up here, as did Logan. My mother, Brianna, was an only child, and Logan was the child of the gamekeeper and his wife. As children, they were allowed to play and explore the woods together, but when my mother came of age, she was married off to my father, Ronan MacInnes, who, like me, is the second son of a laird. Their marriage was, and is, a marriage of politics and alliances between clans, much as mine to Gwyneth was meant to be."

"They were in love, your mother and Logan?"

Roark kissed his perceptive little owl's forehead. "They are still, I believe, though neither one of them has or would ever act against my mother's marriage vows. As far as I know."

"So why?"

"Why does Logan stay?" Roark said with a wry half-grin. "He stays to watch over her. To be her friend and protector, as he was mine for a while."

Alina tilted her head and looked into Roark's eyes. She traced a finger along the line of his clamped jaw to his chin. "What did he protect you from?"

"My father," Roark said on an exhale. "He never beat me or anything like that. It was more that he had his first-born son, his golden boy, Ryan, and so I was never much of a consideration for him until I became of use to send to Roger and all that brought with it."

Alina laid her hand on Roark's cheek. "I'm sorry," she said. "To not know a father's love." She dropped her hand and held his gaze. "What about your mother?"

Roark smiled. "My mother's love made up for the lack of my father's my whole life."

"Are you much alike?"

"My sister, Rowena, and I both look like our mother's side of the family, red-haired and freckled. My brother, Ryan, could be our father's twin in looks and manner. Tall and lean with brown hair, unblemished skin, and giant sticks up their arses."

Alina laughed.

"Logan says that looking into my eyes is like looking into my mother's, which is likely why he let a bothersome lad follow him around day in and day out from the time I was eight 'til the day I left for North Shore Keep at ten and two."

Alina twined her fingers through Roark's and laid her head on his chest. "I cannot imagine how it would feel to be taken from your family at such a young age and made to live amongst that pit of adders."

"I learned how to survive it pretty quickly," he said, touched yet not surprised Alina, out of all his so-called friends and family, understood and sympathized with him. "Luckily, Logan had already taught me how to be patient on the hunt, how to watch and study prey and predator, to make myself seem harmless or threatening, depending on the situation. To know when to strike or when to remain hidden, or even," he gave her shoulder a nudge, "when to flee."

"Because of me," she said. "To protect me."

"Ach, Ali girl," he murmured into her hair. "Don't you know I'd give my life for yours, and gladly."

"I do," she whispered roughly.

The dog's low woofs and a soft persistent knocking roused Roark from the little cocoon he and Alina formed before the fire.

"Logan?" he said through the closed door, short sword in hand.

"Aye, lad, open the door."

By the moon's position, it was late into the night, and by Logan's bright eyes, he had much to tell. Roark poured them all cups of ale while Logan, always a man of sense and order, hung his cloak and cap on their pegs by the door. The three of them sat at the table, the dogs at Alina's feet, and Logan took a long draught of ale and set his cup down.

"Donald and two of the laird's men showed up at the manor house not long after I did," he told them.

"They wasted no time coming after us then," Roark said. He looked at Alina. "You can wager coin on Leif having told them you and I set a trap for him."

Logan shook his head. "It's worse than that, lad. Leif is dead."

"What?" Roark and Alina said at the same time. "How?"

"A scythe to the chest."

"Damnation." Roark shot up and paced from the table to the hearth fire and back again. "He was alive when we left him," he said, trying to make sense of what could've happened. "He was tied, gagged, and unconscious, but he was alive with a strong pulse and steady heartbeat. We checked twice." He held up two fingers. "I wanted to slit the cur's throat, but Alina stopped me. She said it would only make things worse, that I, we, could be hanged for murder. Ah, fuck." He looked to Alina, whose eyes were big and round in her pale face, and swallowed past the fist-size stone in his throat. "They'll think we did it. They'll charge us with Leif's murder." He opened his arms to Alina, and she flew into them. "I'm sorry, Ali," he rasped.

She rolled her forehead into his shoulder and then lifted her gaze to his. "Don't be. You saved me from certain rape and who knows what else. We didn't kill Leif. You and I have nothing to be sorry about."

"We know that," he said, "but without any witnesses, or the actual murderer stepping up and admitting their guilt, it'll be our word against Roger's."

"The lying snake," she hissed. She shuddered and Roark tightened his hold on her. "What do we do now? Will your father stand with you against Roger?"

Logan pressed his lips tight and shook his head. "Laird Ronan has already proclaimed he'll stand with Roger on this."

Roark had to think. To plan. "Tell me everything Donald and my father said," he said as he and Alina sat down, their hands clasped together on the table.

"Donald said Roger was staying at the keep to see to his son's wake and to organize the search for you two. Besides Donald and his men, Roger's sent others to search every port on the eastern coast, starting at Long Firth and going south and north from there. All of them with orders to bring you and the princess, who they're saying's a serving maid you took a shine to, back alive to Roger. They're also supposed to remind all the ships' captains the penalty for knowingly helping murderers is death. He's offering a bounty of ten pounds silver for each 'a you."

"Ten pounds silver each?" Roark repeated. "You can be sure he only wants us brought back alive so he can have the pleasure of watching us hang." He looked from Logan's furrowed brow to Alina's pale face and gave her hand a gentle squeeze. "We can go west. Find a ship to sail from there."

"Or follow the Long River northwest 'til you make the Mounths," Logan said. "Skirt the western hills and cut due north to the Deep Loch, follow its southern shore east to the North Sea Firth. You'd be traveling half the distance Roger's men would up the coast, plus they'd be stopping to search the ships and spreading word of the bounty."

"It would be easier to find a ship to sail from there than the west coast," Roark told Alina. "On the other hand, we'd be riding through naught but wilderness for seven to ten days at least."

"I'm fine with that," she said. "My parents taught all of us children how to survive in many kinds of wilderness. Skills that have served my family well through the generations."

Logan chuckled. "I see why you like her," he told Roark.

"It's more than that," Roark said. *So much more.*

Logan grinned. "I can see that as well."

Roark lifted Alina's hand in his and kissed the backs of her fingers, grinning as she blushed prettily. Logan cleared his throat meaningfully, and Roark brought his attention back to the problem at hand.

"Is Donald staying the night at Thorn Bush?" he asked Logan.

"He is. Your lady mother has already warned him to keep her serving maids out of his bed, and to stay out of theirs."

Alina sat straight up. "I forgot to tell you," she said to Roark. "Jenny is pregnant with Leif's baby. I overheard her and her parents arguing about it before I went to the stables. Before Leif came after me."

"Did Leif know?" Roark asked.

Alina nodded. "Jenny said she'd told him and he'd claim it if it was a boy, but not if it was a girl. 'Just like his uncle, Donald,' her father told her. He sounded angry."

"Who can blame him?" Logan rumbled. "The men in that family spill their seed willy-nilly and dunna give a care where it takes root."

"Well," Roark said wryly, "there's one less to spill his seed now." He drew a deep breath in and let it out. "We'll leave here tomorrow. Take the inland route around the Mounths and up to the North Sea Firth. You agree?" he asked Alina.

"Yes."

"Can you supply us with some food and blankets and rope and maybe a bow and quiver of arrows?" he asked Logan.

"I can do better than that," Logan said. "I only ask that you wait to see your lady mother before you leave tomorrow."

***

Alina stared into silver grey eyes that were mirror images of Roark's and dipped a knee to Lady Brianna, Mistress of Thorn Bush Keep. "It's an honor to meet you, Lady," she said in her best Green Isles tongue.

"And you," Brianna, a handsome, middle-aged woman with dark auburn hair and milky white skin, said kindly. "Logan told me of your and Roark's situation." She clicked her tongue. "Ach, I told my husband no good would come of sending our son to that family." She gave Roark, who'd greeted her with a heartfelt hug almost the moment she'd stepped through the door, a quick shake of her head. "I'm sorry I didn't fight him harder over it. I admit I'd hoped getting away from him might benefit you."

"You did what you had to do at the time, Mother," he said. "I hold no ill will. If you hadn't sent me to Roger, I wouldn't have met Alina, or been there to help get her away from him and his vile plans."

"Ah, yes," Brianna said with an indulgent smile. "Logan told me how it is between you two."

Alina's cheeks flushed hot as Roark twined his fingers through hers. "I'll do whatever I must to get her back to her family," he said. "Though we're both sorry to put you two in the middle of it."

Brianna waved a slim hand dismissively. "You're my son. Where else should I be?" She indicated the wool blanket tied into a pack. "I brought what I could sneak out with." She untied the blanket and pulled out a soft, linen under-tunic, a woolen outer tunic, and a pair of leather breeches and handed them to Alina. "I was told you prefer wearing men's clothing on such occasions," she said with a grin. "So much more practical than trying to ride a horse or traipse around the wilds in skirts."

"Thank you, my lady." Alina took the proffered bundle of clothes. "These will make the journey easier to be sure. Thank you for the food and blanket too." She nodded down at the sack of bread, cheese, dried meat, and field beans.

"You couldn't ask for a more capable companion in the wilds," Brianna said, smiling between Roark and Logan. "My son had the best teacher and Logan the best student."

"The lad was a natural with a bow and arrow," Logan said proudly. "Best aim and steadiest hands I've ever seen." He winked at Roark. "Lad's not bad with a throw net either."

Roark puffed his chest out and Alina laughed, happy to see him with his mother and Logan, two people he actually loved who obviously loved him back, as he deserved.

"Is this your way of warning me we'll be eating a lot of fish?" she asked Logan.

"Best salmon in the world call the Long River and its tributaries home," he boasted.

"Good thing I like salmon then," she said.

"To be supplemented with your knowledge of herbs and greens," Roark added. "She designed a greenhouse at her home," he told his mother, "with roof panes of glass that can be moved to follow the seasonal sun."

Brianna smiled indulgently. "You always did like your inventions." She turned her smile on Alina. "It seems Logan is right. My son has indeed met his match."

"In every way," Roark said, his voice catching.

Alina was suddenly, ridiculously close to tears.

"I wish with all my heart things end well for you two," Brianna told them. She smiled at Logan, her expression sad and bittersweet. "I know how it feels to lose the chance to be with the one person you want most in this world."

Alina's eyes welled and her throat constricted.

"Oh, my dear girl." Brianna wrapped Alina in her embrace. "Don't cry. It's not over yet."

"But when it is, I'll never even get to see Roark again," she sniffed into Brianna's shoulder.

"You never know," Brianna said, holding Alina by the shoulders and staring into her teary eyes. "The fates may have something else in store for you two."

CHAPTER 9

The Stones

Roark and Alina followed the Long River north, avoiding roads, riding through fields, meadows, and woods. As night fell, they stopped along the riverside and made camp in a glen surrounded by willows. Roark tied off the horses to a line between two trees with plenty of spring grass for them to graze on while Alina unpacked bread, cheese, and cherries for their supper.

Logan had given them a small pot along with a store of dried meat, field beans, onions, oats, and hazelnuts, but Roark thought they were still too close to spying eyes to chance a fire. He told Alina that while the Long River would provide them with plenty of food, once it turned west and they continued north to the Mounths, the pickings would be slimmer and the dry stores better used then.

They tucked into the food, refilled their waterskins, and repacked their bags so they'd be able to grab their gear and ride off quickly if needed. Then they unrolled the saddle blankets that were their bedrolls and laid them out under the graceful canopy of a willow tree. Alina sat on her bedroll and stared up into the night sky, finding the Big Bear and the North Star. The stars they'd be following as they skirted the mountain range called the Mounths. She shivered, and Roark pulled around her shoulders one of the otter cloaks his mother had given them.

"Are you all right, Ali?"

"You call me Ali," she said with a small smile as he hunkered down beside her. "That's what my younger brothers, Aaron and Aleksi, call me." She tucked a knee under her chin and craned her head to meet his gaze. "But only you, sir stag, call me lady owl. I like it."

"I'm glad, my lady owl." He gave her one of his slow, easy grins, which made her feel anything but easy inside. He coughed and cleared his throat. "We'd better get to sleep," he said, lying down alongside her. "We need to be on the move at break of dawn."

Alina woke with Roark curled around her as the dark of night was giving way to the grey of dawn. They'd fallen asleep under their cloaks and the shared blanket on their own bedrolls. During the night, their bodies apparently sought the heat and comfort of the other's. Content in the snug cocoon of his big, warm body, she nestled closer into him with a sigh, and felt something long and hard poking into her backside. Roark stirred and yawned and tucked in closer around her, his breath tickling the skin at her nape, and then he stilled.

"Ach, Ali girl," he murmured hoarsely. "I didna mean to…"

"It's fine," she said, her stiffness easing, even if his wasn't. "I have three brothers and numerous male cousins. I grew up listening to them bragging to each other about their morning wood."

Roark chuckled into her hair. "Thank the gods for brothers." He took a deep breath in and blew it out. "We should probably get up now."

"I'd say you already were up," she teased.

Roark's chest rumbled against her back with laughter. "Ah, Ali, me lass." He gave her a smacking kiss on the back of her head. "You never cease to surprise me." He pushed the covers off them and stood and caught her staring at the bulge in his breeches. He grinned and coughed and offered her his hand, pulling her up and into his arms. "Don't think I'm not tempted to lay you right back down and have my way with you, my lady owl. In truth, there's nothing I want more, other than getting you home to your family safe and in one piece."

"Ach, Roark me lad," she replied with her best imitation of his Green Isles burr. "Don't think I'm not tempted to let you. But…"

"But we need to get moving."

They broke camp quickly and silently, each eating a piece of bread and chunk of cheese as they rode. Alina tried to concentrate on the countryside as they followed the river north, sticking to game trails and riding around the farmsteads and villages, keeping watch for any signs of Roger's men. In between, she kept sneaking glances at Roark, admiring the strong lines of his profile, the firm, yet gentle grip he kept on Artur's reins, his well-muscled thighs gripping the stallion's barrel sides whenever they rode abreast.

When she was riding behind him, she couldn't help but marvel at the breadth of his shoulders and how his back tapered down to a trim waist and taut backside. How he rode with such a sure, smooth seat. How he kept sneaking glances at her too, and smiling at her with those rain eyes, and that slow, easy grin of his that could melt glaciers.

At noon, they stopped along the riverside to water the horses and give them a rest. After tying them off to graze, and without a single word, they walked straight into each other's arms and kissed, hard and hungry.

Alina moaned. She couldn't get close enough to him, couldn't get enough of him, and then as suddenly as they'd come together, Roark broke their kiss, their embrace, and turned around and walked fully clothed to the river and dove in head first.

Alina, still panting, followed him in. She came up gasping and spitting water as she pushed her sopping wet braid back to find Roark standing waist deep in the water, grinning down at her.

"Keep grinning at me like that," she told him, "and I'll never make it out of this freezing water."

"Keep kissing me like that," he said, "and I'll be growing gills."

She laughed and dipped her chin and filled her cheeks with river water that she spit at him through her two front teeth. Roark dove at her, splashing water in her face, and then submerged and grabbed her by the ankle and the next thing Alina knew, her leg was in the air and she was on her back underwater. Roark let go of her ankle and she came up splashing and sputtering.

"Your feathers are all wet, my lady owl," he teased.

"As is your hide, sir stag."

Her teeth began to chatter, and she started to unplait her braid, figuring since she was already wet, she might as well give her hair a good rinse. But her fingers were numb and clumsy and her thick plait wasn't cooperating.

"Here," Roark said, stepping behind her. "Let me."

She shivered as he deftly untangled her braid, and when he was done, she dropped down into the water and laid her head back, closing her eyes and letting the current flow through her loose hair. When she lifted her head, Roark was emerging from the water bare chested, his soaking wet tunic in his hand. Alina gaped at the muscled breadth of his lightly furred and heavily freckled chest, and then swallowed hard at the ridged muscles of his belly and the line of darker auburn fur leading to the waist of his breeches and below, which was thankfully underwater.

He held a hand down to her and pulled her up, his own jaw dropping as he stared at her wet tunic clinging to her breasts and frozen nipples, which grew harder at his intent gaze.

"We, ah, we should change into dry clothes and get a move on," he said, his voice deeper than usual. "I want to make the Yew Tree by tonight."

Alina crossed her arms over her chest. "The Yew tree?"

"It's said to be the oldest living tree in all of the Green Isles," Roark told her, "and is the land of my mother's ancestral home."

***

They turned west with the river in the late afternoon and made the yew tree by dark, where they staked out the horses and set up a cold camp under the canopy of the ancient yew, which sat sentry in the graveyard where generations of Roark's family were laid to rest.

"This is the last of the bread," he said, tearing it in half and handing the larger piece to Alina, who handed it back to him and took the smaller piece. "Tomorrow eve we should be far enough away from any keep or village to stop and fish for salmon we can cook over a fire."

"Fresh salmon sounds good," Alina said. "I can gather greens while you fish."

Roark cut her a slice of cheese. "There's a cherry orchard on the north side of the village. If we leave early enough, we can pick some on our way out."

Alina's eyes lit up. "I love cherries."

"I know." Roark grinned. "You smelled like cherry blossoms that day in your greenhouse."

Her eyes widened and her cheeks pinked. "I'd been picking them earlier that morning."

An image of her in a sheer night shift, hair down and barefoot, tripping down a path of fallen cherry blossoms, came to Roark unbidden. He groaned.

"Roark? Are you ill?"

"No. Not exactly."

Alina tilted her head and blinked. "How do you mean?"

The horses nickered and pricked their ears forward. Roark held his hand up, stood, and pulled his short sword. Alina was on her feet too, waist blade in hand. He motioned for her to follow him and they took cover behind the yew's thick trunk. They waited, silent and at the ready, when a robin trilled. Roark looked at Alina and grinned. Robins didn't sing at night. He returned the bird call, which was answered in kind, and he motioned for Alina to stay and stepped out from behind the yew as a man stepped out of the dark beyond the edge of their camp.

"Uncle Bryce." Roark clasped his uncle's hand.

"Roark, my lad." His uncle pulled him in and clapped him on the back. "It's glad I am to see you." He peered around Roark. "Where's your lady friend?"

Roark motioned for Alina to come out from behind the tree. "I take it Roger's men have been here, since you know about her and came looking for us."

"Four of them showed up at the keep yesterday. Said you and she were wanted for murdering the laird's son."

Alina stepped up to Roark's side and he put his arm around her shoulder and gave it a squeeze.

"Uncle Bryce, this is Princess Alina, daughter of King Jerrik and Queen Alyssa of Sea Ridge in the Northlands. Alina, this is my uncle, Bryce MacKay, my mother's cousin and laird of Yew Tree Keep."

"It's an honor to meet you, Laird Bryce," Alina said as he looked her up and down.

"The honor's mine, Princess," Bryce said, and then he grinned at Roark. "I ken why you chose her over that spoilt brat your father sent you away for. Now, how about you tell me your side of this story and I tell you what I know, and we figure out how to get you two safely away to wherever it is you're going."

Roark was getting good at distilling his and Alina's story down to the pertinent facts, which Bryce listened to without comment. Then he told them what Roger's men had told him, which was what they'd told Roark's parents, with a new twist. They'd said that Alina was a servant girl who'd lured Leif into the stables with the promise of a quick rut, where Roark was lying in wait and had slain Leif.

"Even if that were anywhere near to the truth," Roark said, "how would Roger know? Leif couldn't have told him if he was already dead."

"Roger's manservant, Craig, swears he heard Alina invite Leif into the stables. Says he saw them go in together, but only you and she came out."

"Craig, whose daughter, Jenny, is carrying Leif's bastard." Roark met Alina's gaze. "I think we know who stuck the scythe into Leif's chest."

"It could verra well be this Craig," Bryce said. "But unless you somehow get him to confess, you two are on the hook for this. Roger's hired extra men searching for you and offering a reward to whoever brings you back to him, alive. The four who came here said they were splitting up. Two'll be heading west and the other two'll be taking the inland road bordering the Mounths."

Roark rubbed his jaw and spit. "Damnation. We were planning on taking the inland road around the Mounths."

"What do we do now?" Alina asked. "Is there another way around?"

"Not around," Roark told Alina. "Over. We cut due north, across the Mounths."

"The Mounths are a wild, tough crossing," Bryce said. "Not for the timid or the frail."

"Good thing I'm neither then," Alina said. "I'm a Northland woman born and bred. What you call mountains we call hills."

Bryce raised his bushy red brows at Roark.

"I've seen the mountains of the Northlands," Roark said. "Ours are trifling hills compared to theirs."

"Well then." Bryce knelt and opened the pack he'd brought. "Here's some food and supplies for your leisurely trek across our trifling hills." He pulled out a loaf of bread, a wheel of cheese, and a skin of wine. "Who else knows you came this way?"

"My mother and Logan. My father's taken Roger's side on this."

"I coulda guessed as much," Bryce grumbled. He stood and clasped Roark's arm. "Best keep your ears open and your eyes peeled, lad." He winked at Alina. "You're in good hands, Princess," he told her. "From what I've seen, so are you," he told Roark. He slapped Roark on the back and started to walk back into the night's shadows. "If anyone else comes looking for you, I'll be sure to send them in a westerly direction, unless of course it's some Northman king."

"You look like your uncle," Alina told Roark as he packed away the new supplies. "You have his coloring and his eyes."

"Aye. My mother always said I took more after my Uncle Bryce than my father, in looks and temperament."

"Would he protect you from Roger, after I'm gone?"

Roark hadn't even considered this. "He would," he said, and knew it to be true. "But I can't ask that of him."

"You could return to Sea Ridge with me," she said.

Roark held her gaze, soft and pleading. "Even if your father didn't kill me for my part in abducting you, I have to return to my family to try to make things right between them and Roger's." Her gaze dropped, and Roark cupped her chin and gently raised it. "If it were my choice alone, I would sail with you in a heartbeat, Ali girl. But here in this world, there are consequences and repercussions for what we do, what we've done. I have to stay here and deal with mine."

"I understand," she said, blinking back tears. "I do. Your sense of honor is one of the things I respect and lo— regard about you."

***

Roark woke curled around Alina's soft, warm body, his morning wood, as she'd called it, snug against her backside. He lay there sharing her body heat and burying his nose in her nape, breathing in the heady scent of green grass, cool earth, and warm woman. Prolonging his exquisite torture. A torture he'd only suffer for another fortnight if everything went according to plan, which nothing had since the moment he'd laid eyes on her racing her mare along the beach.

He nuzzled her nape and she stirred against him. "Time to wake up, my sleepy owl," he rasped. "The sun is about to rise and so should we."

"Unnnh." She burrowed her nose into the bedroll and nestled her backside into him and he grit his teeth. He backed away from her, missing her soft heat instantly, and when she tried to wiggle close to him again, he threw the blanket and otter cloaks off them and stood abruptly, staring down at her petal pink cheeks, rosy lips, and tousled mane of burnished cedar. She stretched and rolled her lithe, lean body from side to side and then lay on her back and blinked sleep-filled eyes at him. "Why is it I sleep so much better on the cold, hard ground with you than I do in a soft bed without you?"

"Why?" *Because our hearts and souls call out in recognition of the other's.* "Because our bodies instinctively seek out the warmth and comfort of another living being," he said, choosing the practical explanation over the poetic. Determining then and there to continue being a practical companion rather than a moonstruck fool. One would get Alina home safely, the other could get her killed.

"Oh," she said, and though she flashed him a quick smile, it didn't reach her eyes. "I suppose you're right." He offered her his hand, as he had every morning they'd woken together on the ship, in the stables, on the road, yet instead of accepting his hand as she had every other time, she stared at it for a moment and pushed herself up and stood. "I, ah..." She lifted her chin toward the hedgerow and then strode over behind it for her morning relief.

When she returned, she eyed the cold breakfast of bread and cheese and cherries he'd spread out on their bedrolls.

"There should be wild blackberries and bilberries to pick once we make the foothills," he told her.

"That'll be a nice change," she said impassively.

As the sun shone high overhead, they rode in the same uneasy silence since morning, crossing the narrow waterway flowing between the Loch of Bracken and the Loch of Standing Stones. Following the northern shore of the loch for another league, they came upon the ceremonial circle of seven stones, which stood as high as two men standing one on top of the other.

"Can we stay for a bit?" Alina spoke for the first time since they'd woken.

Roark pulled out his spyglass and scanned the area. All he saw were sheep grazing on a far hill. "We can stay for a short while," he said.

Alina dismounted and walked from stone to stone, laying her palms flat along their smoothed sides, running her hands up and down them then pressing her ear to them, listening to their secrets with her eyes closed and a beatific smile on her lovely face. After she'd done this with each and every stone, she stood in the middle of the circle and dropped her head back, lifting her face and arms to the sky as she twirled in slow circles, a graceful, elemental goddess of the earth praising the heavens.

It took every bit of Roark's sorely tested will to keep from laying her down in the grassy circle and claiming her body and soul in the primal ritual of man and woman.

"Keep ahold of yourself, ye randy stag," he muttered. He put the spyglass to his eye and scanned the area again, as much to distract himself as anything else, and spied a shepherd coming up over the hill to the west. "Alina, we need to go."

***

Alina didn't know why Roark was acting so cold and distant, but she knew she didn't like it. She missed the friend who teased her and talked with her about anything and everything, and she ached for the man who kissed her with such bone-melting heat they'd both jumped into the freezing cold river to douse their passions before they ignited.

Most of all, she missed his slow, easy grin and those rain eyes pouring into her.

Eyes that kept sneaking glances at her as they rode away from the stones across fields, staying off the road and avoiding the villages, which grew fewer and fewer as they neared the foothills of the Mounths.

They made good enough time to stop for the night along the Garadh River—famous, Roark told her, for its salmon. Being spring, it was the best time to catch the biggest fish.

Alina watered the horses and staked them in a grassy area while Roark grabbed the net Logan had given him and surveyed the river for the best fishing spot, picking a pool formed by large rocks upriver from their camp. She gathered wood for a fire, and to make a cooking spit with, and then she walked up the shoreline, gathering sorrel and dandelion leaves along the way. At the pool, Roark had already netted two large salmon and was pulling in a third.

"You seem to have found a good spot," she said, sitting down on a grassy hillock.

"Aye." He climbed over the rocks and deposited the fish next to the other two on the ground. He grinned for the first time that day. "I swear I fished this verra same pool with Bryce the summer of my ninth year."

"When is your birthday?" she asked, glad to be having a friendly conversation with him.

"I was born on the seventh day of the seventh moon under the Crab," he told her. "A child of the moon and water."

"That explains your rain eyes."

"My rain eyes?"

"I was born on the first day of the fifth moon," she said, ignoring his question.

"A child of the earth and growing things," Roark said, sitting down beside her. He met her gaze and held it. "With eyes the color of new spring grass."

That grow greener every time your eyes rain on them. Alina's cheeks flushed hot at her unspoken words. She grabbed her bundle of greens and stood. "I'll go start a fire whilst you clean the fish," she said, walking away from a perplexed-looking man.

She struck the flint and lit the dry leaves and kindling while peeking surreptitious glances at Roark, who had four crows strutting and cawing around him for the fish guts he tossed them. He carried the scaled and gutted fish over, spit them, and then hung them over the fire while Alina washed the greens in the river, which she set aside in the pot.

"Do you prefer your greens raw or cooked?"

"Either way," he said. "You pick."

"Raw then," she said. They sat in silence by the fire, soaking up the heat while Roark turned the salmon on the spit, each of them sneaking glances at the other. When Alina could take it no longer, she asked, "What happened between last night and this morning?"

"What do you mean?"

"Why have you been so distant since we woke?"

Roark worked his jaw and toed the ground with his boot. "Because," he said, "if I don't keep my distance from you, Ali girl, I'm afraid I'll be stones deep inside of you. And that, I'll not do."

A surge of liquid heat pooled between her legs. "Why not?"

Roark chuffed. "You and your whys." He turned to face her, his eyes showering hot, sleeting rain into hers. "Believe me," he rumbled, "there's nothing I want to do more, and would if we lived in that faerie world where our actions had no consequences or repercussions. But we don't. I've sworn to right the wrong I've done to you, to get you back to your family safe and sound," he ground out the word "sound." "Which will'na happen if we keep kissing and, well…"

Alina's cheeks were flaming, and the heat between her legs had turned into a deep, pulsing ache. "I see," she said. And she did. He was a man of his word, and his word was his honor.

***

After a night of little sleep and much tossing and turning, her dreams full of Roark's hot, sleeting gaze and his deep voice calling her *Ali girl*, they ate a quick breakfast of leftover cold salmon and bitter greens, and then mounted up. They rode north until noon, when they crossed the Ghar River. Already wet from the crossing, they decided to bathe and wash their dirty clothes while letting the horses rest and fatten up on grass before starting their long climb into the Mounths.

Roark kept watch first as Alina bathed downriver, sneaking glances at him, and catching him pointing the spyglass her way several times, lowering it or turning it toward the countryside whenever she caught him. When she rose up out of the water after rinsing the soap from her hair, he didn't lower the spyglass or turn it away from her.

He could have been a stag in a hunter's sights, he stood so still and rigid. Emboldened by his stance, Alina stood tall and proud, her nipples growing hard under his brazen scrutiny, the ache between her legs actually starting to throb. She smiled boldly, and full of hunger.

Roark lowered the spyglass and set it down on the grassy shore. He removed his short sword and untied his waist belt and blade and set them down beside the spyglass, kicked off his boots and walked into the river for the second time in as many days. Taking pity on him, and herself, Alina strode out of the water and quickly dried and dressed herself. Then she walked upriver to where Roark was treading water chin deep.

"Catch," she said, tossing him the tub of soap.

With the tub in his hand, Roark floated downriver to the small pool where Alina had bathed and stood in the thigh-high water. She watched from afar as he peeled off his wet tunic and breeches and set them on a rock. He scooped a handful of soap from the tub and lathered his hair and body and then dunked to rinse. Alina picked up the spyglass and watched him emerge, admiring his strong, muscular, male body. She followed the line of dark fur down his belly and stopped and stared as his cock grew before her eyes. She swallowed hard and licked her lips. She could've sworn his cock jumped. She lifted the spyglass to his face and her cheeks flamed at the heat of his grin, even fifty paces away.

Lowering the spyglass, she set it down on the grass next to his sword and waist belt and turned and practically ran over to their camp, taking refuge with the horses as he dried and dressed while she set out their meager repast of cheese and hazelnuts.

Hunkering down beside her, Roark met her unsure gaze and grinned. "Well," he said, "that was, uh…"

"Informative?" she said, and they both burst out laughing.

She still couldn't believe she'd stood so boldly while Roark had studied her naked body, or that she'd studied his as brazenly. Nor could she believe how stirring and unsettling it had been to see him naked and proud.

She'd seen her younger brothers naked when they'd been little, and she'd grown up around enough men to have seen bits and pieces here and there, but she'd never seen a naked man in a state of arousal before. Even Leif had only been at half-mast in the stables. Seeing Roark standing naked in the river, his cock at full mast, had been a magnificent sight she would not soon forget, if ever.

After eating their meal and filling their waterskins, they rode due north into the heavily forested foothills of the Mounths. As they left the lowlands behind, Alina glanced back over her shoulder with mixed feelings.

On the one hand, it truly was beautiful country, rich and verdant with thick woods, tilled fields, and rivers and streams flowing with life. This was the country Roark had been born and raised in, the country he loved.

On the other hand, it was the country she'd been forced to by Roger and his venomous family to exact revenge on hers. Turning back around, she faced forward and onward, patting Etain's neck and smiling at Roark and Artur, glad they were on this journey with her.

The foothills rose at a gentle slope compared to the jutting mountains of her homeland, with wooded forests full of birdsong and small creatures scurrying between the trees with no villages or roads to worry about being seen on. The afternoon sun shone down through the leaves of birch, pine, and oak, dappling the forest floor, though not enough to keep the chill of early spring away. Alina was glad for the otter cloak Roark's mother had given her. She and Roark hardly spoke as they rode, though the looks they kept giving each other said plenty. She knew without asking his thoughts kept wandering back to the river, as did hers.

They rode until dark, made camp, and Alina went to search for greens and mushrooms while the grouse Roark had killed roasted over the campfire. She followed the babbling brook and started humming along with the melody of water trilling over rocks as she picked leaves from a patch of sorrel.

"What tune is that?" Roark asked as she strolled back into camp, still humming. He cocked his head and quirked his brows. "I've heard it before."

"It's an old Green Isles love song called 'Somebody,'" she told him. "It's the song Oona the Swan sang to Asad the Lion the first night they met. The song they fell in love to."

"'Somebody.' I've heard it a few times through the years. Will you sing it to me?"

You're the only man I'll ever sing it to. "If you like," she said, setting the sorrel leaves in the pot.

He turned the grouse on the spit and sat cross-legged on a bedroll as Alina drew a deep breath in and let it out slowly, her belly fluttering at the expectant grin on his face. She'd never sung "Somebody" to anyone but herself while riding through the fields on Brynja, dreaming of a love like Oona's and Asad's. Now she would sing it to Roark, the only man she could see herself loving to the end of time. A man she would sail away from if everything went to plan. She drew another breath in and began to sing.

"My heart is sore, I dare not tell,
"My heart is sore, for Somebody.
I would walk a winter's night

All for a sight of Somebody.

If Somebody were to come again
Then one day he must cross the main,
And everyone will get his own
And I will see my Somebody.

Oh, oh, for Somebody,
Oh, hey, for Somebody,
I would do, would I do not
All for the sake of Somebody.

Why need I comb my tresses bright,
Oh, why should coal or candlelight
Shine in my bower day and night,
Since gone is my dear Somebody.

Oh, I have wept for many a day
For one that's banished far away,
I cannot sing and must not say
How sore I grieve for Somebody.

Oh, oh, for Somebody,
Oh, hey, for Somebody,
I would do, would I do not
All for the sake of Somebody."

"Damnation." Roark stood and closed the three paces between them and kissed her as he had on Spring's Eve by the lake. Kissed her as if knew he was her Somebody. And she kissed him back. She kissed him with heat and passion coursing through her veins, never wanting to stop. Mewling with disappointment when he broke the kiss to stare into her eyes, his own heavy-lidded with desire, he muttered, "Damnation."

He pressed featherlight kisses to her eyelids, her ears, her jawline, her lips. He suckled her earlobe and she shuddered and tilted her head, exposing her throat. He nipped and nibbled his way down her neck, and she could feel her pulse pounding beneath his lips. He cupped her backside in his big, strong hands and pressed her pelvis to his. A newly familiar length of hard heat pressed against her belly and Alina moaned.

"Do you trust me, Ali girl?" he said, his voice thick with desire.

Alina stared into eyes the silver grey of a moonlit lake. "With my life," she said with an earthy sough.

Her words, meant to reassure him, brought him up short. With a heavy sigh he held her face in his hands and touched his forehead to hers, caressing her cheeks with the pads of his thumbs. "Which is why, my lady owl, as much as I wish otherwise, we must stop what we were about to do."

"Which was what, exactly?"

"I cannot say for certain, but ah, I can say, pretty much everything but…"

"But?"

Roark dropped his hands and stepped back from her. He laughed, short, quick, and rough. "But consummation, my curious little owl."

"Oh. Why not?" she pushed. "Why can't we do everything but? Nobody would know, and my precious maidenhead would remain intact."

"I would know, Princess Alina. And so would you."

CHAPTER 10

The Storm

Roark watched the grey clouds scudding across the sky from the north. "A storm's coming," he told Alina.

"Will it hit before nightfall?"

"It'll be close enough we should start looking for shelter now."

"I trust you," she said, digging the blade into his self-inflicted wound a little deeper.

He doubted she'd done it intentionally, as he hadn't hurt her intentionally last night by stopping their love play. Still, he had hurt her.

All day, she'd been trying to act like he hadn't, keeping up her end of their conversation with a forced lightness, but she was nowhere near good enough a liar to pull it off. The sad, confused look in her beautiful green eyes gave her away every time.

Roark pulled out his spyglass and searched the stony mountainside ahead of them. "There's plenty of wood to build a lean-to with, if it comes to it," he said. "Though if we're lucky, we'll find a southern-facing overhang large enough to shelter us and the horses."

Alina chuffed. "Neither luck nor the weather have exactly been on my side through any of this," she said, the closest to complaining he'd heard from her since being bound and gagged and dragged away from her home.

She urged the lighter, fleeter Etain forward, and Roark followed, scanning ahead of them with the spyglass. The smaller woodland creatures had already gone to earth and the birds to roost when Roark sighted an opening between an outcropping of several large boulders.

"There." He pointed a quarter league up, grinning as he saw what looked like the entrance to a cave through the spyglass.

The horses didn't show any signs of having smelled a predator at the cave, but Roark told Alina to stay mounted and wait while he checked.

The boulders formed an overhang large enough to protect the horses from the worst of a storm, which was good, because the opening to the cave was only big enough for Roark to squeeze through sideways. Once past the opening, he stopped and waited for his eyes to adjust to the dark as he sniffed around, smelling nothing more than musty dirt and the vague musk of rodents. He coughed and the sound didn't travel far. He didn't hear the scurrying of small creatures or the growl or snuff of a large animal in response.

He squeezed back out into the open. "This will do," he told Alina.

"I'll let the horses graze before the storm hits," she said, dismounting and removing her gear from Etain's saddle.

Roark did the same with Artur and then piled their gear and saddles inside the cave as Alina staked the horses to graze.

"How much firewood should I gather?"

Roark looked up into the sky, which was almost black with storm clouds as far north as he could see. "Three days' worth," he said, and then quickly added, "though I doubt we'll be stuck here that long."

She returned with her first armload of kindling and wood, and Roark stacked it inside the cave and struck his flint, lighting the dry grass and leaves under the kindling and nurturing it to a steady fire. With the fire's light, he inspected the cave, which was high enough to stand in upright, five paces long and wide. Plenty big and comfortable enough for two people.

"More wood." Alina dropped another armload onto a pile outside. "I'm going to forage a little farther for some larger logs," she said, turning on her heels and giving Roark her pert backside.

He finished stowing the wood inside the cave and went to find her. He stood at the edge of the woods, cocking his head and listening for the sound of boot fall or the crunching of twigs, but heard nothing except the wind and the rustling of leaves and grass. He grinned. The little owl moved about the woods as silent as her namesake.

"Alina?"

"Over here."

He followed her voice into a small glen full of dried wood from a fallen tree. "This should keep our fire burning," he said, gathering up an armload and carrying it back to the cave. They managed three more armloads each before the first fat raindrop hit Roark on the nose. "You get Etain, I'll get Artur."

By the time they'd staked the horses under the rocky overhang with a handful of oats each, the sky let loose.

***

Alina entered the cave and looked around. It was small, yet big enough to contain their gear, a fire, and the two of them, with room to lay their bedrolls out next to each other and to move around without bumping into each other.

She glanced at Roark, who stood on the other side of the fire watching her, his rain eyes gleaming, and chided herself for feeling so shy around him. Especially after all they'd already seen and done and been through together. She pulled the pot out of the pile of their gear. "I'm going to catch rainwater to soak beans in for our breakfast," she told him, almost hitting her head on the top of the entrance in her haste to escape the suddenly small, stuffy cave.

Stepping outside, she took in a deep breath of brisk, cooling air and set the pot out past the ledge's edge. At the rate the rain was coming down, it wouldn't take long to fill. She stood outside and double-checked the horses, who looked miserable but dry, chiding herself for being so reluctant to go inside and face Roark in such close quarters for the night.

"Do you think this storm will reach the coast and slow Roger's men?" she asked as she measured two meals' worth of field beans into the pot.

"It's hard to say. The Mounths have their own weather, and the coast is leagues and leagues away. Plus, we're on the opposite side of the peaks from the coast. Odds are the rain clouds'll be too heavy to cross over the peaks."

Alina let her breath out in a rush. "That's what I was afraid of."

"Losing time, or being cooped up in here with me?"

"Both," she answered honestly. "I don't know what to do about either."

Roark grinned, slow and easy, and the cave grew small and sweltering hot. "There's nothing you can do about the storm," he said. "It'll wail and blow until it doesn't. As for me, Ali girl, I'll keep to my word and not bother you. I swear it."

"That's the problem," she said. She, who'd always considered herself a person of sense and intellect, a woman of self-control and practicality, that was until she met Roark and stared into his rain eyes. Until he'd smiled at her with that melting grin of his. Until he'd kissed her. "I don't want you to."

Roark cocked his head. "What do you mean?"

"I mean," she said, closing the distance between them in three strides and standing nose to chin with him, "I want you to bother me. You bothering me is all I think about day and night. The thinking about it gets me bothered to the point where I feel like I'll either erupt or cave in."

He stood still and silent, his nostrils flaring and the black of his pupils almost eclipsing the grey of his eyes. The image of him standing naked in the river came to her as it had a hundred times since yesterday.

"I mean," she said, her voice thick with need pooling deep in her core, "I want to do more than see you naked. I want to feel you, stones deep, inside me."

"Ali, I…" He laid his hand on her shoulder, about to give in or to fight her, she couldn't tell, when a bolt of lightning arced and filled the sky outside with a flash of blinding light, its ear-splitting crack echoing off the cave walls and causing them to jump. "Damnation." He laughed, quick and short, and started to back away from her, but Alina wasn't having it.

"Oh no, you don't." She grabbed him by the tunic and pulled him to her, stood on her toes and kissed him, firmly and none too gently, the pent-up energy in her ready to spark and arc as bright and dangerous as the lightning still cracking outside. She pressed her body against his, breasts to chest, pelvis to pelvis, and smiled as he gave in with a groan and clasped her even closer, one hand in her hair and the other cupping her backside, his mouth slanting over hers.

He broke the kiss and stared hard into her eyes. "Are you sure, Princess?"

Still gripping his tunic, Alina nodded. "In my land," she told him, "a woman doesn't have to be a virgin to marry. Not even a princess."

Roark snorted. "A woman doesn't have to be a virgin to marry in any land," he said. "That doesn't mean a husband wouldn't prefer her to be. Men can be verra territorial when it comes to the woman they love."

"Love?"

"Wed."

"Which is it?" Alina teased. "Love or wed?"

"Both," he said, "if they're lucky. Which most are not."

"My parents were," she said. "As were my grandparents and my great-grandparents. As could we be, for however long we have here in our little cave, our little world, where we could do everything but."

Roark went still everywhere but for the growing heat against Alina's belly. "Are you sure, Ali?" he whispered hoarsely.

She smiled, letting everything she felt for him shine in her eyes. "Yes," she said. "My answer to you has always been yes."

"I know," he said. "I've known since the moment I walked into your greenhouse."

"Knew what?" Alina asked, her brazen courage faltering. That she was an easy mark? That he was bait she couldn't refuse?

He held her face in his hands and grinned, slow and easy. "I knew that you were mine, as I was yours."

Alina let out the breath she'd been holding with a long sigh. "I knew it too," she whispered. "Despite everything that's happened, I've always known it." Her courage building apace with her desire, she bumped her pelvis against his erection, his groan reverberating to her core. "What are we going to do about it?" she asked, her voice low and thick.

He touched his lips to hers. "Everything but," he said, nipping her lower lip. "We are going to do everything but." He claimed her with his mouth, branding her with his lips as he trailed searing kisses along her jaw and down her throat to her shoulder, the neck of her tunic. "Lift your arms," he rasped, grabbing her tunic by the hem and pulling it up over her head and tossing it onto the bedrolls.

Alina stood half-naked before him, basking in the heat of his gaze as he stared at her breasts, her nipples pebbling. He doffed his tunic and embraced her so they were standing skin to skin, her breasts pressed against the hard warmth of his chest. She wrapped her arms around his waist and laid her head on his shoulder, content to absorb the living heat of him, to run her hands up and down the length and breadth of his back, feel the contours of his muscles as he ran his big, tactile hands up and down her bare back. She buried her nose into the crook of his neck where it met his thickly muscled shoulders and breathed in the scent of river water and soap, of rain, sweat, and leather.

He nipped the skin of her shoulder and she shivered. She lifted her head and met his hazed gaze, felt the rumble in his chest. He stepped back and took her by the hand, gently pulling her down to the bedrolls, where she lay on her back and he lay on his side, propped up on his elbow, his eyes raining a soft heat that spread from her face to her breasts to her belly.

"Damnation, Ali," he said, his voice echoing the same need throbbing in her core. "*Tha thu braegha*. You are beyond beautiful."

She reached out a tentative hand and ran it down the length of his arm, stopping at the waist of his breeches. "*Ni ye hen piaoling*. So are you."

One hand under her head and the other on her back, he pulled her onto her side and kissed her senseless, tasting and tangling his tongue with hers. He trailed his lips and tongue down her throat to her breasts and took one nipple into his mouth as he rubbed tantalizing circles around the other with his thumb.

Alina gasped and moaned as he licked and suckled first one breast and then the other. She grasped his shoulders and arched her back to give him more. Gently, he pushed her onto her back and kissed his way down her belly, and she fisted her hands in his hair as he ran a fingertip along the waistband of her breeches. She went still as he pulled the end of her stays with his teeth, untying them.

Kissing her belly, he pulled her breeches down her legs, rubbing his soft beard along the insides of her thighs and nipping her tender skin. She whimpered as he sat back on his heels, desperate to feel his mouth on her again, and then he pulled off her boots, and yanked her breeches down over her knees, her calves, her feet, and tossed them aside with a hungry grin.

He stood and untied the stays to his breeches, and Alina watched, enthralled, as he pulled his breeches down and kicked them off, his erect cock springing free. It had been one thing to ogle him through the spyglass, and quite another to see all of him up close.

She bit her lower lip, glad they'd agreed not to have intercourse. She knew a woman's body was made to fit a man's, yet staring at Roark's thick, engorged cock, she wasn't sure how. He knelt at her feet and lowered his naked body over hers and Alina stopped thinking. All she could do was feel.

The length and the solid weight of him on her, skin on skin. The hard heat of his cock against her belly. His mouth on hers, on her breasts. His hands moving over her, caressing her breasts, roaming down her back and cupping her backside, running his fingertips down the backs of her thighs and up the insides. His fingertip pushing through her thatch of tight curls and touching her intimate flesh.

She moaned.

He covered her mouth with his and swallowed her moan, rubbing delicious, tortuous circles around her flesh. Alina moved her hips with his hand, her need building, to what end, she couldn't have said. She only knew that she wanted, she needed…something. All feeling and thought had gathered between her legs.

Roark slowed his circles and pressed his finger to the nubbin of flesh where all her sensations had pooled. He tapped the nubbin with his fingertip and Alina lifted her pelvis and pressed it into his hand, moving with his finger, his hand, until her muscles tightened and convulsed and ripples of intense pleasure flowed through her, leaving her spent and panting as she gazed at him in awe.

She smiled, boneless, weightless, sated, and he grinned, slow and easy. "My passionate lady owl," he rumbled.

Alina wrapped her arms around his neck and pulled his mouth down to hers. "Tell me how to bring you to your release, sir stag," she whispered hoarsely against his lips.

"It'll be my pleasure," he rasped. He rolled onto his side and placed her hand on his cock, closing his eyes and groaning as she gently wrapped her fingers around it.

"I don't know what to do," she confessed.

Roark opened his eyes, heavy-lidded with desire. "Touch me, pet me, rub me," he told her. "I've dreamt of this, of you, so many times, your touch alone is about to undo me."

Alina unwrapped her fingers and ran them lightly up and down the length of his cock, amazed at how hard, warm, and responsive he was to her touch. How his cock wasn't some separate entity, it was a part of him, his flesh and blood, full of his seed, his life force in her hand.

She splayed her fingers and rubbed them up and down him, her own flesh heating again as he moved with her hand. She wrapped her fingers around him and watched in fascination as he pushed and pulled himself into and through her grip, gripping firmer, tighter, as he moved faster, moving her hand faster and faster until his body went rigid, his cock pulsed in her hand, and he spurt his seed with a shuddering groan.

***

Roark kissed Alina's bare shoulder. "It's stopped raining," he whispered in her ear, grinning as she buried her nose deeper into the bedroll.

He stood and pulled the blanket over her shoulders, stretched his sated body, and went to the cave's entrance. The horses were huddled together under the overhang, cramped but dry. The ground had standing puddles of water and mud, and the clouds were dark and ominous. He figured it was somewhere around noon, but with the sun hidden behind a wall of clouds, it was impossible to tell for certain. He rubbed his beard and gave the sky another look. They wouldn't be riding anytime today.

Back inside the cave, he dressed and stared down at Alina sleeping. Her lush, full lips that'd been wrapped around his cock sometime around dawn, slightly open, her breath, which had been panting and gasping in his ear several times last night, quiet and steady.

Adjusting his randy cock, already half-hard simply from looking at her, he went back outside and led the horses to a patch of grass, letting them relieve themselves and graze while they could. He stayed outside with them, enjoying the brisk air and reliving the most amazing night in his life.

He'd been more right than he knew when he'd said he and Alina belonged together, belonged to each other. The widow had been a skilled and lusty lover, but his princess made love to him with a pure, raw passion, which made up for any lack of skill. She gave all of herself to him, body, heart, and soul, and took all of him in return. Plus, she was a quick learner.

The horses raised their heads and pitched their ears forward, and Roark turned to see Alina coming out of the cave wearing only her boots and an otter skin cloak, her waist-length hair flying around her in the wind, her lips red and swollen from their near-constant love play since yesterday afternoon.

"I, ah, I." She motioned toward a briar of bushes and disappeared behind it, smiling shyly as she came out and up to Roark. "Good morning," she said, and glanced up at the sky. "What time is it?"

"Best I can tell, around noon."

"Are you hungry?" she asked him. "Those beans should be ready to cook."

Roark reached out and hooked a finger in the neckline of her cloak and pulled it down, exposing her bare shoulder. "Famished," he said, nipping the sensitive skin where her shoulder met her neck.

"Ravaging's more like it," she chided.

He nibbled his way up her throat to her lips, cupping her backside with both hands and pulling her close. "You're cold," he said when she shivered.

"So warm me up." She stepped back and threw him a come-hither smile over her shoulder as she headed toward the cave.

"I'll be in after I let the horses graze a little longer," he told her. "I want to take advantage of this break in weather."

"No hurry," she said, stopping at the cave's entrance. "It's obvious we're not going anywhere today." She grinned and flapped her cloak open and closed, teasing Roark with a glimpse of ripe breasts, a trim waist, pale, creamy thighs, and the dark triangle of hair at their apex. "I'll start the beans."

Their bellies full and their lust sated, they sat together before the fire, Alina tucked into his side, her head on his shoulder, staring silently into the flames.

"Are you all right?" Roark asked.

"Mm hmm."

"Not regretting anything?"

She shook her head. "The only thing I regret about all of this is the pain my parents must be going through thinking I'm dead. Not knowing."

Roark hugged her closer. "I regret putting your parents through that. The only thing I regret more is putting you through everything."

She leaned her head back and met his gaze. "I know it's foolish of me, and we're losing precious days of travel, but I'm glad we had to shelter in this cave. I thought the fates against me this whole time, yet the more I think on it, the surer I am the only reason I'm still alive is because of you. Roger was going to try to abduct me no matter what, and Leif, he'd have raped me that first night on *The Rover* if not for you." She scooted around and faced him. "I think the fates brought us together."

"Why?" he said, aware it was him asking her favorite question.

"Because we were meant to be together. Nothing that feels this right can be wrong."

Roark's heart skipped a beat or three. "I agree," he said. "We were. We are. But for how long?" As happy and content as they were right now, the reality was that their sojourn here in the cave would only last another day or two. "Once we make port and find you a ship, we'll be a sea apart."

"I know," she said somberly. "I've known from the moment Leif announced you were betrothed to Gwyneth our time together was preordained by our circumstances in life. Yet here we are. And I'm glad I'm holed up with you, because no matter what happens, I've loved and been loved by you."

"Damnation." Roark pulled her onto his lap and kissed her with everything he felt, everything he had in him. "It's been the privilege of my life to have met you and loved you, and been loved by you, my lady owl."

Her gaze was as deep and fathomless as the sea they'd crossed together. She straddled his hips and untied her stays then lay back and pulled off her breeches as Roark did the same with his. When he was sitting again, she climbed onto his lap, her hot, wet flesh nuzzling his cock.

"Make love to me, sir stag," she murmured. "Let me feel the full measure of you."

"Ali girl…"

She rubbed herself up and down against him. "Did you know," she said, smiling sensually, "that ever since my great-grandmother, Oona the Swan, proposed marriage to Asad the Lion the first night they met, that one or the other of my grandparents and parents proposed to the other the first times they met too?"

"No," Roark said, finding it hard to concentrate. "I didn't know that."

"It's true," she said, rubbing any semblance of sense out of him. "You asked me the first time we met in person, on Spring's Eve, by the lake."

"You started to say yes," he rasped.

"I'm saying yes now," she said, her voice low and throaty. "Here, in our own little world, where only we matter, I'm saying yes. Make me your wife. Be my husband."

Roark blew out his breath and held Alina by the shoulders, locking gazes with her, trying to think rationally. To make them both see reason. "What about when we walk out of this cave and into the real world full of consequences and repercussions?"

Ali, sweet, sensible, rational, reasonable Ali, shook her head. "I don't care," she told him. "I don't care about anything outside of these walls right now. All I care about is you and me, and I want you stones deep inside me. All of you. Now."

She lifted onto her knees and held herself over his straining cock, and then she touched her wet, warm flesh to his and Roark gripped her shoulders. She smiled, slow, sure, and sensuous, as she lowered herself onto him bit by sleek, hot, welcoming bit, until he was fully sheathed inside her, her intimate muscles contracting around him.

Roark groaned and clasped her to him. "Ach, Ali love," he rumbled. "You have undone me."

***

Alina woke to birdsong and sunlight streaming through the cave's entrance, but the fire was out and Roark was gone. The storm had calmed to a light drizzle sometime after midnight, while inside the cave their personal storm had built and spent many times over. She yawned, stretched, and ran her hands down her naked body, sighing and grinning with the newfound knowledge of the pleasures her body was capable of giving and receiving.

She stood and dressed in her tunic and breeches and stepped out into the new day, ready for anything, until she saw Roark's face as he was saddling the horses.

"You should have woken me," she said as he laid Etain's saddle over the mare's back. "I could have helped with the horses." She cinched the strap around the mare's belly and then stepped over to Artur as Roark heaved the saddle onto the stallion. "Roark?" He put his forehead into Artur's side and cinched the saddle strap. "Roark" she said again, waiting for him to look at her. "What's wrong?"

"Nothing," he said, looking away from her while sheathing his short sword at the saddle. She stepped around Artur and laid a hand over his. "Everything." He pulled his hand out from under hers and ran it back through his hair. "Last night should never have happened."

Alina's heart dropped to her feet. Last night had been the most wonderful, amazing night of her life. She'd thought he'd felt the same. He'd certainly acted like it at the time. He'd even called her his love. "What do you mean?" she asked, her voice cracking almost as badly as her heart.

"I never should've let things go as far as they did," he said. "I knew better. I knew how hard it would be to stop once I let myself start with you."

"Are you saying you regret last night?"

"Yes."

Her body went cold and her mind went numb. She stood rooted, her vision unfocused, trying to suck air into her lungs.

"Ali."

"Why?" she cried. "Why would you say that to me?"

He reached for her hand and she slapped his away.

"Ali, love."

"No." She shook her head and glared at him. "You cannot tell me you regret making love to me and then call me love."

"Ali, lass," he said, his voice soft, his eyes pouring into hers. "I could never regret making love to you. What I regret was losing control, going against my word and my oath to not take your maidenhead. Spilling my seed inside you and chancing getting you pregnant with a child. My child." He pulled her to him, holding her tight, and whispered in her ear, "I love you, Ali. I have since the moment I first saw you. I love you so much it pains me because I know I have to let you go. I have to send you away from me and back to your family."

Alina sniffed. "What if I do end up pregnant with your child?"

"Will your family accept it, accept you, without a husband?"

Alina didn't even have to think. "Yes," she said without hesitation. She held his worried gaze, her own pleading. "Come with me," she begged. "Marry me. Raise our child, our children, together in the Northlands."

"I cannot."

"Cannot or will not?"

"I cannot come with you, love, because I will not leave my family to suffer the consequences of my actions. I have to stay and make things right."

"Roger will kill you."

"It's verra likely."

Alina clasped him tight and made her own silent oath. She didn't know how she would accomplish it, but she knew she wasn't going to let Roark die for her. She damned sure wasn't going to let him die for Leif.

***

Alina pulled her otter-skin cloak closer around her shoulders as they rode up the mountain's southern slope. The wind was raw and the air chilled, but they wouldn't suffer from lack of food or water as the high woods of birch and pine were filled with small game and birdsong, and the hillsides crisscrossed with rills and streams overflowing with rainwater. Etain, carrying the lighter Alina, was having an easier time traversing the slogging wet, muddy terrain than the heavier Artur carrying Roark. But like his master, the stallion was strong, sturdy, and sure-footed.

They stopped by a small lake at noon, and Roark set a snare while Alina watered the horses and staked them to graze. They ate the last of the cooked field beans and Alina scoured the mountainside with the spyglass while Roark checked his snare and came back with a hare.

"I'll set another snare when we camp for the night," he said, tying the hare to his saddle.

"The roots your mother gave us will make a good rabbit stew," Alina said. "And there's plenty of fresh greens along the waterways."

They'd lost a day and a half of travel time because of the storm, and almost half of today because of their late start this morning, part of which was them waking up late and the other part their argument, which had ended with Roark declaring his love.

A declaration she would hold close and dear until her dying day, which hopefully would be many years from now. He'd said he regretted consummating their love, but he hadn't said it couldn't happen again. She was determined to make sure it did. If she was going to have to spend the rest of her life without him, then she wanted to get as much of him as she could for as long as she could.

She mounted Etain and resumed their trek up the mountain, keeping an eye out for other riders and dreaming of the night to come. Memories of their lovemaking warming her from the inside out.

They topped the mountain pass as the sun was dipping below the western horizon and rode on until dark, following a stream and making camp in a copse of oak. Alina filled the pot with water, roots, and sorrel leaves she'd picked along the stream while Roark dressed the hare, and then she put the pot over the fire to cook and snuggled up against him on the bedrolls, staring up at the few stars peeking out amongst the clouds.

"If you could do or be anything in our world of no consequences or repercussions," she asked him as the Hunter showed in the southern sky, "what would you choose?"

"Hmmm. I'd like to own land with good, arable acreage to farm, grazing land for sheep, cattle, and horses, and to have a glassmaking shop that would specialize in spyglass lenses and roof panes for greenhouses, and a trading ship or three to trade our wares all over the world."

"Our wares?"

He tucked her into his shoulder and kissed the top of her head. "Our wares. Our glass. Our land. Our keep. Our stable full of horses, cats, and goats. Our bairns."

Alina, who'd always assumed she'd marry and have children someday without feeling the burning desire so many other girls had, laid a hand over her belly where Roark's seed may have already taken hold. "I like your dream," she said.

"What would you choose?"

"You." She ran her fingers through his beard and turned his face to hers. "I love you, Roark. I would choose to be with you all of my days and nights."

He smiled, slow and easy, and more than a little sad. "I would choose the same, Ali love," he said. "While we may not have all our days and nights to be together, we have tonight, and we have now." He nodded toward the pot of stew simmering over the fire. "How much time do we have right now?"

She gave the stew a stir and grinned back at him. "Long enough," she said.

Up to two nights ago, Alina would have said the spyglass was her favorite appendage of Roark's. But that had changed when she'd touched his cock and felt it grow and pulse in her hand. When she'd held it as he shuddered and spilt his hot seed. When she'd licked and nipped, and sucked and swallowed his yeasty essence. When she'd taken his engorged cock deep inside of her and he'd filled her with a need she'd never known she had.

She ran a finger along the inside of his waistband, licking her lips with anticipation as her new favorite appendage rose to meet her fingertip, her laughter low and sultry as he pulled her tunic up and over her head and then doffed his own. They both stood and shucked their boots and breeches and then fell onto the bedrolls together.

"What do you want, my lady owl?" he whispered roughly as he lay on top of her, his thick erection pressing against her belly.

Alina spread her legs beneath him. "You, sir stag. All of you, inside me."

After… They lay together on the bedrolls staring up at the stars in the clearing sky, the stew eaten and the campfire burned to embers. Roark pointed north and west to the Lady in the Chair. "If anything happens to me before we find you a ship," he said, "I want you to go to the MacLeods' at Silver Water Keep."

"Why?"

Roark chuckled at her why. "You're Oona the Swan's great-granddaughter. They're kin. They'll help you."

Alina knew her great-grandmother had come from the Green Isles, but she'd never heard the name of her home, or where in the Green Isles it was. Other than knowing Oona's story, her family had never had any contact with their Green Isles kin from four generations back.

"What if they don't believe me?" she said. "I have no proof she's my great-grandmother."

"The tales all tell of her big, beautiful, emerald green eyes," he said, holding her gaze. "One look into those green eyes of yours and they'll know."

"I suppose." The women in Alina's family were known for the unusual color of their eyes, and though uncommon, green eyes weren't unheard of here in the Green Isles.

"If your eyes don't convince them, sing 'Somebody' for them. There's not a man in this world who could deny you anything if you sang that song to them."

"Perhaps." Roark was the only man she'd ever sung "Somebody" to, the only man she could ever imagine singing it to. "Perhaps I could sing 'The Sailors Tale' if it comes to that."

He sat up and stared down at her, his eyes shining silver in the low glow of the fire's embers. "Promise me," he said, somber, serious. "I want you to promise me that you'll sing whatever song it takes, that you'll do and say whatever you must to survive and get back to your family."

"I promise."

He pulled the vial of White Milk from his pocket and held it out to her. "Take this," he said. "Take it," he repeated, placing the vial in her hand and closing her fingers around it. "You know how to use it, for yourself or anybody else, should the need arise."

Alina nodded, knowing he meant if they were captured and about to be tortured or executed, or in her case, raped, she could take it herself to numb the horror and the pain. Or to escape forever into oblivion.

"Why are you giving this to me, now?" she asked him.

"They would've buried Leif two days ago," he said. "Burying his son was the only thing keeping Roger from sending everything, everyone after us. Or coming after us himself." He stared hard into her eyes. "I know Roger. He spent the past twenty years nursing his grudge and planning his revenge against your parents. He's never going to stop looking for us, for you, until he or we are dead. I wanted to tell you this now to make you understand before something happened. Before it's too late."

CHAPTER 11

White Milk

Roark scanned the mountainside with the spyglass. They'd ridden long and hard the past three days, saddling up at the first light of dawn and riding 'til the dark of night, stopping only long enough to eat, make love, and sleep before rising and doing it all again. By pushing the horses and themselves, they'd made the Mounths' northwest range and would start their slow descent toward the lowlands tomorrow. Which meant farms and villages, and eventually towns to avoid until they reached the North Sea Firth in another three to four days.

He glanced at Alina, who was watering the horses at a stream and checking their hooves. She'd never complained once since they'd fled North Shore Keep, though she'd been on horseback, eating camp food, and sleeping on the hard ground for the past seven days and nights. They'd used the last of the dry stores Roark's mother and uncle had given them two days ago, and had been surviving on the small game they caught, and the wild greens and mushrooms Alina foraged. She could lay a snare as well as Roark, and hadn't exaggerated one whit when she'd claimed she could skin and cook whatever game she caught.

She caught him watching her and smiled. Their time in the wilds hadn't been all drudge and hardship. There'd been dips in streams and ponds, and the nights making love under the stars. Their whispered endearments as they lay huddled together on their bedrolls and their conversations as they rode, covering everything from the natural world they traveled through to the spiritual world they could feel and hope to find one day. Though not yet.

It was that spirit world niggling at the back of his neck that'd had Roark on edge since he'd given Alina the vial of White Milk. He knew Leif was dead and buried, yet he couldn't shake the feeling his ghost was haunting him. He'd shared a brotherly bond with Leif for ten years, and though he'd hated him in the end, and would've killed him if Alina hadn't stopped him, he had left him bound and gagged, a sitting target for whoever it was who had killed him. He felt Leif's presence dogging his every move. This was the one thing he hadn't discussed with Alina, and wouldn't.

Perhaps it was his own pending death preying on him. He knew the odds of him surviving were poor at best if he returned to North Shore Keep to make things right between his family and Roger's. Those odds would go way up if he returned with Alina to Sea Ridge.

It wasn't like he hadn't considered it a hundred times a day since she'd asked him to return with her. He was a young man in his prime with a woman he loved who loved him back. A woman offering him a life he hadn't dared dream of since he'd been sent to Roger and became betrothed to Gwyneth. Yet as much as he wished he could accept her offer, he couldn't live with himself if he left his family and hundreds of others to suffer for his actions. He wouldn't dishonor Alina by marrying her in such a state.

If, by some miracle, he made it back to North Shore Keep alive and survived a public trial and was released from his betrothal to Gwyneth—all big unlikely ifs—then he promised himself he'd go after Alina, and hope she wasn't carrying his child and been forced to marry another man in order to give their child a name.

All big, fucking ifs.

He gave the mountainside one last look as Alina walked the horses over to him, and stopped cold. "There are five riders coming from the south," he said. "Riding hard and fast from the looks of it."

He handed her the spyglass as he checked the cinches on Artur's and Etain's saddles and double=checked the ties on their gear. She handed the spyglass back to him and he booted her up onto Etain's back and swung up onto Artur's.

"Can we outrun them?" she asked as they sent the horses into an easy lope due north.

"We're going to find out." Artur and Etain were both good horses with lots of heart, but they'd been ridden long and hard for days now, their only respite when they'd been huddled damp and cold under the cave's overhang, and that was four days ago.

A lot would depend on where the riders were coming from and how hard they'd ridden to get here. "They're coming from the south, so it's likely they followed us across the Mounths. Hopefully, their horses are as tired as ours."

Alina patted Etain's neck. "My faerie girl has the heart, the will, and the legs," she said. "They'll be hard-pressed to catch us."

Roark pulled out the spyglass and looked over his shoulder. "It's time to put those legs to use," he said, urging Artur into a full gallop.

They kept ahead of the riders for most of the afternoon, and though they hadn't gained any distance on them, they hadn't lost any either. Roark could feel Artur struggling for breath as they climbed, making the pass as the sun was touching the top of the western peak. He could see that Etain was struggling as well. They stopped at the top of the pass to give the horses a quick rest and take a quick piss. Mounting back up, Roark took a look behind them with the spyglass.

"Damnation."

"Are they gaining on us?" Alina asked.

"A little." He turned Artur's head north and urged the stallion forward. Twenty paces in, Artur started limping on his right front leg. "Hold up," Roark called to Alina. He dismounted and lifted Artur's hoof. "Fuck me."

"What is it?"

"A stone bruise." Roark touched the dark swelling and Artur jerked his leg. "It's not too bad yet, but he's done running." Gently, he lowered Artur's hoof and met Alina's worried frown. He untied the spyglass sheath from his waist belt and handed it to her. "Ride due north until you make those woods." He pointed to a thick forest about two leagues down. "Turn west into the woods and do the best you can to hide your tracks. Find a stream to ride down or back and forth across while making your way northwest."

"No." She shook her head. "I'm not leaving you."

Roark pulled his flint out of his saddlebag and his dagger out of his boot, holding them both out to Alina, who was shaking her head even harder, her eyes wide and wild.

"Yes," he told her, shoving the flint and the dagger into her hands. He took the bow and quiver from Artur's saddle and tied them to Etain's. "The mare can't carry us both," he said. "You have to leave me or we'll both die, and this will have all been for nothing." He could see her mind working, arguing against the truth of what he said. "What if you're carrying my bairn?"

She blinked twice, and then she grabbed him by the tunic. "They will grow up knowing they were made of our love. None of this," she said, her voice as fierce as her gaze, "was for nothing. I love you, Roark."

He gave her a smacking kiss on the lips. "I love you too." He took her by the arms and practically threw her up onto Etain's back. "Now fly, my lady owl. Fly to Silver Water Keep, and the gods willing, I'll join you there in a day or three."

"Roark…"

"Go." He slapped Etain on the rump and watched Alina ride away from him, and then he walked Artur over to a log and untied the saddle blanket he'd been using as a bedroll and cut strips off it that he tied around Artur's hoof. When he was satisfied the hoof was sufficiently cushioned, he pulled out his last two strips of rabbit meat and ate them, took a long drink of water from his skin, pulled his short sword, and sat down on the log and waited.

He didn't have to wait long.

He stood and stretched his back and touched his toes and swung his arms from side to side as the riders approached and circled him.

"Where's the woman?" demanded a man of indeterminate age with stringy brown hair and a long, scruffy beard.

"Woman?" Roark glanced around, taking in the four other men. "What woman?"

"The one you was ridin' with," the man, who appeared to be the leader of the motley band, said.

Roark was a laird's son who'd been taught sword fighting since he was eight years old, and by the ragged looks of the men surrounding him, he was at least five years younger than the youngest and outweighed every one of them by three stone of muscle. Still, there were five of them on horseback. The best he hoped to do was stall and give Alina more time to get away, and to take one or two of them down with him.

"You must mean the lad I was riding with," he said. "A fey lad, to be sure. I ken see why you're thinking he was a woman."

"He's messing with ye, Ned," another man, the beefiest of the five, said.

"Shut up, Shaw," the leader, Ned, said. "I know he's messing with me." He glared down at Roark. "An I know who you and the woman be. Now, where is she?"

Roark shrugged and shook his head.

"Rob," Ned barked at the rider to the right of Roark. "Look fer her tracks. She can't've gotten far."

"Aye, Ned."

Roark turned and took two running strides for Rob, leaping into the air and skewering the man through the back of the ribs with his short sword. He pulled the blade from Rob's back as the man slumped forward, and landed on his feet. "Well," he snarled, swinging the short sword and slinging Rob's blood. "Who's next?"

The youngest and twitchiest of the gang charged Roark with his horse, which was as twitchy as his rider. Roark stepped up and bellowed like a bull, waving his arms and shouting at the wall-eyed creature. The horse panicked and reared and threw its rider, who landed on his back with a thud and cracked his head open on a rock. The horse ran off, and the other three men stared at their dead companions for a breath or two, and then they slowly tightened their circle around him.

"Yer a dead man," the one called Shaw spat.

"No, Shaw," Ned snapped. "He ain't worth spit to us dead. We take him alive."

Roark grinned and swung his sword. "You can try."

***

Alina made the woods and picked a winding path in a northwesterly direction over the driest ground she could find, backtracking where Etain's hoofprints would be easiest to track. She came upon a stream a half league into the woods and rode Etain downstream, stopping to look back over her shoulders and listen for the sounds of being followed every twenty paces or so.

The stream flowed in the general direction Roark told her ride, and she could have continued following it as dusk turned to night, putting more distance between herself and the riders who were sure to come after her at some point, yet the farther she got from where she'd left Roark, the more she kept being drawn back.

Roark, who'd stayed to fight and distract the brigands, to give her more time to get away, knowing he couldn't hope to beat five armed men, but would do what damage he could and then let himself be captured to save her.

Roger's orders were to take them alive, so the men shouldn't try to kill Roark. But he would be fighting to kill, not wound them, and men were known to go berserkers in a fight, and fatal wounds were often taken even in practice fights.

Alina reined in Etain to a halt and stared up the mountain. If she didn't keep riding for Silver Water Keep and got caught by the men, then everything Roark had done for her would be for nothing. But what if she kept riding and he died for her? What if she could have saved him?

Alina turned Etain south and rode upstream. She couldn't leave Roark to those men. She wouldn't. She'd simply have to be careful and smart about it.

She rode under the light of a quarter moon until she made the woods' edge sometime before midnight. Pulling out the spyglass, she searched the mountainside and sighted the light of a small campfire at the top of the pass where she'd left Roark to make his stand. She scanned the trail she'd taken down the mountain and saw no movement. The men weren't worried about being seen, or they wouldn't have a fire. They obviously didn't think she'd come back. She was one woman against five men, why would she when she'd gotten away?

"Because they don't know me," she whispered into the tuckered-out mare's ear. Her mother had killed a man with a blade to his chest defending her father, and her grandmother had killed a man with a staff defending her grandfather. Her great-grandmother had killed one of the men sent to kill her in a knife fight, and bore a scar across her back to the end of her days from that battle. "They don't know the women I'm descended from. But they will." She patted Etain's neck. "They will."

Dismounting and staking Etain to graze, Alina pulled off Etain's saddle and went through her packs, taking stock. Keeping the otter cloak out, she packed everything up, refilled her waterskin, resaddled Etain so she could ride at a moment's notice, and lay down on her bedroll with the cloak over her, missing the comfort and warmth of Roark's body curled around hers. She prayed to every god and goddess she knew to keep him safe as she lay trying to figure out how to get him free.

She woke with a start to Etain's worried whinny in the pitch of night. She pulled her waist blade and stood by the mare. "What do you hear?" she whispered. The mare's ears flicked forward. "What is it, eh, girl?"

The mare tugged at Alina's hold on her bridle. Alina held on tight to keep her from throwing her head and letting out a loud whinny, giving them away to whoever or whatever was out there.

"Shhh, Etain," she murmured, stroking the mare's neck and glancing around, though she couldn't see more than ten paces in the dark. "Quiet, girl, let me listen."

She tilted her head this way and that, finally hearing what sounded like shuffling footsteps at the edge of the trees. She let go of her horse and pulled out one of her boot daggers, hiding behind a tree as the shuffling grew closer. Etain tossed her head, snorting, as a great, hulking shadow emerged from the tree line. A different horse whinnied loudly, and Alina peered around the tree, her heart in her throat and her blades at the ready.

A horse stood at the edge of their little camp, its reins dangling as it bobbed its head up and down and neighed softly at Etain. There was a saddle on its back, but no rider. Alina waited and listened, but she didn't see or hear anything beyond the clearing. She stepped out from the tree and went to Etain, laying a hand on the mare's neck.

"It's all right, Etain," she crooned, taking in the rangy roan. "I think the poor beasty is even more frightened than you are, aren't you, beasty?" she said, keeping up her soft patter as she slowly approached the horse. "Are you all alone out here in this scary place?" The horse tossed its head but didn't bolt as she stopped and held her hand out for it to sniff. "Did you run away from those bad men?" The horse dropped its head and Alina placed her palm on its nose and gently rubbed.

"Did Roark unseat your master? Did he send you to find us?" She ran her hand down its neck and over its withers. "You're rather skinny for such a large," she peeked under its belly, "gelding. Would you like to stay here with us for the night? Maybe join us on our journey?" The gelding nickered and Alina chuckled softly. "All right then, Beasty," she said, naming him after her big coursing hound at home who he put her in mind of. "Welcome to our scraggly band of would-be rescuers."

She left the gelding saddled as she went through the bags, finding only a cleanish tunic, a small sack of dried field beans, a few strips of dried meat, and a flint. There was a rope tied to the saddle and two skins, one half full of water and the other half full of wine. She untied the wineskin and took a long drink, then capped it and set it aside on the bedroll. She needed to think.

"I have two horses now, both with saddles, so I can switch off between them, which will keep them fresher than the brigand's mounts." She stared down at the wineskin, and the tale of her grandmother's and grandfather's adventures during the hundred-league race came to her. She patted her tunic pocket with the vial of White Milk. "I know what to do," she told the horses. "I just have to figure out how."

By the moon it was closer to dawn than night. Alina ate one of the meat strips from Beasty's saddle and positioned herself at the woods' edge where she watched the mountain's ridge through the spyglass as dawn broke. Soon enough, she spied horses coming down the northern slope she'd raced down yesterday. Her heart stopped. There were five horses but only four riders, and Artur was the riderless horse. Her heart beating in her ears, she focused on the riders one by one as they got closer. There, in the middle, she was certain she recognized Roark's broad shoulders, the way he sat his mount, the shape of his face, his hair, his cropped beard.

She gave a feral grin. There had been five brigands yesterday, and there were only three today, which likely meant Roark had killed two of them.

She watched until they were less than a league away, and then she tied off Beasty to Etain's saddle, mounted Etain, and rode deep into the woods enough to stay hidden but close enough to watch the men through the spyglass.

***

Roark held on to the saddle horn, his hands bound together at his wrists. The nag he was riding plodded along behind Ned and between Cam and Shaw. The remaining members of the ragtag band that had finally managed to knock him out cold yesterday with the hilt of a short sword to the back of his head. He licked his dry, cracked lips and tugged at the rope around his neck, which Shaw, who seemed to have taken the loss of their two companions the hardest, had control of.

They were following Etain's and Alina's trail down the northern slope of the mountain, and Roark hid his grin when they had to backtrack to find where Alina had turned Etain into the woods. They managed to track the mare's hoofprints to a small stream, where Roark convinced Shaw to let him dismount and drink while Ned and Cam rode up and down the water's course trying to pick up Alina's trail.

After drinking his fill, Roark dunked his head in the water, letting the cold wash away much of his haziness and a little of the throbbing ache in his head. He stood and stretched some of the kinks out of his body after a cramped, uncomfortable night floating in and out of consciousness while tied to a tree, worrying about Alina.

Ned rode back from searching upstream, and he didn't look happy.

"I didn't find a thing," he said. Which was repeated by Cam when he rode back from searching downstream a bit later.

Ned eyed Roark, who worked on keeping his face a blank mask.

"The laird's men said she'd be trying to find a ship to sail out on," Ned said. "Odds are she's riding straight for the North Sea Firth."

"Which is due north," Shaw said. "So why'd she go west into the woods here?"

"To throw us off her trail," Ned said. He looked at Roark, who purposely widened his eyes. "Aye, that's what she's done. That's where she's headed." He jerked his head toward Roark, who glared back at him. "Look at him, he knows I got the right of it." He cackled with anticipation. "Mount up, we're riding north."

Roark let out the grin he'd been holding back. "It won't do you any good," he said. "She's halfway there by now."

"Seeing as how the firth is a three-day ride from here, I doubt it," Shaw said, giving Roark's noose a sharp yank. "Now mount up and shut up."

"Can I at least pack my horse's hoof with mud before we ride again?" Roark asked. Though riderless, Artur's limp had worsened in the two leagues from last night's camp to the stream. "If I don't pack it, his stone bruise will abscess." He'd heard them talking about selling the stallion as soon as they got to a town last night. "He'll be worth nothing to you if that happens."

"Make it quick," Ned said.

Roark held his hands out for Shaw to untie his wrists. "Don't forget I still have a hold of this." Shaw grinned, showing several gaps in his teeth, and gave the rope around Roark's neck another quick yank.

Unwrapping Artur's hoof, Roark frowned. The bruise had grown and darkened. He led the horse into the cold water, hoping it would soak some of the heat and swelling out, and scooped up a handful of black mud he packed into the sole and rewrapped the hoof.

"Next time, tend to yer horse first," Ned said as Shaw retied Roark's wrists. "We're wasting good time."

Roark nodded and bit down on his grin. Wasting time was exactly what he was trying to do. Grabbing the saddle horn of the cob with his tied hands, he leaned back and swayed like he was suddenly dizzy. He lifted his booted foot and missed the stirrup, taking three swipes at it before finally stuffing his boot toe into the stirrup, swung his leg up, missed the saddle, and fell back onto the soft bank of the stream.

"Get him up on his damned horse," Ned ordered.

Roark lay on the ground, his eyes purposely unfocused as Shaw and Cam grabbed him by the shoulders and pulled him to his feet. He swayed against them and let his arms and legs hang like dead weight as they heaved him up onto the cob, belly down, head on one side of the saddle and his legs dangling over the other.

"Sit up, curse you," Shaw spat.

"I'ms trying," Roark slurred as he half-assed swung one leg over the cob's rump, taking two tries before he succeeded. He lay there panting and rolled his eyes. "I'ms a little dizzy, lads."

"You was fine when you was tending yer horse," Shaw grumbled.

"Musta stood up too fasht." Roark slowly pushed himself up to sitting, grabbed the saddle horn to steady himself, and pressed his lips tight when Shaw didn't tie his hands to it.

"Let's go," Ned barked. "Daylight's wasting."

They rode north, keeping the western woods to their shoulders. Roark managed to fall off the cob two more times before they tied him to the saddle. When they stopped at noon to water the horses and relieve themselves, Roark unwrapped Artur's hoof and chipped the dried mud away.

"Damnation." Still kneeling, he motioned for Ned and showed him the stallion's hoof. "The bruise is getting bigger," he told Ned. "And his limp's been getting worse."

Ned pulled on his scraggly beard. "So?"

"So, it's only going to get worse if he keeps walking on it," Roark told him. "He'll move slower and slower until he founders."

Ned eyed Artur's hoof, which the horse wasn't putting any weight on, and spat on the ground. "Damned horse ain't worth spit if he founders." He drew his short sword.

"Wait." Roark threw his tied hands up and swayed a little. "You don't have to kill him. Just leave him here to rest up. There's plenty of water and good grazing. You can come back this way after you've turned me in to the laird's men, catch him and sell him if he's healed. If he hasn't," Roark shrugged, "then you'll likely find his bones picked over by scavengers."

"Do what you need for him and be quick about it," Ned said.

Roark uncinched his saddle and pulled it off Artur. He left the hoof unwrapped and removed Artur's bridle and reins, pressed his forehead to the stallion's and patted his neck. "Take care of yourself, my friend," he said.

He mounted the cob, only taking two swipes at the stirrup before stuffing the toe of his boot into it, and glanced at the woods. The woods Alina should've been long gone from. So why'd he see a flash of light like the sun reflecting on a glass lens blinking at him from the woods' edge?

They continued to ride north until dark without any sign Alina had passed that way, which Roark hoped meant she was on her way northwest to Silver Water Keep. He hadn't seen any more flashes of light from the woods, yet he still had the feeling she was following them. At least Ned and his men seemed to think she was long gone.

"If that girl makes the firth," Cam grumbled as he struck his flint to start the campfire, "odds are some ship captain'll snatch her and get the reward."

"Quit yer whining," Ned told him. "Not that another ten pounds o' silver wouldn't be nice, but we gots our ten pounds guaranteed right here," he said, nodding at Roark, whom Shaw was tying to a tree.

"We're not there yet," Shaw said, yanking the rope tight around Roark's chest. "I fer one ain't gonna count my silver 'til it's in my purse."

"Look, lads," Roark said. "I know you're doing this for the silver and likely don't care, but we didn't kill the laird's son."

"Yer right," Ned said. "We don't care."

"What you should care about though," Roark continued, "is that the girl is no serving wench, she's Princess Alina, daughter of Northland King Jerrik of Sea Ridge."

"So?"

"So, King Jerrik has six warships at his command and will be coming for his daughter any day. That's why we were riding for the North Sea Firth. Why she's still heading there."

"Even if that's true," Ned said, "what's it got to do with us?"

"Northmen are well known for their honor-bound sense of revenge," Roark told them. "Almost as much as they're known for their skill with a long sword."

"So?" Shaw gave the rope around Roark a tug and tied off the ends. "We don't have the princess now, do we?"

"No," Roark said, "you don't. However, you did take her escort, me, from her, and you are chasing her. Somehow, I don't see her father, a fierce Northman king, as caring whether you caught her or not."

"Shut up," Shaw snarled. "Lessen you wanna be gagged."

Roark leaned his head back against the tree trunk and closed his eyes. The men had a tense discussion over continuing their search for her while the beans cooked. Good. He'd spooked them with his talk of Alina's father. He'd learned they were itinerant field workers who'd seen him and Alina riding into the Mounths' southern foothills, and after hearing about them at an inn, they took off after them. They'd spent a miserable two days waiting out the storm while he and Alina had been in their cozy cave.

The cave. Roark let his mind wander back to his memories of those two wonderful, passion-filled days and nights. Memories that would likely have to serve him for the rest of his life, no matter how long or short it turned out to be. His only regret was he wouldn't be spending whatever time he had left with Alina.

An owl hooted in the woods, and Roark sat at attention. It called out again with three short hoots and Roark dipped his head and lifted it, slowly, purposely, and bit down on a grin.

He'd meant for Alina to be on her way to Silver Water Keep, to safety, yet he wasn't surprised she'd stayed. She meant to free him, and though there was only so much he could do to help her in his current position, he could stay alert and at the ready.

***

Alina hunkered down behind a granite outcropping and focused on the camp. The three brigands hadn't even looked up from the fire when she'd let out her owl hoots, but Roark had. He'd not only heard her, but had known it was her. Courage and determination filled her anew. She could do this.

She ate the handful of cold beans she'd packed and waited until the men had eaten their supper, which she was glad to see they shared with Roark, and settled in for the night. Two of the men lay on their bedrolls while the third sat with his back propped up against his saddle, guarding the camp and Roark.

Their horses were tied off to a line, minus Artur, who Alina had crept out and checked on after Roark had cut him free, deciding, as Roark apparently had, that the stallion was better off loose and resting his injured hoof than being forced to keep up with her, Etain, and Beasty.

Alina waited until the guard woke the next man for his shift. By the moon and the stars, they were taking a third of the night each shift, and neither of them had checked the horses once. She let out another three short hoots and slunk back into the cover of the woods and her cold camp and horses. Wrapping the blanket and otter cloak around herself, she propped her back up against a tree and dozed on and off until the sky started to change from black to a misting grey.

Starting out on Etain and leading Beasty, she kept to the woods and followed Roark and the brigands downhill and north toward the foothills. From what Roark had told her, once they made the northern foothills, they would only be one day away from villages and farms, and another day from the shores of the North Sea Firth. Which meant she had tonight to get Roark free.

The lower they got into the foothills, the thicker the woods grew, which made keeping hidden easier, and following a bit trickier. Alina was no trained tracker, but she'd learned enough from her father and Uncle Bors to not fret about losing them.

Besides, tracking four men on horseback who didn't seem worried about being followed wasn't difficult. She hadn't even needed to use the spyglass to keep track of them, but had snuck looks at Roark with it throughout the day.

He rode with his wrists bound and tied to his mount's saddle with another rope around his neck that the same rider kept hold of, and was wont to yank on periodically. Yet he still rode with his head high and a straight spine, unlike his captors, who rode slouched and slumped with their threadbare cloaks pulled tight around their shoulders in the spring chill.

After their noon break, she gave Etain a rest in preparation for the night, and switched to riding Beasty. She was pleased at how well the gelding responded to her. As high strung as he'd acted when he'd first showed up, he turned out to be a gentle soul, as long as you were gentle with him.

"Play your part well tonight, Beasty," she told him, "and you'll be Roark's new mount." She patted the roan's neck and his ears twitched back. "You'll like Roark, he's got good hands and an amazing seat."

They were well into the foothills when the men finally stopped and made camp for the night. Alina ate the last of the beans and tied Etain to a tree, saddled and ready to ride. She left Beasty saddled, took a swig of wine from the skin he'd showed up with, poured the entire vial of White Milk into the skin, shook it to mix it with the wine, and tied it back onto Beasty's saddle. She checked her blades, slung the bow and quiver of arrows over her shoulder, and led Beasty toward the men's camp. She stopped at the wood's edge, hid behind a tree, and set the spyglass to her eye. Then she let out three short hoots.

As before, the brigands didn't seem to take any notice of her hoots as they went about the business of spitting a rabbit over their fire and arranging their gear. Roark, tied to a tree again, lifted his head, cocked it, nodded once, and uncrossed and crossed his legs.

Alina watched and waited until they'd cooked and eaten the rabbit and were beginning to settle for the night, and then she led

Beasty toward the line of horses, one slow, silent step at a time, until they were no more than twenty paces from the horses. Alina let go of Beasty's reins and half ran, half crawled to hide behind a hedge of bushes as the gelding walked up to the other horses.

"Hey," one of the men called out. "Isn't that Rob's horse?" He stood and approached Beasty, who started to back away. "Yeah, it's his gelding all right," the man said, grabbing Beasty's dangling reins. "Always was a twitchy thing." He jerked Beasty's reins and led him over to the line and tied him off with the other horses. Then he looked Beasty's gear over, took the water and the wineskins off the saddle and uncorked them. "Hey." He lifted the wineskin. "It's still half full."

"Bring it over here," another of the men said. "We owe it to Rob to finish it for him."

While she couldn't hear what they were saying as they sat swilling the wine, she could tell when they were starting to feel its drugged effects by how their voices and laughter grew louder like braying asses. Then their voices turned singsong and sporadic, and finally they were silent. She waited a while longer before she crept out from behind the hedge and stopped and stood among the horses.

The brigands made no indications of noticing her as they all lay in various positions of repose around the fire. One on his back, staring up at the night sky, his jaw slack, another on his side, his gaze fixed on the fire, and the third lying on his back, mesmerized by his own hands as he waved them around. Still, she crept around the edges of the camp, one slow, sure step at a time, waist blade in hand until she was standing in front of Roark, who'd been watching her every move.

He grinned, slow and easy, his rain eyes shining in the low glow of the camp's fire. Alina grinned back and untied the rope around him, her grin growing as Roark took a deep breath in and blew it out, and then he held his bound wrists up to her. Alina untied his wrists and he grabbed her and pulled her to him and kissed her. Hard.

"I should be angry with you for not riding out like I told you to," he whispered hoarsely. "But thank you, my lady owl. Thank you for freeing me."

"I wasn't going to let you be taken by the likes of them." She nodded at the drugged men. "Not when I could prevent it." She wound up the two ropes as Roark stood on stiff legs and cocked an eyebrow at her. "You'd have done the same for me, my stubborn stag."

He chuckled. "Aye, lass. I would have." He looked over at his captors, lost in their dreams. "You drugged them with the White Milk?"

Alina grinned. "I did. When Beasty showed up at my camp last night, I remembered the story of my grandmother and grandfather, how they'd been drugged by tainted wine."

"Beasty?"

Alina nodded toward the horses. "The rangy roan. It was as if the fates sent him to me."

"Maybe they did," Roark said, rolling his shoulders and his neck. "If so, they have a twisted sense of humor."

"At the very least," Alina agreed. She looked over at the brigands. "What do you want to do with them?"

"From what I understand, the effects of the White Milk will render them useless until well into tomorrow," he said. "If we tie them up and leave them, chances are they'd die of exposure before they managed to get loose, and we don't need any more murder charges against us. While their motives were purely mercenary, they didn't beat me or starve me, even after I killed two of them in a fair fight," he added. "And they did let me turn Artur loose."

Alina heard the catch of Roark's voice at the mention of Artur. "You did it for his own good," she reminded him. "He would've foundered and died in pain if you hadn't cut him loose. At least this way he'll have a chance to rest and heal."

"Aye, if his hoof doesn't worsen and he doesn't founder anyway, or get attacked and eaten by wolves."

Alina gave Roark's arm a gentle squeeze. "You did what you could for him, and he was doing fine when I last saw him. He's a big, strong stallion who'd give as good as he got. Maybe once we get to Silver Water Keep, you can come back for him."

"Maybe," Roark said. "After you're safely away."

"Speaking of safely away." Alina looped the ropes in her hand over her shoulder and lifted her chin toward the men's gear and horses. "I say we take what we want of theirs, including their horses, and leave them to hoof it out of here."

"Agreed. You go through their gear and I'll saddle their horses."

Alina added another small sack of beans and dried meat to their foodstuff but left the men their waterskins and flints while Roark stripped their saddles of any extra rope, leaving their extra clothes and bedrolls on the saddles.

"Pull off their boots," Roark said. "We'll toss them as we go, slow them down a bit while they're tender-footing it and searching for them."

When they'd finished, he knelt down next to the man who'd controlled the noose around his neck. "Shaw," he said sharply. "Shaw." He grabbed the man's jaw and held his face so that they were nose to nose. "I've no idea if you'll remember this," he told the glassy-eyed man. "But know that I held your life in my hands and I didn't kill you." He tied the short piece of rope that had bound his wrists around Shaw's neck. "Come after me or the girl again, and I won't be so generous."

CHAPTER 12

Silver Water Keep

They rode north down the mountainside, Alina on Etain and Roark on the rangy roan she'd named Beasty, leading the other three horses and tossing the men's boots one at a time every quarter league or so until they made the northern edge of the woods where the country opened into rolling hillsides. They doubled back another half a league, leading the horses in several large circles, and then they removed the saddles and tack from the men's horses, tossed them along the wood's edge and turned the horses loose.

From there they turned into the woods and rode until they came upon a rain-filled stream with a rocky shoreline. Urging the horses into the water, they backtracked south to another large area of rocky shore, where they dismounted and walked the horses out of the water. Remounting, they rode northwest for Silver Water Keep and rode until noon, when they stopped in a little glen of beech fern with a rill running through it.

"When's the last time you slept?" Roark asked Alina as they dismounted and let the horses drink.

"I dozed on and off yesterday night," she said, the dark circles under her eyes telling him it had been more off than on.

"Considering Ned and the lads are likely only now coming out of their daze enough to start looking for their boots and mounts, how about we rest here for a while?" He ran a hand back through his sweaty, grimy hair and rubbed his hands roughly over his face. "I for one could use a dip in the water and a bit of sleep."

She gave him a tired smile. "Sounds good."

They staked the horses and stripped. Bone-tired, sore, and half-starved as he was, Roark's cock still rose at the sight of Alina's lissome limbs and womanly curves. Her weary gaze fixed on his erection. "Don't worry," he told her. "I can wait."

Alina's lips curved up. She stepped up to him and pressed her soft breasts and warm belly against his. "I can't," she whispered roughly.

Roark held her face in his hands, her green eyes reflecting all the fear and rage and determination he'd felt while being held captive, and all the relief, longing, and desire he felt now.

He took her mouth with his, devouring the salty sweet taste of her like a starving man granted the most sumptuous of feasts. He ran his hands down the tautly muscled length of her back and cupped her round buttocks, pressing her pelvis even closer, rubbing his engorged cock against her soft curls. He scooped her up and she wrapped her legs around his waist, her warm flesh nestling his cock. Clinging to him, she lifted herself up so the tip of his cock barely touched her flesh, and Roark held her with one arm as he grabbed his cock and held it and she lowered herself over him, her wet, warm, welcoming sheath taking him in and closing around him, her intimate muscles rippling and contracting around his throbbing cock.

He pushed up as she bore down and ground her pelvis against him in delicious, torturous, flesh-melding, mind-bending circles. Slowly at first, then faster and faster as he thrust harder and deeper, again and again. She arched against him, her fingers gripping his shoulders as he gave one last shuddering thrust and she threw her head back with a raw, primal moan as her muscles convulsed around him.

Panting, she met his lust-hazed gaze, her own heavy-lidded and unfocused. Roark took one of her peaked nipples in his mouth and her groan reverberated from his mouth to his cock. He laved one nipple and then the other as their sweat cooled and then she lowered her mouth to his and kissed him with such need and desire his cock grew inside of her.

"Ach, Ali girl," he rumbled as he walked with her still straddling him to a grassy spot of ground. "I feared I'd never be stones deep in you again, love."

She laughed as she lifted herself up and slid down his belly and legs. "I just found you," she said as her feet touched the ground. "I wasn't about to lose you, to lose this." She bumped her pelvis to his. "Not as long I have any say in the matter."

"Glad I am to hear it," he said, kneeling down on the grass and bringing her with him. He lay on his side, facing her, and trailed his hand over her shoulder, the dip of her waist, the swell of her hip, the soft firmness of her buttocks. He moved his hand over her belly and between her legs. She was as wet and ready for him as he was hard for her. "Glad I am you chose me, my lady owl."

"Glad I am you chose me, sir stag," she breathed, her eyes dark with passion. "Though I'm not sure how much of a choice either of us really had in the choosing."

"I wouldn't have had it any other way," Roark said, moving his hand over her soft, tender flesh. "No matter what happens."

He woke with his nose buried in her nape, his arm hugging her close and his cock nestled against the soft warmth of her backside. Glancing around to get his bearings, he shot up. "Damnation."

Alina stirred and blinked her sleep-filled eyes and yawned. "What's the matter?"

"We've gone and slept our way into the afternoon," he said, standing and running his hands through his still grimy hair. "Which means we've cut any advantage we'd gained over Ned and the lads by a good bit."

Alina sat up and pushed her mane of tangled hair back from her face, her cheeks still rosy from sleep and their lovemaking. "Do you think they'll come after us again? Or consider themselves lucky we didn't slit their throats when we had the chance and call it even?"

"I don't know." Roark grabbed his breeches and pulled them on. "They may consider letting them live reward enough, but the ten pounds of silver they'd planned on getting for me alone was likely more than they'd earn in a year of hard labor, even split three ways." He donned his tunic. "Let's hope their horses wandered away."

Alina eyed the stream and stood. "So much for a wash and a rinse."

She pulled on her breeches and her boots and walked over to the stream, her top half still unclad, and knelt down and splashed water over her face and under her arms. When she stood up, her hair in wild disarray, the gold pearl dangling between her full breasts, her nipples pebbled and pointing straight at him, Roark was sorely tempted to take his chances with the men who may have been coming after them for another romp with the beautiful, wild creature standing before him, staring at his naked chest and smiling like a cat about to lap up a bowl of cream.

Roark stepped toward her, a low growl of male approval rumbling in his chest, when the horses startled, snorting and dancing on their line. Roark and Alina went still, both of them eyeing their waist belts and blades where they lay on the ground several feet away. They let out big sighs of relief when a doe darted across the stream.

"We'd better get riding," Roark said. "With any luck, we should make Silver Water Keep sometime tomorrow afternoon."

***

Roark counted four riders approaching from half a league west, all of them armed. He capped the spyglass and gave Alina a reassuring nod. "They've spotted us," he told her.

"What do we do now?"

"We stay on the road and continue to ride toward them."

It was late afternoon and the sun was in their faces, not a favorable position for a fight, which Roark was hoping to avoid. As the four riders neared, he held out his arms to his sides, palms up and empty, as did Alina. One of the riders stopped twenty paces from them, notched an arrow to his bow, and aimed it at Roark's chest while the other three rode right up to them, two of them pulling their long swords and flanking Roark and Alina.

"What are you doing on MacLeod lands?" the fourth man asked. He was a tall, lanky greybeard with a beaked nose and eyes, a lacquered vest and arm bands.

"We come to speak with your laird," Roark answered. "My name is—"

"Roark MacInnes," the man said. "We know who you be." He jutted his chin toward Alina. "And who she be as well."

"If you know of us by the laird Roger MacKinnon's men," Roark said, "then you're mistaken as to who she is."

"How so?"

"That's for us to tell your laird."

The greybeard chuffed and the two men flanking Roark and Alina edged their mounts closer, their swords still pointed at them.

"What makes you think we won't kill you right here and save the laird the trouble?"

"If you were going to kill us, we'd already be dead," Roark reasoned. "Besides, the reward offered is for us returned to Roger alive." He eyed the greybeard and played his hand. "I don't think you'd want to be killing the laird's own kin."

"Kin?" The greybeard took a closer look at Alina, his perusal stopping and holding at her big, emerald green eyes. "Follow me," he told them, swinging his mount back north.

The road was bordered on the west by a wide, fast-moving river, and on the east by woods of oak and pine covering the hillsides. Roark and Alina rode side by side as they followed the river northwest for another league where it flowed into a loch surrounded by verdant fields of farmland newly planted with spring crops, and low-lying hillsides dotted with sheep, cattle, and horses.

Several small thatch houses lined the road where the river met the loch, and four fishing boats were docked at a wooden pier. They turned northeast for another quarter league and rode up to a two-story manor house of stone and wood the size of North Shore Keep and Thorn Bush Keep combined, with a huge well-kept lawn, a fenced rose garden, and numerous outbuildings.

They followed the greybeard through a stone archway onto the keep's grounds, drawing a crowd as they neared the manor house. The greybeard pulled his horse up near the main entrance to the house and dismounted, indicating they should do the same. Stable hands came running, and Alina held her hands up as they approached Etain.

"Please, move slowly with her," she said to the eager young man reaching for the mare's reins. "She's gentle enough, but skittish with strangers."

"Will do, Mistress," the lad said, taking a step back and eyeing Alina's breeches. He spoke softly to Etain and patted her neck and Alina handed over the mare's reins.

Roark handed Beasty's over to another hand and offered Alina his arm. Laying her hand on his arm, they followed the greybeard up stone steps to the entrance. One of the men-at-arms who'd ridden in with them opened the heavy double doors and they followed the greybeard into a large, open entryway.

"Wait here," the greybeard told them.

Roark patted Alina's hand on his arm and took in the grand staircase leading up to the second story. There was a dining hall to their right with not one, but two high tables and six low tables. To their left was a huge common room with a large hearth built into a stone wall and chairs, benches, and sofas spread all over the room.

He heard voices and footsteps coming from the dining hall and stood at alert as Alina gripped his arm. The greybeard followed behind a handsome man in his middle years with shoulder-length, dark brown hair and a short beard shot through with the first steaks of grey, accompanied by a slim sylph of a woman of the same age with light blonde hair braided and piled high atop her head. Both of them were dressed in good, plain, unadorned linen clothing.

"I'm Owen, laird of clan MacLeod and Silver Water Keep," the man said. "This is my wife, Lady Siusan. I know who you are, Roark MacInnes." His deep green, thickly lashed eyes took Roark in from head to toe before settling on Alina. "Who might you be?"

"I am Alina," she said with a dip of her knee. "Princess of Sea Ridge in the Northlands. Daughter of King Jerrik and Queen Alyssa, granddaughter of King Aleksandr and Queen Sahar, and great-granddaughter of King Asad and Queen Oona, who was the daughter of Aaron and Iseult, who was the daughter of Isolde of the clan MacLeod."

The laird's green-eyed gaze fixed on Alina. "You certainly know the maternal lineage of the MacLeod side of my family," he said. "But then, so do many people."

Alina dipped her head and said nothing. The laird looked to his wife, who glanced from him to Alina and back to her husband.

"She does have the MacLeod eyes," she said.

"Aye," the laird agreed. "That she does." He took in her dirty, ragged state and boy's clothing. "Still, she could as easily be some poor cousin's by-blow."

Alina visibly stiffened. "I assure you I am who I say I am."

"That may be," the laird said, nonplussed. "If it is, I assume you've come here counting on our kinship for protection."

"We have," Roark answered. He held the laird's waiting, watching gaze. "If you know who I am, then you know the story being spread about by Roger MacKinnon, laird of North Shore Keep."

"I do," Laird Owen said. "His story is that you and a serving wench," he indicated Alina, "set a trap for and murdered his son."

"The only trap set was for the princess and her parents," Roark told him. "A trap I was, to my dishonor, a part of. All to settle a twenty-year grievance, which I'm now trying to make right by getting the princess back to her family."

"Did you kill the laird's son?"

"No."

The laird looked to his lady, whose nod was almost imperceptible. He swept his arm toward the dining hall. "You two look half starved," he said. "Come, sit, eat. Tell us your story of how you came to be here."

***

Alina paced herself with the fresh bread, soft cheese, and red, juicy berries the kitchen maids set out as she and Roark sat across the table from Laird Owen and Lady Siusan. Between bites, she couldn't help staring at the laird's eyes, so like her mother's, or her own. The laird kept staring into hers too as Roark told him and his lady of how Roger's scheme to kidnap her for ransom first came about, how he and Leif saw it through, thankfully leaving out the details of how she'd led him like a lovestruck fool to the lake and allowed herself to be taken.

He told them of starting to suspect the veracity of Roger's version of the wrongs done him and his family by Alina's parents, of finding out about Roger's real plan for selling Alina in the same desert slave market where Oona and her sister, Lyrra, had been sold, and of how Roger intended to let her parents think her dead for the rest of their days while he gloated from afar, his coffers full of the gold he'd sold Alina for.

Roark told them of Leif's attempt to rape Alina in the stables, and she found she couldn't meet the lady Siusan's kind eyes, though the shame wasn't hers.

"I wanted to kill him," Roark admitted. "Alina stopped me to avoid the very thing we're accused of and running from now. We left him tied, gagged, and unconscious, but alive. We were leagues away before we heard he'd been killed by a scythe to his chest."

"Why didn't you go to your family for help?" Laird Owen asked.

Alina glanced at Roark. "We would have," she said, not exactly lying. "We were told his father had sided with Roger."

"Ah," Owen said. "I see."

"We decided to cross the Mounths," Roark continued, "to make for the North Sea Firth, where we hope to find a ship to sail Alina home. A storm waylaid us for a few days and then we were overtaken by a band of men intent on collecting the reward Roger offered for us."

"What happened?" Lady Siusan asked.

"Roark's horse went lame so he stayed to fight them and give me time to get away," Alina told her. "He killed two of them before they managed to take him."

"And?" Owen said, glancing at the two of them sitting at his table.

"Alina doubled back and drugged the three remaining men with a vial of White Milk in their wine and rescued me," Roark said, grinning at Alina. "And here we are."

"That's quite a story," the laird said.

Alina pulled the pearl from between her breasts, unclasped the copper chain, and set it on the table. She met and held the laird's serious, green-eyed gaze with her own. "Would a serving wench have a necklace like this?" she said in the Green Isles tongue. "Every word we've told you is true," she said in her Northland tongue. "I swear it on my mother's eyes," she said in her mother's native Rus. "I swear it on my great-grandmother's grave," she said in the desert tongue.

Laird Owen sat back, cocked his head, and turned to the greybeard who'd brought them here, and who'd been standing at his laird's and lady's backs the whole time. "Did you understand any of that, Niels?" Owen asked.

"The first part," Niels answered. "She said that every word they told you was true in the Northern tongue. The rest of it?" He shrugged.

Alina eyed the hawk-nosed Niels. "From what part of the Northlands do you hail?" she asked in their Northern tongue.

"From the western mountains," he answered in kind. "Twenty and five years ago."

"My paternal grandfather, King Anders, would have been recently deceased," she said, "and my great-uncle, Alviss, newly named king."

"Yes," Niels said. "I'd heard of them, and the family's troubles. Something about a cursed throne."

"The only curse was my great-uncle Fenrir and his yellow beards," she said. "It was he who tried to have my father and mother murdered. Roger and his brother Donald were two of Fenrir's yellow beards."

Niles looked to his laird and dipped his head.

"What do you want of us?" Laird Owen asked them.

"Help finding a ship to sail Alina home," Roark said. "Shelter and protection until she sails."

"Only her?"

"I've asked him to sail back with me," Alina told them. "Roark means to stay to try to make things right between his family and Roger's."

"I see." Owen looked from Roark to Alina. "Your father won't seek revenge on this Roger?"

"Revenge?" Alina shook her head. "No. I do think he'll seek justice. He is a king who's sailed much of this world. He'll take the laws and politics of this land into account no matter what he chooses to do."

Laird Owen sat back, his expression one of contemplation. Then he placed both hands palms on the table. "You're both welcome to stay here under my protection while I sort a few things out," he told them. "In the meantime, I suggest we agree on a story about who you are and why you're here that will keep your true identities secret from all but the five of us in this room."

***

Alina returned to her guest chambers from the bathhouse dressed in her old, but relatively clean long tunic and apron to find a mossy green long tunic and darker green apron laid out on the bed. "Thank you, Lady Siusan," she said to the room.

She stared down at the bed and flopped down on it. It was big, soft, and clean, and she would be sleeping in it alone, as much to keep to the propriety of their host's home as to maintain the story that would explain to the rest of the household how and why she and Roark were there. An empty pit formed in her belly when she thought of never sleeping cocooned in Roark's embrace again. Of never feeling his hands and mouth roaming over her bare skin, never making love with him again.

Rolling onto her side, she stared at the closed door to her room and grinned. Roark's room was next to hers. Surely, they could manage sneaking in and out of each other's rooms, each other's beds while here, whether that be for one night or ten.

She stood and doffed her old coarsely woven long tunic and dressed in the soft, finely woven long tunic and apron on the bed. Her hair was still damp from the bath, and she felt a stone lighter with the dirt and grime washed out of it.

She found a comb and brush on the dressing table and set to work on the knots and tangles, remembering how Roark would comb her hair with his fingers, rubbing delightful circles with his fingertips into her scalp, and other places. Squirming on her seat, she concentrated on plaiting her hair in one long braid, pulled on a pair of soft, kidskin boots that were at the foot of the bed, and opened the door to find Roark standing outside of it, his hand raised as if about to knock. His warm smile melting Alina's already overheated body.

"You look beautiful," he told her, offering her his arm. "Not as beautiful as you did in the green worm weave you wore on Spring's Eve, but green is definitely your color."

Alina gave him a sideways grin and ran her hand up and down the sleeve of the dove-grey tunic he was wearing along with dark grey linen breeches hugging his muscular thighs. "Grey is definitely your color," she said. "It brings out your rain eyes."

"Speaking of eyes." Roark stopped at the top of the stairs and smiled into hers. "I told you once they saw yours, they'd know you were a MacLeod."

Alina laughed as light and free as she hadn't been since the first day of spring. "I didn't even have to sing 'Somebody' for them."

"Good." The smile in Roark's eyes went from teasing to scorching. "I find I don't want you singing 'Somebody' to anyone but me, my lady owl."

He glanced around the hallway and cupped her chin and kissed her, soft and tender, the feel of his lips lingering on hers as they descended the stairs and walked into the dining hall arm in arm, where at least thirty people were seated and every single one of them stopped talking and watched them enter.

Alina knew their presence had already been explained to the household. The story was she was a distant cousin of the laird's from the northern Highlands who, with Roark's help, fled an arranged marriage to a man she despised. Laird Owen and Lady Siusan had agreed to mediate between them and the family involved. The question of Roark's and Alina's relationship hadn't been broached by the laird and lady, though they'd all agreed it'd be best to present themselves as childhood friends.

Laird Owen stood. "Our honored guests have arrived," he announced, and indicated the two empty seats to his right. "Please, join us."

Alina gripped Roark's arm as they passed the roomful of curious faces and took their seats, Roark beside Owen and Alina between Roark and a boy who was the spitting image of Owen.

"Roark, Alina," Owen said, "this is our son, Cullen. And this," he turned to indicate a young woman sitting to Lady Siusan's left, "is our daughter, Rose."

"It's a pleasure to meet you, Cullen," Alina told the boy, who looked to be about ten.

"And you, Lady Alina," he said, his green eyes smiling.

"Please, call me Alina," she told the lad. She leaned forward so she could see the daughter and introduced herself. "It's a pleasure to meet you, Rose. I only have brothers and male cousins, so it's a treat to meet a female relative."

Rose, who looked to be about ten and four, and was as blonde and blue eyed as her mother, smiled prettily. "And you, cousin," she said to Alina.

Roark turned his smile on the poor girl and her jaw dropped. Her mother gently cupped her chin and closed her gaping mouth amidst much laughter from the rest of the table. Blushing furiously, Rose stared straight ahead as her father introduced his sister, Agnes, her husband, Gavin, and their three young children.

The servants carried out platters of mutton roasted with carrots, turnips, and onions along with bowls of new spring greens and loaves of fresh baked ryes that had Alina's belly grumbling loud enough to raise the laird's brows.

"My apologies," she said. "It's been a while since I've sat before such a succulent feast."

"How long were you on the road?" Lady Siusan asked.

Alina glanced at Roark. "Ten days?"

Roark nodded. "Sounds right. We got caught in a storm and had to shelter in a cave for two days and nights," he explained to the table at large. "So that stretched the journey out a bit."

"What did you eat?" Cullen asked.

"We left in such a hurry," Roark told him, "all we packed were some dried field beans, stale bread, and salted meat, so we ate those along with whatever small game and salmon we caught, and greens, fruit, and mushrooms we foraged."

"Ten days camping out in the wilds," Cullen said, his expression lit with excitement. "Sounds fun."

"It would've been more fun if half our camps hadn't been cold camps," Roark said, his hand covering Alina's in her lap. "A warm fire in the wilds is a wonderful comfort."

"What was the man's name?" Rose asked Alina. "The man you ran away from marrying."

"I'd, ah, rather not say," Alina demurred. "At least not until everything is settled."

"How kind and brave of you to help her escape," Rose said to Roark with a pretty smile. "He must be a very bad man."

Roark squeezed Alina's hand. "He is, as it turns out."

Lady Siusan whispered something into Rose's ear that caused the girl to turn her attention back to her meal with a pretty pout, and Alina tucked into her meal.

"I saw your mare in the stables," Cullen told her as the main course was being cleared and the cheeses and fruits brought out. "Is she as fast as she looks?"

"She's faster," Alina said, eliciting a huge grin from the lad. "Her name is Etain and she can fly fast as a winged faerie."

"Truly?"

"Truly."

"What's the gelding's name?"

"Beasty," she said. "He's surprisingly fast on those gangly, knobby-kneed legs of his as well."

"Is that why you chose them to run away?"

Alina met Roark's somber gaze, and knew he was thinking of Artur. "It is," she lied.

"Would you like to meet my yearling colt, Damon?" Cullen asked her. "My parents gave him to me for my birthday last spring when he was a newborn. Kirk, the stablemaster, is going to help me train him this summer. I have my old gelding, Godfrey, too. He's a good old horse, but Damon's going to grow up to be a stallion."

Alina laughed lightly, feeling an instant kinship with this boy. "I'd love to meet both horses," she said.

"I can take you tonight," he offered.

"You can take her tomorrow after breakfast," his father told him with an indulgent grin. "Alina and Roark and I have some things to discuss tonight."

"Yes, Father."

"I look forward to tomorrow," Alina told the lad. She leaned in close and whispered. "Maybe we can take the horses a special treat?"

Cullen grinned. "I'll ask cook for some carrots," he whispered back. "They're Damon's favorites."

"Etain's too," Alina said with a conspiratorial wink.

***

Roark sat beside Alina in the laird's private meeting chambers, putting him in mind of their meeting with Roger and Leif the day they'd arrived at North Shore Keep. But where Roger had sat behind his big, imposing table looking down on them, Owen sat on a couch beside his wife with his sister and brother-in-law sitting on another couch together, Roark and Alina on yet another so they all sat facing each other. Niels and another man-at-arms, a burly Green Isler with deep-set brown eyes, curly brown hair, and forearms the size of oak branches, took two chairs to complete the circle. A maidservant carried in a tray laden with cups and two pitchers, set it down on the small, round table around which the couches were arranged, and then left.

Owen poured his own cup of what looked like a dark gold ale and one of wine that he handed to his wife, and then Gavin did the same for himself and Agnes. Yet another difference between the lairds. Roger would never have poured his own drink in front of others.

Taking his cue from Owen and Gavin, Roark asked Alina what she'd like to drink.

"Half a cup of wine, thank you."

He poured her wine and a cup of the golden ale for himself, and took a hearty swallow, choking on the bitter spirits. "What," he sputtered, his eyes watering, "is this?"

Owen and the other men in the room chuckled as Roark swiped at his eyes.

"It's called whisky," Owen said. "The water of life."

"Whisky," Roark repeated. He sniffed at the drink in his cup and took a small sip, letting the dark gold liquid sit on his tongue for a moment, then letting it slide down his throat, savoring the strong, oaken aftertaste. "It's quite tasty," he said. "In small sips."

The men laughed out right, though not unkindly.

"Which is how it's meant to be drank," Owen informed him after having had his chuckle.

He lifted his cup to Roark, as did Gavin and Niels and the brown-haired oak. Roark lifted his to Owen in return, and they all took a sip and set their cups down while the women sipped their wine with amused grins on their faces.

"Now, down to business," Owen said. "Gavin and I know your real story," he told Roark and Alina. "As do Niels and Grant. So, we can all speak freely."

"Good," Roark said. He'd been living with and amongst lies for too many years now and he was heartily sick of them, though he understood they'd still have to maintain several once they left this room. At least until Alina was safely away.

"We've decided to help you two," Owen declared, and Roark and Alina let their breaths out in unison.

"Thank you," Roark said.

"So much," Alina added.

Owen nodded graciously. "Tomorrow, Niels and Grant will ride into the port towns and find out what they can about your situation, as well as search out a ship for Alina to sail home on." He met Roark's gaze and answered his unspoken question. "We'll find a ship. This Roger's arms aren't as long as he thinks, he doesn't have as much sway here as at his home port."

Alina pulled the pearl from her bodice, unclasped the necklace, and laid it on the table. "This should be payment enough for my passage," she said. She turned to Roark with a tremulous smile. "You did it."

"We did it," he said. So why did he feel like his heart had been ripped out of his chest, leaving him an empty, hollowed-out husk? "I'm so glad," he told her. "And so damned sad."

Her big, beautiful, green eyes welled with tears and her lips quivered. She tried to smile, but her face crumpled and she threw her arms around Roark's neck and buried her face into his neck. "I want to go home so badly," she sniffed. "But I don't want to leave you. Ever."

Roark hugged her close and ran a hand through her hair. "I know, love," he whispered in her ear, ridiculously close to tears himself. "I know."

She lifted her head and met his gaze. "Come with me," she said, her eyes pleading with him. "Please."

Aware of the others in the room, none of whom were even pretending not to watch and listen, Roark took her face in his hands. "I wish I could," he told her. "I want to, you know I do."

"But you won't."

"No," he said, "I won't." He touched his forehead to hers. "I love you, Ali girl, so verra much. But I cannot. I will not leave my family and so many others to suffer the consequences of my actions."

She sniffed and nodded her forehead against his and laid her palm on his cheek. "You wouldn't be the man I love if you did." She rolled her forehead against his. "Which leaves us where we've been since the day we met."

Roark kissed her forehead and stared into eyes as bright and green and dewy as new grass after a spring rain. "I wouldn't trade a single moment of our time together for all the moments to come, my lady owl."

"Nor would I, sir stag," she whispered, her cheeks rising. "I will treasure them dearly until I have no more moments left in this life."

A loud sniff and a cough brought Roark's head up. Six pairs of eyes watched them intently as Lady Siusan swiped at her cheeks and Agnes dabbed at hers with her sleeve. Owen cleared his throat while Gavin coughed and snorted, and Niels and Grant looked at Roark with expressions of pity and envy.

Roark took a shaky breath in and blew it out. "Now you know how it is between Princess Alina and me."

Owen coughed and cleared his throat. "I would say so," he said with a low chuckle. "However..."

"However," Roark finished for him. "We are determined nobody outside of this room will." It wouldn't change the gist of their story if anybody did, but it would certainly complicate things.

"Aye, well, we'll see how that goes," Owen said good-naturedly enough. "Well then, unless anybody else has any questions or declarations to make? No?" He stood and offered his wife his arm. "We shall retire for the night and see you all in the morning."

Roark would have preferred to stay in the room alone with Alina, but Niels stood at the door while everyone else filed out, and by the look on his face, he was waiting for them to leave. Roark offered Alina his arm and escorted her past the taciturn greybeard and the few remaining people in the common room and up the stairs.

"I'm going to miss you tonight," he told her as they hovered outside her door, putting off the inevitable.

"I only seem able to sleep with you by my side or wrapped around me," she said with a shy and seductive smile. "Maybe you could come to my room later?"

"It's probably not the smartest thing to do our first night here," he said.

"Probably not," she agreed.

"It would be our first time together in a real bed."

Alina grinned, more seductive than shy, pecked him on the cheek and opened her door, peeking out at him before shutting it. "I won't throw my bolt."

Roark went to his room, undressed, and flopped onto his big, soft, lonely bed, where he tossed and turned so much he had to get up to untangle the bed linens from around his legs.

Once up, he gave up trying to sleep and paced around the room several times before taking the spyglass and looking out the window. He focused on the face of the waning moon as it rose over the tree line of chestnuts bordering the eastern edge of the keep's yard, yet all he could see was a pair of spring green eyes, heavy-lidded and dark with passion, staring dreamily into his.

He tried to focus on the trees when a dark shadow flew across his sight. He followed it to a fence post, where an owl lit and perched, twisting and turning its head this way and that, searching for prey. The owl went still, and Roark followed the direction of its gaze to where an eight-point stag stood at the tree's edge, its head erect and ears twitching.

"Damnation."

Roark set the spyglass on the bed, pulled on a pair of breeches and a tunic, cracked open his door, peered around the quiet, empty hallway, and padded barefoot over to Alina's door. He considered knocking, and then pushed open the unlocked door. He stepped in and glanced at the bed, which was mussed and empty. There was movement at the open window and Roark held his arms out. Alina flew into them. "Damn, Alina," he rasped, burying his nose in her hair, inhaling the sweet perfume of cherry blossoms. "What are we going to do?"

"We're going to make love," she said, kissing and nipping her way up his throat to his jaw. "We're going to make love and love each other as much and as often as we can until we can't anymore."

Roark hooked his finger under her chin and lifted her gaze to his. "I will never not love you, my lady owl."

Her eyes glistened. "I know, sir stag," she said, smiling through her welling tears. "Somehow I've always known. Now kiss me. Kiss me and make love to me and take me to our own special world."

CHAPTER 13

Kith and Kin

Alina woke alone in her bed and burrowed her nose into the pillow that held Roark's scent, her body still thrumming from their night together. She yawned and stretched and luxuriated in the soft bed and warm glow of their lovemaking, remembering how he'd woken her in the first greying of dawn, trailing kisses from her shoulders to her belly and lower, plumbing her depths with his lips, his teeth, and his tongue before slipping out of her room to his own.

By the light pouring in through the eastern-facing window, she'd slept well into the morning, and could've happily rolled over and slept until noon, but then she'd miss what little time she had left with Roark, and she'd promised Cullen she'd visit the stables with him. Plus, she wanted to check on Etain and Beasty.

Throwing off the bedcovers, she got up and splashed cold water on her face, donned the green long tunic and apron, and made her way downstairs to the dining hall, where a few other late stragglers were breaking their fasts. She was eating her bowl of porridge with chopped berries and thinking of the tasteless gruel on *The Rover* when Cullen came into the hall with Roark and Rose.

"You're awake," Cullen said excitedly as they all took seats by her. "We've already been to the stables, Lady Alina, but I'll still take you after you've finished breakfast."

"Thank you, Cullen," she said. She met Roark's smiling eyes. "Good morning, Roark."

He smiled, slow and easy, and melting hot. "Good morning, sleepyhead."

Alina caught the look of pure adoration on Rose's face as she stared at Roark. She'd have to warn him to tone down his charm.

Finished with her porridge, she pushed the empty bowl aside and stood.

"Shall we?"

Cullen led the way and Roark dropped back to walk with Alina. "Niels and Grant left early this morning," he told her as they crossed the yard. "Laird Owen said it would take them a day to reach the port towns, another day or two to take care of business, and a day to return."

"So," she said, as anxious and excited to get home as she was dreading leaving Roark. "We have three to four more days together, at least."

"At least," Roark said, touching his little finger to hers. "It'll depend on whenever the ship they find sails. Owen has assured me we can stay here however long that takes."

Cullen stopped at the stables door and waited for them to catch up while Rose waited and circled behind Roark as they entered.

"Etain and Beasty are over here." Cullen pointed to two stalls next to each other. "I already checked on them this morning, Lady Alina," he said as Etain poked her head over the gate and whinnied. "They've eaten three sheafs of hay and half a bucket of oats each since yesterday."

"Thank you, Cullen," Alina said as she ran her hand down the bridge of Etain's nose. "I can see she's well taken care of."

The mare had calmed down greatly since Alina had fled Roger's stables, and had actually seemed to thrive on the journey here. Alina thought of Artur, and sent a silent prayer to the *bog loshadi,* the horse gods of her mother's homeland, to keep the stallion safe and healing until Roark could go back for him. He'd be riding Beasty and taking Etain with him on his journey back to North Shore Keep, and intended to ride the way they'd come and search for Artur then.

"I wish I could take you home with me," she told Etain. "I think you would like racing along the beach as much as Brynja does."

Etain snorted and shook her head up and down and Alina laughed and gave her a carrot from the bucket. She glanced at Roark, who was feeding Beasty at least his fourth carrot, and caught the moonstruck expression on Rose's face as she watched him treat the gelding. She was of an age to be betrothed, and for the flash of a jealous moment, Alina considered she would make Roark a more loving wife than Gwyneth. A sweet and gentle mother to his children.

She laid a hand over her belly, which had given her no clues as to whether Roark's seed had found purchase in her womb. Under normal circumstances, her moon flow would be due any day. However, circumstances had been anything but normal this past moon. As she'd told Roark, the women in her family were known for having tricky moon flows when under duress. She sighed and dropped her hand. Like everything else in her life, she'd have to wait and see if she was pregnant. And like everything but her love for Roark, she had no idea how she felt about it.

"Are you all right, Ali?" Roark asked.

She shrugged. After the first haze of passion had subsided, he'd cursed himself for spilling his seed in her, yet Alina hadn't been upset at all. She still wasn't. She knew it was foolhardy of her, of both of them, to remain as casual about impregnating her as they'd been, yet she also knew her family would still love her and accept her, no matter what. Something Roark couldn't say about his.

"This way, Lady Alina," Cullen said, pulling on her sleeve. "My colt, Damon, is over here."

Alina turned from Roark's furrowed brow and followed Cullen to a stall with a gorgeous black colt in it. "Oh, Cullen," she said, "he really is a handsome animal." She held out her hand near the colt's head, and when he didn't spook or shy away, she held his halter with one hand and petted the bridge of his nose with the other. "He seems friendly enough," she teased Cullen as the colt nickered and pressed his nose into her hand. "Despite his name."

Cullen grinned and handed Alina a carrot. "He is," he said, "if he likes a person." The colt took the carrot from Alina, blowing softly into her hand. "He sure likes you, Lady Alina."

"There isn't a horse or a cat in this world that doesn't like Lady Alina," Roark said. "Or that she doesn't like back."

Cullen's green eyes grew wide. "Is that true, lady?"

"Please, call me Alina," she told the lad. "And yes, it's true, for the most part. There are few animals I don't like, though horses and cats are my favorites." She gave Roark a quick grin. "Along with stags and goats."

"What's your favorite animal, Roark?" Rose asked.

Roark grinned at Alina. "Owls," he said, and turned his grin on Rose, which really wasn't fair to the poor girl, who practically swooned. "Curious owls who constantly ask why."

"I thought owls asked who?" Cullen said.

Roark laughed. "Most do," he told him. "But there's a verra rare, verra beautiful owl whose favorite word is why."

"Hmm." Cullen seemed to think on this a moment. "My favorite animals are horses, especially stallions."

"Who would've ever guessed?" Roark said, and they all laughed.

Their tour of the clean, well-run stables complete, they went back out into the courtyard.

"I feel like walking," Roark announced. "My backsides spent too many days on a horse lately. Alina, care to join me?"

"A walk sounds nice," she told him. Time alone with Roark sounded even nicer.

"Can Rose and I come?" Cullen asked, all eager boy.

Alina looked to Roark, who arched his brows and shrugged. They were guests here. It wouldn't be polite to turn their host's son away. Plus, Alina liked Cullen. He reminded her of her youngest brother, Aleksi.

"Lead the way," she told the lad.

Rose joined them as Cullen showed them around the extensive grounds of the keep, which had its own smithy and brewing house.

"That's where we brew our ale and whisky," Cullen told them. "Our father lets us have a sip of whisky on feast days," he said, puffing his thin chest out. "Rose doesn't like it, but I do. My father says it's because I'm almost a man, and whisky's a man's drink."

"I can vouch for that," Roark said. "It stands a man upright, it does."

Alina's cheeks flushed as the image of Roark's upright cock came to her, and by the grin on his face, he knew exactly why she was blushing.

"When I'm laird," Cullen told them, "Silver Water Keep will be known for its whisky and its horses."

"I'm sure it will," Alina said. "As I'm sure you'll be as good a laird as your father obviously is."

Cullen puffed his chest out even more. "Rose will be a great lady of her own keep."

"I'm sure she will." Alina met the girl's blushing gaze. "Do you or your family have a young laird in mind?"

Rose glanced at Roark and smiled shyly. "Maybe."

"Will your family choose for you?" Alina asked, playing her part of runaway betrothed.

"No." Rose shook her head. "It does no good to choose for a MacLeod woman. A true MacLeod woman knows her mate at first sight and so must choose her own husband. It's been that way for hundreds of generations."

Roark glanced from Alina to Rose and back to Alina, grinned, and toed the ground with his boot. "So I've been told."

"What of you?" Rose asked him. "Are you allowed to choose your wife?"

"No. My family chose a wife for me when I was younger than you."

"You're married?" The anguish in Rose's voice echoed the voice in Alina's heart.

"No. Not yet."

"Who is she?" Rose asked, more than a little possessively.

"She's the daughter of the laird I live with."

"Do you love her?"

Alina's brows arched into her hairline. Rose wasn't shy about her questions or her feelings.

"No," Roark told her. "I don't love her." He chuffed. "I don't even like her, or her, me."

Rose's big blue eyes widened. "Then you mustn't marry her."

"It's not that simple," Roark explained. "I'm honor-bound to marry her for my family's sake and the sake of many others." His gaze met Alina's, sad, bittersweet, and determined. "Since I cannot marry who I wish, I may as well marry her and keep the alliances formed by our betrothal intact."

"What does your *lady love* think of this?" Rose asked him.

"She doesn't like it," he said, flashing Alina a rueful grin. "But she understands. I think. I hope."

***

Alina snuggled deeper into Roark's shoulder with a satisfied sigh, her passion spent and her skin cooling in the dark before dawn.

"Is it this way for everybody?" she asked, playing with the auburn curls on his chest.

"Nay, lass," he said, tucking her in tighter. "Only for a verra lucky few like us." He placed a tender kiss on her forehead. "I'd say being madly in love is a large part of it."

"Don't let Rose hear you say that," she warned him. "She'd happily strangle me in my sleep and throw my body in the loch if she thought it meant a chance with you."

He chuckled, the low rumble of it reverberating from his chest to Alina's ear. "It's only a girlish notion she has of me. I'm the dashing hero who saved the damsel in distress."

"Hmmph."

"Ach. Are you jealous, my lady owl?"

Alina lifted up onto her elbow so she could see his face. "Should I be?"

"Nah." He gave her a teasing grin. "I promise I won't bring her into my bed until you're well on your way home."

Alina punched him in the shoulder. Hard. "That's not funny."

He rubbed his shoulder, pretending to pout, and then he grabbed her and flipped her onto her back in one swift motion, and pressed his half-hard cock against her belly. "Don't ye ken, Ali love, how you've ruined me for any other woman?"

"Then sail back to Sea Ridge with me."

"You know I cannot."

"I know you will not."

"Ali girl." He held her gaze, his rain eyes pouring into hers. "I wish it could be otherwise. You know I do."

"I know," she said with a resigned sigh. "I do. And I understand your sense of honor and wanting to do the right thing. I respect it." She'd promised herself she wouldn't beg or plead with him about this again, and she'd meant to keep her promise. It was just... "I love you, Roark. So much more than I ever expected to love any man, ever. I was content with my family and my plants and animals, and then you showed up with your earth-kissed face and your rain eyes and the MacLeod woman in me came alive." She laughed, low and throaty. "She came alive with a vengeance."

"So she did," he rumbled, bumping his pelvis to hers. "Glad and honored I am she chose me."

Alina ran her fingers through the soft curls of his beard and rubbed his full lips with the pad of her thumb. "Having chosen you," she told him, "I can never un-choose you." She couldn't foresee ever wanting to. "I hope I carry your babe in my womb," she blurted out.

"You do?"

"I do. Then I'll always have a part of you. Not only memories, but a physical part of you. Of us."

He smiled, slow and easy and heartbreaking. "I confess, I hope you do too," he said, his voice low and rough. "For the vain and selfish reason I too want you to always have a part of me. A part of me to love and cherish, who will love and cherish you as you deserve." He grinned. "A little girl with eyes as green as spring grass."

"And auburn curls."

He chuckled. "I can see her now, elbows deep in soil, planting seeds in her greenhouse, with a tabby cat rubbing against her legs."

"Her rain-eyed brother scouring the sea with his spyglass, searching for the ship carrying his father home to us."

"Brother?"

"Twins do run in my family."

"So they do." His expression turned somber. "What would you tell our children of their father?"

"That we loved each other very much. That they were born of love, and that one day, when he's able, he will come to us." Alina held his gaze, her own serious. "It's what I'll tell myself every day from the day I leave you until I'm in your arms again." He said nothing. "Promise me I won't be waiting in vain." *Or for a ghost.*

"I swear to you, Ali love, I'll come to you as soon as I'm able."

Which could be a moon, a year, a score of years, or never, depending on Roger and whether he or his family insisted on him marrying Gwyneth.

Unlike the night before, Alina didn't fall back to sleep after Roark left her bed. She lay there remembering every glance, every word, and every touch between them since the moment she'd seen him watching her from the deck of *The Rover* until this moment. She lay there in the first real bed they'd shared and thought about how it could be the last, for despite her plea and his promise, she knew how many obstacles there were between their wishes and reality.

She threw off her bedcovers, splashed water on her face, donned the clean, coarse linen long tunic given to her at North Shore Keep, and headed down to the dining hall.

"Laird Owen, Lady Siusan," she greeted them at their table. "Good morning."

"Lady Alina," they said in unison.

"May I speak with both of you in private," she asked them. "After you've finished your breakfast."

"We're finished," Owen told her. "Would now be a good time?"

"Yes. Thank you."

She followed them to the laird's private chambers and sat on a sofa facing Lady Siusan as her husband closed the door. He took a seat beside his wife, reminding Alina of her parents, and how they faced everything together.

"What do you wish to speak with us about?" the laird asked.

"First of all, I cannot thank you enough for taking us in and helping us out as you have."

"Of course," Owen said. "You're kin."

"Aye. Kin you never knew existed until two days ago."

"Kin, nevertheless."

Alina smiled into green eyes as familiar as looking into a mirror. "Yes. We are. I'm so grateful to have found family like you." She took a deep breath in and blew it out. "Roark, however—"

"Is not kin."

"Yet I would ask you to continue to help him after I've sailed. To send a man or two to ride back with him to his home. To make sure he gets there safe and sound." Where his family would either take him in and defend him, or denounce him and let him face Roger and almost certain death alone.

"Does Roark know you're asking us this?" Owen asked.

"No. He wouldn't ask it for himself."

"No," Owen agreed, "he wouldn't. He's a proud man in the best sense of the word."

"Yes," Alina squeezed out past the lump in her throat, grateful Owen could see this about Roark even if his own father couldn't. "He is."

Owen looked to Siusan, speaking that wordless language of long-married partners.

"I'm sure we can find two good, stout Highlanders willing to travel there with him and back," he told Alina.

"Thank you. Thank you both, so much." She broached another subject that had come to her this morning. "My father is always looking for new trade partners," she said. "I think he'd be quite interested in your whisky."

"Do you now?" Owen said with a sparkle in his green eyes.

**

Roark woke so late the dining hall was empty of people and the tables cleared. In the kitchens, the cook gave him a thick slice of bread and cheese and told him he could find the ladies Siusan and Alina at the herb and vegetable garden down by the loch. Stepping out under the noon sun, Roark couldn't remember the last time he'd slept so late, well, except for the two days and nights he and Alina had spent sheltering in the cave, where day and night had made no difference. A time and place he'd remember and treasure for the rest of his life, no matter how long or short it turned out to be.

Swallowing the last of the cheese, he walked past the smithy and the brewery to the path leading to the loch, where he found Alina and Lady Siusan kneeling in the middle of rows of newly sprouting spring seedlings, their heads bent together deep in conversation.

"You could sow the seeds in a greenhouse a moon earlier than in the open ground," Alina was saying, "then transplant the seedlings outdoors after the frosts have gone. By doing this, I've found I can get two good crops in a season. Three, if it's fast growing like greens or beans and radishes."

"A greenhouse with glass panes in the walls and roof," Lady Siusan said. "Intriguing, and quite costly I'm guessing."

"It is," Alina said. "At the onset. But it pays for itself within a few short years with the extra crops it yields." She glanced up, saw Roark, and smiled. "Roark has seen my greenhouse. Is it not a wonder?"

"It is," Roark agreed. "As Alina said, it allows you to plant and harvest early and often. Did she tell you about the herbs she grows year-round in it? Healers from all over the Northlands visit her greenhouse to study and trade for them."

"Impressive," Lady Siusan said. "I admit, I'm not much of an herbalist, but Agnes is. She will definitely want to speak with you about your herbs and greenhouse before you leave."

"I look forward to it," Alina said.

Lady Siusan stood and wiped her hands on her apron. "I'm off to the kitchens to speak with cook about supper. If you'll excuse me."

Roark and Alina both dipped their heads to their hostess, and then Alina turned to Roark.

"You're the sleepyhead today," she said with a teasing grin.

"Aye. A certain lady owl kept me up half the night demanding my favors," he teased. "Glad I am she did," he rumbled, leaning in and nuzzling the tender skin of her nape, thinking of how he'd nuzzled her even more tender flesh this morning.

He glanced around, and saw nobody else nearby, folded her into his embrace and kissed her, long and deep. A thirsty man granted the purest, sweetest spring water. "I look forward to being kept up all night again tonight," he murmured against her lips.

She bumped her pelvis against his eager cock. "If we don't stop now, you'll be up here in broad daylight."

Roark chuckled. "I cannot help it, Ali girl. I swear I've been half-hard since the moment I spied you racing your mare on the beach with your long legs bared." He rubbed his thickening cock against her belly. "Now that I've had those legs wrapped around me, I can hardly think of anything else. You've enthralled me, my lady owl."

Alina laughed, low and sultry. "I suffer from the same enthrallment, sir stag." She twined her hands around his neck, her green eyes darkening with a passion as natural to her as breathing. "Yet unless we wish to be discovered rutting here in the dirt, we should probably find something else to do with our time until tonight."

"Agreed," he said, though every nerve in his body was screaming at him to do it. To lay her down in the garden and have his way with her. But she was right, they needed to act as Lady Alina and Roark MacInnes, not curious little owl and rutting stag, at least in the daylight. He stepped back and offered her his arm. "Shall we let Etain and Beasty graze away the afternoon in the paddock?"

***

When Roark woke under the willow tree with Alina tucked into his side, the sun was low in the western sky and the air had taken on the chill of evening.

"Alina." He gently nudged her arm. "Time to wake up, my sleepy owl."

"Nnnooo." She burrowed her nose deeper into his shoulder. "Not yet."

Roark pushed a lock of hair damp from sleep behind her ear and kissed her on the forehead. "I'm afraid so, love," he said, jostling her again. "By the sun, it's coming on supper time, both ours and the horses. We don't want to be rude to our hosts."

"No," she agreed, rolling away from him and pressing her back against the willow's trunk. "We don't." She yawned and rubbed her eyes and focused her gaze on his. "How is it I sleep so much better with you on the cold, hard ground than I do without you in a warm, soft bed?"

This time he answered her from his heart rather than his head. "Likely for the same reason I cannot look at you without wanting you, Ali lass," he said, his voice low and raw.

She smiled, nodded, sniffed, and crumbled. "What are we going to do?" she cried softly. "How am I ever going to sleep again without you?"

How am I ever going to live without you? "One night at a time, Ali love," he rasped. "One breath, one step, one long, lonely night at a time."

She threw her arms around his neck and held on tight, her heart hammering against his as he clasped her to him.

"I will never love another the way I love you, Roark MacInnes," she whispered fiercely, and then she broke their hold and stood and whistled for the horses, who followed her to the stables, Roark trailing behind them. It would do no good to be seen teary-eyed by the stable hands.

"Did you two have a good sleep?" Lord Owen asked Roark and Alina as they took their seats at the high table.

"We did," Roark answered him. "I think we've both finally caught up."

"Good." Owen perused Roark and then Alina. "You do look more rested."

"Thanks to your hospitality," Roark said. "Again, we cannot thank you enough."

"Actually, there is a way." Owen looked to his lady wife.

"Lady Alina," Lady Siusan said. "The women of your lineage are known for their musical talents. Do you sing or play an instrument?"

"I sing," Alina told her. "Though nothing like my great-grandmother was said to."

"She's being modest, Lady Siusan," Roark said. "She sings beautifully."

"Would you honor us with a song or two after supper?" Lady Siusan asked.

Alina blushed prettily. "It would be my pleasure."

The supper plates cleared and the wine and whisky brought out, one of the laird's men set a stool in a space that had been cleared at one side of the room. Another man, whom Roark recognized as one of the house servants, sat at the stool with a fiddle and played a few warm-up scales while Alina took a good draught of wine and then walked over and stood by the fiddle player.

"Do you know 'The Sailor's Tale'?" she asked him.

"Aye, lady. What tempo would you like played at?"

"Like this." Alina tapped her toe and counted.

The man started to play and Alina to sing. She sang of the sailor leaving his home, and of his wife's and young son's tearful farewells. Her clear, melodic voice instantly capturing the complete attention of everyone in the hall.

The kitchen staff stood at the open door as she sang of the sailor's journey, of his joy in the salty tang of a good wind and the vastness of the sea, swaying her body to the motion of a ship, and the entire room swayed with her. She sang of the sailor's many adventures, of the ports he sailed into, the kings and queens he met, the storms he braved, the monsters he fought and overcame, and every person there was sitting on the edges of their seats, though it was a song known by every Green Isler by the time they could walk and talk.

She sang of the sailor finding the treasure he'd sought, of turning his ship north, sailing for his home, and her voice rang out with determination. She sang joyfully of the sailor sighting his home shore twenty years to the day he'd left, of seeing his wife, grey-haired and ever faithful, waiting on the docks with his two grown sons, and her voice caught as she met Roark's gaze.

She sang of his happy homecoming at last, of him sitting in a rocker by the hearth fire, his wife beside him, at peace and content at last, stringing the last, mellow note out into silence.

A few satisfied oohs and aahs floated about the hall, and then a loud clapping broke out, along with several sharp whistles.

Her cheeks flushing pink, Alina smiled and dipped her head to the low tables and her knee to the high table. "Does anyone have a request?"

"'Somebody,'" Roark said. "Will you sing 'Somebody'?" *To me.*

CHAPTER 14

Goodbyes

Alina stared into eyes the color of rain. A soft, nourishing rain that had brought her to life as a woman. Deep, penetrating, and quenching. A rain whose lack of she would thirst for until she could drink of it freely, whose long absence would leave the woman she'd become a dried-up, hollowed out, withered husk of herself. A rain she would dream of every night and day until she felt its wet pouring over her again. She laid a hand over her belly, hoping Roark's seed had taken root in her womb, praying that he would live to someday see and know their child. A child, or children, born of earth and rain.

"Lady Alina?"

She pulled her gaze from Roark's to the fiddle player. "Do you know 'Somebody'?" she asked.

He nodded and played the first melancholy strains. Alina took a deep breath and blew it out. She sought and found Roark's piercing gaze and began to sing the sad, bittersweet words to Roark as if she could will him to sail to her side again, raising her voice to the gods and the fates.

The fiddle's last long note faded into the hall, the silence broken by a female sniffle or ten and the sound of men coughing and clearing their throats. Roark stood and clapped, his rain eyes glistening as the rest of the assembly stood and clapped, and laughed and cried. Alina dipped her head to the fiddle player and resumed her seat beside Roark as the assemblage took full use of their linen napkins and sleeves.

"Thank you, my lady owl," Roark whispered roughly. "That was…"

"The most beautiful, gut-wrenching song I've ever heard sung," Laird Owen said.

"It truly was," Lady Siusan said, swiping at her wet cheek. She sniffed and laughed lightly. "If there was ever any doubt of you being Oona MacLeod's great-granddaughter, that song put an end to it."

"Thank you, Lady, Laird," Alina said with a tremulous smile. Roark covered her hand with his under the table. "I was inspired."

"Wasn't that the song Oona the Swan sang to Asad the Lion, the first night they met?" Rose asked. She spoke to Alina, but her gaze was on Roark. "The night they first met and fell madly in love?"

"It was," Alina answered. She smiled at Roark. "She was a true MacLeod woman, destined to fall in love with her mate at first sight, as he was destined to fall in love with her." Her smile turned bittersweet. "A love that neither time nor distance could ever lessen."

The hall was silent again. Alina tore her gaze from Roark's only to realize that all eyes and ears were on them, none more intently than Rose's. Clearing her throat, Alina raised her cup to the laird and lady.

"To the MacLeods," she said, her voice steadier than her hand. "May they always find their true loves."

"To the MacLeods," a chorus of voices toasted. "To true love."

***

Alina pushed off the bedcovers, cracked open the door, and peeked into the dark, quiet hallway. It wasn't quite midnight, which was when Roark had come to her room the past two nights, but she couldn't wait any longer. She'd been in an almost constant state of arousal since singing "Somebody" to Roark in front of an entire hall of people, and if she didn't get some release soon, she feared she'd be crawling up the walls like a cat in heat. What was she going to do when they parted?

She padded barefoot to Roark's door and knocked lightly. The bolt slid open almost immediately, and then she was standing eye to eye through the crack in the door with him.

"Ali?" He opened the door, pulled her in, shut and bolted the door, and crushed her to him. "Ach, Ali girl, I've been pacing round and round this room, trying to wait until I was sure everyone else was abed before I went to you." He held her by the shoulders and peered intently into her eyes. "Are you unwell? Is anything amiss?"

Alina shook her head. "Everything's fine. I couldn't wait to be with you. Besides," she said with an unapologetic shrug, "I'm fairly sure the entire household knows we've shared a bed together by now."

"Aye," Roark said, grinning slow and easy, stirring her insides from a simmer to a slow boil. "I'd wager you're right." He leaned in close and whispered in her ear. "After your singing 'Somebody' tonight, I'd wager every couple in this house are doing the verra same thing we're about to do."

Alina placed her palm on his cheek, met and held his gaze. "I sang it to you, Roark, for you, only you."

He took her hand in his and kissed her palm, his lips warm and full of promise. "I know, love," he whispered roughly. "I've been near to bursting with pride and need ever since."

She snaked both hands behind his neck. "Then take me to your bed, sir stag," she breathed into his lips. "Show me what a proud, lusty man you are."

He scooped her up in his arms, grinning at her little shriek. "Your wish is my command, my lady owl." He tossed her onto the bed and shucked his tunic and breeches as Alina hastily doffed her borrowed night shift, and then he stood at the side of the bed, gazing down at her. "Damnation, you're a beautiful woman, Alina."

The warmth of his regard and his praise suffused her limbs with liquid heat and filled her heart to bursting. She reached out and touched the soft tip of his erection, grinning as it jumped.

"And you are a handsome figure of a man, Roark MacInnes." She held out her arms to him. "Come to bed and make love to me. Take me away to our own special world."

"It will be my honor and my pleasure," he said, his voice husky with desire. He laid himself over the length of her and propped himself up on his elbows, nestling his thick erection in her thatch. He lowered his mouth to hers, claiming her with his kiss, and Alina surrendered herself with a soughing sigh. He lifted his head and stared into her eyes, his own shining like rain in moonlight.

"How am I supposed to live without those eyes pouring down on me?" Alina asked him, the gods, the fates. "I'll become like the earth in a drought, all dried up and dying for lack of rain."

"Don't say that, Ali love," he rasped. "Know that wherever I am, I'll be thinking of you, remembering you, remembering this, and dreaming of when we can be together again."

"If we can ever be together again," she whispered, her throat constricting and hot tears blurring her vision. She squeezed her eyes shut. She'd promised herself she wouldn't cry, not in front of him. That she would hold her tears through sheer will if she had to, at least until she was on a ship and sailing away from him. Crying wouldn't change anything. It would only make them feel worse. She met his somber gaze and filled her own with determination. "Promise me," she said. "Swear to me you won't let Roger kill you to satisfy some noble notion of what you owe your family. That you'll fight the lying, vindictive snake with every fiber of your being."

"I promise," he said, his voice rough. "I swear to you I'll not go without a fight." He held her face in his hands, his expression serious. "What I can't promise, love, is that I won't end up dead anyway."

Alina closed her eyes to keep back her tears.

"Or worse," he said. "Married to Gwyneth."

Alina burst out laughing. "A fate worse than death," she agreed. She bumped her pelvis against his. "See that you remember who your first wife is."

"My first." He kissed her forehead. "My last." He kissed her cheek. "My only, as far as my heart is concerned."

Alina drew his head down and kissed him. Kissed him long and hard and searing, branding him with her lips, claiming him, his love. He was hers as she was his. "I love you, Roark, now and always," she told him. "Nothing will ever change that."

He burrowed his face into her neck and kissed and nipped his way to her breast, taking her nipple into his mouth and suckling until she was arching her back to give him more, to give him all. He kissed his way to her other breast, repeating his attentions as he moved his hand down her belly and through her curls, running a fingertip along her folds, wet and eager for his touch. She sighed as his mouth left her breast, and then purred as he kissed his way down her belly, parting her curls and flicking the tip of his tongue over her bud.

"You taste as sweet as honey," he said, his low growl vibrating from her flesh to her bones. He ran blissful, tortuous circles around her nubbin with his tongue until she was writhing in rhythm with him, and then he took her nubbin in his mouth and sucked. She bucked her pelvis straight up and went rigid, all sensation centered in that one tiny piece of flesh as he licked and suckled, pulling her up and up until she soared over the precipice, her body a mass of raw nerves and pulsing pleasure.

She drifted back to reality, to Roark, and moaned as he lifted himself over her and between her legs. He nudged her still-sensitive flesh with the soft, blunt tip of his erection, and Alina opened herself to him, welcoming him, all of him, deep inside her, filling her with his hard, pulsing heat.

He placed his mouth over hers as he began to move inside her, the taste of her on his tongue exciting and stirring. She moved with him in their primal dance whose steps they'd made their own, their pace and rhythm quickening with urgency and need, until with one final thrust Roark shuddered and called out her name, a call reverberating from Alina's core to her soul.

She woke sometime later to his big, warm hand cupping her breast, his thumb teasing her peaked nipple, and his growing erection pressing against her buttocks. She sighed and wiggled her backside closer, and her sigh turned to a soft moan as he kissed her shoulder and ran his hand down her belly and between her thighs. He pushed his fingers through her curls and cupped her mound.

"You're already wet for me," he whispered hoarsely into her ear.

"I'm perpetually wet for you, my rutting stag," she murmured, pushing her pelvis into his palm.

"But this is…" He pulled his hand away and pushed up onto his elbow, holding his hand up to the low glow of the candle's light. "This is blood."

Alina rolled onto her back and stared at the stain darkening his palm. She reached down between her legs and felt the thick, viscous discharge and smelled the coppery scent of her blood.

"My moon-flow has come," she said, and burst into tears.

"Don't cry, Ali girl," he crooned. He sat up and embraced her, running his hand up and down her back as she buried her face into his shoulder. "There's no need to cry. This is a good thing, isn't it?"

"Yes," she cried into his shoulder. "No. I don't know." What was wrong with her? Of course, it was a good thing. Her being pregnant with his child would've complicated things even more than they already were.

So why did it feel as if her soul had been ripped out of her? How was it possible to mourn a child who had never been? To feel bereft of something she'd never had? She lifted her tear-streaked face to Roark's. "I kn...know it's foo...foolish of me," she bawled. "But I...I wanted our chiiilld."

"I know, love," he soothed. "I know you did. Crazy as it was, so did I."

He held her and let her cry, whispering sweet, tender words of love and endearment as she sobbed her heart out over the child they would never have, the love they'd have to walk away from for the sake of others. Over losing her one true love. Her Somebody.

When she had no tears left to shed, he laid her down on the bed and gently wiped the salt of her drying tears from her face with a wet washrag, kissed the tip of her nose, and handed her the washrag to serve as a temporary bleeding rag.

"It's coming on dawn, lass," he murmured, leaning over her and kissing her cheek. "You should go back to your room before the household starts to stir."

***

Roark stepped out of his room and almost smack into Lady Siusan and two maidservants, one carrying a basin and ewer, and the other a stack of small absorbent cloths to Alina's room.

"Is Alina unwell?" he asked Lady Siusan.

"She is indisposed," she told him, "and will likely remain so for another day or two."

Roark eyed the basin and the bleeding cloths. "Ah, I see," he said, acting like he'd figured out that Alina's moon-flow had come, but not fooling the lady in the least. It was perfect timing it happened here, instead of their long journey through the wilds, and before she'd set sail with a ship full of strange men.

But she'd been bereft, crying over a babe that was never to be. Crying over leaving him when she'd never once cried over what had been done to her. Her sad expression when she'd left him early this morning, assuring him she'd be fine, had been troubling him since. "If I may ask, how is she?"

The lady of the manor gave him a stern, motherly look. "She is as well as can be expected," she said, not exactly easing his worries. "I'll tell her you asked after her."

"Thank you."

Lady Siusan nodded and waved the maidservants on.

"Lady Siusan," he called. She stopped and looked over her shoulder. "Will you give her my love, please?"

The lady's stern expression softened. "Of course." She stepped up to him and lowered her voice to a whisper. "Shall I tell her to expect you tonight?"

"I, ah, um."

"I'll take that as a yes."

Roark was still shaking his head as he walked down the stairs to a mostly empty dining hall and grabbed a piece of bread, a slice of cold mutton, and a handful of cherries from the serving table, eating them as he strolled over to the stables where he found Cullen feeding Etain carrots.

"My mother said Lady Alina wasn't feeling well today," he told Roark, "so I'm making sure Etain gets her treats."

"That's verra considerate of you," Roark said. He grabbed two carrots from the bucket and fed one to Beasty. "I'm sure Alina will appreciate it almost as much as Etain." He fed Beasty the other carrot and sent out a prayer to the *bog loshadi,* the horse gods Alina had told him about, for Artur's healing and safe return. "I was going to let Etain and Beasty out in the paddock for a bit," he said. "Would you like to help me with them?"

Cullen nodded eagerly. "Do you think they'll get along with Godfrey and Damon?"

"They should," Roark said. "Beasty here seems to get along with anyone as long as they're friendly, Etain too." As long as they didn't try to nurse from her.

The image of an auburn-haired babe with eyes as green as spring grass suckling at Alina's breast came unbidden, hitting him like a blow to the chest. He braced his hands on his knees pulling in air, but he still couldn't breathe.

"Roark?"

He looked over at Cullen's big green eyes, so like Alina's, so like the child he'd envisioned, and lowered his head. "I'm all right," he lied. "I need a moment, lad."

After his breathing returned to normal, they led the horses out two by two, keeping an eye on them as they approached the other horses, sniffing and flicking their tails before settling down to graze under the late morning sun. Roark was showing Cullen how to use the spyglass when Owen and Gavin came into the paddock, and he showed them as well.

"Here," Roark said, holding the spyglass out to Owen. "I want you to have this as thanks for all you've done. For all you intend to do for Alina and myself."

Owen eyed the spyglass for a moment and then waved it away. "While I appreciate the offer," he said, "you should hold on to it. You'll have more need of it on your journey back to—" he glanced at Cullen, "your home. Which you'll be accompanied on by Niels and Grant."

"While I appreciate your offer," Roark said, "may I ask why you'd be willing to send two of your men on such a long, arduous journey with me, and back?"

"Because it is such a long, arduous journey," Owen said. "And because Lady Alina asked me to."

Roark snorted. "Of course she did." He toed the ground with his boot and rubbed his jaw. He hated bringing more people further into his mess, but the company of two armed men would almost guarantee his return to clean up the rest of it. He held his hand out to Owen. "Of course, I accept."

"Good," Owen said, clasping Roark's forearm and giving it a shake. "Now that's settled, we were about to go taste test a batch of whisky. Care to join us?"

***

Roark woke fully clothed on top of a bed in a strange room that spun when he tried to sit up. He fell back on his elbows and squinted at the glaring daylight streaming in through the open window shutters and groaned as his head started pounding.

"Water," he croaked, forcing himself to sit up slowly and scan the room for a drinking pitcher. Spying one on a table, he pushed himself onto unsteady legs, grabbed his throbbing head with both hands, and stumbled over to the pitcher. His hands shook as he poured himself a cup of water and drank it in three long swallows. He refilled his cup and gulped down the water until the pitcher was empty. Now he recognized where he was.

He remembered going to the distillery with Owen and Gavin and drinking whisky, telling tall tales, and laughing until his belly hurt. He was fairly sure they'd sung a few bawdy songs before staggering across the yard to the manor house sometime after dark. He had a vague memory of attempting to climb the stairs to their rooms, and thought they may have fallen a time or two—which his sore backside and shoulder attested to. He'd obviously made his room, where he must've passed out in a drunken stupor and remained the rest of the night.

A night he was meant to spend with Alina. "Damnation."

Ignoring the constant, throbbing ache in his head, he splashed water on his face and left his room to end up standing in the hall trying to decide whether to go straight to Alina's room or go down to the dining hall and get something solid into his empty, queasy belly. With his belly threatening to revolt and the smell of whisky sweating out of his pores, he decided it would be best to eat and bathe first. Alina would understand. He hoped.

Loud, boisterous voices assailed his head as he entered the dining hall, and then the heat and smell of bodies and food hit his nose and belly. He glanced at the bowls of porridge people were eating as he headed for the high table and almost retched, twice.

He took a seat by a dour-faced Owen and peered into the laird's bloodshot eyes. "How much whisky did we taste yesterday?" he croaked.

"Gallons," a sallow-skinned Gavin answered from Owen's other side.

Roark took in the fried eggs, buttered bread, and ale the laird and his brother-in-law were eating and asked the serving maid for a plate and a cup of the same.

"O'course, m'lord," she answered.

He started to raise his hand, to stop her and tell her he was no bloody lord, but it took too much effort. He propped his elbows on the table and laid his head in his hands instead and tried to remember more of yesterday, but it only made his headache worse.

The maid brought his food and drink, and by the time he'd sipped half the cup and eaten most of the food, his belly was feeling almost normal and the pounding in his head had dulled enough for him to think without hurting, though his memory was still muddled.

"I've been drunk a few times before," he told Owen, who'd finished eating his food and was nursing his second cup of ale. "But never like that."

"I'm not surprised, lad," Owen said with a subdued chuckle. "Whisky's a stronger drink than most men are used to."

Gavin turned a jaundiced eye to Roark. "I must say, lad, you handled it better than most their first time overindulging. Right up until you started singing."

"I apologize," Roark said. He sounded like a stag in rut when he tried to sing. "Anything else I said or did I should be aware of since I can't remember a thing after the third, or maybe it was the fourth, cup?"

"Not much," Owen told him, "other than your entire life history up until the moment you spied Alina racing her horse on the beach with her legs bare and her long mane flowing."

Roark buried his head in his hands and groaned.

"Then you went all moon-eyed and introspective," Owen continued. "After that, I admit I don't recall much either, other than Gavin and me helping you up the stairs. It's all still a bit hazy."

Roark shook his head in his hands, thankful he'd apparently not told them any more details of his time with Alina. "I have a vague memory of being hauled up the stairs by you two. Did we fall?"

Both men laughed good-naturedly. "Aye, lad," Owen said. "Twice, according to my lady wife, with a great deal of thumping around and colorful cursing that woke half the household."

"Alina?" Roark asked.

"Siusan said Alina found it quite amusing."

"She would." Roark chuckled, relieved he wouldn't have much explaining to do as to why he hadn't visited her rooms last night. Not that Alina was the type to get mad at him for it, but she'd been so disappointed about her moon-flow, the last thing he wanted to do was disappoint her more. "Speaking of which," he said, standing and taking a moment for his legs to work and his head to stop spinning. "I should give her a visit."

"Do yourself and her a favor, lad," Owen said, giving the air around Roark a sniff and a grimace. "Visit the bathhouse first."

***

Roark knocked on Alina's door, preparing to apologize for last night and to ask her if she'd like supper brought up to her room. She'd been asleep when he'd gone to visit her after his bath, so he'd gone back to his room and slept the afternoon away. He'd woken feeling much revived, and seeing Alina's face as she answered her door dressed and ready for supper made him genuinely pleased.

"I'm heartily sick of four walls and a bed," she said, closing the door behind her and looping her arm through his. She peered intently at him. "How are you feeling?"

"Better now," he said. Now that he'd gotten some sleep and had her on his arm. "That whisky has quite a kick."

She giggled. "No broken bones or permanent injuries from tumbling down the stairs, I take it?"

"Only a few sore spots," he said, grinning, and rubbed the back of his head, the only part of his head that still ached. "One advantage to falling when you're verra drunk apparently."

"Or dumb luck," she said with a teasing grin.

"Or that." He stopped at the top of the stairs and cupped her chin. "I'm sorry I missed spending time with you last night."

She shrugged. "I wouldn't have been good company anyway."

He peered into her eyes and saw the telltale redness of shed tears. "Alina…"

"I'll be fine."

He wasn't sure he believed her. He wasn't sure she believed herself. But the tone of her voice told him she didn't want to talk about it. He kissed her lightly on the lips and then deepened the kiss.

"Ahem." They both turned around to see the laird and lady standing arm in arm outside their chamber's door. "Shall we?" Owen said, stepping past them with his lady and heading down the stairs.

Alina laced her arm through Roark's and they followed, the smell of roasted meat making his belly growl and rumble as they took their seats. They had no sooner tucked into their meal when Niels and Grant strode into the hall with a nod to the laird and then to Roark as they too sat, but at a low table, still covered in the dust and grime from their trip.

"They made good time," Owen said, "which bodes well for you two. We'll meet with them after supper."

Roark met Alina's too-bright gaze and squeezed her hand under the table. For all he knew they could be leaving here tomorrow, Alina for her ship and Roark back to North Shore Keep. He made himself eat, though he barely tasted the food, and saw that Alina did the same. At last, the laird and lady stood.

"Roark, Alina, Gavin, Agnes," Owen said. "If you would come with us to my council chambers."

Niels and Grant joined them, Grant closing the door behind them as the three couples chose their sofas and the men their chairs.

"What news?" Owen asked Niels.

"We found a ship docked at the southern port, the *Trade Wind,* that sails under a Captain Wallis, who's willing to take the Lady Alina to Sea Ridge for the price of her pearl. They sail in four days' time on the morning tide."

"Do you trust this Wallis?" Roark asked.

"We asked around," Niels said. "Got nothing but good reports on him, and he owns the ship he sails, so he's not beholden to any laird who's likely to side with this Roger. Wallis says he's traded at Sea Ridge before, and he's always found the trading there fair."

"So then," Owen said. "We have two days to prepare, one day to travel, and one day to get Lady Alina aboard the *Trade Wind* and on her way home."

Four days. Roark twined his fingers through Alina's, glad she'd be safely away, but desolate to be saying good-bye to her. Maybe forever.

"Any word on Roger's men?" Owen asked.

"Aye," Niels said. "We heard they've been up and down the firth's ports, spreading their accusations of murder and the bounty price on these two, along with Roger's threat of retribution to anyone who dares help them. Which Wallis says doesn't bother him any." He looked to Grant and both men grinned.

"What else?" Owen said.

Niels chuckled and pulled on his beard. "We were in a tavern our last night there," he said, "where we happened to overhear three men bragging about how they'd captured Roark, who they said was traveling alone, and how they had him all nice and hog-tied, and were on their way to port to turn him in to the laird's men and collect their reward when they were set upon by a gang of thieves in the middle of the night atop the northern pass. How many men did they say?" he asked Grant. "Eight, nine?"

"The number kept changing with each telling and cup of ale," Grant said. He grinned at Alina. "I believe it was ten by their last telling."

"Anyway," Niels continued, "they said they fought off this gang of men and claimed they killed two," he glanced at Roark, "before the thieves took their prisoner and ran." He winked at Alina. "Guess it sounded a mite better than being outsmarted by one woman."

Alina shrugged and her eyes grew wide. "This is good," she told Roark. "This will keep people from blaming you for killing those two men, even though it was self-defense."

"And it keeps you out of it altogether," Roark said. "People will think we've split up and gone our separate ways."

Which they would be doing in four days.

After some time spent in the common room conversing with the family and sipping only half a cup of whisky, which Roark had taken a liking to despite everything, he walked Alina up to her room.

"I'll be back shortly," he told her. "I'm going to get my things from my room, for our room."

She rewarded him with a happy smile. "It was nice of Owen and Siusan to permit us to share a room."

"Yes, it is," he agreed. All he'd had to do was promise not to make any babies with her. "It appears we haven't fooled a single adult here about our relationship."

"Good. I'm tired of trying to hide it. This way we can be Roark and Alina for the time left us here."

He went to his room and piled all his personal belongings onto his otter cloak, wrapped them up, and carried them to Alina's room, where she was already changed into a night shift, sitting on the bed, her knees tucked under her chin. She watched him with a shaky smile on her beautiful face as he arranged his belongings, her green eyes wide with appreciation as he stripped and joined her on the bed. Their bed, for three more nights anyway.

He leaned against the headboard, her head nestled on his shoulder. "Niels and Grant agreed to ride back with me," he said. He kissed her on the crown of her head, breathing in the scent of spring grass, cherry blossoms, and her. "Thank you."

"They might come in handy," she said, "since you won't have your gang of ten with you this time."

He chuckled low. "No gang of ten could've handled those brigands as well as you did, my brave, intelligent owl."

"I'm glad you'll have their company. Do they intend to ride all the way to North Shore Keep with you?"

"No. Only as far as Thorn Bush Keep. I don't wish to drag the MacLeods any deeper into this mess than they already are."

"I'm glad we came here," she said. "I like them. I like knowing they're kin. Knowing where my great-grandmother, Oona, came from. It makes me feel connected to her. To all the women of my line."

"From Swan to Tigress to Lynx to Owl," Roark said. "You've come full circle." He hugged her tight. "The women of your line would be proud."

CHAPTER 15

North Sea Firth

They left the keep at dawn and rode northeast along the southern shore of Silver Water Loch, Laird Owen and Niels in the lead, Alina on Etain and Roark on Beasty behind them, and one of the laird's men named Liam driving a wagon laden with barrels of whisky, batts of wool, and crates of cherries behind them. Grant and a fourth man named Duncan were riding rear guard. Alina, traveling as Al, wore the linen tunic and breeches Brianna had given her, along with the otter cloak. Her hair was braided and tucked tight under a woolen cap.

Roark too wore a woolen cap over his auburn waves and a scarf around his neck, which could be pulled up over his nose to hide his freckled face. But there was no hiding his eyes, which Alina sought and held every chance she got.

The past three days and nights had been bittersweet. They'd enjoyed a close contentedness, petting and kissing, walking and talking, eating and sleeping together, doing everything *but*. They'd even taken baths together, giving Alina a new appreciation for why her parents enjoyed bathing together so much.

Saying her good-byes to Lady Siusan, Agnes, Cullen, and Rose, who'd given up chasing Roark after the night Alina sang "Somebody," had been gut-wrenching. They'd all been so welcoming and gracious, and had accepted her. She would never be able to repay their kindness, though she intended to do her best. Which was why the wagon carried two barrels of whisky bound for Sea Ridge. She'd meant what she'd told Owen about her father being interested in trading for the spirits, and looked forward to opening a trade line between them.

They left the shores of Silver Water Loch by midmorning, and by midday made the Long Loch, which looked more like an inland sea than a lake. Long, wide, and deep, the loch ran ten leagues south to north, where it joined the mouth of the North Sea Firth, Owen explained. He also told them of a giant sea creature as big as a small ship living in the loch's depths that could sometimes be seen breaching the shallows, its shiny, grey-black body undulating in the wind-blown waters.

"Could it be whales?" Alina asked him.

"Nay, lassie." Owen shook his head as Niels rolled his eyes behind his laird's back, causing Alina to stifle a laugh. "It's never been seen coming up for air or blowing like a whale."

"Have you ever seen it?"

"I've not," he admitted. "It's mostly fishermen or shepherds who've spent their lives on or near the loch who have."

"Along with faeries and unicorns," Niels added sardonically. "A direct result, I would say, of spending so much time staring at the water."

The men all laughed, yet Alina kept an eye on the loch's murky waters all the same. Her father, who was not a fanciful man but had sailed much of the known world, had often told her there was more and stranger things in it than anyone knew.

By late afternoon, when they'd reached the loch's northernmost point where it emptied into the firth, she'd yet to see anything resembling such a creature, though the search had helped keep her mind off this being her last ride through the countryside with Roark.

They arrived in the port town of River's Mouth in the late afternoon, where it was decided she and Roark would share a room with Owen at the inn, while the four men would share another, taking shifts two by two between resting in the room and staying with the wagon outside the inn's stable.

Liam and Duncan took the first shift, while the others went to their rooms. Almost as soon as she stepped into theirs, Alina pulled her cap off and let down her hair, scratching her overheated scalp. Owen left the room to meet with Niels and Grant downstairs to sup while Alina and Roark hid out in the room. Owen would bring up their supper later.

The door had barely shut behind Owen when Alina flew into Roark's arms and his lips were in her hair.

"I thought he'd never leave," Roark whispered huskily. "I've been aching all day to hold you and kiss you."

She nuzzled his neck, breathing him in. "I've been yearning to be held and kissed by you all day."

He tilted up her chin and grinned. "I love you, my lady owl. No matter what happens, never forget that. Never forget me."

Alina gazed into eyes the color of rain, eyes that poured love sweet and bitter into hers. "I could never forget you, sir stag," she whispered fiercely. "You are the air I breathe, the heat of my sun, the earth I stand on, the blood in my veins. Your love has kept me going when it felt like all was lost. It's what will keep me going forward from here. What will keep me hoping and believing we'll be together again, whether in this world or the next. For this moment in time, your love is all that matters to me here in our own little world."

"A world without consequence or repercussion."

She nodded, smiled, and shut her eyes tight against the welling of hot tears. As soon as Owen walked back into the room with their supper, their wonderful little world would give way to the real one. The one where they'd soon be parted. For how long, neither of them knew.

Roark wrapped his hand around the back of her head and pressed her forehead to his chest, his lips moving wordlessly in her hair. They stood there holding each other, chest to aching chest, heart to breaking heart, until a knock on the door broke their bittersweet reverie.

***

Alina quickly tucked her hair back up under her woolen cap and Roark held the door open as Owen walked in, followed by two maidservants carrying trays laden with bowls of stew, half a loaf of bread, three cups, and a pitcher of ale. As soon as the maids left the room, Roark slid the bolt shut, Alina tossed her cap, and Owen lay down flat on his back on one of the two beds in the room with a groan.

"Ahhh. A full day in the saddle takes a greater toll on me than it used to," he said. He closed his eyes with a heavy sigh and was snoring lightly before Roark and Alina had swallowed their second spoonful of mutton stew.

They ate and drank in companionable silence, the stew under-salted and the ale flat, but it filled their bellies and revived them after a long day on the road.

When they were finished, Roark set the empty tray of dishes outside the door and shut and bolted it. He sat down on the edge of the bed and patted the space beside him. Alina sat next to him and leaned her head on his shoulder as he wrapped his arm around her and held her close.

"Come with me," she said.

"You know I can't."

"I know you won't."

It was the same argument, and it would end the same way it always had. It wasn't that he didn't want to go with her. He did. He wanted to be with her more than anything. But he needed to settle things between his family and Roger's first.

"Ali girl, I—"

A knock at the door had Roark and Alina on their feet and Owen sitting up quickly enough to prove himself a light sleeper.

"Who is it?" Owen demanded.

"Niels."

Owen nodded to Roark, who opened the door to Niels.

"Your gang of three is downstairs in the common room," Niels said to Roark. "They've been bragging about how they're working for this Laird Roger's men directly and asking questions about what we're doing here." He glanced over at Owen. "My first inclination was to tell them to fuck off, pardon my language, lady. But seeing as how we're trying to keep our presence here nice and quiet like, I told them we're here to load up a trade ship with our whisky and wool. They pushed, wanting to know whose whisky and what ship." He shrugged. "That's when I told them to fuck off, pardon my language, lady."

Roark chuckled, Owen shook his head, and Alina laughed out loud.

"What was their response to that?" Owen asked.

Niels grinned and tugged on his beard. "They sized me up and decided their three against my one wasn't the odds they were looking for, so they took themselves back to their table and commenced to drink and brag about how they'd beat back the ten men who'd stolen their valuable prisoner." He winked at Alina.

"Anyway, whilst they were drinking and bragging, I went on over to the stables and warned Liam and Duncan they'd likely be having visitors as soon as our friends got drunk enough to be stupid brave."

"Think they'll try to steal anything?" Owen asked.

"Nah. They'll likely poke their noses around and ask the lads questions they'll get no answers to. Though it wouldn't surprise me if they showed up at the docks tomorrow."

"With or without Roger's men?"

"As much as they were blabbing about everything else, the one thing they didn't say was where Roger's men are. 'Course, they may not know. Want me to ask around?"

Owen nodded. "Aye, I do. Tell Grant and the others they'll be rotating shifts between the three of them, two on and one off at a time. I want you rested up for tomorrow."

As soon as Niels left the room, Owen went to his pack and pulled out his short sword, stuffed it under his mattress with the hilt sticking out, shifted his waist belt so the blade was center of his belly, checked his boot blade, and lay down on his bed, fully clothed and with his boots still on. Roark did the same with his short sword and blades, as did Alina. Then they set their backs against the wall and sat sprawled on their bed shoulder to shoulder.

"You should get some sleep," he said, wrapping his arm around her and tucking her in to him.

"So should you," she said, leaning her head on his shoulder.

"We both should," he agreed.

"But it's our last night together. For a time."

Roark hugged her even closer. "Ahh, Ali girl," he said, his voice cracking. "Your optimism is one of the myriad things I love about you."

Alina sniffed and nestled her nose into his neck. "I refuse to believe the fates brought us together only to lose each other forever."

"I believe in making our own fate, my lady owl. If we hadn't, you'd be sailing for the desert lands and life as a pleasure woman instead of sailing home to your family, and I'd be making arrangements to marry Gwyneth rather than going back to confront my family and hers."

"And to face charges of murdering Leif, without any proof other than your word you didn't." She sat up and grabbed him by the neck of his tunic. "Promise me you'll not leave Owen's keep for Roger's right away. Give me time to get home and sail back here with my father. Then you can sail back to North Shore Keep with us, and we can confront Roger over his lies and deceit together."

"How much time are we talking?"

"Four to six days for me to sail to Sea Ridge, two days there to prepare, and four to six days to sail back here, a day to ride to Silver Water Keep for you and a day to get back to the ship, then two days to sail from here to North Shore Keep, so ten and four to ten and eight days before we made it back to confront Roger. It took us ten days to ride from there to here, with a few stops on the way," she said with a sensuous smile. "So even figuring for bad weather, it would take you ten days to ride back there. Another six to eight days shouldn't matter too much."

"I don't know. Roger could get frustrated at not finding us and start taking it out on my family. Besides, how long I stay at Silver Water Keep is up to Laird Owen. I don't want to impose on him anymore than I already have."

"You're no imposition, Roark MacInnes," Owen said from his bed. "You're welcome to stay as long as you wish."

***

Roark woke the same way he'd fallen asleep in the wee hours of the night, with his arm wrapped around Alina, and her head tucked under his chin. They'd spent most of the night sitting on the bed and whispering their thoughts, dreams, and hopes to each other while their time together sifted away. Alina had sung "Somebody" to Roark, her voice soft, pure, and achingly beautiful. It had been the most tender, sad, bittersweet night of his life. And now it was at an end.

"Alina." He nuzzled her cheek as Owen stirred in his bed. "Time to wake up, my sleepy little owl."

"Nnnooo." She burrowed her nose deeper into his tunic.

Roark grinned. She really wasn't a morning person.

"Aye, Ali girl," he said, hugging her and placing a kiss on the crown of her head. "Dawn is breaking."

She yawned, shifted, and blinked her sleepy green eyes up at him. "Not yet," she pleaded. "Surely we can sleep in a little long…" Her sleepy eyes widened. "Damnation."

"Aye," Roark said, pushing a lock of hair from her sleep-dampened cheek. "Damnation." He lowered his mouth to hers and kissed her, long, soft, and tender. He started to pull his mouth away and she threw her arms around his neck and deepened their kiss, branding his lips with hers, branding him, his heart, and his very soul.

"I, ah, I hate to break this up," Owen said from across the room. "But we need to get going if we want to make the *Trade Wind* in time."

Roark held Alina by both shoulders and stared into her eyes. "We can do this," he told her. Told himself. "We can do this."

She smiled and blinked back her welling tears, sniffed, and nodded. "We can do this."

They met up with Niels in the common room, where he told them he'd been right about the raggedy band of three nosing around the wagon last night, though not too close or too long when Duncan and Liam confronted them. He'd heard Roger's men had left town shortly after their group had arrived.

Owen bought two loaves of bread, a wheel of cheese, and a pitcher of ale from the innkeeper that they took to the stables, where the draft horses were already hitched to the wagon and their mounts all saddled. They split the food and drink amongst themselves and ate it quickly, and then it was time to go.

Unable to resist the chance to touch Alina, Roark took her by the waist and boosted her onto Etain, running his hand down her breeches-clad thigh and booted calf, guiding her foot into the stirrup. Loath to remove his hand from her, her gave her ankle a gentle squeeze and then broke his hold and mounted Beasty.

The docks were only a short ride away, yet each step felt like a league as they made their way down the road in the thick, early morning mist.

Roark sidled Beasty closer to Etain and held out his hand, his throat constricting as Alina reached out and twined her fingers through his. He tried to smile, to reassure her, and himself, and was pretty sure it came out more of a grimace.

They held on tight to each other's hands as the docks came into view. Niels pointed out the *Trade Wind* tied off at the nearest pier, and men appeared on the deck of the ship. The mist cleared and other men appeared on the road, all of them mounted and all of them armed, blocking their way to the ship.

Roark recognized them immediately. Three of them were Ned, Shaw, and Cam, and the other four were Roger's men-at-arms. He pulled his scarf up over his nose and Alina pulled her woolen cap lower over her forehead.

"What is the meaning of this?" Owen demanded as Liam pulled the wagon to a stop. "I am Owen MacLeod, laird of Silver Water Keep. Who are you to block our way?"

Scott, the captain of Roger's men-at-arms, urged his horse forward, his gaze flicking over Roark and Alina before he addressed Owen. "We are the men of Laird Roger MacKinnon of North Shore Keep," he said. "Sworn to apprehend the murderers of his only son and return them to him for a fair trial and public hanging."

"What is that to us?" Owen said.

Scott lifted his chin toward Roark and Alina. "I see the murderers, Roark MacInnes and the serving wench, Alina, amongst you there. I demand you turn them over to us."

"Or?"

Scott glanced from his men, who were all armed with short and long swords and wore lacquered chest plates and arm guards, to Owen's who, though armed with short swords, wore no armor other than their thick leather jerkins. Among whom only Owen and Niels had long swords. "Or we will take them by force and you will suffer the consequences of Laird Roger's wrath."

Owen laughed, short and harsh. "This laird Roger must think his arms long indeed if he thinks they can reach me here."

"Will you give the man and woman over?" Scott asked, his question more of a demand than a request as Ross, his second, urged his horse forward.

"I will not," Owen said as curious onlookers began to line up along the road.

On board the *Trade Wind,* three of the crew started to descend the gangplank, each one armed with a short sword and various blades, while three more stayed on board, brandishing their blades from the rails. Scott and Ross both glanced behind them to see the three crewmen spreading out around them, and Owen grinned. It was now Roger's group who were outnumbered.

"Well," Owen called out to Scott. "What's it to be?"

Scott and Ross sat taller in their saddles and pulled their long swords, as Douglas and Todd, the other two of Roger's men, did the same. Ned, Shaw, and Cam brandished their short swords. Owen and his men pulled their weapons too, and Alina had a death grip on her waist blade with one hand and her boot dagger in the other.

Roark had been in enough fights to realize no one was going to back down, and people were going to get injured and die if a fight broke out. Laird Owen could be hurt, or killed, leaving his wife and children without him. Alina could be injured or killed, or taken prisoner and sold as a slave, and then all of what they'd gone through would be for naught.

"I'm sorry, Ali," he said. "I know I promised I'd wait to go back and face Roger, but if I don't go with them now, people will die. You could die. I won't be responsible for that, not if I can stop it."

"No." She shook her head, her eyes pleading with him. "Roark, no."

He let his eyes tell her what he couldn't and urged Beasty forward between Owen's and Niels's mounts and lowered his scarf.

"What are you doing, lad?" Owen said.

"Stopping this before it gets bloody." Roark urged Beasty forward a few more steps. "Scott, Ross," he addressed Roger's men. "You know me. You know I'm a man of my word."

"Aye, you were," Scott said. "Before you killed Leif."

"I didn't kill Leif," Roark said. "I did beat him senseless when I came upon him trying to rape Princess Alina." Both Scott's and Ross's heads shot up. "I wanted to kill him," Roark admitted, "and would have, but Princess Alina stopped me. We left him tied and gagged and alive in the stables, defenseless, apparently, against whoever did kill him. But it wasn't me or Princess Alina."

"That'll be for you and the laird to work out," Scott said.

"So it will," Roark agreed. "Which is why I always meant to go back to North Shore and deal with it all, after the princess, who's an innocent in all of this, is on her way home."

Scott scoffed. "You say that now."

"He has said that since the day he and my cousin, Princess Alina, came to me for aid and shelter," Owen said as he and Niels brought their mounts forward to flank Roark.

Roark nodded his thanks to Owen and then made a point of looking at the growing crowd of townspeople, as did Scott and Ross.

"My offer is this," Roark said, speaking loud enough for the crowd to hear. "Let Princess Alina board the *Trade Wind,* let her sail home to her family at Sea Ridge in the Northlands. Let her safe return assuage her father's, King Jerrik's, anger at her having been abducted by Laird Roger MacKinnon of North Shore Keep for his own vengeful purposes, and I will leave here with you the moment the *Trade Wind* sails out of this port."

"We were told to bring back both of you," Scott said.

Roark squared his shoulders and shook his head. "The deal is me and only me. In which case, I go with you peacefully. If you try to take the princess, you will have to fight for her."

Scott shifted uneasily on his saddle and looked over Owen's men, the ship's crew both on and off the deck, and the buzzing crowd.

"You're outnumbered, Scott," Roark pointed out. "Even including Ned, Shaw, and Cam there, who'll as likely turn tail and run as fight." He saluted the raggedy brigands with his short sword and they cackled and squirmed on their mounts, their shifty gazes already searching for a way out of any fight to come. "Be smart about this, Scott. Don't make Pam a widow and Robbie fatherless." He looked the other three men in the eyes one by one. "Ross, Douglas, Todd, don't lose your lives or limbs over this. No matter what, you're not getting the princess, so take me, let me deal with Roger. Too many people know who Princess Alina is now. Too many know what Roger has done, what he'd intended to do to the princess. As will her father, King Jerrik, soon enough."

"What happens when her father, this King Jerrik, exacts his revenge against Roger?" Ross, who was married with two young children, asked. "What happens to us and our families then?"

"He will not exact his revenge on the people of North Shore," Alina said loudly, sidling Etain up beside Beasty. "You have my word on this."

Scott held a hand up and spoke with Ross, speaking low and glancing around several times.

"You don't have to do this, you know," Owen told Roark as Scott and Ross continued to talk it over. "We've got them outnumbered two to one."

"Yes," Roark said. "I do." He met Alina's worried gaze. Alina, who'd forgiven him everything. Who he hoped would forgive him this. "I got everyone into this and I'll get them out. No one else should pay for my actions any more than they already have. Scott, Ross, and the others are decent men doing their laird's bidding. They don't deserve to die today. None of you do. I'll not chance Alina getting hurt or taken, and I won't let anyone die today if I can help it."

Owen nodded. "You're a good man, Roark."

"Thank you, Laird Owen. You saying that means a lot." He glanced at Alina, who was biting her lips and shaking her head. He looked to Scott and Ross. "Do we have a deal?"

"We do," Scott said.

"Damn," Niels grumbled. "I was really hoping for a go at those three idiots from the inn."

Roark quirked his brow. "You may get your chance yet," he told the Northman. "Roger's men will have no need of them once they have me. My guess is they'll toss them a copper each and cut them loose within a league's distance of here."

Niels grinned as Owen ordered Liam and Duncan to load the whisky and wool onto the *Trade Wind.* Roark offered his hand to the laird and Niels. "Thank you," he told them. "For everything."

Owen clasped his forearm, his green MacLeod eyes serious. "If you get out of this alive, Roark MacInnes, you'll always have a place at Silver Water Keep."

Roark nodded, unable to speak for the sudden lump in his throat. His own father had never offered him such praise and acceptance his entire life. Roger had only praised him for a job well done when it was to Roger's benefit. He nodded to each of Owen's men in turn and then met Alina's wide-eyed gaze, his heart splintering into a thousand shards at the pain and grief he saw reflected there.

He took Etain's reins from her trembling hands and led them past Owen and his men, past Roger's men, and up to the gangplank of the *Trade Wind.* He dismounted from Beasty, wrapped his hands around Alina's slim waist, and helped her down from Etain, groaning as she slid her body against his until her feet hit the ground. She leaned into him, embracing him as tightly as he embraced her, as if they could hold on against everything and everyone pulling them apart.

"I wish it could be otherwise, Ali love," he whispered in her ear. "I wish we truly were in a world where our actions had no consequences or repercussions for anyone other than ourselves."

"But we don't," she whispered into his neck. "We never did." She lifted her head and met and held his gaze, her crystalline green eyes glistening with tears. "I love you, Roark MacInnes." She grabbed him by the arms and shook him. "You stay alive, sir stag," she told him. "You stay alive until I can come back for you. And I will. I swear it."

Roark nodded and pressed his forehead to hers. "I will, my lady owl. I will do whatever I can and must. I swear it."

She rolled her forehead against his. "I know you will," she said. "You will do whatever you think right and necessary. That's what worries me."

He tilted up her chin and smiled down into her beautiful, sad face, and she smiled back through her tears. He lowered his mouth to hers and kissed her, soft, tender, and lingering sweet, and then he broke the kiss, offered her his arm, and walked her up the gangplank.

***

Alina stepped onto the *Trade Wind*'s deck, loath to let go of Roark's arm. To let go of him. They stood there for an eternity as the ship's crew loaded the barrels of whisky and batts of wool in the hold, neither of them speaking a word. What was there left to say? They'd been saying good-bye for days now, all the words had been spoken, all the endearments whispered, their love proclaimed.

When the last of the trade goods had been loaded, and the hatches battened down, Roark lifted Alina's hand from his arm, kissed the backs of her fingers, untied the sheath from his waist belt, and placed the spyglass in her hand. He gave her one last, slow, melting grin, and then he turned and walked back down the gangplank.

Holding the spyglass in her numb fingers, Alina stood rooted to the deck as she watched Roark walk away from her. She clamped her jaw tight to keep from calling out after him, to beg him not to give himself up to almost certain death for the sake of others. For her. Yet she knew she couldn't. She couldn't ask him to give up his honor for her. She'd tried, many times, and he'd refused every time, and she loved him all the more for it.

She stood and watched him mount Beasty as the ship's captain gave the orders to set sail. She watched him take Etain's reins and led her over to stand between Scott's and Ross's mounts. She watched as he looked up and found her gaze and held it. He smiled, and she tried to smile back but couldn't, else her fragile mask of fortitude would crack and break.

She startled at the creak of rigging and the snap of sails unfurling and closed her ears to the shouts of the sailors throwing off tie lines to the dock.

Beneath her feet the ship lurched forward as the wind filled the sails. She touched her fingertips to her lips and held her hand up to Roark, her tears falling freely as the wind and the tide pulled the ship, and her, away from her one true love.

CHAPTER 16

The Road Back

Riding away from Alina was like cutting out his own heart with a dull, rusted spoon. Yet Roark was bound by his word, and his love for her to do it. He'd helped get her free of Roger and on her way home to her family, his atonement for having helped bring her to Roger in the first place. He'd done what his heart and his honor demanded. If Roger killed him for it, so be it. His only regret would be never seeing her again. Never gazing into her brilliant green eyes, never talking to her again. Never tasting her sweet kiss or touching her warm, smooth skin. Never making love with her.

He pulled his otter cloak closer around his shoulders as a chill set into his bones, though it wasn't a particularly cold day. He glanced back toward the firth as the road turned south, but the ship was already out of sight. Alina was out of sight, but not his mind.

She would haunt him for the rest of his days and nights. His own bittersweet ghost whose memory was already dearer to him than life. If he was meant to die, then it would be with her image in his mind, legs bare and hair blowing in the wind as she raced her mare along the sea's shore. Free.

"Don't look so hangdog," Scott said over his shoulder. "You'll have plenty more to brood over than your princess soon enough."

Scott and Ross rode ahead of Roark with Douglas and Todd behind him. As he'd predicted, Scott had already paid Ned and his cohorts a copper each and sent them down the road, where they'd likely drink and piss their three coppers' worth of ale away at the closest inn.

Roark had always gotten along with these four men-at-arms. Better than Leif, who'd never hesitated to throw his weight around.

He'd sworn he wouldn't try to run, and they'd taken him at his word and let him ride unbound. Whether they tied him up when they camped for the night remained to be seen. Either way, he'd given his word and he intended to keep it.

"How's the family taking Leif's death?" he asked.

"As you'd expect," Scott answered. "His mother is distraught, his aunt and uncle are angry, his sister is using it as an excuse to be even more lazy and demanding, and his father is…" Scott shook his head. "I've never seen the laird in such a rage."

Which was understandable, and Roark doubted had abated in the time he and Alina had been on the run. Knowing Roger and his penchant for holding grudges and seeking revenge, his rage had grown white hot.

Roark edged Beasty up alongside Scott's horse. "What have you heard about my family?" he asked.

"Your father remains loyal to Roger," Scott told him. "Other than that, I haven't heard."

Which meant his brother would stand by Roger too, and his mother was staying circumspect. Smart.

The road turned southeast and would be turning more southerly tomorrow when it connected to the road running along the coastal side of the Mounths. Roark had left Artur on the far west side of the mountain range. He figured Artur's hoof had either healed by now, or he'd foundered. He chose to imagine the stallion thriving and living free as king of the mountain rather than having died a slow and painful death from sepsis.

His mind traveled from the mountain pass to the cave. To his time there with Alina, cocooned in their own little world, a world of love, laughter, and passion. A world he couldn't think of without his gut twisting into knots of yearning. He shook his head and squared his shoulders. Better to think of Alina onboard the *Trade Wind,* her face to the wind, tousling her hair. He'd savor the memories of their time together in the cave when he was alone.

He took in the grassy foothills dotted with sheep and shaggy highland cows, the small fishing villages and stone manor houses, and the roadside towns, yet all he saw in his mind's eye was Alina. Riding on the beach. Bent over her herbs, her hands covered in soil, the look of surprise and recognition on her face when he'd stepped out from behind Leif. Her look of betrayal when she'd realized he was abducting her.

She may have forgiven him for his betrayal, but Roger would never forgive him for switching his loyalties. Roger thought they'd killed Leif, and Roark only had six or seven days to figure out how to convince him otherwise. Which, knowing Roger, would be difficult at best even with proof, and he had none.

Day turned into night as his thoughts still went round and round the same circle of events, and no solutions presented themselves. At least making camp and seeing to Beasty and Etain gave him something to do besides ride and fret. Unlike Ned and his companions, Scott and his men shared their supper fairly, and though they did tie him to a tree for the night, they cushioned the rope around his wrists with strips of felt from Etain's saddle blanket, much as he had done for Alina on *The Rover*. Alina, who would be sleeping in the hold of the *Trade Wind*, unbound and uncuffed, and without Roark by her side.

He recalled the times she'd sworn she slept better on the cold, hard ground or a stables floor with him than she did in a soft, warm bed without him. He concentrated on sending his thoughts across the land and over the sea to her. Thoughts of calm, peace, and love.

He fell asleep thinking of her and he woke up thinking of her. He thought of her all day as he rode, and all night as he lay awake and eventually fell asleep and dreamt of her. He was definitely thinking of her when he woke with his cock as hard as forged iron and no sweet Alina to release him. His only ease was knowing her ship would be out of the firth by now and on its way across the North Sea.

Their third day of riding was much like the first two, except they were heading almost due south now, and the skies were threatening rain. The rain held off until dusk, and made for a cold, wet, miserable night of fitful sleep spent huddled under a canopy of trees that was as far from his and Alina's cozy cave as their little world had been from reality.

By morning they could start a fire, and they all sat around it drying off and warming up while the beans they'd soaked overnight cooked. By Roark's reckoning, they were only three to four days away from North Shore Keep. It was time to quit moping and figure some things out.

"Are Munroe and Gwyneth still sneaking off into the woods together?" he asked. "I'm not jealous," he added when no one answered. "Only curious. I care for Gwyneth about as much as she cares for me. Which is not at all." The men said nothing, though the looks they exchanged spoke plenty. "What?" he said. "Tell me."

"They were," Ross said. "Until Gwyneth caught him sneaking off with Jenny."

"Leif's Jenny?"

"Aye," Ross said. "They've been keeping company almost since the day Leif was—"

"Killed," Roark finished for him. He'd always thought Jenny was mad for Leif, if not in love with him, so why would she take to Munroe so quickly when the entire household knew Munroe and Gwyneth were sweet on each other?

Gwyneth wasn't someone you wanted as an enemy, especially if you were a servant and she the daughter of the laird. Unless… "Does Munroe know Jenny's pregnant?"

All four men sat back.

"How'd you know?" Douglas, who was good friends with Munroe, asked. "She didn't tell Munroe until after you'd run off with the princess."

"Jenny's pregnant with Leif's child," he told them. "Alina heard her and her parents arguing about it in the kitchens, right before she went to the stables and Leif tried to rape her."

The men exchanged another round of looks, and Roark found it interesting not one of them had questioned his accusations against Leif.

"Did Leif know?" Scott asked.

"He did," Roark said. "That's what the argument was about. Leif had told Jenny he'd claim a boy bairn, but if it was a girl, she was on her own."

"Just like his ruttin' uncle," Scott spat.

"That's why Jenny went after that fool Munroe so quick and sudden after Leif's death," Douglas exclaimed. "She needed a father for her bairn."

Roark let this sink in for a moment, then asked, "Who found Leif's body?"

"Craig did," Scott answered.

"Jenny's father," Roark said, though they all knew who he was. "Interesting."

The men chewed on this for a bit.

"Can you tell me something?" Scott asked Roark. "Will Alina keep her word? Will she keep her father from wreaking vengeance on the North Shore?"

"Alina always keeps her word," Roark assured him.

Scott shook his head. "She didn't keep her word to stay and wait for her father to ransom her."

"She meant to," Roark told them, "and would have, except we found out Roger had no intention of ransoming her, or of ever letting her parents know what had become of her. He meant for Murtaugh to sail her to the desert lands and sell her as a slave, a pleasure woman, to whatever desert king would pay his price in gold."

"Why would Roger do that?" Ross asked.

"It would be his secret revenge against her parents," Roark explained. "Against her whole family, sending her to suffer the same fate that had befallen her great-grandmother, Oona the Swan."

"Alina's the great-granddaughter of Oona the Swan?" all four men asked at once.

"Princess Alina is the daughter of Queen Alyssa, who's the daughter of Queen Sahar, who was the daughter of Queen Oona. Which is why Laird Owen MacLeod took us in and gave us shelter. She's kin to him."

"She does have the MacLeod eyes." Todd spoke for the first time.

Roark grinned. "You should hear her sing."

They finished their breakfast and were breaking camp when the horses lifted their heads and pricked their ears forward. Roger's men drew their weapons while Roark grabbed a heavy stick.

"Hello, the camp," a man's voice called from the road. "It's Niels and Grant, Laird Owen's men. We come as friends."

Roger's men looked to Roark, who relaxed his stance as two men on horseback rode into the clearing.

"Is it Alina?" Roark asked as they dismounted. "Is she all right?"

"The princess is fine as far as we know," Niels said, nodding to Roger's men, whose stances had relaxed, if not their grips on their weapons. "Last we saw, she was sailing safely away on the *Trade Wind*."

"Then what are you doing here?" Roark said. "Not that I'm not glad to see you."

"Laird Owen wanted someone at your trial to speak for the MacLeods," Niels said. "So here we are." He held his empty hands up to Roger's men, palms up, as did Grant, though they both had short swords sheathed at their waist belts and long swords on their saddles. "We're not here to interfere with you taking Roark back to your laird. In fact, our laird's expressly forbidden it." He lifted his chin toward his and Grant's bulging saddlebags. "We've brought extra food supplies. Figured yours were growing thin by now."

Scott sheathed his long sword and stepped up to Niels. "I'm Scott," he said, offering Niels his hand. "Welcome."

***

Alina was perched in the crow's nest of the *Trade Wind*, scanning the open sea with Roark's spyglass and seeing nothing but the late morning sun's light reflecting off the water. Lowering the glass, she stared out over the vast expanse without really seeing, her gaze as vacant as the hole in her chest. She missed Roark so much her heart actually ached. She'd heard of people and animals dying of a broken heart, but had never really believed it possible. Now she knew it was.

She'd almost called out for the captain to stop the ship and let her off at least ten times before they'd sailed out of the firth and into the open sea. To find a port town and beg, buy, or steal a horse and go after Roark. To try to get him free of Roger's men. Yet she'd ended up clamping her mouth shut every time.

Going after him, trying to free him, would've gone against his given word. She wouldn't do that to him. Worse, if she did try and got caught and hauled back to Roger, then everything they'd done, everyone they'd asked favors of, would have been for nothing. So, she'd said nothing.

She'd paced the ship's deck like a madwoman for the first day, and climbed up to the crow's nest the second, and that's where she'd been every day since, searching the sea and missing Roark.

If she closed her eyes, she could see his shining like rain in moonlight, pouring heat and desire into her. She could see his slow, easy, melting grin, could feel his strong hands roaming over her skin, his hot, throbbing cock filling her body and soul.

She could hear his deep, resonant voice telling her he loved her. Only her. His lady owl. Then she would squeeze her eyes tight to keep her tears from spilling. Tears that wouldn't do her or Roark any good. If the *Trade Wind* made it to Sea Ridge in good time, she could sail back to the North Shore with her father and defend Roark against Roger. If the winds didn't hold and they didn't make it back in time…

Alina shook her head and looked steadfastly east, refusing to even consider what could happen. She couldn't bear to think of a world without Roark in it, even if it wasn't with her.

She laid a hand over her barren womb, the grief she still felt at the loss of a babe she'd never had nearly doubling her over. She knew if, by some miracle, Roger let Roark live, he would likely be forced to marry Gwyneth. It would be Gwyneth who bore his children. Yet as much as that possibility tore at her, at least he would still be alive. That was what mattered.

She glanced down at the captain and crew going about their duties. They'd all been nothing but polite and accommodating to her the four days they'd been at sea, and had turned a corner of the hold into her own private little antechamber with a hammock she'd gotten little sleep in. She sighed, wondering if she'd ever sleep well without Roark next to her again. The last three nights at Silver Water Keep, when they'd been able to sleep through the nights together, had been a wonderful gift. One she silently sent out her thanks to Laird and Lady MacLeod for.

Lifting the spyglass, she put it to her eye, scanning the sea without really expecting to see anything, but needing something, anything, to occupy her mind. A dark spot blinked in and out of sight to the northeast and Alina held the spyglass steady, watching as the spot slowly grew in size from a black bobbing blob to the solid mass of a ship's hull with white sails overhead. She started to call down to the captain and then stopped and refocused. There were two smaller ships flanking the larger one.

"Captain Wallis," she yelled and pointed. "There's a trading ship flanked by two long-boats heading our way from the northeast."

"Longboats?" he yelled up at her. "Northern longboats?"

Alina took another look through the spyglass. "By the looks of them, aye, Northern long-boats." *Warships*.

"Have they seen us?"

"I don't know. I can't tell."

The captain gave orders to turn the *Trade Wind* south. Alina watched with growing dread as the ship and the longboats turned south as well.

"They've not only seen us," she called down to the captain. "They're coming after us. The longboats are gaining on us."

The *Trade Wind* was already at full sail and was still no match for longboats being oared by ten and two burly Northmen, especially when the wind chose to die down to a gentle breeze.

"Damnation." What was it with the wind on this cursed sea?

The longboats were closing in fast enough she didn't need the spyglass to watch them. Below her, the crew started readying for a fight, bringing up long and short swords and positioning themselves along the rails with bows and arrows. Alina palmed the hilt of her waist blade, a paltry weapon against a man with a sword, though it would at least give her the choice of taking her own life before a marauder was able to climb the mast to the crow's nest. She could still end up a slave in some king's household, or more likely held for ransom once the Northmen found out who she was. Either way, she would lose her chance to save Roark.

She put the spyglass back to her eye and focused on the man standing at the prow of the nearest longboat. A big, barrel-chested Northman with short-cropped hair and a square jaw whose gaze was as sharp as honed steel even from a distance.

"Uncle Bors?"

She moved her focus to the trade ship's prow, which was carved into the shape of a screaming eagle's head. She focused on the deck, where a tall man with white-blond hair stood beside a woman whose golden-brown hair was blowing around a familiar oval face.

"Captain Wallis," she yelled, laughing and pointing. "It's the *Sea Eagle*, my father's ship." And her father and her mother were on it.

Alina was off the small boat and climbing the rope ladder onto the *Sea Eagle* before Captain Wallis had tied the small boat off to the ship's side. When she reached the top rung, her father's face was beaming down at her. He held out his hand and helped pull her up and over the rail.

"Oh, Father," she cried as he pulled her into his arms. "I thought I might never see you or Mother again." She laughed through her tears as her mother joined their embrace, and it was as if the weight of the world had been lifted from her shoulders. She kissed her mother's cheek, which was as wet with tears as her own, and grinned as her father ruffled her hair and took in her tunic and breeches.

"It's a long story," Alina said.

"One I look forward to hearing," her father said, and then pulled her and her mother into his arms once more.

"We were so afraid we'd lost you," her mother whispered. "Oh, Alina, my beautiful girl. Are you, you've not been...?"

"I'm well, Mother, truly."

Her mother sniffed and nodded, and held tight to Alina's hand as the crew shouted out greetings to her.

"Uncle Han," she cried as the slim, black-haired Far Easterner bristling with blades stepped up and hugged her. "I'm so glad to see you."

"Not as glad as I to see you, missy," he said, grinning from ear to ear. He nodded toward the longboat pulling up beside the ship from which Bors stood glaring up at them. "Bors's gonna be so jealous I get hug you first."

Alina laughed. As scary-looking as he was, her Uncle Bors was a big old softy. "He'll get over it," she said.

The captain and the first mate from the *Trade Wind* climbed aboard and Alina introduced them.

"Father, Mother, this is Captain Wallis and his first mate, Brady. They were taking me back to Sea Ridge."

"Captain." Her father held out his hand to Wallis. "Thank you. We owe you a great debt for bringing our daughter to us."

"It's my honor, King Jerrik," Wallis said, shaking his hand. He reached into his tunic pocket and pulled out Alina's pearl necklace and held it out to her. "Seeing as how I didn't take you all the way to Sea Ridge, I'd feel wrong keeping this."

"It's yours," Alina told him. "You got me back to my parents. You've fulfilled your part of the bargain."

"I tell you what, Captain," her father said, taking the necklace from Wallis and looping it over Alina's head. "I'll make sure you're paid what the necklace is worth, either in coin or trade." He glanced at the *Trade Wind.* "You've traded in Sea Ridge before. I never forget a face or a ship."

"Aye, King Jerrik, three times. This trip'll be our fourth, which is one of the reasons I agreed to take your daughter onboard."

Her father cocked his head, his blue eyes piercing. "Why would you not?"

Wallis looked to Alina.

"As I said, it's a long story," she told her father. "One I will explain in detail once we're on our way to the Green Isles."

"To Silver Water Keep?" her mother said.

"No." Alina shook her head, curious her mother asked about the keep by name. In all the tales of the Lion and the Swan she'd heard, it had only ever been told that Oona the Swan had come from the Green Isles. The name of her family home had never been mentioned. She wanted to ask her mother how she knew of Silver Water Keep, but like many other things, the explanation would have to wait. "We need to sail to North Shore Keep, on the Long Firth," she said. "The home of Laird Roger MacKinnon, Roark's patron, the man he and Leif abducted me for. The sooner we get there, the better."

The *Trade Wind* would continue on to Sea Ridge, where her father made arrangements with Captain Wallis to have the wool and whisky and other trade goods taken directly to the palace warehouse to be traded for furs and worm weave, and for the captain to receive a bolt of his choice as payment for letting Alina sail on his ship.

Alina said her farewells to the captain and Brady, and as soon as they'd oared their small boat away, Bors brought his longboat alongside the *Sea Eagle* and bounded onto the deck. Alina flew into his arms, laughing as he gave her a big bear hug.

"Don't you go scaring us like that again, missy," he mock scolded. "You left grown men in tears thinking you were dead. Not me, of course, but others," he said with a sniff and a wink. "And poor Beast, the hound sat at the end of the dock and wouldn't leave for three days after you disappeared. He must've followed your scent to where it ended." He snuffled and wiped his nose on his sleeve. "We followed the blood trail and searched the forests and mountains for a fortnight, looking for any trace of you."

"I know what Leif and his men did with my gown and cloak, and the pig's blood to make you all think I'd been dragged off into the woods by some wild beast," she said, and saw the deep shadows of grief flit across her uncles' and parents' faces. "I'll tell you everything that's happened to me, I promise, but first, I have to ask, how did you know where to come looking for me?"

"It was your mother," her father said, wrapping his arm around her shoulder and hugging her to him. "When we couldn't find any signs of you…" His voice, always so strong and sure, broke. "Once the shock and grief of your supposed death had ebbed enough to think and function again, she looked into the scrying bowl."

As far as Alina knew, her mother had only looked into the scrying bowl once before, on the night before she and her father were to have been married. What she'd seen there had scarred her so deeply she'd never looked again.

"I wanted, I needed to see you one more time," her mother said, her voice, her smile, cracking. "I needed to know if you were…at peace."

"What did you see?" Alina squeezed out around the lump in her throat.

"I saw an owl perched on a stag's horns. The stag was swimming into the sunset across a great sea, and then it was walking through a thick wood until it came upon a lake of silver waters. Two girls were playing at the lake's shore, one was you at eight years of age, and the other had long, white-blonde hair and eyes that shone green as cut emeralds when she looked up at me and told me to go where it all began."

"Oona the Swan," Alina whispered. "It was Great-Grandmother telling you where I was." She rubbed the goosebumps that had risen on her arms. "I was there," she said. "Roark and I went to Silver Water Keep, where our cousin, Laird Owen MacLeod, gave us shelter and found Captain Wallis to sail me home to you."

"Roark was there with you?" her father said.

Alina nodded. "I've so much to tell you," she said with a catch in her voice, "and I will. I will tell you all." Well, almost all. "But first, can we start sailing for the Long Firth? Now? There's no time to waste."

***

"This is Beasty," Roark told Gare as he handed the gelding's reins over. Gare said nothing, though his glare spoke plenty. "I didn't kill Leif," Roark said. "I swear it." He handed Etain's reins over to Gare as well. "She gets along well with Beasty," he said, patting the mare's sleek neck. "They've been through a lot together. How's the colt, Ash, doing?"

Gare's expression softened. "He's doubled in weight since you and Alina's been gone and is completely off the goats' milk." He chuckled. "He and Smokey are pretty much inseparable, the rascals."

"I'm glad to hear it."

"If'n you don't mind me asking," Gare said, "where's Alina?"

"Don't know," Roark told him, which wasn't a complete lie. He didn't know exactly where the *Trade Wind* was right now. "She and I became separated when we were attacked by a band of brigands."

"Brigands?"

"She and Artur got away," Roark assured him with another half-truth. "She rode north."

"I hope she's all right," Gare said. "I always liked her."

Roark clapped a hand on Gare's shoulder. "I hope so too."

Gare shook his head and started to say something else when Scott called for Roark to follow him and his men to the manor house. According to the men, Roger intended to put Roark through a public trial before giving him a public hanging, which meant Roark would be held prisoner at the keep until his family and whoever else Roger wanted to witness the trial showed up. Which they'd all agreed wouldn't include Roark's uncle, Bryce, who not only wielded a great deal of clout as laird of the MacKay clan, but had never liked Roger, and was why Niels and Grant had ridden for Yew Tree Keep two days ago.

Roark had told Roger's and Owen's men about everything that had happened to him and Alina since the day he'd met her without going into the more personal details, and was fairly certain they'd come to believe most of what he'd told them. It hadn't been difficult to convince them of Leif's attempt to rape Alina, and to a man they'd condemned his soul for it. They'd also agreed not to tell Munroe or anybody else the babe Jenny carried was Leif's. Not until the trial.

They headed for the manor house as they'd ridden, with Scott and Ross leading Roark. Douglas and Todd followed behind.

The aroma of roasted meat and baked bread wafted from the dining hall, making Roark's belly rumble. They stopped at the hall's entrance, and one by one the voices quieted as their presence was noted. Roark caught Craig's and Peg's quick glances before Roger stood at the high table. Roark had been at the receiving end of Roger's rebukes through the years, but never had he felt such white-hot hatred before. He reminded himself the man thought he'd killed his only son, which didn't absolve him of what he'd done, and had intended to do to Alina.

"Take the murdering piece of offal to my private chambers," Roger ordered.

Roark sat on the bench between Scott and Ross, the same bench he'd sat on beside Alina what felt like a lifetime ago. Then, he'd had suspicions about Roger's deceit and lies. Now he had first-hand knowledge, if little actual proof.

He sat up straight and squared his shoulders. Whatever Roger had in store for him, Roark would face it knowing he'd gotten Alina away from the sick bastard and on her way back to her family, safe and in one piece, if not a virgin. Yet she'd given her virginity to Roark of her own free will. He hadn't taken it, as Leif had tried to do. Roark didn't regret accepting her gift. He could never regret loving her or her loving him. Even if it meant his death by hanging for a crime he didn't commit.

He sat stiffly as Roger entered the room along with Donald and Munroe.

"Where's the girl?" Roger demanded.

"We don't know where the girl is," Scott said. "We were only able to take Roark."

Roark clamped his jaw tight and looked straight ahead at nothing. Scott hadn't lied. He'd phrased the truth in a way that would keep to the story they'd all agreed on. One that would keep Scott and the others from having to explain why they'd let Alina sail away, and keep Roger from putting all their lives in more danger by preparing for a fight if and when King Jerrik showed up at North Shore Keep. A fight that Roark had convinced them they would not win and would do better to let Jerrik deal with Roger.

Roger stepped in front of Roark and stood there until Roark looked up at him. "Where's the girl?" he snarled.

Roark shrugged. "Princess Alina and I went our separate ways when a gang of men came after us in the Mounths. I was captured. She got away."

Roger looked to Scott.

"That's how we found him," Scott said. "The gang who'd caught him were bragging about it at an inn. We paid them off with a few coppers."

Roger furrowed his brow and glared at Roark. "Why isn't he bound?"

"He swore he wouldn't run," Scott told him. "He wanted to come back and face the charges against him."

Roger snorted. "You believed him?"

"He kept his word and was no trouble."

"What did you hope to gain by coming back here?" Roger asked Roark. "Sympathy? Leniency? Your family's forgiveness? An honorable death for a heinous crime?"

"The truth," Roark told him.

"The truth," Roger sneered. "What would you know about the truth?"

Roark flashed a quick grin. "We'll find out soon enough."

***

Roark paced his old bedchambers, his prison cell for the past two days now. Word had come: his parents would be arriving at North Shore Keep sometime this afternoon, and his trial would take place tomorrow.

He'd slept little and fitfully, missing Alina so much his chest ached. He wished she'd been pregnant with his child, that there would be a living, breathing testament to his life and their love in the world, because the closer his trial got, the less faith he had in being exonerated. The only things he had to argue his innocence were his word and hearsay. He still didn't have a single piece of hard evidence someone else killed Leif, and it was unlikely the real murderer would confess.

He was sorry for putting his family through all of this, for dragging their name through the mud and likely leaving it besmirched for years to come. But he wasn't sorry for what he'd done or why he'd done it. He didn't feel bad Leif was dead. He'd tried to rape Alina, and would have, had Roark not stopped him. He'd deserved what he'd gotten. Unfortunately, Roark doubted Roger or any of the MacKinnons would see it that way. They'd lost their only male heir, as well as their hostage, who, unbeknownst to them, should be safely back in the fold of her family by now.

Roark hoped she was. Otherwise, this would have all been for nothing. Well, not nothing. If Roger hadn't sent him to kidnap Alina, Roark never would have met her. Never would have loved and been loved by her. If he died, it would be a small price to pay for that privilege.

"Damnation." He had to change the directions of his melancholy thoughts or he was going to go mad. Mad for want of Alina. Mad at the unjustness of the world. Mad for dreaming of a world where the consequences and repercussions they were about to suffer matched what they'd actually done.

The outside bolt, which had been installed on his door during his absence, slid open and his mother walked in. He threw his arms around her and hugged her tight.

"I'm so glad to see you," he said as she hugged him back. "Though I am sorry about the cause."

"Don't be," she said with a soft smile. "I know the truth of things. The truth of you."

Her steadfast faith in him warmed him to his core. "Thank you, Mother. For everything. Truly."

She sniffed and stepped away from him as his father stepped up. "Well, Roark," he said coldly. "What have you to say for yourself? For the shame you've brought on your family?"

"Any shame you feel is based on Roger's many lies," Roark told him, aware that Roger stood at the open door.

"I lie?" Roger hissed. "My son is dead because of you."

"Your son is dead because of his own actions," Roark said. "Because he tried to rape Princess Alina." Roark looked directly at his father, spoke directly to his father. "I did not kill Leif. I swear it."

His father held his gaze for a long moment, his expression implacable. "We'll see," he said, and then he took his wife by the arm and led her out of the room and down the hall with Roger as Bryce stepped in.

"Roark, me lad. Glad I am to see you."

"Uncle Bryce." Roark actually laughed as he was embraced in his uncle's bear hug. "Not half as glad as I am to see you."

"Your friends from the north filled me in on everything," Bryce whispered into Roark's ear. "Roger thinks they're my men for now. He won't be hanging you without a fight, lad." He stepped back and grinned. "An old friend of yours showed up at Yew Tree Keep a few days ago. He was limping a bit, so I left him to rest up in my stables."

"Artur?" Roark asked. "Artur is at Yew Tree?"

Bryce touched the side of his nose.

Roark took his first deep breath in what felt like days. "Can you do me a couple of favors, Uncle?" he said in a low voice. "Can you keep Artur's return a secret?"

"Of course, lad."

"Also, can you take my friends from the north and ride into port today, look for a ship called *The Rover* and ask to talk to Kerry and Kerwin? Offer them your protection if they'll speak at my trial about where they were to sail with Alina."

Bryce slapped him on the shoulder. "Will do, lad."

CHAPTER 17

True Lies

Roark walked out of his chambers flanked by Scott and Ross, and descended the stairs where Bryce was waiting for him at the bottom.

"Sorry, lad," his uncle told him. "*The Rover* was at full sail and heading seawards by the time we got to the docks yesterday."

"Thanks for trying."

Roark's hopes, which had been tenuous at best, unraveled further. He should've expected Roger would make sure the ship was gone and the crew unavailable for any questioning. Lengthening his spine and squaring his shoulders, he walked into the dining hall, where his parents sat at the high table with Roger, Lynette, Gwyneth, Donald, and Myrna.

He took his seat at a low table set sideways to the high table and the other low tables, where everyone could view him, as Bryce took his seat beside Roark's mother.

Craig, Peg, and Jenny sat at a low table with the other house servants, and he noticed while everyone else was looking at him and whispering among themselves, those three were silent and studiously avoiding his gaze.

Roger stood and the hall went quiet. He glared at Roark before he spoke, his voice thick with rage. "Roark MacInnes, second son of Ronan MacInnes and Brianna MacKay, ward of Roger MacKinnon, friend to Leif MacKinnon and betrothed of Gwyneth MacKinnon, you are hereby charged with the murder of Leif MacKinnon. How do you plead?"

"Not guilty," Roark said. "I did not kill Leif."

Roger stared down his beak of a nose at him. "We have witnesses who will prove otherwise."

Roark raised a brow. "Do you?"

"Craig Maxwell," Roger said. "If you would take the witness stand."

Jenny's father stood and walked over to the table directly across from Roark's and took a seat, facing the assemblage and Roark.

"Tell us, Craig, what you witnessed the day my son was murdered."

"I, ah, the missus and me was in the kitchen, having a bite to eat, when we heard a ruckus going on outside. We went out to see what was what, when we seen Roark and the pri… the servant girl, Alina, come running out of the stables, Roark's blade dripping blood. They, ah, they jumped onto their horses, what were already saddled up and their packs bulging, and they hightailed it outta here, riding north like a pack of banshees was after them. I went to the stables, and it was there I come upon Leif, tied, gagged, and dead, a scythe sticking out of his chest."

"Thank you, Craig," Roger said, his voice strained, Lynette visibly weeping beside him.

"My laird." Craig stood.

"Not so fast, Craig." Roark held his hand up. "First you must answer my questions."

Craig nodded and remained standing, wringing the cap in his hands and licking his lips.

Roark stood. "Did you actually see me kill Leif?" he asked.

Carig shook his head. "But I seen you and the girl leaving the stables and no one else right before I went in and found him dead."

"So, the answer is no," Roark said. "You didn't actually see me or Alina stab Leif with the scythe, was it?"

"No. I mean, aye." Craig swiped at the sweat beading on his forehead. "I mean, I didna see you or Alina stick the scythe into Leif, but you and she was the only ones come running out of the stables."

"With my blade dripping blood?"

"Aye."

"Why would my blade be dripping blood if Leif was killed by a scythe to the chest?"

"I dunna know," Craig said, shifting from one foot to the other. "Maybe it's what you cut the tip of his ear off with."

"First," Roark said, "cutting off the tip of a person's ear wouldn't leave a blade dripping with enough blood to see from the kitchens to the stables. And second, the tip of Leif's ear was bitten off by *Princess* Alina when Leif tried to rape her."

"That's a lie," Roger thundered, pushing up to his feet as a low buzzing filled the hall. "Why would my son need to rape a woman he despised when he had his choice of women willing to warm his bed?"

"I would say the answer to your question is one of character, Laird," Roark answered. "Not one of need."

"It's not enough your son killed mine?" Lynette shrieked at Brianna. "Now he slanders him as well?"

To her credit, Roark's mother simply pressed her lips tight and said nothing, while Roger wrapped his arm around Lynette's shoulder and whispered in her ear. The most outwardly attentive Roark had ever seen him with his wife.

Roark turned his attention back to Craig. "What were you, Peg, and Jenny arguing about in the kitchen before Alina came in that day?"

"Wha… what?"

"What were you, your wife, and daughter arguing about when *Princess* Alina came into the kitchen and interrupted you?"

"Nu… nothing of import."

Roark was sorry to out Jenny's secret in such a crude manner, but the fact of her pregnancy would be known soon enough, as would the child's sire if it was blond and blue-eyed. "Your daughter being pregnant with Leif's babe was of no import?"

"Leif's babe?" Munroe erupted as the hall filled with gasps and whispers. He glared at Jenny, who quailed beside her mother. "You told me the babe was mine, you cuckolding bitch."

Roark glanced at the high table, the shock still evident on Roger's and Lynette's faces. They hadn't known.

"The babe is Leif's," Roark said loudly. "Jenny had told Leif, and he'd told her he'd only claim a boy bairn. If it was a girl, she was on her own." He turned back to Craig, who'd sagged onto his chair. "To which you cursed Leif for being just like his Uncle Donald, who'd only ever claimed his male by-blows."

"How'd you… that's a lie," Craig said, rallying.

"No," Roark said. "It's not, is it?" he asked Jenny, who went white-faced and said nothing. Roark looked over at the high table, at a furious Roger and a tight-lipped Lynette. At Gwyneth, who was glaring daggers at Jenny, and at Donald, whose usual smug expression had turned dour. He didn't even bother glancing at Myrna's perpetually sour face. "My point is," he said to the assembly at large, "I wasn't the only person with a reason to kill Leif."

"Yet you admit you had a reason to," Roger said.

"I did," Roark said. "I likely would have if not for Alina. I admit I pulled him off her where he had her pinned to the floor, clothes torn and struggling against him. I admit I beat him senseless, and I would've continued beating him until he was dead if she hadn't stopped me to keep me from being in the exact position I'm in now. Accused of his murder.

"I admit I beat him, bound him, and gagged him. I left him alive and breathing in the stables with his useless cock hanging out of his breeches so whoever found him would know what kind of man he was.

"I admit I helped Princess Alina ride away from here, from you," he told Roger. "A man so full of his own poison he lied to all of us so we'd kidnap an innocent woman from her home in order to exact his revenge on her parents over a twenty-year-old grudge." He turned to face the assemblage. "Roger was never going to ransom Princess Alina," he told them. "He was going to have her sold to some desert king as a slave in some twisted reenactment of what happened to her great-grandmother, Oona the Swan, of the clan MacLeod. All because he and his family were exiled from Sea Ridge for helping try to murder the new king and queen twenty years ago."

Still standing, Roger clapped slowly. "That was quite a story."

"It's true," Roark, who'd never made a speech that long or impassioned in his life, said. "Every word of it."

"Yet you have no proof."

"Nor do you," Roark countered. He glanced over at Craig, who was looking at Jenny with pure fear on his face. "All you have is hearsay."

Roger smiled, cold and deadly. "I am laird," he said. "Your laird. I don't need proof to hang you." He looked to Roark's father, who sat stone faced and silent. "Unless your father wishes to stand for you, which would rend asunder our alliance." He smirked as Roark's father maintained his stony silence, despite his mother's whispered pleas. "Does anyone here wish to stand for this murdering cur, Roark MacInnes?" Roger said, his gaze threatening anyone who dared.

Bryce started to stand, and Roark shook his head and motioned for him to stay seated. The last thing he wanted to do was start a feud between his uncle's and Roger's clans.

"Anyone?" Roger asked again.

Roark looked to Craig, who refused to meet his eyes. He looked to Peg, who was rocking a sobbing Jenny in her arms, her gaze meeting Roark's over Jenny's head, pleading with him. He glanced at Roger, who was determined to see him hang for Leif's death. No matter the cause. Roark took a deep breath in and blew it out. There was no reason to drag Jenny and her family further into this mess. If Craig did kill Leif, Roark couldn't really blame him. He understood protecting your family, no matter the cost.

With a thin smile as cold and deadly as an adder's, Roger raised his hand and the hall went silent.

"Roark Bruce MacInnes," he said loudly. "I declare you guilty of the murder of Leif Andrew MacKinnon, my only son and heir to North Shore Keep, for which you shall hang by the neck until you are dead, tomorrow at high noon in the town square for all to witness what a dishonorable and murderous traitor you are."

***

Roark stood on the gallows with his hands tied behind his back and looked up into a spring sky filled with grey clouds scudding from south to north. He would've liked to feel the sun on his face one last time, but had learned a long time ago a person didn't always get what they wanted.

He dropped his gaze from the sky and found his mother standing between his father and Logan, front and center in the crowd of family and friends and onlookers, her eyes bright with welling tears. He'd told her she didn't have to be here today when she'd visited him in his cell last night. He couldn't blame her for not wanting to watch him die in such an undignified manner. She'd tsked and told him she'd been there when he took his first breath and she'd be there when he took his last. He lifted his lips in a toothless smile and dipped his head to her and she lifted trembling lips to him in return.

He looked to Logan, standing by his mother as he always had and always would, and dipped his head in thanks and farewell. He looked to his Uncle Bryce, who'd offered to help him fight his way free as they rode from the keep this morning, with Niels and Grant offering their sword arms as well. Men he liked and respected. Men who knew the truth of almost all that had happened. Men he'd made swear not to raise arms against his family or Roger's, lest the alliance he was willing to die for splintered and broke. Men to whom he nodded his farewells.

Refusing to even look at Roger and his family of lying, vindictive snakes, Roark looked to his father, who stood as stiff and unmoved as he had yesterday. Roark had lived his entire life aware of his father's indifference, yet it still gutted him. He sucked a deep breath of salt-tanged air in and blew it out. At least his mother, Logan, and Uncle Bryce, the three people closest to him in the world except for Alina, believed the best of him.

Alina.

He'd told her he would fight to stay alive for her, to be with her again, and he hadn't kept that promise. He couldn't. Not without causing even more harm and death to his family and hundreds of others. He'd apologized to her so many times in his mind and heart over the last several days and nights he thought surely her soul had heard his.

He knew she would understand why he'd done what he had, as he knew she would grieve him for the rest of her days, and she would haunt him in the otherworld. They'd loved each other body, mind, and soul, and he would never regret it.

The hangman stepped up next to Roark and held out a black linen hood. Roark gave him a grim grin and shook his head. He wanted his last sight of this world to be one of light, not darkness. With a shrug, the hangman tossed the hood to the gallows deck and then tugged down on the rope, testing its strength before looping the noose around Roark's neck.

Roark closed his eyes and saw a pair as bright and green as new spring grass smiling into his. He felt her soft, warm skin beneath his fingers, tasted her kiss, her flesh. He breathed in the scent of sweet cherry blossoms and earthy woman, and heard her throaty laughter.

He saw her walking out of the woods toward him, singing "Somebody," her voice pure and lilting. He watched her racing along the sea's shore on her mare, her long legs bare and her mane of cedar blowing in the last, brisk breeze of winter.

He saw her lift her face to the sun and felt its warmth on his. He smiled. At peace.

A flash of light streaked across his eyelids and he opened them and looked out over the sea of people waiting to watch him hang. A ship was docking at the pier.

The Rover.

He opened his mouth to call out that there would be witnesses onboard and felt the jolt of the hangman's hand hitting his back and shoving him into oblivion.

***

"Rrroooaaarrrk!" Alina's scream tore out of her throat as Roark's body swung out over the gallows and fell with a jerk. "Nnnooo!" The spyglass dropped from her hands and she ran down the gangplank as it was being lowered, jumping the last three feet to the ground. "Han, Bors," she yelled. "With me."

She raced for the gallows as factions of the crowd ran screaming from the armed men flanking her, giving her a straight path to Roark, whose body twisted and turned in the air.

"Help him," she cried.

A man grabbed Roark by his thighs and held his body up, taking the pressure from his neck, while another red-headed man held off two of Roger's men, who had their swords pulled but made no effort to fight or stop them from helping Roark.

Two other men jumped up onto the gallows and sawed at the rope with their short swords, cutting through it as Alina reached Roark. Her heart stopped as Logan and Bryce lowered an unconscious Roark to the ground and loosened the noose from his neck.

Alina dropped to the ground at Roark's head and pressed her fingers to his throat as the shouts of men and scraping of blades rang out.

"I can't feel a pulse," she cried. "I can't feel a pulse."

"He isn't breathing either," Logan said.

"No." Alina squeezed back tears. "No." She straddled Roark's belly and pressed her hands palm down on his chest as she'd seen

Hamar do with a newborn foal who hadn't breathed on its own in a timely manner. "No." She pressed down on his chest again. "You cannot die on me." She pressed on his chest again and again. "Not now. Not like this." She pressed on his chest again. "You will not die on me, Roark MacInnes," she whispered savagely. She pumped his chest again and again, stopping to watch for his chest to rise on its own. "Please, Roark," she cried when his chest lay still. "You promised me." She hit his chest with her fist. "You promised me." She felt hands on her shoulders, heard kind voices telling her to let him go. She shook the hands off and lowered her mouth to Roark's ear. "Come back to me, sir stag," she pleaded. "Come back to your lady owl."

He lay there unmoving, his eyes closed, his face ashen.

Gentle hands pulled her up and she stared into the grief-stricken eyes of Lady Brianna. Into Roark's eyes.

"He's gone, Alina," his mother said. "Roark is gone." She hugged Alina to her and whispered in her ear. "He sacrificed himself to save you, to save all of us."

Alina went ice cold, and then she went raging hot. She stepped back from Roark's mother and met his father's stony gaze. "He died for you," she seethed. "Your son died for you. To keep the alliances between your clan and Roger's intact. To keep the hundreds of families dependent on your houses from suffering the consequences of such a breach. And you stand there like a, a bloodless statue." She shook her head and swiped at the hot tears falling down her cheeks. "What manner of man are you to have never seen what a good, honorable man your son is?" she said, her voice cutting. "What manner of man he was."

"Ali girl?"

Alina's sob stuck in her throat and she whipped around and dropped to her knees beside Roark, who lay watching her with a quizzical expression on his face.

"I though you dead," she cried, her tears flowing freely. "We all thought you dead."

"Dead?" he rasped. He started to raise his head and stopped, put a hand to his bruising throat, and another to his ribs, which Alina had been pounding on. He turned his gaze to Bryce, Logan, and his mother, all of them kneeling around him, and Alina knew the moment he remembered where he was and why by the pain reflected in his eyes.

"Help me sit up," he croaked to Logan, who stood and lifted him by the shoulders until he could sit on his own. He lifted an arm and Alina scooted under it, nestling into his side. "I don't know how it is you're here and I'm alive," he whispered hoarsely, "but I'm glad on both accounts."

"As am I, my love." Alina exhaled, her voice as shaky as her body all of a sudden. "As am I."

She lifted her head from his shoulder and became aware of her father's Northmen holding Roger's men and the few villagers who hadn't fled at sword point. The two men who'd cut Roark loose from the noose stepped down from the gallows, their short swords in their hands, their long swords still sheathed.

"Niels, Grant," she said. "It's good to see you again."

"Princess Alina." Niels tipped his short sword to her.

"Help me stand," Roark said, and she scooted out from under his shoulder as Bryce and Logan pulled him to his unsteady feet. He leaned on their shoulders as Alina's parents approached, flanked by three Northmen bristling with swords and war axes. Roark's father stepped over to stand by Roark's mother.

"Roark," her father said in the Northern tongue. "It's a good thing you have a strong neck."

"So it would seem," Roark answered in kind. "Thank you, King Jerrik, for coming, for saving my life."

"Thank our daughter."

Roark nodded and stepped away from Logan's and Bryce's support to stand before her father. "I owe her more than my life, King Jerrik. I owe her my soul." He looked at Alina and smiled, slow and melting. "She already owns my heart." He turned back to her father. "I owe you an apology and an explanation."

Her father held up his hand. "All of which we will deal with later," he said. He turned toward where the MacKinnons stood, perusing Roger, Lynette, Donald, Myrna, and Gwyneth one by one. "Rigil Fenrirson," her father said in the Green Isles tongue for all to hear. He lifted his chin toward Donald. "Delling Fenrirson. I told you both if you ever came after me or my family again, I would kill you, did I not, cousins?"

Alina's jaw dropped as a great buzzing swarmed through the crowd.

"Rigil is Roger?" she asked Roark, who didn't look half as surprised as she felt.

Roger drew himself up. "You have no power here, Jerrik the Usurper," he declared.

Alina's father simply raised a brow and glanced around the square, where his men held Roger's at sword point. He turned toward the dock, where one of his warships was being pulled up onto the shore by four Northmen. The second longboat had stayed with the *Sea Eagle* where it lay anchored at the port's mouth, which was where they'd intercepted *The Rover* as she was heading out to sea and boarded her, sailing her into the North Shore port with Alina, and twenty armed Northmen hidden aboard.

"You, Rigil, are the one with no power here," her father said. He turned to address the gathering. "These men are Rigil and Delling Fenrirson, my cousins. Sons of a dead father killed by my hand twenty years ago for murdering my father, my mother, my two brothers, and my wife's brother, and for attempting to murder me and my wife, all to sit on a throne not rightfully his." He paused for breath and effect and Alina smiled. Her father knew how to capture a crowd's attention. "I banished Rigil and Delling and their families for their parts in their father's murderous schemes on the condition they never return or bother my family again." He glared at Rigil and shook his head. "In return for my letting them live, he had my only daughter kidnapped, not to ransom her, but to sell her as a slave. His revenge on me and her mother would be to let us think her dead the rest of our lives."

"You lie," Rigil spat.

Alina's father looked over to where Captain Murtaugh stood with Kerry and Kerwin.

"It's true," Murtaugh said. "We were to sail to the desert lands with Princess Alina, but then she escaped with Roark."

"So what?" Rigil sneered. "Even if true, none of this changes the fact I am laird and Roark a convicted killer, sentenced to hang for the murder of my son."

The rage that had been simmering in Alina since Leif had pulled the hood over her head boiled over. She quickly closed the distance between her and the man whose twisted sense of vengeance had caused all of this and stood with her waist blade to Rigil's throat before he or anybody else could react.

"Nobody's going to hang Roark again," she growled. "Especially not for the murder of your rapist son. A crime Roark did not commit."

She held Rigil's impotent glare as Han and Bors stepped to her sides, long swords drawn. Alina smiled. She could slit Rigil's throat right here and nobody could stop her. He certainly deserved to die for all his lies and deceit, for all the trouble and grief he'd caused.

Roark's big, familiar hand reached out and he laid it on her forearm, gently wrapping his fingers around her wrist. "Don't do this, my fierce little owl," he said, his voice low and steady.

"Why not?" she asked, never taking her eyes from Rigil's, which had grown wide with real fear. "He tried to kill you. To sell me into slavery."

Roark placed his other hand on Alina's shoulder and leaned in so that only she could hear him. "You don't want the memory of thrusting your blade into his throat haunting you the rest of your life. In this world, where all our actions have consequences and repercussions, I need you, Princess Alina, King Jerrik's daughter, to trust me on this. I need you to let me, Roark MacInnes, deal with Roger MacKinnon, laird of North Shore Keep."

Alina glanced at Roark. He'd called her princess and used the other's titles for a reason. She didn't know what that reason was, but she trusted him. She lowered her blade and wagged the tip at him. "Don't you dare die on me again."

Rain eyes poured in hers, filling her with everything she'd ever felt with or about Roark.

"You should go stand with your parents and their guard," he told her.

***

Roark stood to his full height and faced Rigil and his family. "I did not kill Leif," he said. He looked to where Craig and Peg stood like a protective shield around Jenny. "Did I, Jenny?" he asked, playing a hunch that'd grown stronger throughout his sham of a trial.

Jenny's face drained of all color under Roark's steady stare, and then it crumpled.

"He, he called me a useless whore," she cried. "He, he told me to, to cut him loose. To ma, make myself useful and su, suck his cock while I was down theeere."

"So you stabbed him with the scythe," Roark said gently.

Jenny glanced wildly about as the crowd's whispers grew louder and harsher. "I, I didna mean to," she said, holding out her hands and staring blankly at them. "It, it just happened."

She broke into sobs and Craig pulled his daughter into his chest as Peg mumbled and cried into his shoulder.

"Seize her." Rigil pointed at Jenny. "Seize the murdering bitch," he screamed when his men-at-arms didn't move.

"You would kill the child in her womb?" Scott accused, he the father of a young son he adored. "Your own grandchild?"

Rigil pulled his long sword. "I'll deal with the bitch myself," he snarled. "And I'll deal with the four of you later."

Roark looked to Logan and made the motion of grasping a sword. Before Logan could pull his sword, Roark's father tossed him his, and Roark's chest filled with an unfamiliar pride as he caught it, nodded his thanks, and stepped in front of Rigil, stopping him in his tracks.

"Rigil Fenrirson," he said, the half-formed plan that'd come to him when he'd talked Alina out of slitting Rigil's throat spilling out. "I, Roark MacInnes, challenge you for the lairdship of North Shore Keep."

Rigil sneered. "What makes you think you have the right?"

"I am a true-born son of the clans MacKay and MacInnes," he said. "Whose people have lived and died on the Green Isles for a hundred generations. You are a Northman who lied and cheated his way into a lonely old man's house and claimed false kinship." Rigil said nothing, and Roark continued to make his case. "How much did you pay the old laird to claim you were his long-lost nephew?" The crowd began to stir and mutter. "Did you kill Ronald with the same slow poison your father killed King Jerrik's brother with?"

The crowd's mutterings burst into gasps of comprehension as Rigil drew himself up to his full height and haughtiness. "What lies has your Northern whore been filling your head with?" he hissed.

Behind him, Roark heard the shifting of stances and angry murmurs. This was his chance to settle this mess with as little bloodshed as possible. King Jerrik had shown considerable restraint so far, but it would only last so long. It'd been the story of how King Jerrik had sealed his rule by killing Fenrir in a trial by combat that had given Roark the idea to challenge Rigil for the lairdship.

Though still hale and hearty, Rigil had twenty and five years on Roark, and weighed two stones less at least. Roark had kept up his fighting skills, sparring with Leif on a regular basis, while Rigil had let his skills grow rusty. He was, however, as crafty as ever. And desperate.

Rigil glanced around at his out-armed, outnumbered men, who'd shown no interest in coming to his defense. Especially with twenty heavily armed Northmen at the ready. He looked at his family, his wife, brother, and daughter, and gave them a sickly grin. He grasped his long sword with both hands and dipped his chin to Roark, who did the same. Rigil stepped back on his heels in a defensive posture and Roark charged him with a mighty roar, swinging his father's sword in a wide arc, catching Rigil under his chin on the uppercut, slicing his throat open.

The square was silent as a grave as Rigil's body slumped to the ground in his pooling blood, and then a high-pitched scream rent the air. "You've killed him," Lynette shrieked. "You've killed the laird."

His heart pounding in his ears, Roark held his father's blood-tipped sword high. "By right of blood and battle, I claim North Shore Keep."

"By the gods, you shall not." Delling charged Roark with his sword drawn and Roark held a hand out toward King Jerrik to keep his men from joining the fight as he jumped aside, avoiding the thrust of Delling's sword.

Where Rigil had been a plotter and a schemer, his brother, Delling, had always been blunter and bolder in his actions, and had kept his fighting skills sharp. As much as Roark would've liked the Northmen's help fighting Delling, it was important Roark be the one to defeat him in order to maintain his claim to the lairdship.

To bring the rest of his plan to fruition, he had to stay alive.

He met Delling's attack, blocking and feinting until Delling began to slow. Tired of being on the defensive for the past ten years, Roark pressed his attack, raining blows down on Delling until sweat was pouring down both their faces. Working to slow his breath as Delling panted, Roark lunged. Delling stumbled and went down to one knee, gasping for air, the expression on his face that of a man who knew he was about to die.

With one last, hard thrust, Roark plunged his father's sword into Delling's breast. "May the gods have mercy on your soul."

***

Alina started toward Roark. It was her mother's gentle but firm hand that held her back.

"You must wait," she said. "We are strangers here. We must let certain things fall out where they may. Where they must."

"But what if..." What if the people didn't accept Roark as the new laird? What if they did and he was still expected to marry Gwyneth for the sake of their people, their families? Would he go along with it to keep the old alliances intact, or would he fight for Alina and their love? Her mother squeezed her arm and Alina let her breath out in a ragged sigh. Roark had asked her to trust him, to let him deal with the clans. She could do no less than honor his request.

She looked up from her unhappy musings and caught his gaze. He smiled, slow and easy, and Alina took in a shaky breath and let it out with a quick smile.

Roark wiped the sweat from his face and pointed the tip of his father's sword toward the men-at-arms he'd given himself up to and ridden back here with. "Scott, Ross, see to Rigil's and Delling's bodies."

"Aye, Laird Roark."

"Laird Ronan, Lady Brianna, Laird Bryce, King Jerrik, Queen Alyssa," he said. "If you would join me. Niels and Grant, if you would as well."

"That's it?" Lynette screeched. "He kills my son, my husband, my husband's brother, and that's it?"

"Silence, woman," Laird Ronan commanded, his voice, his countenance, brooking no argument. "It's been established Roark did not kill Leif." He glared from Lynette to Myrna. "From this moment on, neither of you have any say in anything pertaining to the title and lands you and your husbands took by lies and larceny."

"What of me?" Gwyneth smiled prettily at Roark, and Alina glared daggers at the simpering flirt. "I had nothing to do with any of this. I haven't forfeited my right to be Roark's lady wife."

Alina took a step forward, ready to grab Gwyneth by her hair until she confessed her affair with Munroe, but then she recalled her mother's wise words and stopped herself as Roark turned to Gwyneth.

"All will be considered in any decisions made," he told her.

He glanced at Alina, his expression unreadable while her heart was in her eyes. She paced between Han and Bors as Roark and those he'd asked to join him gathered on the other side of the gallows, her father's Northmen maintaining a loose circle around the edges of the crowd, weapons still drawn and at the ready, but not pointing at anyone.

"You not worry, missy," Han told her. "Only fool choose Gwyneth over you, and your Roark, he no fool."

"Aye," Bors seconded. "We've seen the way he looks at you, and has since Spring's Eve. He'll choose you. I'd wager coin on it."

"Thanks," she said. "But it may not be his choice. There's many things to be considered other than what Roark and I want in this life." *In this world.*

"We about to find out," Han said, lifting his chin toward Roark and the others as heads nodded and arms were clasped.

They stood in front of the gallows Roark had been swinging from only a short time ago, though so much had happened since, it felt like days had passed. Alina licked lips gone dry as Laird Ronan stepped forward.

"It has been agreed. Roark Bruce MacInnes is now laird of North Shore Keep. All lands and titles are rightfully his to be passed down to his future heirs."

Alina let out her breath in a rush of relief and apprehension. Her heart swelled with pride as the keep's men-at-arms and the villagers cheered and set up a chant of "Laird Roark, Laird Roark." Aware, she was certain, they'd been given a better laird than the one they'd been living under for the past twenty years.

Alina's father stepped forward and the crowd quieted.

"For your part in your family's abduction of our daughter, Princess Alina, with the intention of selling her into slavery, you Linnea, who call yourself Lynette, and you Mildri, who call yourself Myrna, wives of Rigil and Delling, will be taken and sold in a desert slave market in Alina's place." Lynette and Myrna both went ashen. "Captain Murtaugh," her father said. "You will sail them there for your part in my daughter's kidnapping, and all debts will be considered paid."

The captain doffed his cap. "Thank you, King Jerrik." He'd gotten off easy and he knew it.

Neither her father nor Roark's had mentioned Gwyneth, who looked to have taken it as a sign that she would retain her position as Roark's betrothed by her preening smiles. Alina's heart dropped to her feet. She'd always known it was the most likely outcome, and she told herself she understood why. But she'd always held out hope she and Roark would find a way for their love to transcend their dream world, allowing them to be together in the real world.

Gwyneth giggled and smirked, and Alina swayed on unsteady legs, an empty, hollowed-out husk.

"I've got you, missy." Bors's deep boom echoed in her spinning head and his strong arm held her steady. "You can do this." He joggled her against his solid side. "Don't give that blonde bitch the satisfaction of thinking she's won for even a moment."

"But she has."

"Not yet," he told her. "I will not believe it 'til I hear your young man say it."

Alina buried her face into Bors's shoulder, fighting tears. "I can't," she whimpered, hating how pitiful she sounded. How hopeless she felt.

"Yes, you can, Princess. You are the daughter of Alyssa, granddaughter of Sahar, great-granddaughter of Oona the Swan. Warrior queens all."

Alina sniffed back unshed tears and lifted her head. She straightened her back, squared her shoulders, and faced forward as Roark stepped up to stand beside her father and his. His gaze met hers for a moment and his lips twitched up, but there was no slow, easy grin for her. She raised her chin, took a deep breath in and blew it out.

"My first order of business as laird," Roark said, "will be to deal with Leif's death."

"With his murder, you mean," Lynette roused herself enough to shrill out.

Roark ignored her. "We've agreed. Jenny, pregnant with Leif's child, distraught and provoked by Leif's cruelty, acted rashly and without forethought or malice." He looked to Jenny and her parents, who didn't move, blink, or even breathe. "We absolve you of Leif's murder." Loud gasps of collective relief filled the square as Lynette stood with her mouth hanging slack. "We offer you the choice of staying here at North Shore Keep to work as you have been and raise your child, or moving to Thorn Bush or Yew Tree." Roark smiled kindly as Jenny burst into sobs. "You have plenty of time to decide."

"Thank you, Laird Roark," Craig said, hugging his wife and daughter to him. "Thank you, all of you."

Roark nodded, looked out over the crowd, toed the ground with his boot, squared his shoulders, and met Alina's worried, waiting gaze.

"As laird, I will need to marry," he said. "As you all know, my family betrothed me to Gwyneth, the only daughter of Roger and Lynette MacKinnon, ten years ago now." Gwyneth giggled again and dimpled. Alina swallowed her heart. "However, since the MacKinnons were not who or what they presented themselves to be, I have been allowed to withdraw from this betrothment."

"What?" Gwyneth shrieked. "No. You cannot. I am your betrothed. I am to be lady of North Shore Keep."

Ignoring the still-shrieking Gwyneth, Roark closed the chasm between him and Alina with sure, steady strides, took both her hands in his, and grinned, slow, easy, and melting.

"Will you marry me, my curious little owl?" he asked. "Will you consent to be my wife and take me as your husband? To ask me why every day and night for the rest of our lives?" He stepped in closer and whispered in her ear. "Will you be my wife in this world and ours, where the consequences and repercussions of our actions will matter to more than only ourselves?"

Alina stared into eyes as warm, soft, and giving as summer rain. Eyes that poured a deep, enduring love into hers. "Yes," she said, answering him as she almost had the night of Spring's Eve by the lake. As her heart had answered him every night since. "Yes, I will marry you, sir stag. With pleasure and with honor."

Roark laid his open palm on her cheek. "*Tha thu braegha,*" he whispered huskily.

Alina placed her hand on his cheek, rubbing the pad of her thumb over his freckled cheek. "*Ni ye hen piaoling.*"

Loud sniffing caught their attention, and they turned to where Bors and Han stood.

"What?" Bors said, tears tracking down his cheeks. "I'm not crying." He elbowed a grinning Han in the side. "He's crying."

EPILOGUE

"Mama, Mama, Mama."

Alina straightened from over the seed bed she'd been planting, wiped her soil-covered hands on her apron, and turned in time to brace herself for the onslaught of her son barreling into her legs.

"What is it, Owain?" she laughed, snatching him up and twirling him around.

"Da wet me wook in pie gwas."

"He did?" she said as he squirmed out of her arms. "What did you see in the spyglass?"

"I see wagon. I see Unco Wen dwive wagon."

"You saw Uncle Owen driving the wagon?"

"Uh-huh."

"Mama, Mama, Mama."

Alina grinned as her daughter came skipping into the greenhouse. "What is it, Oona?"

"I see wagon in pie gwass."

"Did you?" She scooped up her daughter and nuzzled her neck, eliciting girlish giggles. "Was Uncle Owen driving the wagon?"

"Uh-huh." Oona wiggled her way out of Alina's arms and started inspecting the herbs that had made it through the winter. "What dis?"

"That," Alina told her, "is fennel."

"Is fenny?" Oona said, whisking her toddler's fingers though the herb's ferny leaves.

Alina laughed lightly. "So it is," she said. "Fenny ferny fennel."

"Fenny fenny," Owain repeated. "Fenny fenny." He started chasing his twin sister around the planter boxes, the sound of their high-pitched laughter music to Alina's ears.

They'd been born on the first day of spring three years ago tomorrow, exactly one year to the day their parents had first met. Owain, the first born, had curly brown hair and eyes the color of rain, like his father's, MacKay eyes. Oona, the second born, had auburn curls, a light dusting of freckles across her nose and cheeks, and the green MacLeod eyes. They were the light and heart of not only their parents' lives, but of the entire household. Alina and Roark gave thanks to the gods and the fates for them every day.

Alina laid a hand over her belly and smiled. There would be another child come the autumn, a boy child she'd seen in her dreams, with his grandfather's white-blond hair and green eyes flecked with gold and grey. A child she would tell Roark about tomorrow night as they celebrated the fourth anniversary of their first meeting.

"Dada," the twins said in unison.

Roark walked into the greenhouse and met Alina's smiling gaze. He grinned, slow and easy, and Alina's insides melted.

"I'm told Owen is arriving," she said as the twins ran up to him, squealing with delight as he scooped them up and tucked one under each arm.

"Aye, the *Sea Hawk* sailed into port this morning," he said, jiggling his progeny up and down. "Owen said he'd be bringing three barrels of whisky for the glass panes for Siusan's new greenhouse."

"Was Siusan with him?"

"She was riding in the wagon with him," he said, setting the twins down to run around. "Cullen was riding Damon."

The *Sea Hawk* was Owen's trade ship, built two years ago with the proceeds of his whisky trade with Alina's father and other Northland ports, as well as North Shore, Thorn Bush, and Yew Tree keeps. After hearing Jerrik's and Alyssa's stories, Owen had made sure to build a horse pen on the deck, as Roark had done with *The Swan,* a wedding present from Alina's parents Kerry and Kerwin captained together.

The MacLeods were now as well known for their whisky and horses as the MacInneses were for their horses and glass. One of the first things Roark had done after becoming laird was to build a glass-making shop. If Alina ever needed to find her husband, that was the first place she looked, even though he had plenty of craftsmen working it for him.

"Come, children," she said, holding out her hands. "We should get cleaned up and ready for our visitors. Grandmama Brianna and Granddad Ronan will be here any time too."

"For our birfday?" Owain asked.

"Yes," Alina said, taking hold of their hands. "For your birthday. Shall we go tell Ompa Jerrik, Oma Alyssa, Uncle Anders, and Auntie Rose her parents are here?"

True to her MacLeod blood, Rose had taken one look at Anders at Roark and Alina's wedding and that had been that. They'd been betrothed within a fortnight and married at Silver Water Keep two moons after their betrothal. Their son, Jerrik, had been born ten moons later, and Rose was four moons along with their second child.

Both families traveled to North Shore Keep every spring to celebrate the twins' birthday and visit for a fortnight, along with Roark's parents and his Uncle Bryce and Aunt Jeanine. From the moment Ronan had given Roark his sword to fight Rigil and Delling, their rift had mended, and Roark's parents were frequent visitors since the twins' birth.

Jenny had chosen to live and work at Yew Tree Keep, deciding it would be too painful to stay at North Shore with her memories of Leif and what she'd done. She'd be coming down with Bryce and Jeanine, and Peg and Craig were beside themselves with their daughter's and granddaughter's pending arrival.

Gwyneth had guilted Munroe into marrying her, and the last anybody had heard, they were living at a keep on the west coast where Munroe was a man-at-arms for the local laird. Word was that they were miserable together and childless. Alina tried hard not to gloat, but was glad that no child would have to grow up with Gwyneth as a mother.

Owain swung Alina's hand. "Yet's go tell Oma an Ompa dat Unco Owen coming."

"Yesh," Oona said. "Yet's go tell Oma an Ompa."

Roark held open the door to the greenhouse as the twins ran out toward the manor house, where Peg stood outside the door, waving them over. He wrapped an arm around Alina's shoulder and pulled her in close, nuzzling her neck. "You were in the orchard this morning," he murmured. "You smell of cherry blossoms."

"And you smell of horse," she teased. "How's Etain's new colt doing?"

"Nursing well and gaining weight according to Gare," he said. "I swear Artur knows the colt's his. He put up such a fuss when Etain went into the brooding stall Gare and Fergus had to move him into the stall next to it."

Alina glanced over at the paddock where Ash, who'd grown into a fine, deep-chested stallion, grazed alongside Smokey, Beasty, Brynja, and Flame, Brynja's and Artur's yearling foal. She looked back over her shoulder at the panes of glass on her greenhouse shining in the last of winter's afternoon light, at the vegetable garden's soil, newly turned over in readiness for the greenhouse transplants. She gazed lovingly at her husband's profile, his broad forehead, high cheekbones, and strong jaw. She touched her fingers to the earth-kissed skin on his forearm and smiled into eyes the color of rain.

"If you could say or do anything you wanted without fear of consequences or repercussions—"

"I'd be exactly where I am, telling you I love you, Ali girl. It's all I've wanted since the day I first set eyes on you racing along the beach, legs bare and mane flying."

AUTHOR'S NOTE

Thank you to everyone who read the MacLeod women's stories: Oona the Swan, Sahar the Tigress, Alyssa the Lynx, and Alina the Owl. Warrior women all. And, of course, their men who were strong enough to love them and stand by their sides throughout the Destined series.

I hope you enjoyed reading their stories as much as I enjoyed writing them.

Michele James

ABOUT THE AUTHOR

Michele James lives in a southern California beach town with her understanding husband, two lazy house cats, and two crazy cattle dogs. She is the proud mother of an adult son and daughter, and is Oma to the world's most adorable grandson.

A mostly retired veterinarian technician, she enjoys reading everything from cereal boxes to serious tomes, watching movies without commercials, cooking, gardening, walks on the beach (especially in winter), and practicing yoga.

CONNECT WITH MICHELE:

website: michelejamesauthor.com
instagram: @michelejamesauthor
facebook: michelejamesauthor

www.BOROUGHSPUBLISHINGGROUP.com

If you enjoyed this book, please write a review. Our authors appreciate the feedback, and it helps future readers find books they love. We welcome your comments and invite you to send them to info@boroughspublishinggroup.com. Follow us on Facebook, Twitter and Instagram, and be sure to sign up for our newsletter for surprises and new releases from your favorite authors.

Are you an aspiring writer? Check out www.boroughspublishinggroup.com/submit and see if we can help you make your dreams come true.

Love podcasts? Enjoy ours at www.boroughspublishinggroup.com/podcast.

www.ingramcontent.com/pod-product-compliance
Lightning Source LLC
Chambersburg PA
CBHW030132180626
46812CB00002B/663